Here is TITAN: the alien that is, itself, a world.

Here is TITAN: the heralded novel by one of SF's most spectacular talents, the Hugo and Nebula Award winner who has been compared by Isaac Asimov with the early Heinlein.

Here is TITAN: the story of a journey through the awesome interior of a moon-sized being that leads to an encounter with a vast and lonely intelligence. And a proposal.

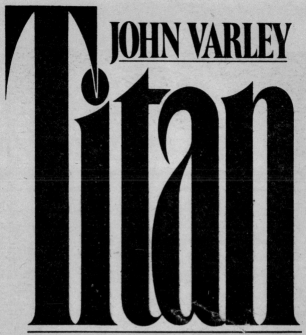

JOHN VARLEY

Titan

Illustrated by Freff

ACE BOOKS, NEW YORK

This Ace book contains the complete
text of the original hardcover edition.
It has been completely reset in a typeface
designed for easy reading and was printed
from new film.

TITAN

An Ace Book / published by arrangement with
the author

PRINTING HISTORY
Berkley/Putnam edition published March 1979
Berkley edition / March 1980
Twelfth printing / June 1986
Ace edition / April 1987

ISBN: 0-441-81304-6

Ace Books are published by The Berkley Publishing Group,
200 Madison Avenue, New York, New York 10016.
The name "Ace" and the "A" logo
are trademarks belonging to Charter Communications, Inc.
PRINTED IN THE UNITED STATES OF AMERICA

10   9   8   7   6   5   4   3

For
John E. Varley
and for
Francine and Kerry

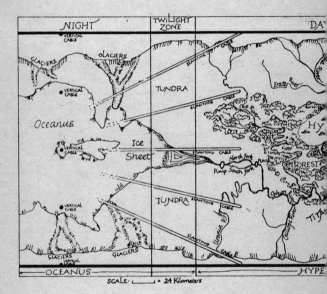

NIGHT   TWILIGHT ZONE   DAY

VERTICAL CABLE

GLACIERS   GLACIERS

Erato River

VERTICAL CABLE

TUNDRA

SLANTING CABLE

Io River

Oceanus

SLANTING CABLE

Hy

Ice Sheet

VERTICAL CABLE

SLANTING CABLE

North Fork

FOREST

Pump   South Fork

TUNDRA

SLANTING CABLE

Ophir

VERTICAL CABLE

Livonia River

TITA

SLANTING CABLE

Calliope River

GLACIERS   GLACIERS

VERTICAL CABLE

OCEANUS   HYPE

SCALE   = 24 Kilometers

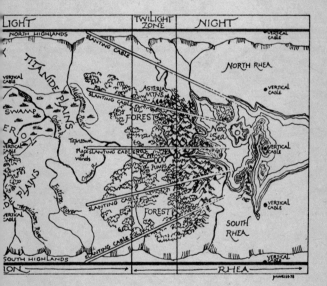

LIGHT   TWILIGHT ZONE   NIGHT

NORTH HIGHLANDS

VERTICAL CABLE

SLANTING CABLE

NORTH RHEA

TITANIDE PLAINS

VERTICAL CABLE

VERTICAL CABLE

ASTERIA MTNS.

SLANTING CABLE

FOREST

Nox Sea

SWAMP

Ophion R.

Ophion R.

Titantown

VERTICAL CABLE

Place of Winds

SLANTING CABLE

VERTICAL CABLE

Ringmaster R.

PUMPS

PLAINS

Feather River

Ophion R.

VERTICAL CABLE

SLANTING CABLE

FOREST

SOUTH RHEA

VERTICAL CABLE

SOUTH HIGHLANDS

SLANTING CABLE

VERTICAL CABLE

ION   RHEA

YARMEISS-78

GAEA

© Feff 24/2 1977

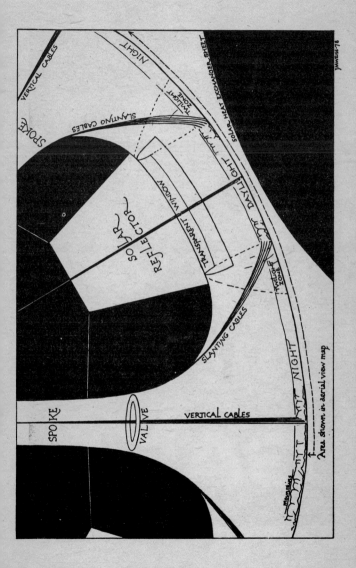

VERTICAL CABLES

SPOKE

NIGHT

TWILIGHT ZONE

SLANTING CABLES

SOLAR HEAT EXCHANGER SHEET

DAYLIGHT

SOLAR REFLECTOR

WINDOW

TRANSPARENT

TWILIGHT ZONE

SLANTING CABLES

NIGHT

SPOKE

VALVE

VERTICAL CABLES

Mountains

Area shown in aerial view map

JMW266.78

Chapter One

"Rocky, would you take a look at this?"

"That's Cap'n Jones to you. Show me in the morning."

"It's sort of important."

Cirocco was at her wash basin, her face covered in soap. She groped for a towel and wiped the greenish goop away. It was the only kind of soap the recyclers would eat.

She squinted at the two pictures Gaby handed her.

"What is it?"

"Just the twelfth satellite of Saturn." Gaby was not entirely successful at hiding her excitement.

"No fooling?" Cirocco frowned from one picture to the other. "Just a lot of little black dots to me."

"Well, yeah. You can't see anything without the comparometer. That's it right there." She indicated an area with her little finger.

"Let's go take a look."

Cirocco rummaged through her locker and found a pea-green shipsuit that smelled as good as any of them. Most of the handy velcro patches were peeling.

Her room was at the bottom of the carousel, midway between ladders three and four. She followed Gaby around the curving floor, then pursued her up the ladder.

Each rung was a little easier than the last until, at the hub, they were weightless. They pushed off from the slowly rotating ring and drifted down the central corridor to the science module: SCIMOD in NASA-ese. It was kept dark to make the instruments easier to read, and was as colorful as the inside of a jukebox. Cirocco liked it. Green lights blinked and banks of television screens hissed white noise through confetti clouds of snow. Eugene Springfield and the Polo sisters floated around the central holo tank. Their faces were bathed in the red glow.

Gaby handed the plates to the computer, punched up an image-intensifying program, and indicated the screen Cirocco should watch. The pictures were sharpened, combined, then rapidly alternated. Two miniscule dots blinked, not far from each other.

"There it is," Gaby said proudly. "Small proper motion, but the plates are only twenty-three hours apart."

Gene called to them.

"Orbital elements are coming in," he said.

Gaby and Cirocco joined him. Cirocco glanced down and saw his arm go possessively around Gaby's waist, looked quickly away, noting that the Polo sisters had seen it and were just as careful not to notice. They had all learned to stay out of each other's affairs.

Saturn sat in the middle of the tank, fat and brassy. Eight blue circles were drawn around it, each larger than the last, each in the equatorial plane of the rings. There was a sphere on each circle, like a single pearl on a string, and beside the pearls were names and numbers: Mnemosyne, Janus, Mimas, Enceladus, Tethys, Dione, Rhea, Titan, and Hyperion. Far beyond those orbits was a tenth one, visibly tilted. That was Iapetus. Phoebe, the most distant, could not be shown on the scale they were using.

Now another circle was drawn in. It was an eccentric ellipse, almost tangent to the orbits of Rhea and Hyperion, cutting right across the circle that represented

Titan. Cirocco studied it, then straightened. Looking up, she saw deep lines etched on Gaby's forehead as her fingers flew over the keyboard. With each program she called up, the numbers on her screen changed.

"It had a very close call with Rhea about three million years ago," she noted. "It's safely above Titan's orbit, though perturbations must be a factor. It's far from stabilized."

"Meaning what?" Cirocco asked.

"Captured asteroid?" Gaby suggested, one eyebrow raised doubtfully.

"The proximity to the equatorial plane would make that unlikely," one of the Polo sisters said. April or August? Cirocco wondered. After eighteen months together she still couldn't tell them apart.

"I was afraid you'd see that." Gaby chewed a knuckle. "Yet if it was formed with the others, it ought to be less eccentric."

The Polo shrugged. "There are ways to explain it. A catastrophic event in the recent past. It would be easy to move it."

Cirocco frowned. "Just how big is it, then?"

The Polo—August, she was almost sure it was August—looked at her with that calm, strangely unsettling face. "I should say about two or three kilometers. Possibly less."

"Is *that* all?"

Gene grinned. "You give me the numbers, I'll land on it."

"What do you mean, 'Is that all'?" Gaby said. "It couldn't have been very much bigger, not to have been sighted by the Lunar scopes. We would have known about it thirty years ago."

"All right. But you interrupted my bath for a damn pebble. It hardly seems worth it."

Gaby looked smug. "Maybe not to you, but if it was a tenth that size, I'd still get to name it. Discovering a comet or an asteroid is one thing, but only a couple people each century get to name a moon."

Cirocco released her toehold on the holo tank strut and twisted toward the corridor entrance. Just before she left she glanced back at the two tiny dots still flashing on the screen overhead.

Bill's tongue had started at Cirocco's toes and was now exploring her left ear. She liked that. It had been a memorable journey. Cirocco had loved every centimeter of it; some of the stops along the way had been outrageous. Now he was worrying her earlobe with his lips and teeth, tugging gently to turn her around. She let it happen.

He nudged her shoulder with his chin and nose to get her turning faster. She began to rotate. She felt like a big, soft asteroid. The analogy pleased her. Extending it, she watched the terminator line crawl around her to bring the hills and valleys of her front into sunlight.

Cirocco liked space, reading, and sex, not necessarily in that order. She had never been able to satisfactorily combine all three, but two was not bad.

New games were possible in free-fall, like the one they had been playing, "no hands." They could use feet, mouths, knees, or shoulders to position each other. One had to be gentle and careful, but with slow bites and nips anything could be done, and in such an interesting way.

All of them came to the hydroponics room from time to time. *Ringmaster* had seven private rooms, and they were as necessary as oxygen. But even Cirocco's cabin was crowded when two people were in it, and it was at the bottom of the carousel. It took one act of love in free-fall to make a bed seem as limiting as the back seat of a Chevrolet.

"Why don't you turn this way a little?" Bill asked.

"Can you give me a good reason?"

He showed her one, and she gave him a little more than he had asked for. Then she found herself with a little more than *she* had asked for, but as usual, he knew what he was doing. She locked her legs around his hips and let him do the moving.

Bill was forty, the oldest of the crew, and had a face

dominated by a lumpy nose and jowls that could have graced a bassett hound. He was balding and his teeth were not pretty. But his body was lean and hard, ten years younger than his face. His hands were neat and clean, precise in their movements. He was good with machinery, but not the greasy, noisy kind. His tool kit would fit in his shirt pocket, tools so tiny that Cirocco wouldn't dare handle them.

His delicate touch paid off when he made love. It was matched by his gentle disposition. Cirocco wondered why it had taken her so long to find him.

There were three men aboard *Ringmaster,* and Cirocco had made love to them all. So had Gaby Plauget. It was impossible to keep secrets when seven people lived in such a confined space. She knew for a fact, for instance, that what the Polo sisters did behind the closed doors of their adjoining rooms was still illegal in Alabama.

They had all bounced around a lot, especially in the early months of the voyage. Gene was the only married crew member, and he had taken care to announce quite early that he and his wife had an arrangement about such matters. Still, he had slept alone for a long time because the Polos had each other, Gaby didn't seem to care about sex at all, and Cirocco had been irresistibly drawn to Calvin Greene.

Her persistence was such that Calvin eventually went to bed with her, not just once, but three times. It didn't get any better, so before he could sense her disappointment she had cooled the relationship and let him pursue Gaby, the woman he had been drawn to from the first. Calvin was a general surgeon trained by NASA to be competent as ship's biologist and ecologist as well. He was black, but attached little importance to it, having been born and raised in O'Neil One. He was also the only crew member who was taller than Cirocco. She didn't think that had much to do with his appeal; she had learned early to be indifferent to a man's height, since she was taller than most of them. She thought it was more in his eyes, which were soft and brown and liquid. And his smile.

Those eyes and that smile had done nothing for Gaby,

just as Cirocco's charms had not interested Gene, her second choice.

"What are you smiling about?" Bill asked.

"Don't you think you're giving me enough reason?" she countered, a little breathlessly. But the truth was she had been thinking of how amusing the four of them must have looked to Bill, who had stayed out of the shuffle of bodies. That seemed to be his style, to sit back and let people sort themselves out, then move in when it began to be depressing.

Calvin had certainly been depressed. So had Cirocco. Whether from preoccupation with Gaby or just inexperience, Calvin had not been much of a lover. Cirocco thought it was a little of both. He was quiet, shy, and bookish. His records showed he had spent most of his life in school, carrying an academic load that left little room for fun.

Gaby just didn't care. The Science Module of *Ringmaster* was the finest toy a girl ever had. She loved her work so much she had joined the astronaut corps and graduated at the top of her class so she could watch the stars without an annoying atmosphere, even though she hated to travel. When she was working she noticed nothing else, did not think it odd that Calvin spent almost as much time in SCIMOD as she did, waiting for the chance to hand her a photographic plate or a lens cloth or the keys to his heart.

Gene didn't seem to care, either. Cirocco sent out signals that could have drawn her five to life if the FCC had known about them, but Gene wasn't receiving. He just grinned with that boyish, tousle-haired Aryan ideal face and talked about flying. He was to be the pilot of the Satellite Excursion Module when the ship reached Saturn. Cirocco liked flying, too, but there came a time when a woman wanted to do something else.

But eventually Calvin and Cirocco got what they had wanted. Soon after, neither wanted it anymore.

Cirocco didn't know what the problem was with Calvin and Gaby; neither of them talked about it, but it was obvious that it worked only passably at best. Calvin continued to see her, but she saw Gene, too.

Gene had apparently been waiting for Cirocco to stop chasing him. As soon as she did, he began to sidle up and breathe heavily in her ear. She didn't like that much, and the rest of his technique was no better. When he was through making love, it almost seemed he expected to be thanked. Cirocco had never been easily impressed; Gene would have been astonished to learn where he fell on her scale of one to ten.

Bill had happened almost by accident—though she had since learned that few accidents happened around Bill. One thing led to another, and now they were about to provide a pornographic demonstration of Newton's Third Law of Motion, the one that used to refer to "action and reaction."

Cirocco had done some calculations on the matter, and had found that the force of ejaculation was not nearly enough to account for the orgasmic acceleration she always observed at that moment. The cause was certainly spasms of the large muscles of the leg, but the effect was beautiful and a little frightening, as though they had become big, fleshy balloons losing air, forced away from each other at the moment of closest approach. They would careen and carom, and finally come to rest together again.

Bill felt it building, too. He grinned, and the hydroponic lamps made his crooked teeth luminescent.

PUB/REL DISPATCH #0056
5/12/25
DSV RINGMASTER (NASA 447D, L5/1, HOUSTON-COPERNICUS GCR BASELINE)
JONES, CIROCCO, MISCOM
FOR PARAPHRASING AND IMMEDIATE RELEASE
BEGINS:
Gaby has settled on Themis as the name of the new moon. Calvin agrees with her, though they arrived at the name from different directions.
Gaby mentions the alleged sighting of (what would have been) a tenth moon of Saturn by William Henry

Pickering—discoverer of Phoebe, Saturn's outermost moon—in 1905. He named it Themis, and no one ever saw it again.

Calvin points out that five of the Saturnian moons are already named after the Titans of Greek myth (which is a special interest of his; see PUB/REL DISPATCH #0009, 1/3/24) and a sixth is called Titan. Themis was a Titan, so Calvin's mind is appeased.

Themis has things in common with the moon Pickering thought he saw, but Gaby is not convinced he actually sighted it. (If he did, she would not be listed as its discoverer. But to be fair, it seems too small and dim to be seen in even the best Lunar scopes.)

Gaby is formulating a cataclysmic theory of Themis' formation, the result of a collision between Rhea and a wandering asteroid. Themis might be the remnant of the asteroid, or a chunk knocked off of Rhea itself.

So Themis is proving an interesting challenge for

"—that wonderful gang of idiots you all know so well by now, the crew of the *DSV Ringmaster*." Cirocco leaned back from the typer touchplate, stretched her arms over her head, and cracked her knuckles. "Tripe," she muttered. "Also bullshit."

The green letters glowed on the screen in front of her, still with no period at the bottom.

It was a part of her job she always delayed as long as possible, but the NASA flacks could no longer be ignored. Themis was an uninteresting chunk of rock, by all indications, but the publicity department was desperate for something to hang a story on. They also wanted human interest, "personality journalism," as they called it. Cirocco tried her best, but could not bring herself to go into the kind of detail the release writers wanted. Which hardly mattered anyway, since what she had just written would be edited, re-written, discussed in conference, and generally jazzed up to "humanize" the astronauts.

Cirocco sympathized with their goal. Few people gave a damn about the space program. They felt the money could be better spent on Earth, on Luna, and at the L5 colonies. Why pour money down the rat-hole of exploration when there was so much benefit to be derived from things that were established on a businesslike basis, like Earth-orbital manufacturing? Exploration was terribly expensive, and there was nothing at Saturn but a lot of rock and vacuum.

She was trying to think of some fresh, new way to justify her presense on the first exploratory mission in eleven years when a face appeared on her screen. It might have been April, and it might have been August.

"Captain, I'm sorry to disturb you."

"That's okay. I wasn't busy."

"We have something up here for you to see."

"Be right up."

She thought it was August. Cirocco had worked on keeping them straight since twins generally resent being mistaken for each other. She had gradually realized that April and August didn't care.

But April and August were not ordinary twins.

Their full names were April 15/02 Polo and August 3/02 Polo. That was what was written on their respective test tubes, and that is what the scientists who had been their midwives had put on the birth certificates. Which had always struck Cirocco as two excellent reasons why scientists should not be allowed to fool around with experiments that lived and breathed and cried.

Their mother, Susan Polo, had been dead for five years at the time of their births, and could not protect them. Nobody else seemed ready to give them any mothering, so they had only each other and their three clone-sisters for love. August had told Cirocco once that the five of them had only one close friend while growing up, and that had been a Rhesus monkey with a souped-up brain. He had been dissected when the girls were seven.

"I don't want to make it sound too brutal," August had said on that occasion, a night when some glasses of Bill's soybean wine had been consumed. "Those scientists were not monsters. A lot of them behaved like kindly aunts and uncles. We had just about anything we wanted. I'm sure a lot of them loved us." She had taken another drink. "After all," she said, "we cost a lot of money."

What the scientists got for their money was five quiet, rather spooky geniuses, which is just what they ordered. Cirocco doubted they had bargained for the incestuous homosexuality, but felt they should have expected it, just as surely as the high I.Q. They were all clones of their mother—the daughter of a third-generation Japanese-American and a Filipino. Susan Polo won the Nobel prize in physics and died young.

Cirocco looked at August as the woman studied a photo on the chart table. She was exactly like her famous mother as a young woman: small, with jet-black hair and a trim figure, and dark, expressionless eyes. Cirocco had never thought Oriental faces were as similar as many Caucasians found them to be, but April and August's faces gave nothing away. Their skin was the color of coffee with lots of cream, but in the red light of the Science Module August looked almost black.

She glanced at Cirocco, showing more excitement than usual for her. Cirocco held her eye for a moment, then looked down. Against a field of pinpoint stars, six tiny lights were arranged in a perfect hexagon.

Cirocco looked at it for a long time.

"It's the damdest thing I ever saw on a starplate," she conceded. "What is it?"

Gaby was strapped to a chair on the other side of the compartment, sucking coffee from a plastic bulb.

"It's the latest exposure of Themis," she said. "I took it over the last hour with my most sensitive equipment and a computer program to justify the rotation."

"I guess that answers my question," Cirocco said. "But what *is* it?"

Gaby waited a long time before replying, taking another sip.

"It is possible," she said, sounding detached and dreamy, "for several bodies to orbit around a common center of gravity. Theoretically. No one's ever seen it. The configuration is called a rosette."

Cirocco waited patiently. When no one said anything, she snorted.

"In the middle of Saturn's satellite system? For about five minutes, maybe. The other moons would perturb them."

"There's that," Gaby agreed.

"And how would it happen in the first place? The chances against it are tremendous."

"There's that, too."

April and Calvin had entered the room. Now Calvin looked up.

"Isn't anyone going to say it? This isn't a natural arrangement. Somebody made this."

Gaby rubbed her forehead.

"You haven't heard it all. I bounced radar signals off it. They came back telling me Themis was over 1300 kilometers in diameter. Density figures all cockeyed, too, making it less dense than water by quite a bit. I thought I was getting screwed-up readings because I was working at the limits of my equipment. Then I got the picture."

"Six bodies or one?" Cirocco asked.

"I can't tell for *sure*. But everything points to one."

"Describe it. What you think you know."

Gaby consulted her printout sheets, but obviously did not need them. The figures were clear in her mind.

"Themis is 1300 klicks across. That makes it Saturn's third largest moon, about the size of Rhea. It must be flat black all over, except those six points. This is by far the lowest albedo of any body in the solar system, if that interests you. It's also the least dense. There's a strong possibility it's hollow, and a good chance it's not spherical. Possibly disc-shaped, or toroidal, like a donut. Either way, it seems to turn like a plate rolling along its edge, once every hour. That's enough spin so nothing could stay on its surface; the centripetal force would overpower the force of gravity."

"But if it's hollow, and you were on the inside..." Cirocco kept her eyes on Gaby.

"Inside, *if* it's hollow, it would be equivalent to a force of one-quarter gee."

Cirocco looked her next question, and Gaby couldn't meet her eyes.

"We're getting closer every day. The seeing can only get better. But I can't promise you when I could be sure about any of this."

Cirocco headed for the door. "I'll have to send what you have."

"But no theories, okay?" Gaby shouted after her. It was the first Cirocco had seen her less than happy with what she'd seen through a telescope. "At least don't attribute them to me."

"No theories," Cirocco acknowledged. "The facts ought to be plenty."

Chapter Two

INFORMATIONAL DISPATCH #0931
(REPLY TO HOUSTON TRANSMISSION #5455, 5-20-25)
5-21-25
DSV RINGMASTER (NASA 447D, L5/1, HOUSTON-COPERNICUS GCR BASELINE)
JONES, CIROCCO, MISCOM
SECURITY INTERLOCK *ON*
CODE PREFIX DELTADELTA
BEGINS:

1. Concur your analysis of Themis as interstellar space vehicle of the generation type. Don't forget we suggested it first.

2. Latest photo follows. Note increased resolution of bright areas. Still no luck finding docking facilities at hub; will keep looking.

3. Concur your mid-course scheduled 5/22.

4. Request updated tracking as new orbital insertion is approached, beginning 5/25 and continuing until insertion commences, then upgraded. I don't care if this means shifting in another computer; I don't think our on-board will handle this volume.

5. Turnaround 5/22, 0400 UT, after the mid-course burn.
INFORMATIONAL ENDS
PERSONAL (CIRCULATION LIMITED TO RINGMASTER
MISSION CONTROL COMMITTEE) BEGINS:
Re the Contact Committee which has been bending my ear: *buzz off!* I don't care WHO'S on the damn thing. I've been getting contradictory instructions that sound like they have the force of direct orders. Maybe you don't like my ideas of how to handle this, maybe you do. The fact is it's going to have to be my show. Time-lag alone is enough to make that necessary. You gave me the ship and the responsibility, so *GET OFF MY BACK!*
ENDS

Cirocco hit the ENCODE button, then TRANSMIT, and leaned back in her chair. She rubbed her eyes. A few days ago there had been too little to do. Now she was snowed under with the status check to ready *Ringmaster* for orbital insertion.

Everything was changed, and all by those six tiny points of light in Gaby's telescope. There seemed little sense in exploring the other Saturnian moons now. They were committed to an early rendezvous with Themis.

She called up the schedule of things still to be done, then the duty roster, saw it had been re-arranged again. She was to join April and Calvin outside. She hurried to the lock.

Her suit was bulky and tight. It murmured at her while the radio hissed quietly. It smelled comfortably like herself, and like hospital plastic and fresh oxygen.

Ringmaster was an elongated structure consisting of two main section joined by a hollow tube three meters in diameter and a hundred meters long. Structural strength for the tube was provided by three composite girders on the outside, each of which transmitted the thrust of one engine to the life system balanced on top of the tube.

At the far end were the engines and a cluster of detachable fuel tanks, hidden from sight by the broad plate of the radiation shield which ringed the central tube like the rat guard on the mooring line of an ocean-going freighter. The other side of that shield was an unhealthy place to be.

On the other end of the tube was the life system, consisting of the science module, the control module, and the carousel.

Control was the extreme front end, a cone-shaped protuberance rising from the big coffee can that was SCIMOD. It had the only windows on the ship, more for tradition than practicality.

The Science Module was almost hidden behind a thicket of instrumentation. The high-gain antenna rose above it all, perched on the end of a long stalk and trained on Earth. There were two radar dishes and five telescopes, including Gaby's 120-centimeter Newtonian.

Just behind it was the carousel: a fat, white flywheel. It rotated slowly around the rest of the ship, with four spokes leading up from the rim.

Strapped to the central stem were other items, including the hydroponics cylinders and the several components of the lander: life system, tug engine, two descent stages and the ascent engine.

The lander had been intended for exploring the Saturnian moons, in particular Iapetus and Rhea. After Titan—which had an atmosphere and was therefore unsuited for exploration this trip—Iapetus was the most interesting body in the neighborhood. Until the 1980's, it had been significantly brighter in one hemisphere, but it had changed over a twenty-year period until its albedo was nearly uniform. Two troughs in the graph of luminosity now occured at opposite points on its orbit. The lander had been designed to discover what had caused it.

Now that trip had been scrapped in the face of the much more compelling object called Themis.

Ringmaster resembled another spaceship: the fictional *Discovery*, the Jupiter probe from the classic movie *2001: A Space Odyssey*. It was not surprising that it should. Both ships had been designed from similar parameters, though one sailed only on celluloid. Cirocco was EVA to remove the last of the solar reflection panels which wrapped the life system of *Ringmaster*. The problem in a space vehicle is usually one of disposing of excess heat, but they were now far enough from the sun that it paid to soak up what they could get.

She hooked a safety line around a pipe that went from the carousel hub to the airlock, and faced one of the last panels. It was silver, a meter square, made of two sheets of thin foil sandwiched together. She touched the screwdriver to one corner and the device clucked as it found the slot. The counterweight rotated. It gulped the loose screw before it could drift away.

Three more times and the panel floated away from the layer of anti-meteorite foam beneath. Cirocco held it and turned to face the sun, conducting her own informal puncture survey. Three tiny, bright lights marked where the sheet had been hit by grains of meteoritic dust.

The panel was held rigid by wires along the edges. She bent two of these in the middle. After the fifth fold it was small enough to fit in the thigh pocket of her suit. She fastened the flap, then moved to the next panel.

Time was at a premium. Whenever possible they combined two chores, so the end of the ship's day found Cirocco reclining on her bunk while Calvin gave her a weekly physical and Gaby showed her the latest picture of Themis. The room was crowded.

"It's not a photo," Gaby was saying. "It's a computer-enhanced theoretical image. And it's in infra-red, which seems to be the best spectrum."

Cirocco raised herself on one elbow, careful not to dislodge any of Calvin's electrodes. She chewed on the end of the thermometer until he frowned at her.

The print showed a fat wagon wheel surrounded by broad-based, bright red triangular areas. There were six red areas on the inside of the wheel, but they were smaller, and square.

"The big triangles on the outside are the hottest parts," Gaby said. "I figure they're part of the temperature control system. They soak up heat from the sun or bleed off the excess."

"Houston already decided that," Cirocco pointed out. She glanced at the television camera near the ceiling. Ground control was monitoring them. If they thought of something Cirocco would hear of it in a few hours, asleep or not.

The wheel analogy was almost literally true, except for the heating or cooling fins Gaby had indicated. There was a hub in the center, and it had a hole which could have taken an axle if Themis had actually been a wagon wheel. Radiating from the hub were six thick spokes which flared gradually just before joining the outer portion of the wheel. Between each pair of spokes was one of the bright, square areas.

"This is what's new," Gaby said. "Those squares are angled. They're what I originally saw; the six points of light. They're flat, or they'd scatter a lot more light. As it is they only reflect light to Earth if they're at just the right angle, and that's rare."

"What kind of angle?" Cirocco lisped. Calvin took the thermometer out of her mouth.

"Okay. Light comes in parallel to the axis, from *this* angle." She moved an extended finger toward the print. "The mirrors are set to deflect the light ninety degrees, into the wheel roof." She touched the paper with her finger, turned the finger, and indicated an area between two spokes.

"This part of the wheel is hotter than the rest, but not so hot that it could be soaking up all the heat it gets. It's not reflecting it or absorbing it, so it's transmitting it. It's transparent or translucent. It lets most of the light go through to whatever's underneath. Does that suggest anything to you?"

Cirocco looked up from her careful examination.

"What do you mean?"

"Okay. We know the wheel is hollow. Maybe the spokes are, too. Anyway, picture the wheel. It's like a car tire, big and fat and flat on the bottom to give more living space. Centrifugal force pushes you away from the hub."

"I've got all that," Cirocco said, slightly amused. Gaby could be so intense when explaining something.

"Right. So when you're standing on the inside of the wheel, you're either under a spoke, or under a reflector, right?"

"Yeah? Oh, yeah. So—"

"So it's always either daytime or nighttime at any particular spot. The spokes are rigidly attached, the reflectors don't move, and neither can the skylights. So it *has* to be that way. Permanent day or permanent night. Why do you think they'd build it that way?"

"To answer that, we'd need to meet them. Their needs must be different from ours." She looked back at the picture. She had to keep reminding herself of the size of the thing. Thirteen hundred meters in diameter, 4000 around the outer rim. The prospect of meeting the beings who built such a thing was worrying her more each day.

"All right. I can wait." Gaby was not that interested in Themis as a spacecraft. To her it was a fascinating problem in observation.

Cirocco again looked at the picture.

"The hub," she began, then bit her lip. That camera was still running, and she didn't want to say anything too hastily.

"What about it?"

"Well, it's the only place you could dock with the thing. The only part that's motionless."

"Not the way it is now. That hole in the middle is pretty big. The first time you reach anything solid, it's moving at a pretty good clip. I can calculate—"

"Never mind. It's not important right now. The point is, only at the very dead center of rotation could you dock with Themis without a great deal of trouble. *I* sure wouldn't want to try it."

"So?"

"So there must be a compelling reason why there's no docking facilities visible there. Something important enough to sacrifice that location, some reason for leaving a big hole in the center."

"Engine," Calvin said. Cirocco glanced at him, got a glimpse of his brown eyes before he turned back to his work.

"That was my thought. A real big fusion ramscoop. The machinery is in the hub, electromagnetic field generators to funnel the interstellar hydrogen into the center, where it gets burned."

Gaby shrugged. "Makes sense. But what about docking?"

"Well, *leaving* the thing would be easy enough. Just drop out a hole in the bottom and get escape velocity for free, plus some to fool around with. But there ought to be some sort of dingus that would telescope out to the center of rotation when the engine isn't running, to pick up scout ships. The main engine *has* to be there. The only other way would be to space engines around the rim. I'd want three, at least. More would be better."

She turned to face the camera.

"Send me what you can about hydrogen ramscoop engines," she said. "See if you can give me some idea of what to look for if Themis has one."

"You'll have to take your shirt off," Calvin said.

Cirocco reached up and switched off the camera, leaving the sound on. Calvin thumped her back and listened to the results while Cirocco and Gaby continued to study the picture of Themis. They came up with no new insights until Gaby brought up the matter of the cables.

"As far as I can tell, they form a circle about midway between the hub and the rim. They support the top edges of the reflecting panels, sort of like the rigging on a sailing ship."

"What about these?" Cirocco asked, indicating the area between two of the spokes. "Any idea what they're for?"

"Nope. There's six of them, and they run midway between the spokes, from the hub to the rim, radially. They pass through the reflecting panels, if that tells you anything."

"Not exactly. But if there's any more of these things, maybe smaller ones, we should look for them. These cables are about—what did you say? Three kilometers around?"

"More like five."

"Okay. So one that's just a tiny thing—say about as big around as *Ringmaster*—might be invisible to us for a long time, especially if it's as black as the rest of Themis. Gene's going to be nosing around there in the SEM. I'd hate for him to hit one."

"I'll get the computer on it," Gaby said.

Calvin began packing his equipment.

"As disgustingly healthy as usual," he said. "You people never give me a break. If I don't try out that five-million-dollar hospital how am I going to make them believe they got their money's worth?"

"You want me to break somebody's arm?" Cirocco suggested.

"Nah. I already did that, back in medical school."

"Broke one, or fixed it?"

Calvin laughed. "Appendix. Now *there's* something I'd like to try. You don't hardly get busted appendixes anymore."

"You mean you've never taken out an appendix? What do they teach you in medical school these days?"

"That if you get the theory right, the fingers will follow. We're too intellectual to get our hands dirty." He laughed again, and Cirocco could feel the thin walls of her room shaking.

"I wish I knew when he was serious," Gaby said.

"You want serious?" Calvin asked. "Here's something you might never have thought of. Elective surgery. You folks have one of the best surgeons around—" He paused to allow the rude noises to die away. "One of the best surgeons there is. Does anyone take advantage of it? Not hardly. A nose job, now that's going to cost you seven, eight thousand back home. Here you got it on the Blue Cross."

Cirocco drew herself up and gave him an icy glare.

"You couldn't be talking about *me*, could you?"

Calvin held out a thumb and sighted along it to Cirocco's face, squinting. "Of course, there's other types of elective surgery. I'm pretty good at all of them. It was my hobby." He moved his thumb lower. Cirocco aimed a kick at him and he ducked out the door.

She was smiling when she sat down. Gaby was still there, the picture tucked under her arm. She perched on the tiny folding stool beside the cot.

Cirocco raised one eyebrow.

"Was there something else?"

Gaby looked away. She opened her mouth to say something, didn't manage to make a sound, then slapped her bare thigh with her palm.

"No, I guess there wasn't." She started to get up, but didn't.

Cirocco looked at her thoughtfully, then reached up and turned the television sound off.

"Does that help any?"

Gaby shrugged. "Maybe. I would have asked you to turn it off anyway, if I could ever have started talking. I guess I figure it's none of my business."

"But you felt you ought to say something." Cirocco waited.

"Yeah, okay. It's your business how you run this ship. I want you to know I realize that."

"Go on. I can take criticism."

"You've been sleeping with Bill."

Cirocco laughed quietly. "I don't ever *sleep* with him. The bed's too small. But I get the idea."

Cirocco had hoped to put Gaby at ease, but apparently it hadn't worked. Gaby stood and paced slowly, even though she could only go four steps before she reached the wall.

"Captain, sex is no big thing to me." She shrugged. "I don't hate sex, but I'm not all that crazy about it, either. If I don't have sex for a day or a year, I don't even notice it. But most people aren't like that. Especially men."

"I'm not like that, either."

"I know. That's why I wondered how you. . . . just what your feelings are toward Bill."

It was Cirocco's turn to pace. It was even less satisfactory to her, since she was bigger than Gaby and could only take three steps.

"Gaby, human interactions in confined environments is a well-researched field. They've tried all-male ships.

Even all-female once. They've tried it with all-married crews, and with all singles. They've had rules forbidding sex, and they've had no rules at all. *None* of them worked well. People will get on each other's nerves, and they're going to have sex. That's why I don't tell anybody what to do in private."

"I'm not trying to say that you—"

"Just a minute. I said all that so you'd know I'm not un-aware of potential problems. I should hear about specific ones."

She waited.

"It's Gene," Gaby said. "I've been making it with both Gene and Calvin. Like I say, it's no big thing for me. I know Calvin's got this thing for me. I'm used to that. At home, I'd just cool him off. Here, I fuck with him to keep him happy. It makes very little difference to me either way.

"But I'm fucking Gene because he.... he has this.... this *pressure*. You know?" She had balled her hands into fists. Now she opened them and looked to Cirocco for understanding.

"I've had some experience with it, yes." Cirocco kept her voice even.

"All right, he doesn't satisfy you. He told me that. It bothers him. That kind of intensity scares me, maybe because I don't understand it. I've been seeing him try to ease his tension."

Cirocco pursed her lips.

"Let me get this straight. Are you asking me to take him off your hands?"

"No, no, I'm not asking you anything. I told you, I'm just making you aware of the problem, if you weren't already. What you do about it is up to you."

Cirocco nodded. "All right. I'm glad you told me. But he's going to have to live with this. He's stable, well-adjusted, a bit of a dominating personality, but he's got it well under control or he wouldn't be here."

Gaby nodded. "Whatever you think best."

"One more thing. It's no part of your duty to keep anyone sexually satisfied. Any burden you feel in that direction is self-assumed."

"I understand that."

"Just so you do. I'd hate to think you thought I expected it of you. Or that you expected it of me." She searched the other woman's eyes until Gaby looked away, then reached over and patted her knee.

"Besides, it'll take care of itself. We're all going to be too busy to think much about screwing."

Chapter Three

From a ballistic standpoint, Themis was a nightmare.

No one had ever tried to orbit a toroidal body. Themis was 1300 kilometers across and only 250 kilometers wide. The torus was flat along the outside, and 175 kilometers from top to bottom. The density of the torus varied radically, supporting the view that it was composed of a thick floor along the outside, an atmosphere about that, and a thin canopy arching overhead holding the air inside.

Then there were the six spokes, 420 kilometers tall. They were elliptical in cross-section, with major and minor axes of 100 kilometers and 50 kilometers, respectively, except near the base where they flared out to join the torus. In the center was the hub, more massive than the spokes, 160 kilometers in diameter, with a 100-kilometer hole in the center.

Trying to cope with a body like that was tantamount to a nervous breakdown for the ship's computer, and for Bill, who had to make a model the computer would believe in.

The easiest orbit would have been in the equatorial plane of Saturn, enabling them to use the velocity they

already had. But that was not possible. Themis was
oriented with its axis of rotation parallel to the equatorial
plane. Since the axis passed through the hole at the center
of Themis, any Saturn-equatorial orbit Cirocco might
assume would have *Ringmaster* passing through areas of
wildly fluctuating gravitational attraction.

The only viable possibility was an orbit in the
equatorial plane of Themis. Such an orbit would be
expensive in terms of angular momentum. It had the
single advantage of being stable, once achieved.

The maneuvering began before they reached Saturn.
During the last day of approach their course was
re-calculated. Cirocco and Bill relied on Earth-based
computers and navigational aids as far away as Mars and
Jupiter. They lived in CONMOD and watched Saturn
grow larger in the aft television screens.

Then the long burn was initiated.

During a lull in her work, Cirocco turned on the
camera in SCIMOD. Gaby looked up with a harried
expression.

"Rocky, can't you do something about that vibration?"

"Gaby, the engine function is, as they say, nominal.
They're just going to shake, that's all."

"Best observing time of the whole fucking *trip*," Gaby
muttered. In the seat next to Cirocco, Bill laughed.

"Five minutes, Gaby," he said. "And I really think we
ought to let them burn as long as we planned. It would
work out so much nicer that way."

The engines shut down on the tick and they watched
for final confirmation that they were where they wanted
to be.

"This is *Ringmaster*; C. Jones commanding. We have
arrived in Saturn orbit at 1341.453 hours, Universal
Time. I'll send up the prelims for a correcting burn when
we come out from behind. Meanwhile, I'm going off this
channel."

She slapped the appropriate switch.

"Anybody who wants to take a look outside, this is
going to be your only chance."

It was tight, but August and April and Gene and Calvin

managed to squeeze into the cramped room. After checking with Gaby, Cirocco turned the ship ninety degrees.

Saturn was a dark gray hole, seventeen degrees wide, covering 1000 times the area of the moon as seen from Earth. The rings were an incredible forty degrees from side to side.

They looked like solid, brilliant metal. *Ringmaster* had come in north of the equator, so the upper face was presented to them. Each particle was being lit from the opposite side, presenting a thin crescent, like Saturn. The sun was a brilliant point of light in the ten o'clock position, approaching Saturn.

No one spoke as the sun drew nearer to eclipse. They saw Saturn's shadow fall across the part of the ring nearest them, cutting it like a razor.

Sunset lasted fifteen seconds. The colors were deep and changed rapidly, pure reds and yellows and blue-blacks like those seen from an airliner in the stratosphere.

There was a soft chorus of sighs in the cabin. The glass depolarized and everyone gasped again as the rings grew brighter, bracketing the deep blue glow that outlined the northern hemisphere. Gray striations became visible on the planetary surface, illuminated by ringlight. Down there were storms as big as the Earth.

When she looked away at last, Cirocco saw the screen to her left. Gaby was still in SCIMOD. There was an image of Saturn on the screen above her head, but she didn't look up at it.

"Gaby, don't you want to come up and see this?"

Cirocco saw her shake her head. She scanned the numbers marching across a tiny screen.

"And lose the best observing time of the whole trip? You've got to be out of your mind."

They first assumed a long, elliptical orbit with a low point 200 kilometers above the theoretical radius of Themis. It was a mathematical abstraction because the orbit was tilted thirty degrees from Themis' equator, which put them above the dark side. They passed the

spinning toroid to emerge on the sun side. Themis lay
spread out before them as a naked-eye object.

Not that there was a lot to see. Themis was nearly as
black as space, even with the sun shining on it. She studied
the huge mass of the wheel with the triangular solar
absorption sails rimming it like sharp gear teeth,
presumably soaking up sunlight and turning it into heat.

The ship moved over the interior of the great wheel.
The spokes became visible, and the solar reflectors. They
seemed nearly as dark as the rest of Themis, except where
they mirrored some of the brighter stars.

The problem that still worried Cirocco was the lack of
an entrance. There was a lot of pressure from Earth to get
into the thing, and Cirocco, despite her cautious instincts,
wanted to as badly as anyone else.

There had to be a way. No one doubted Themis was an
artifact. The debate concerned whether it was an
interstellar space vehicle or an artificial world, like O'Neil
One. The differences were movement and orgin. A
spaceship would have an engine, and it would be at the
hub. A colony would have been built by somebody close
at hand. Cirocco had heard theories that included
inhabitants of Saturn or Titan, Martians—though no one
had found so much as a flint arrowhead on Mars—and
ancient space-faring races from the Earth. She didn't
believe any of them, but it hardly mattered. Ship or
colony, Themis had been built by someone, and there
would be a door.

The place to look was the hub, but the constraints of
ballistics forced her to orbit as far from the hub as she
could get.

Ringmaster settled into a circular orbit 400 kilometers
above the equator. They traveled in the direction of spin,
but Themis turned faster than their orbital speed. It was a
black plane outside Cirocco's window. At regular
intervals one of the solar panels would sweep by like the
wing of a monstrous bat.

Some details could now be seen on the outer surface.
There were long, puckered ridges that converged on the

solar panels, presumably covering huge pipes to carry a fluid or gas to be warmed by the sun. Scattered widely in the darkness were a few craters, some of them 400 meters deep. There was no rubble scattered around them. Nothing could stay on the outer surface of Themis that wasn't fastened down.

Cirocco locked her control board. At her elbow, Bill nodded in his couch, asleep. The two of them had not left CONMOD in two days.

She moved through SCIMOD like a sleepwalker. Somewhere down there was a bed with soft sheets and a pillow, and a comfortable quarter gee now that the carousel was turning again.

"Rocky, we've got something strange here."

She stopped with one foot on the ladder of D Spoke, stood very still for a moment.

"What did you say?" The edge in her voice made Gaby look up.

"I'm tired, too," she said, irritable. She palmed a switch, and an image appeared on the overhead screen.

It was a view of the approaching edge of Themis. There was a swelling on it that seemed to grow larger as it caught up with them.

"That wasn't there before." Cirocco's brow furrowed as she tried to shake off the exhaustion.

A buzzer sounded faintly and for a moment she could not place it. Then things became sharp and clear as adrenalin ate the cobwebs. It was the radar alarm in CONMOD.

"Captain," Bill said over the speaker, "I've got a strange reading here. We're not getting closer to Themis, but something's getting closer to us."

"I'll be there." Her hands felt like ice as she grabbed a stanchion to swing herself up. She glanced at the screen. The object exploded. It looked like a starburst, and it was growing.

"I can see it now," Gaby said. "It's still attached to Themis. It's like a long arm or a boom, and it's opening out. I think—"

"The docking facilities!" Cirocco yelled. "They're

gonna grab us! Bill, start the engine sequence, stop the carousel, get ready to move."

"But it'll take us thirty minutes—"

"I *know*. Move!"

She caromed off the viewport and into her seat, reached for her microphone.

"All hands. Emergency status. Depressurization alert. Evacuate the carousel. Acceleration stations. Strap *in*." She slammed the alarm button with her left hand and heard the eerie hooting begin in the room behind her. She glanced to her left.

"You too, Bill. Get suited."

"But—"

"Now!"

He was out of his seat and diving through the access hatch. She turned and called over her shoulder.

"Bring my suit back with you!"

The object was visible out the window now, approaching fast. She had never felt so helpless. By overriding the attitude control system's programing she was able to fire all the thrusters on the side of the ship facing Themis, but it was not nearly enough. The great mass of *Ringmaster* barely moved. Other than that, she could only sit and monitor the automatic engine sequencing and count the seconds as they dragged by. In a short time she knew they could not escape. That thing was big, and moving faster.

Bill appeared, suited, and she scrambled into SCI-MOD to don her own suit. Five anonymous figures sat belted to acceleration couches, not moving, staring at the screen. She clamped her helmet, and heard chaos.

"Quiet down." The chatter died away. "I want silence on the suit channel unless I ask you to speak."

"But what's happening, Commander?" It was Calvin's voice.

"I said no talking. It looks like an automatic device is going to pick us up. This must be the docking facilities we were looking for."

"It looks more like an attack to me," August muttered.

"They must have done this before. They must know how to do it safely." She wished she could convince herself of that. It didn't help her credibility when the whole ship shuddered.

"Contact," Bill said. "It's got us."

Cirocco hurried back to her station, just in time to miss seeing the grapple sweep over them. The ship jumped again, and awful noises came from the rear.

"What did it look like?"

"Great big octopus tentacles without the suckers." He sounded shaken. "There were hundreds of them, waving around all over."

The ship gave an even greater lurch, and more alarms began to sound. A firestorm of red lights spread across her controls.

"We've got a hull rupture," Cirocco said, with a calmness she did not feel. "Losing air from the central stem. Sealing off pressure doors 14 and 15." Her hands moved over the controls without conscious guidance. The lights and buttons were far away, seen through the wrong end of a telescope. The accelerometer dial began to spin as she was thrown violently forward, then to the side. She came to rest on top of Bill, then struggled back to her seat and strapped in.

When the buckle clicked around her waist the ship jerked backwards again, worse than before. Something came through the hatch behind her and hit the viewport, which developed a network of cracks.

She hung from her seat, her body straining forward against the belt. An oxygen cylinder flew through the hatch. The glass shattered and the sound of the impact was sucked away with the burst of cold, hard glass knives that turned and dwindled before her eyes. Everything in the cabin that wasn't tied down leaped up and hurtled through the mouth of jagged teeth that had once been a viewport.

Blood pulsed in her face as she hung above a bottomless black hole. Large objects turned lazily in the sunlight. One of them was the engine module of *Ringmaster*, out there in front of her where it had no right to be. She could see the broken stump of the connecting stem. Her ship was coming apart.

"Oh, shit," she said, then had a vivid recollection of a

tape she had once heard from the flight recorder of an airliner. That had been the last word the pilot had uttered, seconds before impact, when he knew he was going to die. She knew it, too, and the thought filled her with a vast disgust.

She watched in dull horror as the thing that had the engines wrapped more tentacles around it. It reminded her of a Portuguese man o' war with a fish snared in its poisonous grip. A fuel tank ruptured—soundlessly, with a strange beauty. Her world was coming apart with no noise to mark its passing. A cloud of compressed gas quickly dispersed. The thing did not seem to mind.

Other tentacles had other parts of the ship. The high-gain antenna almost seemed to be swimming away, but it moved too slowly as it tumbled down the well below her.

"Alive," she whispered. "It's alive."

"What did you say?" Bill was trying to hold himself secure with both hands on the instrument panel. He was strapped solidly to his chair, but the bolts which held it to the floor had broken.

The ship shuddered again, and Cirocco's chair came free. The edge of the panel caught her across the thighs and she cried out as she struggled to free herself.

"Rocky, things are falling apart in here." She wasn't sure whose voice it was, but the fear reached her. She pushed, and managed to open her seat belt with one hand while holding herself away from the panel with the other. She slipped out to the side and saw her chair bounce across the shattered array of dials, stick briefly in the frame of the broken port, and launch into space.

She thought her legs were broken, but found she could move them. The pain lessened as she drew on reserves of strength to help Bill out of his chair. Too late, she saw that his eyes were closed, his forehead and the inside of his helmet smeared with blood. As his body slithered loosely over the control panel she saw the dent his helmet had made in it. She fought for a grip on his thigh, then his calf, his booted foot, and he was falling, falling in the middle of a glittering shower of glass.

She came to her senses crouched in the leg well under

the control panel. She shook her head, unable to recall what had put her there. But the force of deceleration was not so great now. Themis had succeeded in bringing *Ringmaster*—or what was left of it—up to its own rotational speed.

No one was talking. A hurricane of breathing came through the speaker in her helmet, but no words. There was nothing to say; the screams and curses had exhausted themselves. She got to her feet, grabbed the edge of the hatchway above her, and pulled herself through into chaos.

No lights worked, but sunlight spilled harshly across broken equipment from a large rip in the wall. Cirocco moved through the debris and a suited figure got out of her way. Her head throbbed. One of her eyes was swollen shut.

There was a lot of damage. It would take a while to get it cleaned up so they could get underway.

"I'll want a complete damage report from all departments," she said, to no one in particular. "This ship was never meant for that kind of treatment."

Only three people were standing. One figure knelt in the corner, holding the hand of another who was buried in the wreckage.

"I can't move my legs. I can't move them."

"Who said that?" Cirocco shouted, trying to make the dizziness go away by shaking her head, succeeding only in making it worse.

"Calvin, attend to the injuries while I see what can be done for the ship."

"Yes, Captain."

No one moved, and Cirocco wondered why. They were all watching her. Why were they doing that?

"I'll be in my cabin if you need me. I'm not . . . feeling so good."

One of the suits took a step toward her. She moved, trying to avoid the figure, and her foot went through the deck. Pain shot through her leg.

"It's coming in, over there. See? It's after *us* now."

"Where?"

"I don't see anything. Oh, God. I see it."

"Who said that? I want silence on this channel!"

"Look out! It's behind you!"

"Who said that?" She broke out in a sweat. Something was creeping up behind her, she could feel it, and it was one of those things that only come out into your bedroom after you switch off the light. Not a rat, but something worse that had no face but only a patch of slime and cold, dead, clammy hands. She groped in the red darkness and saw a writhing snake dart through a patch of sunlight in front of her.

It was so quiet. Why didn't they make any noise?

Her hand closed around something hard. She lifted it and began to chop, up and down, over and over as the thing flashed into view.

It wouldn't die. Something wrapped around her waist and started to pull.

The suited figures jumped and ran around in the small space, but the tentacles shot out strings which stuck like hot tar. The room was laced with them, and something had Cirocco by the legs and was trying to pull her apart like a wishbone. There was a pain like she had never felt before, but she continued to chop at the tentacle until awareness slipped from her.

Chapter Four

There was no light.

Even that bit of negative knowledge was something to cling to. The realization that the swaddling darkness was the result of the absence of something called light had cost her more than she would have believed possible, back when time had consisted of consecutive moments, like beads on a string. Now the beads scattered through her fingers. They rearranged themselves in a mockery of causality.

Anything needs a context. For darkness to mean anything there must be the memory of light. That memory was fading.

It had happened before, and would happen again. Sometimes there was a name to identify the disembodied consciousness. More often, there was only awareness.

She was in the belly of the beast.

(What beast?)

She couldn't remember. It would come back to her. Things usually did, if she waited long enough. And waiting was easy. Millennia were worth no more than milliseconds here. Time's stratified edifice was a ruin.

Her name was Cirocco.

(What's a Cirocco?)

"Shur-*rock*-o. It's a hot wind from the desert, or an old model Volkswagen. Mom never told me which she had in mind." That had been her standard answer. She recalled saying it, could *almost* feel intangible lips shape the meaningless words.

"Call me Captain Jones."

(Captain of what?)

Of the *DSV Ringmaster,* DSV for Deep Space Vessel, on its way to Saturn with seven aboard. One of them was Gaby Plauget....

(Who is....)

...and...and another was...Bill...

(What was that name again?)

It was on the tip of her tongue. A tongue was a soft, fleshy thing...it could be found in the mouth, which was...

She had it a moment ago, but what was a moment?

Something about light. Whatever that was.

There was no light. Hadn't she been here before? Yes, surely, but never mind, hold onto it, don't let the thought go. There was no light, and there was nothing else, either, but what was something else?

No smell. No taste. No sense of touch. No kinesthetic awareness of a body. Not even a sense of paralysis.

Cirocco! Her name was Cirocco.

Ringmaster. Saturn. Themis. Bill.

It returned all at once, as if she was living again in a split second. She thought she would go mad from the flood of impressions, and with that thought came another, later memory. This had happened before. She had remembered, only to see it all slip away. She had been insane, many times.

She knew her grip was tenuous, but it was all she had. She knew where she was, and she knew the nature of her problem.

The phenomenon had been explored during the last century. Put a man in a neoprene suit, cover his eyes and restrain his arms and legs so he can't touch himself, eliminate all sounds from the environment, and leave him floating in warm water. Free-fall is even better. There are refinements like intravenous feeding and the elimination of smells, but they are not really necessary.

The results are surprising. Many of the first subjects had been test pilots—well-adjusted, self-reliant, sensible men. Twenty-four hours of sensory deprivation turned them into pliable children. Longer periods were quite dangerous. The mind gradually edited the few distractions: heartbeat, the smell of neoprene, the pressure of water.

Cirocco was familiar with the tests. Twelve hours of sensory deprivation had been part of her own training. She knew she should be able to find her breathing, if she looked for it long enough. It was something she could control; a non-rhythmic thing if she chose to make it so. She tried to breathe rapidly, tried to make herself cough. She felt nothing.

Pressure, then. If something was restraining her it might be possible to pit her muscles against it, to at least feel that something was holding her, however gently. Taking one muscle at a time, isolating them, visualizing the attachments and location of each, she tried to make them move. A twitch of the lip would be enough. It would prove that she was not, as she was beginning to fear, dead.

She retreated from the thought. While she had the normal fear of death as the end of all consciousness, she was glimpsing something infinitely worse. What if people did *not* die, ever?

What if the passing of the body left *this* behind? There might be eternal life, and it might be passed in eternal lack of sensation.

Insanity began to look attractive.

Trying to move was a failure. She gave it up, and began ransacking her most recent memories, hoping the key to her present situation could be found in her last conscious seconds aboard *Ringmaster*. She would have laughed, had she been able to locate the muscles to do so. If she was not dead, then she was trapped in the belly of a beast large enough to devour her ship and all its crew.

Before long, that began to look attractive, too. If it was true, if she *had* been eaten and was somehow still alive, then death was still to come. Anything was better than the nightmare eternity whose vast futility now unfolded before her.

She found it possible to weep without a body. With no tears or sobs, no burning in the throat, Cirocco wept hopelessly. She became a child in the dark, holding the hurt inside herself. She felt her mind going again, welcomed it, and she bit her tongue.

Warm blood flowed in her mouth. She swam in it with the desperate fear and hunger of a small fish in a strange salt sea. She was a blind worm, just a mouth with hard round teeth and a swollen tongue, groping for that wonderful taste of blood which dispersed even as she sought it.

Frantically, she bit again, and was rewarded by a fresh spurt of red. Can you taste a color? she wondered. But she didn't care. It *hurt*, gloriously.

The pain carried her into her past. She lifted her face from the broken dials and shattered windscreen of her small plane and felt the wind chill blood in her open mouth. She had bitten her tongue. She put her hand to her mouth and two red-filmed teeth fell out. She looked at them, not understanding where they had come from. Weeks later, checking out of the hospital, she found them in the pocket of her parka. She kept them in a box on her bedside table for the times she woke up with the deadly quiet wind whispering to her. *The second engine is dead, and there's nothing but trees and snow down there.* She would pick up the box and rattle it. *I survived.*

But that was years ago, she reminded herself.

—as her face throbbed. They were removing the bandages. So cinematic. It's a damn shame I can't see it. Expectant faces gathered around—camera cuts quickly among them—dirty gauze falling beside the bed, layer upon layer unwinding—and then...why...why, Doctor...she's *beautiful*.

But she hadn't been. They had told her what to expect. Two monstrous shiners and puffed, angry red skin. The features were intact, there were no scars, but she was no more beautiful than she had ever been. The nose still looked vaguely like a hatchet, and so what? It hadn't been broken, and her pride would not allow her to have it changed for purely cosmetic reasons.

(Privately, she hated the nose, and thought that it, along with her height, had secured her command of *Ringmaster*. There had been pressure to select a woman, but those who decided such things could still not put a pretty five-footer in command of an expensive spaceship.)

Expensive spaceship.

Cirocco, you're wandering again. Bite your tongue.

She did, and tasted blood—

—and saw the frozen lake rush up to meet her, felt her face hit the panel, lifted her head from shattered glass which promptly tumbled down a bottomless well. Her seat belt held her above the abyss. A body slipped through the ruins and she reached out for his boot...

She bit again, hard, and felt something in her hand. Ages passed, and she felt something touching her knee. She put the two sensations together and realized she had touched herself.

She had a slippery one-woman orgy in the dark. She was delirious with love for the body that she now re-discovered. She curled tight, licked and bit everything she could reach while her hands pinched and pulled. She was smooth and hairless, slick as an eel.

A thick, almost jellied liguid rippled through her nostrils when she tried to breathe. It was not unpleasant; not even frightening once she was used to it.

And there was sound. It was a slow bass, and it had to be her heartbeat.

She could touch nothing but her own body, no matter how she stretched. She tried swimming for a while, but could not tell if she was getting anywhere.

While pondering what to do next, she fell asleep.

Waking was a gradual, uncertain process. For a time she could not tell if she was dreaming or conscious. Biting herself didn't help. She could dream a bite, couldn't she?

Come to think of that, how could she *sleep* at a time like this? Having thought of that, she was no longer sure she had slept at all. It was becoming rather problematic, she realized. The differences in states of consciousness were tiny with so little sensation to give them shape. Sleeping, dreaming, daydreaming, sanity, madness, alertness, drowsiness; she had no context to give any of them meaning.

She could hear her terror in the increased rate of her heartbeat. She was going to go crazy, and she knew it. Fighting it, she held tenaciously to the personality she had reconstructed from the whirlwind of madness.

Name: Cirocco Jones. Age: thirty-four. Race: not black, but not white, either.

She was a stateless person, legally an American but actually a member of the rootless Third Culture of the multi-national corporations. Every major city on Earth had its Yankee Ghetto of tract houses, English schools, and fast-food franchises. Cirocco had lived in most of them. It was a little like being an army brat, but with less security.

Her mother had been an unmarried consulting engineer who often worked for the energy companies. She had not intended to have children, but had not counted on the Arab prison guard. He raped her when she was captured after a border incident between Iraq and Saudi Arabia. While the Texaco ambassador negotiated her release, Cirocco was born. A few nukes had been sown in the desert by then, and the border incident was a brush-fire war by the time Iranian and Brazilian troops overran the prison. As political balances shifted, Cirocco's mother made her way toward Israel. Five years later she had lung cancer from the fallout. She spent the next fifteen years undergoing treatments slightly less painful that the disease.

Cirocco had grown up big and lonely, having only her mother for a friend. She first saw the United States when she was twelve. By then she could read and write, and could not be developmentally harmed by the American school system. Her emotional development was another matter. She did not make friends easily, but was fiercely loyal to those she had. Her mother had firm ideas on how to raise a young lady, and they included handguns and karate as well as dancing and voice lessons. Outwardly, she did not lack self-confidence. Only she herself knew how frightened and vulnerable she was beneath it all. It was her secret—one she kept so well that she fooled the NASA psychologists into giving her command of a ship.

And how much of that was true? she wondered. There was no point in lying here. Yes, the responsibility of command frightened her. Perhaps all commanders were secretly unsure of themselves, knew deep inside that they were not good enough for the responsibility thrust upon them. But it wasn't the sort of thing one asked about. What if the others *weren't* scared? Then your secret was out.

She found herself wondering how she had come to command a ship, if it was not what she wanted. What *did* she want?

I'd like to get out of here, she tried to say. *I'd like something to happen.*

Presently, something did happen.

She felt a wall with her left hand. In time, she felt another with her right. The walls were warm, smooth, and resilient, just as she imagined the inside of a stomach would be. She could feel them moving past her hands.

And they began to narrow.

She lodged, headfirst, in an uneven tunnel. The walls began to contract. For the first time, she felt claustrophobic. Tight spaces had never bothered her before.

The walls pulsed and rippled, pushing her forward until her head slipped through into coolness and a rough texture. She was squeezed; fluid bubbled out of her lungs and she coughed, inhaled, found her mouth filled with grit. She coughed again and more fluid came out, but now her shoulders were free and she ducked her head in the darkness to avoid getting another mouthful. She wheezed and spit, and began to breathe from her nose.

Her arms came free, then her hips, and she began

digging at the spongy material that enclosed her. It smelled like a childhood day spent in a cool, bare earth basement, in the narrow space adults visit only if the plumbing is acting up. It smelled like nine years old and digging in the dirt.

One leg came free, then the other, and she rested with her head bent into the air pocket formed by her arms and chest. Her breath came in wet spasms.

Dirt crumbled behind her neck and rolled down her body until it nearly filled her air space. She was buried, but she was alive. It was time to dig, but she could not use her arms.

Fighting panic, she forced herself up with her legs. Her thigh muscles knotted, her joints cracked, but she felt the mass above her yielding.

Her head broke through into light and air. Gasping, spitting, she pulled one arm out of the ground, then the other, and clawed at what felt like cool grass. She crawled from the hole on hands and knees and collapsed. She dug her fingers into the blessed ground and cried herself to sleep.

Cirocco didn't want to wake up. She fought it, pretending she was asleep. When she felt the grass fading away and the darkness returning she opened her eyes quickly.

Centimeters from her nose was a pale green carpet that looked like grass. It smelled like it, too. It was the kind of grass found only on the greens of the better golf courses. But it was warmer than the air, and she couldn't account for that. Perhaps it wasn't grass at all.

She rubbed her hand over it and sniffed again. Call it grass.

She sat up and something clanked, distracting her. A gleaming metal band circled her neck, and other, smaller ones were on her arms and legs. Many strange objects dangled from the large band, held together by wire. She slipped it off and wondered where she had seen it before.

It was amazingly difficult to concentrate. The thing in her hand was so complex, so various; too much for her scattered wits.

It was her pressure suit, stripped of all the plastic and rubber seals. Most of the suit had been plastic. Nothing remained but the metal.

She made a pile of the parts, and in the process realized just how naked she was. Beneath a coating of dirt her body was completely hairless. Even her eyebrows were gone. For some reason that made her very sad.

She put her face in her hands and began to cry.

Cirocco did not cry easily, nor often. She was not good at it. But after a very long time she thought she knew who she was again.

Now she could find out where she was.

Perhaps a half hour later she felt ready to move. But that decision spawned a dozen questions. Move, but to where?

She had intended to explore Themis, but that was when she had a spaceship and the resources of Earth's nest technology. Now she had her bare skin and a few bits of metal.

She was in a forest composed of grass and one species of tree. She called them trees by the same reasoning she had used on the grass. If it's seventy meters tall, has a brown, round trunk and what looks like leaves far above, then it's a tree. Which did not mean it might not cheerfully eat her if given the chance.

She had to get the worries down to a manageable level. Rule out the things you can do nothing about, don't fret too much about the things you can do little about. And remember that if you're as cautious as sanity would seem to dictate, you'll starve to death in a cave.

The air was in the first category. It could contain a poison.

"So stop breathing, at once!" she said, aloud. Right. At least it smelled fresh, and she was not coughing.

Water was something she could do little about. Eventually she would have to drink some, assuming she could find it—which should go right to the top of her list. When she found it, perhaps she could make a fire and boil it. If not, she would drink, microscopic bugs and all.

And then there was food, which worried her more than anything. Even if there was nothing around that wanted to make a meal of her, there was no way of knowing if the food she ate would poison her. Or it might be no more nourishing than cellophane.

If that wasn't enough, there was the calculated risk. How do you calculate what is risky when a tree might not be a tree?

They didn't even look that much like trees. The trunks were like polished marble. The high branches were parallel to the ground and ran for a precise distance before making a right angle. Above, the leaves were flat, like lily pads, and three or four meters across.

What was foolhardy and what was overcautious? There was no guidebook, and the dangers would not be marked. But without a few assumptions she could not move, and she had to get moving. She was getting hungry.

She set her jaw, then stamped over to the nearest tree. She smacked it with the palm of her hand. It just stood there, supremely indifferent.

"Just a dumb tree."

She examined the hole she had emerged from.

It was a raw brown wound in the neat expanse of grass. Patches of sod, held together by a feathery root structure, lay upside-down around it. The hole itself was only half a meter deep; the sides had crumbled to fill the rest.

"Something tried to eat me," she said. "Something ate all the organic parts of my suit, and all my hair, then excreted the junk right here. Including me." She noted in passing that she was glad the thing had classified her as junk.

It was a hell of a beast. They knew the outer part of the torus—the ground she was sitting on—was thirty kilometers thick. This thing was large enough to snag *Ringmaster* while the ship orbited 400 kilometers away. She had spent a long time in its belly and for some reason had proved indigestible. It had burrowed through the ground to this point, and expelled her.

And that just didn't make sense. If it could eat plastic, why couldn't it eat her? Were ship's captains too tough?

It had eaten her whole *ship*, pieces as large as the engine module, others just tiny bits of glass or rumbling, dwindling spacesuited figures with dented helmets...

"Bill!" She was on her feet, every muscle in her body straining. "Bill! I'm *here*. I'm alive! Where are you?"

She slapped her forehead with her hand. If only she could get through this muddy-headed feeling when thoughts were coming so slowly. She had not forgotten about the crew, but it was not until that moment that she connected them with the new-born Cirocco standing naked and hairless on the warm ground.

"Bill!" she shouted again. She listened, then collapsed with her legs folded under her. She plucked at the grass.

Think it through. Presumably, the creature would have treated him as another piece of debris. But he had been injured.

So had she, now that she thought of it. She examined her thighs and found not even a bruise. It told her nothing. She might have been inside the creature for five years, or only a few months.

Any of the others might arrive and be pushed out of the ground at any time. Somewhere down there, about a meter and a half deep, was some kind of excretory outlet for the creature. If she waited, and if the creature didn't like the taste of all humans and not just ones named Cirocco, they might all get together again.

She sat down to wait for them.

Half an hour later (or was it only ten minutes?) it didn't make sense. The creature was *big*. It had eaten *Ringmaster* like an after-dinner mint. It must extend through a great part of the underworld of Themis, and it didn't make sense to think this one orifice could handle all the traffic. There could be others, and they could be scattered all over the countryside.

A little later she had another thought. They were coming far apart, but they were coming, and she was grateful for that. The thought was simple: she was thirsty, she was hungry, and she was filthy. What she wanted most in the world was water.

The land sloped gently. She was willing to bet there would be a stream down there somewhere.

She stood and poked at the pile of metal pieces with one foot. There was too much to carry, but the junk was all she had for tools. She took one of the smaller rings, then picked up the larger one which had been the bottom of her helmet and was still connected to the dangling electronic components.

It wasn't much, but it would have to do. She slung the large ring over her shoulder and started down the hill.

The pool was fed by a two-meter fall from a rocky stream which wound through a little valley. The huge trees arched overhead, completely blocking her view of the sky. She stood on a rock near the edge of the pool, trying to judge its depth, thinking about jumping in.

Thinking about it was all she did. The water was clear, but there was no telling what might be in it. She jumped over the ridge which produced the waterfall. It was easy in the one-quarter gee. A short walk brought her to a sandy beach.

The water was warm, sweet, and bubbly, and easily the best thing she had ever tasted. She drank all she wanted, then squatted and scrubbed with sand, keeping an eye open. Watering holes were places for caution. When she was through she felt reasonably human for the first time since her awakening. She sat on the wet sand and let her feet trail in the water.

It was cooler than the air or the ground, but still suprisingly warm for what looked to be a glacier-fed mountain stream. Then she realized it would make sense if the heat source in Themis was as they had deduced: from below. The sunlight at Saturn's orbit wouldn't provide much ground heating. But the triangular fins were under her now, and were probably designed to capture and store solar heat. She envisioned huge subterranean rivers of hot water running a few hundred meters under the ground.

Moving on seemed to be the next order of business, but which way? Straight ahead could be ruled out. Across the stream the land began to rise again. Downstream should be easiest, and should bring her to flatlands soon.

"Decisions, decisions," she muttered.

She looked at the tangle of metal junk she had been carrying all... what was it? Afternoon? Morning? Time could not be measured that way in here. It was possible only to speak of elapsed time, and she had no idea how much had gone by.

The helmet ring was still in her hand. Now her brow furrowed as she looked closer.

Her suit had once contained a radio. Of course it was not possible that it had come through the ordeal intact, but just for the hell of it she hunted for and found the remains. There was a tiny battery, and what was left of a switch, turned on. That ended that. Most of the radio had been silicon chips and metal, so there had been some faint hope.

She looked again. Where was the speaker? It should be a little metal horn, the remains of a headset unit. She found it, and lifted it to her ear.

"...fifty-*eight,* fifty-*nine,* ninety-three-*sixty*..."

"Gaby!" She was on her feet, shouting, but the familiar voice kept counting, oblivious. Cirocco knelt on the rock and arrayed the remains of her helmet on it with fingers that trembled, holding the speaker to one ear while pawing through the components. She found the pinhead throat mike.

"Gaby, Gaby, come in please. Can you hear me?"

"...eighty—Rocky! Is that you, Rocky?"

"It's me. Where... where are..." She calmed down deliberately, swallowed, and went on. "Are you all right? Have you seen the others?"

"Oh, *Captain.* The most horrible things..." Her voice broke, and Cirocco heard sobs. Gaby poured out an incoherent stream of words: how glad she was to hear Cirocco's voice, how lonely she had been, how sure she had been that she was the only survivor until she listened to her radio and heard sounds.

"Sounds?"

"Yes, there's at least one other alive, unless that was you crying."

"I ... hell, I cried quite a bit. It might have been me."

"I don't think so," Gaby said. "I'm pretty sure it's Gene. He sings sometimes, too. Rocky, it so *good* to hear your voice."

"I know. It's good to hear yours." She had to take another deep breath and relax her grip on the helmet ring. Gaby's voice was back in control, but Cirocco was on the edge of hysterics. She didn't like the feeling.

"The things that have *happened* to me," Gaby was saying. "I was dead, Captain, and in heaven, and I'm not even religious, but there I was—"

"Gaby, settle down. Get a grip on yourself."

There was silence, punctuated by sniffs.

"I think I'll be all right now. Sorry."

"It's all right. If you went through anything like what I did, I understand perfectly. Now, where are you?"

There was a pause, then a giggle. "There's no street signs in the neighborhood," Gaby said. "It's a canyon, not very deep. It's full of rocks and there's a stream down the middle. There's these funny trees on both sides of the stream."

"It sounds pretty much like where I am." But which canyon? she wondered. "Which way are you going? Were you counting steps?"

"Yeah. Downstream. If I could get out of this forest, I could see half of Themis."

"I thought of that, too."

"We just need a couple landmarks to tell if we're in the same neighborhood."

"But I thought we must be, or we wouldn't be able to hear each other."

Gaby didn't say anything, and Cirocco saw her mistake.

"Right," she said. "Line of sight."

"Check. These radios are good for quite a distance. In here, the horizon curves *up*."

"I'd believe it better if I could see it. Where I am right now could be the enchanted forest at Disney World in late evening."

"Disney would have done a better job," Gaby said. "It would have had more detail, and monsters popping out of the trees."

"Don't say that. Have you seen anything like that?"

"A couple insects, I guess they were."

"I saw a school of tiny fish. They looked like fish. Oh, by the way, don't go in the water. They might be dangerous."

"I saw them. *After* I was in the water. But they didn't do anything."

"Have you passed anything that's remarkable in any way? Some unusual surface feature?"

"A few waterfalls. Two fallen trees."

Cirocco looked around and described the pool and waterfall. Gaby said she had passed several places like that. It might be the same stream, but there was no way to know.

"All right," Cirocco said. "Here's what we do. When you find a rock facing upstream, make a mark on it."

"How?"

"With another rock." She found one the size of her fist and attacked the rock she had been sitting on. She scratched a large "C" on it. There could be no mistaking its artificiality.

"I'm doing that now."

"Make a mark every hundred meters or so. If we're on the same river one of us will come up behind the other, and the one in front can wait for the other to catch up."

"Sounds good. Uh, Rocky, how long are these batteries good for?"

Cirocco grimaced, and rubbed her forehead.

"Maybe a month of use. It could depend on how long we were . . . you know, how long we were inside. I don't have any ideas on that. Do you?"

"No. Do you have any hair?"

"Not a strand." She rubbed her hand over her scalp, and noticed that it did not feel quite as smooth. "But it's growing back in."

Cirocco walked downstream, holding the speaker and mike in place so they could talk to each other.

"I feel hungriest when I think about it," Gaby said. "And I'm thinking about it right now. Have you seen any of these little berry bushes?"

Cirocco looked around but didn't spot anything like that.

"The berries are yellow, and about as big as the end of your thumb. I'm holding one now. It's soft and translucent."

"Are you going to eat it?"

There was a pause. "I was going to ask you about that."

"We'll have to try something sooner or later. Maybe one won't be enough to kill you."

"Just make me sick," Gaby laughed. "This one broke on my teeth. There's a thick jelly inside, like honey with a minty taste. It's dissolving in my mouth...and now it's gone. The rind is not so sweet, but I'm going to eat it anyway. It might be the only part with any food value."

If even that, Cirocco thought. There was no reason why any part of it should sustain them. She was pleased that Gaby had given her such a detailed description of her sensations while eating the berry, but she knew the purpose of it. Bomb de-fusing teams used the same technique. One stayed away while the other reported every action over the radio. If the bomb went off, the survivor learned something for the next time.

When they judged enough time had passed with no ill effect, Gaby began eating more of the berries. In time, Cirocco found some. They were almost as good as that first taste of water had been.

"Gaby, I'm about dead on my feet. I wonder how long we've been awake?"

There was a long pause, and she had to call again.

"Hm? Oh, hi. How did I get here?" She sounded slightly drunk.

Cirocco frowned. "Where's here? Gaby what's happening?"

"I sat down for a minute to rest my legs. I must have fallen asleep."

"Try to wake up enough to find a good place for it." Cirocco was already looking around. It was going to be a problem. Nothing looked good, and she knew it was the worst possible idea to lie down alone in strange country. The only thing worse would be trying to stay awake any longer.

She went a short distance into the trees, and marveled at how soft the grass felt under her bare feet. So much better than the rocks. It would be nice to sit down for a minute.

She awoke on the grass, sat up quickly and looked all around. Nothing was moving.

For a meter in every direction from where she had slept, the grass had turned brown, dried out like hay.

She stood and looked down at a large rock. She had approached it from the downstream side while looking for a place to sleep. Now she walked around it, and on the other side was a large letter "G."

Chapter Five

Gaby insisted on turning back. Cirocco didn't protest; it sounded good to her, though she could never have suggested it.

She walked downstream, often passing the marks Gaby had made. At one point she had to leave the sandy shore and go up onto the grass to avoid a large pile of boulders. When she reached the grass she saw a series of oval brown spots spaced like footprints. She knelt and touched them. They were dry and brittle just like the grass where she had slept.

"I've found part of your trail," she told Gaby. "Your feet couldn't have touched the grass more than a second, and yet something in your body killed it."

"I saw the same thing when I woke up," Gaby said. "What do you think of it?"

"I think we secrete something that's poison to the grass. If that's true, we might not smell very good to the kind of large animals that might normally take an interest in us."

"That's good news."

"The bad part is that it might mean we have very

different sorts of biochemicals. That's not so good for eating."

"You're so much fun to talk to."

"Is that you up ahead?"

Cirocco squinted into the pale yellow light. The river ran straight for a good distance, and just where it started to bend was a tiny figure.

"Yep. It's me, if that's you waving your arms."

Gaby whooped, a painful sound in the tiny earphone. Cirocco heard the sound again a second later, much fainter. She grinned, and then felt the grin getting bigger and bigger. She hadn't wanted to run, it was so like a bad movie, but she was running anyway and so was Gaby, taking absurdly long hops in the low gravity.

They hit so hard they were both breathless for a moment. Cirocco embraced the smaller woman and lifted her off her feet.

"D-d-d-damn, you look s-s-so *good*!" Gaby said. One of her eyelids was twitching, and her teeth chattered.

"Hey, hold on, take it easy," Cirocco soothed, rubbing Gaby's back with both hands. Gaby's smile was so wide it hurt to look at it.

"I'm sorry, but I think I'm going to be hysterical. Isn't that a laugh?" And she did laugh, but it was flat and hurt the ear, and before long turned into shudders and gasps. She held Cirocco strongly enough to break ribs. Cirocco didn't fight it, but eased her down to the sandy river bank and held her close while huge, low-gravity tears dripped onto her shoulders.

Cirocco was not sure at what point the comforting hugs turned into something else. It was so gradual. Gaby was quite insensible for a long time, and it seemed the natural thing to hold and stroke her while she calmed down. Then it seemed natural that Gaby should stroke her, and that they should press close together. The first moment when it began to seem a little unusual was when she found herself kissing Gaby, and Gaby kissing back.

She thought she might have stopped it then, but she didn't want to because she could not tell if the tears she tasted belonged to her or Gaby.

And besides, it never really turned into love-making. They rubbed against each other and kissed mouth-to-mouth, and when the orgasm came it almost seemed irrelevant to what had gone before. At least that's what she kept telling herself.

One of them had to say something when it was over, and it seemed best to stay away from what they had just done.

"Are you all right now?"

Gaby nodded. Her eyes were still bright, but she was smiling.

"Uh-huh. Probably not permanently, though. I woke up screaming. I'm really afraid to go to sleep."

"It's not my favorite thing, either. You know you're about the funniest-looking critter I ever saw?"

"That's because you don't have a mirror."

Gaby couldn't stop talking for hours, and she didn't like it when Cirocco let go of her. They moved to a less exposed position up in the trees, then sat with Cirocco's back against a trunk and Gaby reclining against her.

She spoke of her trip down the river, but what she kept wanting to go back to, or what she couldn't get away from, was her experience in the belly of the creature. It sounded to Cirocco like an extended dream that had little in common with what she herself had experienced, but that might have been just the inadequacy of words.

"I did wake up in the darkness a few times, like you did," Gaby said. "When I did, I couldn't feel or see or hear anything, and I didn't really want to stay there very long."

"I kept going back to my earlier life. It was extremely vivid. I could ... *feel* it all."

"Me, too," Gaby said. "But it wasn't a repeat. It was all new things."

"Did you always know who you were? That was the worst part for me, remembering and then forgetting. I don't know how many times that happened."

"Yeah, I always knew who I was. But I got to be pretty

tired of being me, if that makes any sense. The possibilities were so *limited*."

"What do you mean by that?"

Gaby moved her hands indecisively, trying to pull something out of the air. She gave up and twisted in Cirocco's arms to look intently into her eyes for a long moment. Then she rested her head between Cirocco's breasts. Cirocco found it disturbing, but the warmth and companionship of their closeness was too good to give up. She looked down at Gaby's bald head and had to fight an urge to kiss it.

"I was in there for twenty or thirty years," Gaby said quietly. "And don't try to tell me that's impossible. I've got a pretty good idea that nothing like that amount of time passed in the rest of the universe. I'm not crazy."

"I didn't say you were." Cirocco rubbed her shoulders when Gaby began to tremble, and it subsided.

"Well, I shouldn't have said I'm *not* crazy, either. I never had to have somebody baby me so I wouldn't cry before. I'm sorry."

"I don't mind," Cirocco murmured, and she really did not. She found it surprisingly easy to whisper assurances in the other woman's ear. "Gaby, there's no way either of us could have come through that without some twitches. I cried for hours. I threw up. I may do it again, and if I can't help myself, I'd like for you take care of me."

"I will, don't worry about that." She seemed to relax a little more.

"Real time isn't important," Gaby said at last. "It's internal time that matters. And by the clock, I was in there for many years. I went up to heaven on a goddam staircase of glass, and as sure as I'm sitting here I can see every step in my mind, and I can feel the clouds whipping by and hear my feet squeak on the glass. And it was Hollywood heaven, with red carpet for the last three or four kilometers, and golden gates like skyscrapers, and people with wings. And I didn't believe in it, you understand, and yet I did. I knew I was dreaming, I knew it was ridiculous, and finally I wouldn't have any more of it and it went away."

She yawned, and laughed quietly.

"Why am I telling you all this?"

"Maybe to get rid of it. Does it make you feel better?"

"Some."

She was quiet for a while after that and Cirocco thought she had gone to sleep, but it was not so. She stirred, and nuzzled deeper into Cirocco's chest.

"I had time to take a good look at myself," she said, slurring her words. "I didn't like it. I got to wondering what I was doing with myself. It never bothered me before."

"What's wrong with the way you were?" Cirocco asked. "I kind of liked you."

"You did? I don't see how. Sure, I didn't cause a lot of trouble to anybody, I could take care of myself. But what else? What *good*?"

"You were very good at your job. That's all I really demanded of you. You're the very best there is, or you wouldn't have been picked for this mission."

Gaby sighed. "Somehow, that doesn't impress me. I mean, to *get* that good I sacrificied just about everything that makes a human being. Like I said, I did some real soul-searching."

"What did you decide?"

"For one thing, I'm through with astronomy."

"Gaby?"

"It's the truth. And what the hell? We'll never get out of here, and there's no stars to look at. I'd have needed to find something else to do anyway. And it's not that sudden. I had a long, *long* time to change my mind. You know, I don't have one lover in the whole world? Not even one friend."

"I'm your friend."

"No. Not the way I'm talking about. People respected me for my work, men desired me for my body. But I never made any friends, even as a kid. Not the kind you can open your heart to."

"It's not that hard."

"I hope not. Because I'm going to be a different person. I'm going to tell people about the real me. This is the first time I can do it, because it's the first time I've really known myself. And I'm going to love. I'm going to care about people. And it looks like you're it." She raised her head and smiled at Cirocco.

"What do you mean?" Cirocco asked, frowning slightly.

"It's a funny feeling, and I knew it as soon as I saw you." She rested her head again. "I think I love you."

Cirocco could not say anything for a time, then forced a laugh.

"Hey, honey, you're still in that Hollywood heaven. There's no such thing as love at first sight. It takes time. Gaby?"

She tried several times to talk to her, but she was either asleep or faking it very well. She let her head fall back wearily.

"Oh, my God."

Chapter Six

The smart thing would have been to post watches. Cirocco wondered as she struggled to wakefulness why she had so seldom managed to do the smart thing since she got to Themis. They would have to adjust to the strange timelessness. They couldn't go on walking until they dropped.

Gaby was sleeping with her thumb in her mouth. Cirocco tried to get up without disturbing her, but it wasn't possible. She moaned, then opened her eyes.

"Are you as hungry as I am?" she yawned.

"That's hard to say."

"You think it's the berries? Maybe they're no good."

"Impossible to tell so soon. But take a look over there. That might be breakfast."

Gaby looked where Cirocco pointed. There was an animal down by the stream, drinking. As they watched, it raised its head and looked at them from no more than twenty meters away. Cirocco tensed, ready for anything. It blinked, and lowered its head.

"A six-legged kangaroo," Gaby said. "With no ears."

It was a fair description. The animal was covered with

short fur and had two large hind legs, though not as large as a kangaroo's. The four front legs were smaller. The fur was light green and yellow. It was not taking any special care to protect itself.

"I'd like to get a look at its teeth. It might tell us something."

"The smart thing is probably to get the hell out of here," Gaby said. She sighed, and looked around on the ground. She got up before Cirocco could stop her, and was walking toward the creature.

"Gaby stop it," Cirocco hissed, trying not to alert the animal. She saw now that Gaby had a rock in her hand.

The creature looked up again. It had a face that would have been hilarious in other circumstances. The head was round, with no visible ears or nose—just two big soft eyes. But the mouth looked as if the creature was chewing on a bass harmonica. It stretched twice as wide as the rest of the head, giving the animal a foolish grin.

It lifted all four front feet from the ground and bounded three meters in the air. Gaby jumped just about as high in surprise, and had time to twist wildly in the air before coming down on her buttocks. Cirocco reached her and tried to take the rock away.

"Come on, Gaby, we don't need meat that badly."

"Be quiet," Gaby said through clenched teeth. "I'm doing this for you, too." She wrenched her arm away and ran forward.

The thing had taken two leaps, but each had been good for eight or nine meters. Now it stood quietly, forelegs touching the ground, head lowered. It was eating the grass.

It looked up placidly as Gaby stopped two meters away. It seemed to have no fear of her, and resumed cropping as Cirocco came up behind Gaby.

"Do you think we should—"

"Hush!" Gaby hesitated only a moment longer, then stepped up to the beast. She raised her arm and brought the rock down hard on the top of its head, then jumped away.

The beast made a coughing noise, staggered, and fell

on its side. It kicked once, and was still.

They watched it for a while, then Gaby walked over and prodded it with a toe. Nothing happened, so she went down on one knee beside it. It was no larger than a small deer. Cirocco squatted, elbows on her knees, trying not to feel disgusted by it. Gaby seemed short of breath.

"Do you think it's dead?" she asked.

"Looks like it. Kind of anti-climatic, don't you think?"

"It's okay with me."

Gaby wiped a hand across her forehead, then smacked the rock repeatedly into the creature's head until red blood flowed. Cirocco winced. Gaby dropped the rock and wiped her hands on her thighs.

"That's that. You know, if you could gather up some of that dry underbrush I think I might be able to make a fire."

"How're you going to do that?"

"Never mind. Just get the wood."

Cirocco had half an armload of it before she stopped to wonder when Gaby started giving the orders.

"Well, the theory was good," Gaby said gloomily.

Cirocco tore again at the stringy red meat that clung so tenaciously to the bone.

Gaby had sweated for an hour with a piece of her spacesuit and a rock she had hoped was flint but which proved not to be. They had a pile of dry wood, a fine moss-like substance, and splinters carefully shaved from tree branches with the sharp edge of Cirocco's helmet. They had all the essential ingredients of fire except the spark.

In that hour Cirocco's opinion of Gaby's kill had undergone a revolution. By the time she had it skinned and Gaby had given up on the fire she knew she would eat it raw and be thankful for it.

"That thing didn't have any predators," Cirocco said, around a mouthful. The meat was better than she had expected, but could have used some salt.

"It sure didn't act like it," Gaby agreed. She squatted on the other side of the carcass and her eyes roamed the ground over Cirocco's shoulder. Cirocco was doing the same thing.

"That could mean no predators big enough to bother us."

Dinner was a drawn-out affair because of all the chewing necessary. They spent the time examining the carcass. The animal didn't seem too remarkable to Cirocco's untrained eyes. She wished Calvin was there to tell her if she was wrong. The meat, skin, bones and fur were of the usual colors and textures, and even smelled right. There were organs she couldn't identify.

"The skin ought to be good for something," Gaby pointed out. "We could make clothes out of it."

Cirocco wrinkled her nose, "If you want to wear it, go ahead. It's probably going to stink pretty soon. And it's warm enough so far without clothes."

It didn't seem right to leave the biggest part of the animal behind, but they decided they had to. They both kept a leg bone for use as a weapon, and Cirocco hacked off a large chunk of meat while Gaby cut strips of skin to tie the spacesuit parts together. She made a crude belt for herself and tied her things to it. Then they started downstream again.

They saw more of the kangaroo creatures, both singly and in groups of three or six. There were other smaller animals that moved up and down the tree trunks almost too fast to see, and still more that stayed close to the water's edge. None of them were hard to approach. The tree animals, when they held still long enough to examine, didn't seem to have heads. They were blue balls of short fur with six clawed feet sticking out around the edges, and they moved in any direction with equal ease. The mouth was on the underside, centered in a star of legs.

The countryside began to change. Not only did they see more animals, but there were more varieties of plant life. They plodded on through light that turned pale green by the forest canopy, one hundred thousand steps to the twenty-four-hour day.

Unfortunately, they soon lost count. The huge,

simplified trees gave way to a hundred different species, and a thousand kinds of flowering shrubs, trailing vines, and parasitic growths. The only things that remained constant were the stream that was their only guide, and the tendency of Themis trees to be gigantic. Any one of them would have rated a plaque and a tourist turn-out in Sequoia National Park.

It was no longer quiet, either. During their first day of travel Cirocco and Gaby had only the sounds of their own footsteps and the clatter of their salvaged suits to keep them company. Now the forest twittered and barked and yammered at them.

The meat tasted better than ever when they stopped for a rest. Cirocco wolfed it down, sitting back to back with Gaby beside the gnarled trunk of a tree that was warmer than any tree should have been, with soft bark and roots that knotted into burls bigger than houses. Its upper branches were lost in the incredible tangle overhead.

"I'll bet there's more life in those trees that there is on the ground," Cirocco said.

"Look up there," Gaby said. "I'd say somebody wove those vines together. You can see water leaking out the bottom."

"We ought to talk about that. What about intelligent life in here? How would you recognize it? That's one of the reasons I tried to stop you from killing this animal."

Gaby munched thoughtfully. "Should I have tried to talk to it first?"

"I know, I know. I was more afraid it would turn around and bite your legs off. But now that we know how unaggressive it is, maybe we ought to do just that. Try to talk to one."

"How stupid, you mean. That thing didn't have half the brain of a cow. You could see that in its eyes."

"You're probably right."

"No, *you're* right. I mean, I'm right, but you're right that we should be more careful. I'd hate to eat something I ought to be talking to. Hey, what was that?"

It wasn't a noise, but the realization that noise had ceased. Only the splash of water and the high hiss of leaves disturbed the silence. Then, building so quietly and so slowly that they had been hearing it for minutes before they could identify it, came a vast moan.

God might moan like that, If He had lost everything He had ever loved, and if He had a throat like an organ pipe a thousand kilometers long. It continued to build on a note that somehow managed to rise without ever straying from the uttermost lower limits of human hearing. They felt it in their bowels and behind their eyeballs.

It already seemed to fill the universe, and yet still it got louder. It was joined by the sound of a string section: cellos and electronic basses. Treading lightly on top of this massive tonal floor were supersonic hissing overtones. The ensemble grew louder when it was not possible that it could grow louder.

Cirocco thought her skull would shatter. She was dimly aware of Gaby hugging her. They stared slack-jawed as they were showered by dead leaves from the vault overhead. Tiny animals fell, twisting and bouncing. The ground began to throb in sympathy. It yearned to fly apart and hurl itself into the air. A dust-devil skittered indecisively, than dashed itself to pieces on the bones of the tree where they huddled. They were lashed with debris.

There was crashing above them, and a wind began to reach down to the forest floor. A massive branch embedded itself in the middle of the stream By then the forest was swaying, creaking, protesting: gunshots, and nails wrenched from dry wood.

The violence reached a plateau and stayed at that level. The winds seemed to be about sixty kilometers per hour. Higher up it sounded much worse. They stayed low in the protection of the tree roots and watched the storm rage around them. Cirocco had to shout to be heard above the bass moaning.

"What do you suppose could cause it to come up so fast?"

"I have no idea," Gaby yelled back. "Local heating or cooling, a big change in the air pressure. I don't know what would cause that, though."

"I think the worst is over. Hey, your teeth are chattering."

"I'm not scared anymore. I'm *cold*."

Cirocco was feeling it, too. The temperature was plunging. In just a few minutes it had gone from balmy to chilly, and now she judged it was getting down around zero. With the wind coming at sixty klicks, it was no laughing matter. They huddled together, but she could feel the heat being sucked from her back.

"We've got to get to some kind of shelter," she yelled.

"Yeah, but what?"

Neither of them wanted to move from what little shelter they had. They tried covering each other with dirt and dead leaves, but the wind blew it away.

When they were sure they would freeze to death, the wind stopped. It did not diminish; it stopped dead, and Cirocco's ears popped so hard it hurt. She could not hear until she forced a yawn.

"Wow. I've heard of pressure changes, but nothing like that."

The forest was quiet again. Then Cirocco found that if she listened carefully she could hear the dying ghost of whatever had made the moaning sound. It made her shiver in a way that had nothing to do with the cold. She had never thought of herself as imaginative, but the moan had sounded so human, though on such a mighty scale. It made her want to lie down and die.

"Don't go to sleep, Rocky. We've got something else."

"What now?" She opened her eyes and saw a fine white powder drifting through the air. It sparkled in the pale light.

"I'd call it snow."

They went as fast as they could to keep their feet from getting numb, and Cirocco knew it was only the still air that saved them. It was cold; even the ground was cold for a change. Cirocco felt drugged. It could not be possible. She was a spaceship captain; how had she ended up trudging through a snowstorm in her bare skin?

But the snow was transitory. At one point it was a few centimeters deep on the ground, but then the heat began to well up from below and it melted quickly. Soon the air was getting warmer. When they felt it was safe, they found a place on the warm ground and went to sleep.

The haunch of meat did not smell too good when they awoke, and neither did Gaby's hide belt. They threw it all away and washed in the stream, then Gaby killed another of the animals they had begun to call smilers. It was as easy as it had been the last time.

They felt much better after breakfast, which they supplemented with some of the less exotic fruits they found in great profusion. Cirocco liked one that looked like a lumpy pear but had meat like a melon. It tasted like sharp cheddar cheese.

She felt as if she could march all day, but it turned out that they could not. The stream, their guide for the whole journey so far, vanished in a large hole at the base of a hill.

The two of them stood on the edge of the hole and looked down. It gurgled like the drain of a bathtub, but at long intervals make a sucking sound followed by a deep belch. Cirocco didn't like it, and edged away.

"Maybe I'm crazy," she said, "but I wonder if this is where the thing that ate us gets its water?"

"Could be. I'm not diving in to find out. So what's next?"

"I wish I knew."

"We could go back to where we started and wait there." Gaby did not seem enthusiastic about this idea.

"Damn! I thought sure we'd find a place to look around if we went far enough. Do you think the whole inside of Themis is one big rain forest?"

Gaby shrugged. "I don't have enough information, obviously."

Cirocco chewed it over for a while. Gaby was apparently willing to let her make the decisions.

"Okay. First we go to the top of this hill and see what it's like. One more thing I'd like to try if there's nothing worthwhile up there is to climb one of these trees. Maybe we could get high enough to see something. Do you think we could do it?"

Gaby studied a trunk. "Sure, in this gravity. That's no guarantee we'll be able to stick our heads out, though."

"I know. Let's go up the hill."

It was steeper than the countryside they had come through. There were places where they had to use hands and feet, and Gaby led the way through those because she had more experience in rock climbing. She was agile, much smaller and more limber than Cirocco, and soon Cirocco felt every month of the age difference between them.

"Holy shit, take a look at that!"

"What is it?" Cirocco was a few meters behind. When she looked up she saw only Gaby's legs and buttocks, from a distinctly unusual angle. It was odd, she thought, that she had seen all the male crew members naked, but had to come to Themis to see Gaby. What a strange creature she was with no hair.

"We've found our scenic viewpoint," Gaby said. She turned around and gave Cirocco a hand.

There were trees growing on the brow of the hill, but they did not approach the height of the ones behind them. Though they were dense and overgrown with vines, none was over ten meters tall.

Cirocco had wanted to climb the hill to see what was on the other side. Now she knew. The hill didn't have an other side.

Gaby was standing a few meters from the edge of a cliff. With every step Cirocco took the view adjusted itself, receding, encompassing more area. When she stood beside Gaby she still could not see the cliff face, but she had some idea of how long the drop was. It would be measured in kilometers. She felt her stomach lurch.

They stood at a natural window formed by a twenty-meter gap between the outermost trees. There was nothing in front of them but air for 200 kilometers.

They were at one edge of the rim, looking across the breadth of Themis to the other side. Over there was a hairline shadow that might have been a cliff like the one they were standing on. Above the line was green land, fading to white, then to gray, and finally becoming a brilliant yellow as her eyes traveled up the sloping side to the translucent area in the roof.

Her eyes were drawn back down the curve to the distant cliff. Below it was more green land, with white clouds hugging the ground or towering up higher than she was. It looked like the view from a mountaintop on Earth, but for one thing. The ground seemed level until she looked to the left or right.

It bent. She gulped, and craned her neck, twisting, trying to make it level, trying to deny that far away the land was higher than she was without ever having risen.

She gasped and clutched at the air, then went down on hands and knees. It felt better that way. She edged closer to the abyss and kept looking to her left. Far away was a land of shadow, tilted on its side for her examination. A dark sea twinkled in the night, a sea that somehow did not leave its shores and come spilling toward her. On the other side of the sea was another area of light, like the one in front of her, dwindling in the distance. Beyond it her view was cut off by the roof overhead, seeming to belly down to meet the land. She knew it was an illusion of the perspective; the roof would be just as high if she stood beneath it at that point.

They were on the edge of one of the areas of permanent day. A hazy terminator began to blanket the land to her right, not sharp and clear like the terminator of a planet seen from space, but fading through a twilight zone she estimated to be thirty or forty kilometers wide. Beyond that zone was night, but not blackness. There was a huge sea in there, twice as large as the one in the other direction, looking as if bright moonlight was falling on it. It sparkled like a plain of diamond.

"Isn't that the direction the wind came from?" Gaby asked. "Yeah, if we didn't get turned around by a curve in the river."

"I don't think we did. That looks like ice to me."

Cirocco agreed. The ice sheet broke up as the sea narrowed to a neck, eventually becoming a river that ran in front of her and emptied into the other sea. The country over there was mountainous, rugged as a washboard. She did not understand how the river could thread its way through the mountains to join the sea on the other side. She decided the perspective was fooling her. Water would not flow uphill, even in Themis.

Beyond the ice was another daylight area, this one brighter and yellower than the others she could see, like desert sands. To reach it, she would have to travel across the frozen sea.

"Three days and two nights," Gaby said. "That worked out pretty well from the theory. I said we'd be able to see almost half the inside of Themis from any point. What I didn't figure on were *those* things."

Cirocco followed Gaby's pointing finger to a series of what looked like ropes that started on the land below and angled upward to the roof. There were three of them in a line almost directly in front of them, so that the nearest partially concealed the other two. Cirocco had seen them earlier, but had skipped over them because she could not understand it all at once. Now she looked closer, and frowned. Like a depressing number of things in Themis, they were huge.

The nearest one could serve as a model for all the rest. It was fifty kilometers away, but she could see that it was made of perhaps one hundred strands wound together. Each strand was 200 or 300 meters thick. Further detail was lost at that distance.

The three in the row all angled steeply over the frozen sea, rising 150 kilometers or more until they joined the roof at a point she knew must be one of the spokes, seen from the inside. It was a conical mouth, like the bell of a trumpet that flared to become the roof and sides of the rim enclosure. At the far edge of the bell, some 500 kilometers away, she could make out more of the ropes.

There were more cables to her left, but these went straight up to the arched ceiling and disappeared through it. Beyond them were other rows that angled toward the spoke mouth she could not see from her vantage point, the one over the sea in the mountains.

Where the cables joined the ground, they pulled it up into broad-based mountains.

"They look like the cables on a suspension bridge," Cirocco said.

"I agree. And I think that's what it is. There's no need for towers to support it. The cables can be fastened in the center. Themis is a circular suspension bridge."

Cirocco eased herself closer to the edge. She stuck her head over and looked down two kilometers to the ground.

The cliff was as near perpendicular as an irregular surface feature can be. Only near the bottom did it begin to flare out to meet the land below.

"You aren't thinking of going down that, are you?" Gaby asked.

"The thought had entered my mind, but I sure don't feel good about it. And what would be better down there than up here? We've got a pretty good idea we could survive up here." She stopped. Was that to be their goal?

Given the chance, she would take adventure to security, if security meant building a hut from sticks and settling down to a diet of raw meat and fruit. She would be crazy in a month.

And the land below was beautiful. There were impossibly steep mountains with shining blue lakes set in them like gems. She could see waving grasslands, dense forests, and far to the east, the brooding midnight sea. There was no telling what dangers that land concealed, but it seemed to call to her.

"We might shinny down those vines," Gaby said, reaching over the edge and pointing out a possible line of descent.

The cliff face was encrusted with plants. The jungle spilled over the edge like a frozen torrent of water. Massive trees grew from the bare rock face, clinging like barnacles. The rock itself could be seen only in patches, and even there the news was not all bad. It looked like a basaltic formation, a closely packed sheaf of crystal pillars with broad hexagonal platforms where columns had broken off.

"It's do-able," Cirocco said, at last. "It wouldn't be easy

or safe. We'd have to think of a pretty good reason for trying it." Something better than the formless urge she felt to be down there, she thought.

"Hell, I don't want to be stuck up here, either," Gaby said, with a grin.

"Then your troubles are over," said a quiet voice from behind them.

Every muscle in Cirocco's body tensed. She bit her lip, forcing herself to move slowly until she was safely away from the edge.

"Up here. I've been waiting for you."

Sitting on a tree limb three meters from the ground, his bare feet dangling, was Calvin Greene.

Chapter Seven

Before Cirocco quite had a chance to settle down, they were all sitting in a circle and Calvin was talking.

"I came out not far from the hole where the river disappears," he was saying. "That was seven days ago. I heard you on the second day."

"But why didn't you call us?" Cirocco asked.

Calvin held up the remains of his helmet.

"The mike is missing," he said, extricating the broken end of wire. "I could listen, but not transmit. I waited. I ate fruit. I just couldn't kill any of the animals." He spread his broad hands, and shrugged.

"How did you know this was the place to wait?" Gaby asked.

"I didn't know, for sure."

"Well," Cirocco said. She slapped her palms on her legs, and then laughed. "Well. Fancy that. Just when we'd about given up hope of finding anybody else, we stumble over you. It's too good to be true. Isn't it, Gaby?"

"Huh? Oh, yeah, it's great."

"It's good to see you folks, too. I've been listening to you for five days now. It's nice to hear a familiar voice."

"Has it really been that long?"

Calvin tapped a device on his wrist. It was a digital watch.

"It's still keeping perfect time," he said. "When we get back, I'm going to write a letter to the manufacturer."

"I'd thank the maker of the watchband," Gaby said. "Yours is steel and mine was leather."

Calvin shrugged. "I remember it. It cost more than I made in a month, as an intern."

"It still seems like too much time. We only slept three times."

"I know. Bill and August are having the same trouble judging time."

Cirocco looked up.

"Bill and August are alive?"

"Yeah, I've been listening to them. They're down there, on the bottom. I can point to the place. Bill has his whole radio, like you two. August only had a receiver. Bill picked out some landmarks and started talking about how we could find him. He sat still for two days, and August found him pretty quick. Now they call out regular. But August only asks for April, and she cries a lot."

"Jesus," Cirocco breathed. "I guess she would. You don't have any idea where April is, or Gene?"

"I thought I heard Gene once. Crying, like Gaby said."

Cirocco thought it over, and frowned.

"Why didn't Bill hear us, then? He'd be listening in, too."

"It must have been line-of-sight problems," Calvin said. "The cliff was cutting you off. I was the only one who could listen to both groups, but I couldn't do anything about it."

"Then he'd hear us now, if—"

"Don't get excited. They're asleep now, and they won't hear you. Those earphones are like a gnat buzzing. They ought to wake up in five or six hours." He looked from one of them to the other. "The smart thing for you folks is to get some sleep, too. You've been walking for twenty-five hours."

This time, Cirocco had no trouble believing him. She knew she was existing on the excitement of the moment; her eyelids were drooping. But she couldn't give in yet.

"What about yourself, Calvin? Have you had any trouble?"

He raised one eyebrow. "Trouble?"

"You know what I'm talking about."

He seemed to draw in on himself.

"I'm not talking about that. Not ever."

She was inclined not to push it. He seemed peaceful, as if he had come to terms with something.

Gaby stood up and stretched, yawning hugely.

"I'm for the sack," she said. "Where do you want to stretch out, Rocky?"

Calvin stood up, too. "I've got a place I've been working on," he said. "It's up here in this tree. You two can use it, and I'll stay up and listen for Bill."

It was a bird's nest woven from twigs and vines. Calvin had lined it with a feathery substance. There was plenty of room, but Gaby chose to get close, as they had been doing before. Cirocco wondered if she ought to call a halt to it, but decided it didn't matter.

"Rocky?"

"What is it?"

"I want you to be careful around him."

Cirocco came back from the edge of sleep.

"Mummph? Calvin?"

"Something's happened to him."

Cirocco looked at Gaby with one bloodshot eye. "Go to sleep, Gaby, okay?" She reached around and patted her leg.

"Just watch out," Gaby muttered.

If only there was some sign to mark the morning, Cirocco thought, yawning. It would make getting up a lot easier. Something like a rooster, or the sun's rays coming in at a different slant.

Gaby was still asleep beside her. She disentangled herself and stood on the broad tree limb.

Calvin was not around. Breakfast was within arm's

reach: purple fruit the size of a pineapple. She picked one and ate it, rind and all. She began to climb.

It was easier than it looked. She went up almost as fast as she could have climbed a ladder. There were definitely things to be said for one-quarter gee, and the tree was ideal for climbing, better than anything she had seen since she was eight years old. The knobby bark provided handholds where limbs were scarce. She picked up a few scratches to add to her collection, but it was a price she was willing to pay.

She felt happy for the first time since her arrival in Themis. She didn't count the meeting with Gaby and Calvin, because those had been so emotional they had verged on hysteria. This was just feeling good.

"Hell, it's been longer than that," she muttered. She had never been a gloomy person. There had been some good times aboard *Ringmaster*, but little out-and-out *fun*. Trying to recall the last time she had felt this good, she decided it was the party when she learned she had her command after seven years of trying. She grinned at the memory; it had been a very good party.

But she soon put all thought from her mind and let her soul flow into the endeavor itself. She was aware of every muscle, every inch of skin. There was an astonishing amount of freedom in climbing a tree with no clothes on. Her nudity, until now, had been a nuisance and a danger. Now she loved it. She felt the rough texture of the tree under her toes, and the supple flex in the tree limbs. She wanted to yodel like Tarzan.

As she approached the top, she heard a sound that had not been there before. It was a repeated crunching, coming from a point she couldn't see through the yellow-green leaves, in front of her and a few meters down.

Proceeding more cautiously, she eased herself onto a horizontal limb and sidled toward the open air.

There was a blue-gray wall in front of her. She had no idea what it might be. The crunching came again, louder, slightly above her. A tuft of broken branches moved in front of her and out of sight. Then, with no warning, the eye appeared.

"Wow!" she yelped, before she could get her mouth shut. Without quite recalling how she got to be there she was three meters back, bouncing with the motion of the tree and staring transfixed at the monstrous eye. It was as wide as her outstretched arms, glistening with moisture, and astonishingly human.

It blinked.

A thin membrane contracted from all sides, like a camera aperture, then snapped open again, literally quick as a wink.

She broke all records getting down, not feeling it when she scraped her knee, yelling all the way. Gaby was awake. She had a thighbone in her hand, and looked ready to use it.

"Down, down!" Cirocco yelled. "There's something up there. It could use this tree for a toothpick." She levitated the last eight meters, hit the ground on all fours, and was on her way down the hill when she collided with Calvin.

"Didn't you hear me? We've got to get out of here. There's this thing—"

"I know, I know," he soothed, putting out his hands, palms toward her. "I know all about it, and it's nothing to worry about. I didn't have time to tell you before you went to sleep."

Cirocco felt deflated, but far from soothed. It was terrible to have that much nervous energy and nothing to do with it. Her feet wanted to run. Instead, she blew up at him.

"Well *shit*, Calvin! You didn't have *time* to tell me about a thing like *that*? What is it, and what do you know about it?"

"That's our way off this cliff," he said. "His name is—" he pursed his lips and whistled three clear notes with a warble at the end, "—but I see that's awkward to use mixed with English. I call him Whistlestop."

"You call him 'Whistlestop,'" Cirocco repeated, numbly.

"That's right. He's a blimp."

"A blimp."

He looked at her oddly and she gritted her teeth.

"He looks more like a dirigible, but he's not, because he

doesn't have a rigid skeleton. I'll call him and you can see for yourself." He put two fingers to his lips and whistled a long, complex tune with odd musical intervals.

"He's calling him," Cirocco said.

"So I heard," Gaby said. "Are you okay?"

"Yeah. But my hair's going to come back in gray."

There was an answering series of trills from above, then nothing happened for several minutes. They waited.

Whistlestop bulged into view from the left. He was 300 or 400 meters from the cliff face, traveling parallel to it, and even that far away they could see only a little of him. He was a solid blue-gray curtain being drawn across their view. Then Cirocco spotted the eye. Calvin whistled again, and the eye swiveled aimlessly, eventually finding them. Calvin looked back over his shoulder.

"He don't see so good," he explained.

"Then I'm for staying out of his way. Like in the next county."

"That wouldn't be far enough," Gaby said, awed. "His ass would *be* in the next county."

The nose disappeared and Whistlestop continued to glide past. And glide past. And glide, and glide, and glide. There seemed to be no end to him.

"Where's he going?" Cirocco asked.

"It takes him a while to stop," Calvin explained. "He'll get squared away pretty soon."

Cirocco and Gaby finally joined Calvin at the edge so they could see the whole operation.

Whistlestop the blimp was a full kilometer from stem to stern. All he needed to look like a bigger-than-life-size replica of the German airship *Hindenberg* was a swastika painted on his tail.

No, Cirocco decided, that was not quite true. She was an airship enthusiast, had been active in the NASA project to build one almost as big as Whistlestop. While working with the project engineers, she had come to know the design of the LZ-129 quite well.

The shape was the same: an elongated cigar, blunt at the nose, tapering to a point at the stern. There was even some sort of gondola slung beneath, though farther back than in the *Hindenberg*. The color was wrong, and the texture of the skin. No bracing structure was visible; Whistlestop was smooth, like the old Goodyear blimps, and now that she could see him in the light he shone with a mother-of-pearl iridescence and a hint of oiliness over the basic blue-gray.

And *Hindenberg* had not had hair. Whistlestop did, along a transverse ventral ridge, growing thicker and longer amidships, thinning out to a sparse blue down toward the ends. A clutch of delicate tendrils hung beneath the central nodule, or gondola, or whatever it was.

Then there were the eyes, and the tail fins. Cirocco saw one side-looking eye, and thought there were probably more. Instead of four flight surfaces at the tail Whistlestop had only three: two horizontal ones and one rudder. Cirocco could see them flexing as the monstrous thing struggled to turn its nose toward them, at the same time backing up half its length. The fins were thin and transparent, like the wings of a man-powered O'Neil flyer, and supple as a jellyfish.

"You . . . uh, you *talk* to this thing?" she asked Calvin.

"Pretty well," He was smiling at the blimp, happier than Cirocco had ever seen him.

"It's an easy language to learn, then?"

He frowned. "No, I don't think you could say that."

"You've been here—how long? Seven days?"

"I tell you, I know how to talk to it. I know a lot about it."

"Then how did you learn it?"

The question obviously troubled him.

"I woke up knowing it."

"Say again?"

"I just *know* it. When I first saw him, I knew all about him. When he talked, I understood. As simple as that."

It was far from simple, Cirocco was sure. But he obviously did not want to be pressed on the question.

It took the better part of an hour for Whistlestop to position himself, then to nose in carefully until he nearly touched the side of the cliff. During the operation, Gaby

and Cirocco moved well back. They felt better when they saw its mouth. It was a meter-wide slash, ridiculously tiny for a creature of Whistlestop's size, set twenty meters below the forward eye. There was a separate orifice below the mouth: a sphincter muscle that doubled as a pressure-relief valve and whistle.

A long, rigid object protruded from the mouth and extended to the ground.

"C'mon," Calvin said, beckoning to them. "Let's get aboard."

Neither Gaby nor Cirocco could think of a line to go with that. They just stared at him. He looked exasperated for a moment, then smiled again.

"I guess it's hard for you to believe, but it's true. I do know a lot about these things. I've already been for a ride. He's perfectly willing; he's going our way anyhow. And it's *safe*. He only eats plants, and very little of that. He can't eat too much, or he'd sink." He put a foot on the long gangplank and walked toward the entrance.

"What's that thing you're standing on?" Gaby asked.

"I guess you could call it his tongue."

Gaby started to laugh, but it had a hollow sound, and died in a cough. "Isn't that all just a bit too . . . I mean, Jesus, Calvin! There you stand on the damn thing's tongue, asking me to walk into his *mouth*, dammit. I suppose at the end of . . . shall we call it the throat? At the end of the throat is something that's not really a stomach but just serves the same purpose. And those juices that start flowing over us, you'll have a nice, glib explanation for that, too!"

"Hey, Gaby, I promise you, it's as safe as—"

"No, *thank* you!" Gaby shouted. "I may be Mama Plauget's dumbest daughter, but nobody ever said I didn't have the sense to stay out of some fuckin' monster's *mouth*. Jesus! Do you *know what you're asking*? I've already been eaten alive once on this trip. I'm not going to let it happen again."

She was screaming by now, shaking, and her face was red. Cirocco agreed with everything Gaby said, on an emotional level. She stepped onto the tongue, anyway. It was warm, but dry. She turned, and held out her hand.

"Come on, shipmate. I believe him."

Gaby stopped shaking and looked stunned.

"You wouldn't leave me here?"

"Of course not. You're coming with us. We have to get down there with Bill and August. Come on, where's the courage I know you have?"

"That's not fair," Gaby whined. "I'm not a coward. You just can't ask me to do *that*."

"I *am* asking you. The only way to deal with your fear is to face it. Come on in."

Gaby hesitated a long time, then squared her shoulders and marched up as if going to her execution.

"I'll do it for you," she said, "because I love you. I have to be with you, wherever you go, even if it means we die together."

Calvin looked at Gaby strangely, but said nothing. They went into the mouth, found themselves in a narrow, translucent tube with a thin floor over even thinner air. It was a long walk.

Amidships was the large pouch she had seen from the outside. It was thick, clear material, a hundred meters long by thirty wide, and the bottom was covered in pulverized wood and leaves. There were small animals inside with them: several smilers, a selection of smaller species, and thousands of tiny smooth-skinned creatures smaller than shrews. Like the other animals they had seen in Themis, these paid no attention to them.

They could see out on all sides, and found they were already some distance from the cliff face.

"If this place isn't Whistlestop's stomach, what is it?" Cirocco asked.

Calvin looked puzzled.

"I never said it wasn't his stomach. This is his food we're standing on."

Gaby moaned and tried to run back the way she had come in. Cirocco grabbed her and held her down. She looked up at Calvin.

"It's all right," he said. "He can only digest with the

help of these little animals. He eats their end product. His digestive juices can't hurt any more than weak tea."

"You hear that, Gaby?" Cirocco whispered in her ear. "We're going to be all right. Calm down, honey."

"I h-hear. Don't be mad at me. I'm frightened."

"I know. Come on, stand up and look out. That'll take your mind off it." She helped her up, and they wallowed over to the clear stomach wall. It was like walking on a trampoline. Gaby pressed her nose and hands to it and spent the rest of the trip sobbing and staring fixedly into space. Cirocco left her alone, and went to Calvin.

"You've got to be more careful of her," she said, quietly. "The time in the darkness has affected her more than us." She narrowed her eyes and searched his face. "Except I don't really know about you."

"I'm all right," he said. "But I don't want to talk about my life before my re-birth. That's over."

"Funny. Gaby said pretty much the same thing. I can't see it that way."

Calvin shrugged, plainly not interested in what either of them thought.

"All right. I'd appreciate it if you told me what you know. I don't care how you learned it if you don't want to tell me."

Calvin thought it over, and nodded.

"I can't teach you their language quickly. It's mostly tone and duration, and I can only speak a pidgen version based on the lower tones I can hear.

"They come in all sizes from about ten meters to slightly larger than Whistlestop. They often travel in schools; this one has some smaller attendants which you didn't see because they stayed on his other side. There's some of them now."

He pointed out the window, where a flight of six twenty-meter blimps jostled for position. They looked like ponderous fish. Cirocco could hear shrill whistles.

"They're friendly, and quite intelligent. They don't have any natural enemies. They generate hydrogen from their food and keep it under a slight pressure. They carry water for ballast, drop it when they want to rise, valve off hydrogen when they want to go down. Their skin is tough, but if it gets torn they usually die.

"They're not very maneuverable. They don't have much fine control, and it takes them a long time to get moving. A fire can trap them sometimes. If they can't get away, they go up like a bomb."

"What about all these creatures in here?" Cirocco asked. "Do they need all of them to digest their food?"

"No, just the little yellow ones. Those things can't eat anything but what a blimp prepares for them. You won't find them anywhere but in a blimp's stomach. The rest of these critters are like us. Hitchhikers or passengers."

"I don't get it. Why does the blimp do it?"

"It's symbiosis, combined with the intelligence to make his own choices and do as he pleases. His race gets along with other races in here, the Titanides in particular. He does them favors, and they return it by—"

"Titanides?"

He smiled uncertainly, and spread his hands. "It's a word I substitute for a whistle he uses. I only get a hazy idea of what they're like because I can't do too well with complex descriptions. I gather they're six-legged, and they're all females. I call them Titanides because that's the name in Greek mythology for female Titans. I've been naming other things, too."

"Such as?"

"The regions and the rivers and the mountain ranges. I named the land areas after the Titans."

"What...oh, yeah, I remember now." Calvin had studied mythology as a hobby. "Who were the Titans, again?"

"The sons and daughters of Uranus and Gaea. Gaea appeared from Chaos. She gave birth to Uranus, made him her equal, and they produced the Titans, six men and six women. I named the days and nights here after them, since there's six days and six nights."

"If you named all the nights after women, I'm going to think up names of my own."

He smiled. "No such thing. It's pretty much at random. Look back there at the frozen ocean. That seemed like it ought to be Oceanus, so that's what I called it. The country we're over now is Hyperion, and that night over there in front of us, with the mountains and the irregular sea, is Rhea. When you face Rhea from Hyperion, north is to your left and south is to your right. After that, going around the circle—I haven't seen most of these, you understand, but I know they're there—I call them Crius, which you can just see, then around the bend are Phoebe, Tethys, Thea, Metis, Dione, Iapetus, Cronus, and Mnemosyne. You can see Mnemosyne on the other side of Oceanus, behind us. It looks like a desert."

Cirocco tried to string them all together in her head. "I'll never remember all that."

"The only ones that matter right now are Oceanus, Hyperion, and Rhea. Actually, not all the names are Titans. One Titan is Themis, and I thought that would be confusing. And, well...." He looked away, with a sheepish grin. "I just couldn't recall the names of two Titans. I used Metis, which is wisdom, and Dione."

Cirocco did not really care. The name were handy, and in their own way, systematic. "Let me guess about the rivers. More mythology?"

"Yeah. I picked the nine largest rivers in Hyperion—which has got a hell of a lot of them, as you can see—and named them after the Muses. Down south over there is Urania, Calliope, Terpsichore, and Euterpe, with Polyhymnia in the twilight zone and feeding into Rhea. And over here on the north slope, starting at the east—is Melpomene. Closer to us are Thalia and Erato, which look like they make a system. And the one you came down is a feeder of the Clio, which is just about below us now."

Cirocco looked down and saw a blue ribbon winding through dense green forest, followed it back to the cliff face behind them, and gasped.

"So *that's* where the river went," she said.

It arched from the cliff face, nearly half a kilometer below where they had been standing, looking solid and hard as metal for fifty meters before it began to break up. It fragmented rapidly from that point, reaching the ground as mist.

There were a dozen more plumes of water issuing from the cliff, none so close or spectacular, each with its attendant rainbow. From her vantage point, the rainbows were lined up like croquet wickets. It was breathtaking, almost too beautiful to be real.

"I'd like to have the post card concession for this place," she said. Calvin laughed.

"You sell film for the camera, and I'll sell tickets to the rides. What do you think of this one?"

Cirocco glanced back at Gaby, still frozen to the window.

"Reactions seem mixed. I like it okay. What's the name for the big river? That one that all the others join?"

"Ophion. The great serpent of the north wind. If you'll look closely, you can see that it comes out of a small lake back there at the twilight zone between Mnemosyne and Oceanus. That lake must have a source, and I suspect it's Ophion flowing underground through the desert, but we can't see where it goes under. Other than that, it flows without a break, into seas and out of them on the other side."

Cirocco traced the convoluted path and could see that Calvin was right. "I think a geographer would tell you that it's not the same river going into a sea as it is coming out," she said. "But I know all the rules were made for Earth rivers. Okay, so we'll call it a circular river."

"That's where Bill and August are," Calvin said, pointing. "About halfway down the Clio, where that third tributary—"

"Bill and August. We were supposed to try and contact them. With all that commotion about getting on the blimp—"

"I borrowed your radio. They're up, and waiting for us. You can call them now, if you like."

Cirocco got her helmet ring and radio from Gaby.

"Bill, can you hear me? This is Cirocco."

"Uh . . . yeah, yeah? I hear you. How are you doing?"

"About as well as you'd expect, riding in the stomach of a blimp. What about you? Did you come through all right? No injuries?"

"No, I'm fine. Listen, I wish . . . I wish I could say how good it feels to hear your voice."

She felt a tear on her cheek, and brushed it away.

"It's good to hear *you*, Bill. When you fell out that window—oh, damn! You wouldn't remember that, would you."

"There's a lot of things I don't remember," he said. "We can straighten it all out later."

"I'm dying to see you. Do you have any hair?"

"It's growing in all over my body. We'd better let all this wait. We've got lots to talk about, me and you and Calvin and . . ."

"Gaby," she prompted, after what seemed like a very long pause.

"Gaby," he said, without much conviction. "You see I'm a bit confused about some things. But it shouldn't be a problem."

"Are you sure you're all right?" She felt cold suddenly, and rubbed her forearms briskly.

"Sure thing. When will you be here?"

Cirocco asked Calvin, who whistled a short tune. He was answered by another tune from somewhere overhead.

"Blimps don't have much idea of time," he said. "I'd say three or four hours."

"Is that any way to run an airline?"

Chapter Eight

Cirocco chose the front end of the gondola—it didn't help anything to think of it as a stomach—to be by herself. Gaby was still petrified and Calvin was not much fun to talk to once he'd said everything he knew about Whistlestop. He wouldn't discuss the things Cirocco wanted to know.

A handrail would have been nice. The gondola wall was clear as glass right down to her feet, and would have been clear there too but for the carpet of half-digested leaves and branches. It made for a dizzying view.

They were passing over thick jungle, much like the country higher up on the cliff. The land was dotted with lakes. The river Clio—broad, yellow, and sluggish—wound through it all: a rope of water thrown to the ground to coil where it wished.

She was astonished at the clarity of the air. There were clouds over Rhea that built to thunderheads on the north shore of the sea, but she could see over them. She could see to the limits of the curve of Themis in both directions.

A school of big blimps hovered at various heights around the suspension cable nearest Whistlestop. She couldn't tell what they were doing there, but thought they might be feeding. The cable was massive enough that trees could very well grow on it.

Looking straight down, she could see the huge shadow Whistlestop cast. The lower they went, the larger the shadow became. After four hours it was tremendous, and they were still above the treetops. Cirocco wondered how Whistlestop proposed to set them on the ground. There was no clear area remotely large enough to accommodate him.

She was startled to see two figures standing at a bend in the river, on the west shore, waving at her. She waved back, unsure if she could be seen.

"So how do we get down?" she asked Calvin.

He grimaced. "I didn't think you'd like this, so I didn't bring it up. No sense in having you worry. We parachute."

Cirocco did not react, and he seemed relieved.

"It's a cinch, really. Nothing to it. Safe as can be."

"Uh-huh. Calvin, I love parachuting. I think it's loads of fun. But I like to inspect and pack my own chute. I like to know who made it, and if it's a good one." She looked around her. "Correct me if I'm wrong, but I didn't see you carrying any aboard."

"Whistlestop has 'em," he said. "It never fails."

Again Cirocco said nothing.

"I'll go first," he said, persuasively. "So you can see."

"Uh-huh. Calvin, do I understand this is the only way down?"

"Short of going about a hundred kilometers east to the plains. Whistlestop will take you there, but you'll have to walk back through a swamp."

Cirocco looked at the ground, not really seeing it. She breathed in deeply, then exhaled.

"Right. Let's see these chutes." She went to Gaby and touched her shoulders, pulled her gently away from the side wall, and guided her toward the back of the gondola. She was docile as a child. Her shoulders were stiff, and she was shaking.

"I can't really show them to you," Calvin said. "Not until I jump. They're produced when you bail out. Like this."

He reached up and grasped a handful of dangling, white tendrils. They stretched. He began separating them until he had a loose netting. The stuff was like taffy, but held its shape when it wasn't pulled.

He forced one leg through a gap in the netting, then the other. He pulled it up around his hips and it formed a tight basket. He pushed his arms through more holes until his body was wrapped in a cocoon.

"You've jumped before; you know the drill. Are you a good swimmer?"

"Very good, if my life is at stake. Gaby? You swim well?"

It took her a few moments to become aware of them, then a flickering interest grew in her eyes.

"Swim? Sure. Like a fish."

"Okay," Calvin said. "Watch me, and do what I do." He whistled, and a hole irised into being on the floor in front of him. He waved, stepped over the lip, and fell like a stone. Which was not all that fast in one-quarter gravity, but fast enough, Cirocco felt, with an untested chute.

The shrouds spun out behind him like spider silk. Then came a solid, pale blue sheet, tightly bunched together and gone in a second. They looked down in time to see and hear the flutter and crack as the chute opened and grabbed air. Calvin floated down, waving to them.

She gestured to Gaby, who donned the harness. She was so eager to be out that she jumped before Cirocco could check the arrangement.

That's two out of three, she thought, and put her foot through the third set of webs. They were warm and elastic, and comfortable when she had them in place.

The jump was routine, if anything inside Themis could be so. The chute made a blue circle against the yellow sky above her. It seemed smaller than it should be, but apparently it was enough in the low gravity and high pressure. Grabbing a handful of shrouds, she guided herself toward the river's edge.

She hit standing up and got out of the harness quickly. The chute collapsed on the muddy bank, almost covering Gaby. She stood in knee-deep water and watched Bill coming toward her. It was hard not to laugh. He looked like a pale, plucked chicken with short stubble growing on his chest, his legs, arms, face, and scalp.

She put both hands on her forehead and rubbed them back over her fuzzy scalp, grinning wider as he got closer.

"Am I like you remember me?" she said.

"Even better." He splashed through the last few steps between them. He put his arms around her and they kissed. She did not cry, did not feel the need to though she was brimming over with happiness.

Bill and August had done wonders in only six days, working with just the sharp edges of their suit rings. They had built two shacks; a third had two sides and half a roof. They were made from branches tied together and caked with mud. The roofs were slanted and thatched.

"The best we could do," Bill said, as he showed them around. "I was thinking in terms of adobe, but the sun won't dry the mud fast enough. They keep out the wind, and most of the rain."

Inside, the huts were two by two meters, covered with a thick layer of dry straw. Cirocco could not stand erect, but didn't think of objecting. Being able to sleep inside was nothing to laugh at.

"We didn't have time to finish the other one before you got here," he went on. "One more day, with the three of you helping. Gaby, this one is for you and Calvin. Me and Cirocco will move into the one over there that August used to have. She says she wants the new one." Neither Calvin nor Gaby said anything, but Gaby was sticking close to Cirocco.

August looked like hell. She had aged five years since Cirocco last saw her. She was a thin, hollow-eyed ghost with hands that shook constantly. She looked incomplete, as if half of her had been hacked away.

"We didn't have time to make a fresh kill today," Bill was saying. "We were too busy on the new house. August, is there enough left over from yesterday?"

"I think so," she said.

"Would you get it?"

She turned away. Bill caught Cirocco's eye, pursed his lips, and shook his head slowly.

"Nothing at all from April, huh?" he said softly.

"Not a word. Gene, either."

"I don't know what's going to happen to her."

After the meal Bill put them to work finishing the third hut. With two for practice, he had it down to a routine. It was tedious, but not physically difficult; they could move large logs easily, but had a terrible time cutting even the smallest ones. As a result, the fruit of their labors was not pretty to look at.

When it was done, Calvin went into the hut he had been assigned while August moved into another. Gaby seemed at a loss, but finally managed to stammer that she was going to look around the area, and would not be back for several hours. She wandered off, looking forlorn.

Bill and Cirocco looked at each other. Bill shrugged, and gestured toward the remaining hut.

Cirocco sat awkwardly. There were many things she wanted to ask, but she was hesitant to start.

"How was it for you?" she asked finally.

"If you mean the time between the collision and waking up in here, I'm going to have to disappoint you. I don't remember any of it."

She reached over and probed gently at his forehead.

"No headaches? Dizziness? Calvin should take a look at you."

He frowned. "Was I hurt?"

"Pretty bad. Your face was bloody and you were out cold. That's all I could see in a few seconds I had. But I thought your skull might be broken."

He felt his forehead, ran his fingers around to the sides and back of his head.

"I can't find any tender places. There weren't any bruises, either. Cirocco, I—"

She put her hand on his knee. "Call me Rocky, Bill. You know you're the only one I didn't mind it from."

He scowled, and looked away from her.

"All right, Rocky. That's what I need to talk to you

about. It isn't just the . . . the dark period, August called it. It isn't just that I can't remember. I'm pretty hazy about a lot of things."

"Just how many things?"

"Like where I was born, how old I am, or where I grew up or went to school. I can see my mother's face, but I can't remember her name, or if she's dead or alive." He rubbed his forehead.

"She's alive and very well in Denver, where you grew up," Cirocco said, quietly. "Or she was when she called us on your fortieth birthday. Her name's Betty. We all liked her."

He seemed relieved, then downcast again.

"I guess that means something," he said. "I *did* remember her because she's important to me. I remembered you, too."

Cirocco looked into his eyes. "But not my name. Is that what you're having trouble telling me?"

"Yeah." He looked miserable. "Isn't that a hell of a thing? August told me your name, but she didn't tell me I called you Rocky. That's kind of cute, by the way. I like that."

Cirocco laughed. "I've been trying to kill that name most of my adult life, but I always weaken when somebody whispers it in my ear." She took his hand. "What else do you remember about me? You recall I was the Captain?"

"Oh, sure. I remember you were the first female Captain I'd ever served under."

"Bill, in free-fall, it doesn't matter who's on top."

"That's not what I—" He smiled when he realized he was being kidded. "I wasn't sure about that, either. Did we . . . I mean were we . . . ?"

"Did we fuck?" She shook her head, not in negation, but in wonder. "Every chance we got, as soon as I stopped chasing Gene and Calvin and noticed that the most man on board was my chief engineer. Bill, I hope I don't hurt your feelings, but I kind of like you like this."

"Like what?"

"You couldn't bring yourself to ask if we'd . . . been

*in*timate." She made the pause as dramatic as she could, lowering her eyes shyly, and he laughed. "You were like that before we got to know each other. Shy. I think this is going to be like the first time all over again, and the first time is always special, don't you agree?" She blinked at him and waited what she felt was a reasonable time, but he made no move, so she went to him and pressed close. It had not surprised her; she had needed to make her feelings quite clear the other first time, too.

When they broke the kiss he looked up at her and smiled.

"I wanted to tell you that I love you. You didn't give me any time."

"You never said that before. Maybe you shouldn't commit yourself until you get your memory back."

"I think I might not have known I loved you before. Then . . . all I was left with was your face and a feeling. I'll trust that. And I meant what I said."

"Mmm. You're nice. Do you remember what to do with that?"

"I'm sure it'll come back to me with practice."

"Then I think it's time for you to start serving under me again."

It was as joyous as a first time, but without the awkwardness that usually goes along with it. Cirocco forgot everything else. There was just enough light to see his face, just enough gravity to make the heaps of straw softer than the finest silk.

The timeless quality of that long afternoon had little to do with the unchanging light of Themis. She didn't have any place she needed to be; there was no need to go anywhere, ever, for anything.

"Now's the time for a cigarette," he said. "I wish I had one."

"And drop your ashes down on me," she teased. "Filthy habit. I wish I had some cocaine. It all went down with the ship."

"You can go straight."

He had not withdrawn from her. She remembered how

much she had liked that in *Ringmaster*, waiting to see if things would get going again. With Bill, they usually did.

This time was a little different.

"Bill, I'm afraid I'm getting a little irritated like this."

He eased his weight onto his hands. "The straw hurting your back? I can take a turn underneath if you want."

"It's not the straw, honey, and it ain't my back. It's a little more personal than that. I'm afraid you feel like sandpaper."

"So do you, but I was much too polite to say it." He rolled off and put his arm under her shoulders. "Funny I didn't notice it a few minutes ago."

She laughed. "If you'd grown spikes, I wouldn't have noticed it a few minutes ago. But I wish we had our hair back. I feel pretty silly like this, and it's uncomfortable as hell."

"You think you got it bad? I'm growing it back all over. It's like fleas square-dancing on my skin. Pardon me while I scratch." He did so, lustily, and Cirocco helped him get the impossible places on his back. "Aaaah. Did I say I loved you? I was crazy, I didn't know what love meant. *Now* I know."

Gaby chose that moment to walk in the door.

"Pardon me, Rocky, but I was wondering if we should do something about the parachutes. One of them already floated down the river."

Cirocco sat up quickly. "Do what with them?"

"Save them. They might be useful."

"You . . . sure, Gaby. You might be right."

"I just thought it would be a good idea." She looked at the floor and shuffled her feet, glanced at Bill for the first time. "Uh . . . okay. I thought maybe I . . . could make something nice for you." She hurried from the hut.

Bill sat up and put his elbows on his knees.

"Was I reading too much into that?"

Cirocco sighed. "I'm afraid not. Gaby's going to be a big problem. She thinks she's in love with me, too."

Chapter Nine

"What do you mean, good-bye? Where are you going?"

"I've been thinking it over," Calvin said, quietly. He removed his wristwatch and handed it to Cirocco. "You people can use this better than I can."

Cirocco was about to burst with frustration.

"And that's all the explanation we get? 'I've been thinking it over.' Calvin, we've got to stick together. We're still an exploration party, and I'm still your Captain. We've got to work together toward getting rescued."

He smiled faintly. "And just how are we going to do that?"

She wished he hadn't asked that question.

"I haven't had time to work out a plan on that," she said, vaguely. "There's bound to be something we can do."

"You let me know when you think of something."

"I'm ordering you to stay with the rest of us."

"How are you going to stop me from leaving if I want to go? Knock me out and tie me up? How much energy is it going to take to guard me all the time? Keeping me here makes me a liability. If I go, I can be an asset."

"What do you mean, an asset?"

"Just that. The blimps can talk around the whole curve of Themis. They're great with news; everybody here listens to them. If you ever need me for anything, I'd come back. All I'd have to do is teach you a few simple calls. Can you whistle?"

"Never mind that," Cirocco said, with an annoyed wave of her hand. She rubbed her forehead, and allowed her body to relax. If she was to make him stay, she had to talk him out of it, not restrain him.

"I still don't see why you want to go. Don't you like it here with us?"

"I . . . no, not all that much. I was happier when I was alone. There's too much tension. Too much bad feeling."

"We've all been through a lot. It ought to get better when we get some things straightened out."

He shrugged. "Then you can call me, and I'll try it again. But I don't care for the company of my own kind anymore. The blimps are freer, and wiser. I've never been happier than during that ride."

He was showing more enthusiasm than Cirocco had seen since the meeting on the cliff.

"The blimps are old, Captain. Both as individuals and as a race. Whistlestop is maybe 3000 years old."

"How do you know that? How does *he* know?"

"There are times of cold, and times of warmth. I figure they must be because Themis always stays pointed the same direction. The axis points close to the sun right now, but every fifteen years the rim blocks the sunlight until Saturn moves and brings the other pole back toward the sun. There's years in here, but each of them is fifteen years long. Whistlestop has seen 200 of them."

"Okay, okay," Cirocco said. "That's what we need you for, Calvin. Somehow you're able to talk to these things. You've been learning from them. Some of it might be important to us. Like these six-legged things, what did you call them . . . ?"

"Titanides. That's all I know about them."

"Well, you might learn more."

"Captain, there's too much to know. But you've landed in the most hospitable part of Themis. Stay put, and you'll be all right. Don't go into Oceanus, or even Rhea. Those places are dangerous."

"See? How could we have known that? We *need* you."

"You don't understand. I can't learn about this place without going to *see* it. Whistlestop's language is mostly out of my range."

Cirocco could feel the bitterness of defeat welling up inside her. Damn it, John Wayne would have keelhauled the bastard. Charles Laughton would have clapped him in irons.

She knew it would make her feel a lot better just to take a swing at the obstinate son of a bitch, but that would wear off quickly. She had never commanded like that. She had won and kept the respect of her crew through showing responsibility and using the best wisdom she could bring to bear on any situation. She could face facts, and knew Calvin was going to leave them, but it just didn't feel right.

And why not? she wondered. Because it lessened her authority?

That had to be part of it, and part of it was her responsibility for his welfare. But it came back to the problem she had faced from the beginning of her command: the lack of enough role models for a female ship's Captain. She had determined to examine all assumptions and use only those that felt right to her. Just because it was right for Admiral Nelson in the British Navy did not mean it was right for her.

There had to be discipline, surely, and there had to be authority. Naval Captains had been demanding one and enforcing the other for thousands of years, and she did not intend to throw away all that accumulated experience. Where a Captain's authority was questioned, disaster usually followed.

But space was not the same, generations of science-fiction writers to the contrary. The people who explored it were highly intelligent, individualistic geniuses, the very best the Earth had to offer. There had to be flexibility, and the NASA legal code for deep-space voyages acknowledged it.

Then there was the other factor she could never forget.

She no longer had a ship. The worst thing that could ever happen to a Captain had happened to her. She had lost her command. It would be a bitter taste in her mouth for the rest of her life.

"All right," she said, quietly. "You're right. I can't spare the time and energy to guard you, and I don't feel like killing you, except in a figurative sense." She made herself stop when she realized she was gritting her teeth, and deliberately relaxed her jaw. "I'm telling you now that if we get back, I'm bringing you up on charges of insubordination. If you go, it will be against my wishes, and against the interests of the mission."

"I accept that," he said, without emotion. "You'll come to see that the last part is not true. I'll be more use where I'm going that I would be here. But we're not going back to Earth."

"We'll see. Now, why don't you teach somebody how to call blimps? I find I'd rather not be around you."

In the end, Cirocco had to learn the whistle code, because she had the most musical ability. Her sense of pitch was near-perfect, and it was critical to the blimp speech.

There were only three phrases to learn, the longest being seven notes and a trill. The first translated as "good lifting," and was nothing but a polite greeting. The second was "I want Calvin," and the third was "Help!"

"Remember, *don't* call a blimp if you've got a fire going."

"How optimistic you are."

"You'll make a fire soon enough. Uh, I was wondering...do you want me to take August off your hands? She might feel better if she was with me. We can cover more ground looking for April."

"We can take care of our own casualties," Cirocco said, coldly.

"Whatever you think is best."

"She's barely aware that you're leaving, anyway. Just get out of my sight, will you?"

August proved to be not as comatose as Cirocco had thought. When she heard Calvin was leaving, she insisted on joining him. After a brief battle, Cirocco gave in, though with even more misgivings than before.

Whistlestop came in low and began spinning a cable. They watched it whip and twist in the air.

"Why is he willing to do this?" Bill asked. "What does he get out of it?"

"He likes me," Calvin said, simply. "Also, he's used to carrying passengers. The sentient species pay for their rides by moving food from his first stomach into the second. He doesn't have the muscles for it. He has to save on weight."

"Does everything here get along so well?" Gaby asked. "We haven't seen anything like a carnivorous animal so far."

"There are carnivores, but not many. Symbiosis is the basic fact of life. That, and worship. Whistlestop says all the higher life forms owe allegiance to a godhead, and the seat of divinity is in the hub. I've been thinking of a goddess that rules the whole circle of the land. I call her Gaea, for the Greek mother."

Cirocco was interested, in spite of herself. "What is Gaea, Calvin? Some sort of primitive legend, or maybe the control room of this thing?"

"I don't know. Themis is a lot older than Whistlestop, and a lot of it is unknown to him, too."

"But who runs it? You said there were many races in here. Which one? Or do they cooperate?"

"Again, I don't know. You've read the stories of generation ships where something went wrong and everybody slipped back to savagery? I think something like that might be going on here. I know something's working somewhere. Maybe machines, or a race that stays in the hub. That may be the source of the worship. But Whistlestop is sure there's a hand on the wheel."

Cirocco scowled. How could she let him go, with all that information in his head? It was spotty and they had no way of knowing how much of it was true, but it was all they had.

But it was too late for second thoughts. His foot was in the stirrup at the end of the long line. August joined him and the blimp reeled them in.

"Captain!" he shouted, just before they disappeared. "Gaby shouldn't have called this place Themis. Call it Gaea."

Cirocco brooded about their departure, plunging into a black depression during which she sat on the side of the river and thought about what she should have done. No course seemed right.

"What about his Hippocratic oath?" she asked Bill at one point. "He was sent along on this trip for one damn thing, to take care of us if we needed it."

"It changed us all, Rocky."

All but me, she thought, but did not say. At least, as far as she could tell, she had suffered no lasting effects from her experience. In a way, that was stranger that what it had done to the others. It should have driven them all catatonic. Instead, there was an amnesiac, an obsessive personality, a woman with an adolescent crush, and a man in love with living airships. Cirocco's was the only level head.

"Don't kid yourself," she muttered. "You probably look as crazy to them as they do to you." But she discarded that notion, too. Bill, Gaby, and Calvin all knew they had been changed by their experience, though Gaby would not admit that her love for Cirocco was a side-effect. August was too distracted by her loss to think about anything at all.

She wondered again about April and Gene. Were they still alive, and if so, how were they taking it? Were they alone, or had they managed to link up?

They had a regular routine of listening and broadcasting, trying to contact the two, but nothing came of it. No one heard a man crying again, and no one heard anything from April.

Time drifted by, all but unmarked. Cirocco had Calvin's watch to tell them when to sleep, but it was hard to adjust to the unfailing light. She would never have suspected it of a group of people who had lived in the artificial environment of *Ringmaster*, where the day was set on the ship's computer and could be varied at will.

Life was easy. All the fruit they tried was edible, and

seemed to be nourishing them. If there were vitamin deficiencies they had yet to make themselves known. Some fruits were salty, and others had a tang they hoped was vitamin C. Game was plentiful, and easy to kill.

They were all used to the strict time-lines of an astronaut, where every chore is assigned by ground control and the chief pastime is bitching about how it was impossible and yet doing it anyway. They had been prepared to struggle for survival in a hostile environment, but Hyperion was about as hostile as the San Diego Zoo. They had expected Robinson Crusoe, or at least the Swiss Family Robinson, but Hyperion was a creampuff. They had not yet adjusted enough to think in terms of a mission.

Two days after Calvin and August left, Gaby presented Cirocco with clothes she had made from the discarded chutes. It touched Cirocco deeply to see the expression on Gaby's face when she tried it on.

The outfit was half toga and half loose pants. The material was thin, but surprisingly tough. It had taken Gaby a lot of hard work to cut it into usable sizes and sew it together with thorn needles.

"If you can work out something for mocassins," she told Gaby, "I'll promote you three grades when we get home."

"I'm working on it." Gaby glowed for a day after that, and was frisky as a puppy, brushing against Cirocco and her fine clothing at the slightest excuse. She was pathetically eager to please.

Cirocco was sitting by the side of the river, alone for once, and glad of it. Being the bone of contention between two lovers was not to her taste. Bill was starting to get annoyed by Gaby's behavior, and seemed to feel he should do something.

She reclined easily with a long limber pole in one hand and watched a small wooden float bob at the end of her line. She let her thoughts drift over the problem of aiding any rescue party that might come for them. What might be done to make rescue easier?

It was a certainty that they couldn't get out of Gaea on their own. The best she could do would be to try contact with the rescue party. She had no doubt one would arrive, and few illusions that its primary purpose would be rescue. The messages she had managed to send during the break-up of *Ringmaster* described a hostile act, and the implications of that were enormous. *Ringmaster*'s crew would certainly be presumed dead, but Themis-Gaea would not be forgotten. A ship would arrive soon, and it would be loaded for bear.

"All right," she said. "Gaea should have some communications facilities somewhere."

Probably in the hub. Even if the engines were there too, its central location seemed the logical place for controls. There might be people up there running things, and there might not. There was no way to make the trip look easy, or the destination safe. It could be carefully guarded against entry and sabotage.

But if there was a radio up there, she should see what she could do about getting to it.

She yawned, scratched her ribs, and idly moved her foot up and down. The float bobbed in and out of the water. It seemed a good time for a snooze.

The float jerked, and vanished beneath the muddy waters. Cirocco looked at it for a moment, then realized with mild surprise that something had taken the bait. She stood and began pulling in the line.

The fish had no eyes, no scales, and no fins. She held it up and looked at it curiously. It was the first fish any of them had caught.

"What the hell am I doing?" she asked aloud. She tossed it back into the water, coiled her fishing line, and started around the bend in the river toward camp.

Half-way there, she began to run.

"I'm sorry, Bill, I know you put a lot of work into this place. But when they come to get us, I want to be working as hard as I can toward getting ourselves out," Cirocco said.

"I agree with you, basically. What's your idea?"

She explained her thinking about the hub, the fact that if there was a central technological control for this vast construct, it would be up there.

"I don't know what we'd find. Maybe nothing but cobwebs and dust, and everything down here is still going by sheer inertia. Or maybe the Captain and a crew waiting to blow us to pieces for invading their ship. But we have to look."

"How do you propose to get up there?"

"I don't know for sure. I'm assuming the blimps can't do it or they would know more about this goddess they talk about. There may not even be any air in the spokes."

"That would make it a bit tough," Gaby pointed out.

"We won't know until we look. The way to get up the spokes is the support cables. They should go all the way up the insides, right to the top."

"My God," Gaby muttered. "Even the slanted ones are a hundred kilometers high. And that just brings you to the roof. From there it's another 500 kilometers to the hub."

"My aching back," Bill groaned.

"What the matter with you?" Cirocco demanded. "I didn't say we'd climb them. We'll decide that when we get a good look. What I'm trying to tell you is that we're *ignorant* of this place. For all I know, there's an express elevator sitting in the swamp that would take us all the way to the top. Or a little man selling helicopter tickets, or magic carpets. We'll never know unless we start looking around."

"Don't get excited," Bill said. "I'm with you."

"What about you, Gaby?"

"I go where you go," she said, matter-of-factly. "You know that."

"All right. Here's my thinking. There's a slanted cable to the west, toward Oceanus. But the river flows the other way, and we could use that for transportation. We might even get to the next row of cables faster that way than beating through the jungle. I think we should head east, toward Rhea."

"Calvin said we should stay out of Rhea," Bill reminded.

"I didn't say we'd go into it. If there's anything that would be harder to take than this perpetual afternoon, it would have to be perpetual night, so I'm not anxious to go there anyway. But there's a lot of country between here and there. We could take a look at it."

"Admit it, Rocky. You're a tourist at heart."

She had to smile. "Guilty. I thought a while ago, here we are in this incredible place. We know there are a dozen intelligent races in here. What do we do? Sit around and fish. Well, not me. I feel like nosing around. It's what they were paying us for, and hell, it's what I like. Maybe I want some adventure."

"My god," Gaby said again, with a hint of chuckle. "What more could you ask? Hasn't enough happened?"

"Adventures have a way of turning around and biting you," Bill said.

"Don't I know it. But we're heading down that river, anyway. I'd like to get going after the next sleep period. I feel like I've been drugged."

Bill considered that for a moment. "Do you think that's possible? Something in one of the fruits?"

"Huh? You've been reading too much sci-fi, Bill."

"Listen, you don't knock my reading habits and I won't knock your old black and white flat films."

"But that's *art*. Never mind. I guess it's possible we've eaten something that tranquilizes but I really think it's just old-fashioned laziness."

Bill stood and reached for his non-existent pipe. He looked annoyed to have forgotten yet again, then dusted off his hands.

"It'll take a while to knock a raft together," he said.

"Why a raft? What about those big seed pods we've seen floating down the river? They're big enough to hold us."

Bill frowned. "Yes, I guess they are, but do you think

they'll handle well in rough water? I'd like to get a look at the bottoms before—"

"Handle? You think a raft would be better?"

He looked startled, then chagrined.

"You know, maybe I *am* getting slow. Lead on, Commander."

Chapter Ten

The seeds grew from the tops of the tallest trees in the forest. Each tree produced only one seed at a time, and when it reached maturity it exploded like a cannon shot. They had heard them going off at long intervals. What was left after the explosion was something like a walnut shell, evenly and smoothly divided.

When they saw a large one float by, they swam out and pulled it to shore. It rode high in the water when empty. Loaded, it still had plenty of freeboard.

They took two days outfitting it and trying to rig a rudder. They fashioned a long pole with a broad blade on the end, and hoped that would be enough. There was a primitive oar for each of them in case they ran into rough water.

Gaby cast off the line. Cirocco put her back into poling them out to the middle of the river, then took her post at the stern, one hand lightly on the tiller. A breeze came up, and she wished once again for her hair. What a fine thing, to have hair whipping in the wind. It's the simple things we miss, she thought.

Gaby and Bill were excited, forgetting their animosity

for the time being as they sat on opposite sides of the boat, watching the river ahead and calling out hazards to Cirocco.

"Sing us a sea chantey, Captain!" Gaby yelled back.

"You've got it mixed up, stupid," Cirocco laughed. "It's you low-life types in the fo'c'sle who pump the bilge and sing the songs. Haven't you ever seen *The Sea Witch*?"

"I don't know. Has it been on the treedie?"

"It's a flat movie starring good ol' John Wayne. The *Sea Witch* was his ship."

"I thought it might be the Captain. You've just picked yourself a nickname."

"You watch yourself, or I'll see if I can rig up a plank for you to walk."

"What about a name for *this* boat, Rocky?" Bill asked.

"Hey, it should have a name, shouldn't it? I was so busy trying to scrounge up champagne for the launching I forgot all about it."

"Don't mention champagne to me," Gaby moaned.

"Any suggestions? Here's your chance for a promotion."

"I know what Calvin would have named it," Bill said, suddenly.

"Don't talk to me about Calvin."

"Nevertheless, we've committed ourselves to Greek mythology. This ship should be named the *Argo*."

Cirocco looked doubtful. "Wasn't that tied up with the search for the golden fleece? Oh, yeah, I remember the movie now."

"We're not searching for anything," Gaby pointed out. "We know where we want to go."

"Then how about..." Bill paused, then looked thoughtful. "I'm thinking of Odysseus. Did his ship have a name?"

"I don't know. We lost our mythologist to that overgrown tire advertisement. But even if it did, I wouldn't want to use it. Odysseus had nothing but trouble."

Bill grinned. "Superstitious, Captain? I never would have believed it."

"It's the sea, lad. It does strange things to a body."

"Don't give me your late-show dialogue. I vote to call the boat *Titanic*. There was a ship for you."

"A bucket of rust. Don't tempt the fates, matey."

"I like *Titanic*, too," Gaby laughed. "Who'd believe it, on a boat made out of a glorified peanut?"

Cirocco looked up, thoughtfully. "Let it be on your heads, then. *Titanic* it is. Long may she sail. You may whoop, and otherwise make merry."

The crew cheered three times, and Cirocco grinned and took a bow.

"Long live the Captain," Gaby shouted.

"Say," Cirocco said. "Shouldn't we be painting the name on the fender, or whatever the hell it is?"

"On the *what*?" Gaby looked horrified.

Cirocco grinned. "This is a fine time to be telling you, but I don't know shit about boats. Who's done some sailing?"

"I've done a little," Gaby said.

"Then you're ship's pilot. Change places with me," She released the tiller and walked forward carefully. She reclined on her back, stretched, and folded her arms under her head. "I'll be making important command decisions," she said, with a big yawn. "Don't disturb me for anything less than a hurricane." She closed her eyes to a chorus of hoots.

The Clio was long, winding, and slow. In the middle, their four-meter poles would not touch bottom. If they put them in the water they could feel things bump into them. They never knew what was doing it. They kept *Titanic* midway between the middle of the river and the port side shore.

Cirocco had planned for them to stay on the boat, going ashore only to gather food—a project which never took more than ten minutes. But standing watch did not work well. Too often, *Titanic* would run aground, making it necessary to wake the sleepers. It took all three of them to move the boat when the bottom was on mud. They quickly learned that *Titanic* was not very maneuverable, and it took two people with poles to push the boat away from approaching shallows.

They decided to camp every fifteen or twenty hours. Cirocco made a schedule which assured that two people were always awake while they sailed, and one when they camped.

Clio meandered through the almost-level terrain like a snake doped with Nembutal. One night's camp might be only half a kilometer in a straight line from the one of the night before. They would have lost their orientation but for the support cable which attached to the ground in the center of Hyperion. Cirocco knew from her air survey that the cable would be east of them until long after they joined the river Ophion.

The cable was always there, towering like some unimaginable skyscraper, rising, seeming to lean toward them until it vanished through the roof and into space. They would pass near it on their way to the angled support cables which led into the spoke over Rhea. Cirocco hoped to get a close look at it.

Life settled into a routine. Soon they were working flawlessly as a team, seldom needing to talk. Most of the time there was little to do but stay alert for sand bars. Gaby and Bill spent a lot of time making improvements in everyone's clothing. They both got to be handy with thorn needles. Bill continually tinkered with the rudder and worked to make the interior of the boat more comfortable.

Cirocco spent most of her time daydreaming, watching the clouds drift by. She considered ways and means of reaching the hub, trying to anticipate problems, but it was a futile occupation. The possibilities were too varied to allow reasonable planning. She much preferred woolgathering.

She eventually did sing to them, and surprised them both. She had taken voice and piano lessons for ten years as a child, had considered a career as a singer before the lure of space grew too strong. No one knew about it until the trip in the *Titanic*; she had thought it not in keeping with her image to entertain the crew with songs. Now she didn't care, and the singing brought them closer together. She had a rich, clear alto that worked best with old folk music, ballads, and Judy Garland songs.

Bill made a lute from a nutshell, parachute shrouds, and a smiler skin. He learned to play it, and Gaby joined in on a nutshell drum. Cirocco taught them songs and assigned harmonies: Gaby had a passable soprano, Bill a tone-deaf tenor.

They sang drinking songs from the taprooms of O'Neil One, songs from the hit parade, from cartoons and old movies. One quickly became their favorite, considering their circumstances. It spoke of a yellow brick road and the wonderful wizard of Oz. They bellowed it every morning when they set out, shouting all the louder when the forest shrieked back at them.

Several weeks went by before they reached the Ophion. Only twice did anything interrupt their peaceful routine.

The first incident was three days into the trip, when an eyeball at the end of a long stalk emerged from the water not five meters from *Titanic*. There was no doubt that it was an eye, any more than there had been with Whistlestop. It was a ball twenty centimeters in diameter, set in a flexible green socket that at first glance appeared to be a green hand with fingers wrapped around the eye from behind. They eyeball itself was lighter green with a gaping pupil.

They began poling for shore at the first sight of the creature. The eye had been pointing at them, betraying neither interest nor emotion but only a fixed stare. It did not seem to mind when they moved away. It watched for two or three minutes, then vanished as quietly as it had appeared.

The consensus, once ashore, was that there was little they could do about it. The creature had not tried to harm them—which said nothing about its future conduct. But they could not end their trip just because there were big fish in the river.

They soon saw more of the eyes, and eventually became accustomed to them. They looked so much like periscopes that Bill named them U-boats.

The second incident was something they were more prepared for because it had happened before. It was the vast moaning wind Calvin had dubbed Gaea's Lament.

There was time before the worst of the winds to beach *Titanic* and seek shelter on the downwind side of the boat. Cirocco did not want to go under the trees, recalling the near-miss by a falling branch in the highlands.

The observing conditions were not good with the wind whipping her face and the clouds rolling overhead, but she managed to catch glimpses of the storm coming out of Oceanus. It came from above. Clouds billowed down from the vast spoke above the frozen sea like the icy breath of God. The wind hit the sheet of ice and broke on it, whipped into tornadoes that looked tiny from that distance, but which must have been huge.

Through the clouds that rapidly advanced toward Hyperion, Cirocco could see the angled support cables that joined the ground to the sky over Oceanus. If they were moving in the wind it was far too slowly to be seen, but there must have been some swaying or stretching motion. The cables were shedding a fine gray mist. She watched it drift down into the narrow angles the cables made with the ground and had to remind herself that the particles she could see from so far away must be as large as trees. Then the clouds obscured all vision, and snow began to fall. Soon after that the river grew agitated, rising almost to the beached *Titanic*. Cirocco thought she could feel the ground moving.

She knew she was seeing some part of Gaea's air circulation system in operation, and wondered how the air was drawn into the spoke and what mechanism forced it back out again. She also wondered why the process had to be so violent. Calvin's watch said it had been seventeen days since the last Lament; she hoped it would be at least as long until the next.

As before, the cold did not last more than six or seven hours, and the snow did not stick to the ground. They weathered it better this time, finding that the blimpsilk clothes were more protective than they looked, working as windbreakers.

The thirtieth day since their emergence was marked by two things: something that happened, and something that didn't happen.

The first was their arrival at the confluence of the Clio and the mighty river Ophion. They were deep in south Hyperion by then, equidistant between the central vertical cable and the southern one, both of which now towered over them.

Ophion was blue-green, wider and swifter than the Clio. It swept *Titanic* into its center, and after a time of alertness and soundings with their poles, the travelers decided it would be safe to stay there. In size and speed, Ophion reminded Bill and Cirocco of the Mississippi, but with more vegetation and tall trees along the banks. The land was still jungle, but Ophion was wide and deep.

Cirocco was far more concerned with the non-event— the one she had waited for as the days ticked by on Calvin's watch. She had been regular as the tides for twenty-two years, and it was disturbing to miss a period.

"Did you know it's been thirty days now?" Cirocco asked Gaby that evening.

"Has it? I hadn't thought about," She frowned.

"Yeah. And I'm more than late. I've always been twenty-nine days; sometimes early by a day, never late."

"You know, I'm late, too."

"I thought you were."

"Christ, that just doesn't make sense at all."

"I was wondering what sort of protection you used on *Ringmaster*. Could you have forgotten about it back then?"

"Not bloody likely. Calvin gave me monthlies."

Cirocco sighed. "I was afraid it'd be something as infallible as that. Me, I can't take pills; they make me swell up. I used one of those wear-ever diaphragms. I had it in when we went under. I didn't really think to look for it until . . . well, after we joined up with Bill and August and it might already have been too late." She was hesitant to discuss that part with Gaby. It was no secret that she and Bill had made love, and also no secret that there had been no time or place or privacy for it on *Titanic* with Gaby always around.

"Anyhow, it's gone. I presume it was eaten by the same thing that ate our hair. Which makes my skin crawl, by the way."

Gaby shivered.

"But I thought it could be Bill. Now I don't really think so." She got up and went over to Bill, who was sleeping on the ground. She woke him, and waited until he looked alert.

"Bill, we're both pregnant."

Bill was not as awake as she had thought. He blinked in surprise, then his brow furrowed.

"Well don't look at *me*. Not even for yours. The last time with Gaby was not long after we left Earth. Besides, I've got a valve."

"I wasn't saying anything like that," she soothed. With Gaby, huh? she thought. She hadn't known about that, and she thought she had been aware of everything that occurred on *Ringmaster*. "That just makes it more certain that something very strange is going on. Somebody or something is playing a big joke on us, but I'm not laughing."

Calvin was as good as his word. Two days after Cirocco hailed a passing blimp, Whistlestop hovered overhead and a blue flower blossomed with their wandering surgeon dangling beneath it. August was close behind him. They hit the water just off shore.

Cirocco had to admit that Calvin looked good. He was smiling, and there was a bounce in his step. He greeted everyone and didn't seem to mind having been summoned. He wanted to talk about his travels, but Cirocco was too anxious to hear what he thought of the new situation. He turned very serious long before they had finished telling him about it.

"Have you had a period since we got here?" he asked August.

"No, I haven't."

"It's been thirty days," Cirocco said. "Is that unusual for you?" From the way August's eyes widened, Cirocco assumed it was. "When was the last time you had intercourse with a man?"

"I've *never*."

"I was afraid you'd say that."

Calvin was quiet for a while, considering it. Then he frowned more deeply.

"What can I say? You all know it's possible for a woman to skip a period for other reasons. Athletes sometimes skip a whole lot of them, and we're not sure why. Stress can do it, emotional or physical. But I think the chances of it happening to all three of you at the same time are slim."

"I would tend to agree," Cirocco said.

"It could be dietary. There's no way to know. I can tell you that the three of you, and...uh, April, were undergoing some convergence."

"What's that?" Gaby asked.

"It sometimes happens to women who live together, like on a spaceship where they're in close quarters. Some hormonal signal tends to synchronize their menstruation. April and August have been in rhythm with each other for a long time, and Cirocco was only a few days off their cycle. Two early periods and she was in step. Gaby, you were getting erratic, if you recall."

"I never paid much attention to it," she said.

"Well, you were. But I can't see what that would have to do with what we have here. I only brought it up to point out that strange things happen. It's *possible* that you all just skipped one."

"It's also possible that we're all knocked up, and I

shudder to think who the father is," Cirocco said, sourly.

"That's just flat impossible," Calvin said. "If you're saying that the thing that ate us did it to you all . . . I can't buy that. There isn't another animal even on Earth that can impregnate a human. You tell me how this alien creature did it."

"I don't *know*," Cirocco said. "That's why it's alien. But I'm convinced it got inside us and did something that might seem perfectly reasonable and natural to it, but is alien to what we know. And I don't like it, and we want to know what you can do if we *are* pregnant."

Calvin rubbed the tight curls on his chin, then smiled slightly. "They didn't prepare me for virgin births at med school."

"I'm not in the mood for jokes."

"Sorry. You and Gaby aren't virgins, anyhow." He shook his head in wonder.

"We were thinking of something more immediate and less sacred," Gaby said. "We don't want these babies, or whatever the hell they are."

"Look, why don't you wait another thirty days before you start getting excited? If you miss another period, call me again."

"We'd like to get it over with now," Cirocco said.

Calvin looked upset for the first time. "And I'm saying I won't do it yet. It's too risky. I might make the tools for a D. and C., but they'll have to be sterilized. I don't have a speculum, and the thought of what I might have to improvise to dilate the cervix is enough to give you nightmares."

"The thought of what I've got growing in my belly is *giving* me nightmares," Cirocco said, darkly. "Calvin, I don't even want a *human* baby now, much less whatever this might be. I want you to do the operation."

Gaby and August nodded their agreement, though Gaby looked slightly ill.

"And I say wait another month. It won't make any difference. The operation would be the same, just scraping out the inner walls of the uterus. But maybe a month from now you'll have found a way to make a fire, to boil some water, to *sterilize* whatever instruments I manage to make. Doesn't that make sense? I assure you, I can do the operation with a minimum of risk, but only with clean tools."

"I just want to get it over with," Cirocco said, "I want to get this thing out of me."

"Captain, take it easy. Settle down and think it out. If you get infected, I'm helpless. There's different country to the east. You might find a way to make a fire. I'll look, too. I was clear over in Mnemosyne when your call came. It could be there's somebody who uses tools and could make a decent speculum and dilator."

"They you're leaving again?" she asked.

"Yes, I am, after I give you all a check-up."

"I'm asking you again to stay with us."

"I'm sorry. I can't."

Nothing Cirocco could say would change his mind, and though she flirted again with the idea of holding him, the same reasons still made that a bad idea. And one more thing had occurred to her since his departure; it might not be wise to harm someone with a friend as big as Whistlestop.

He pronounced all four of them fit and healthy, despite the missed periods of the women, then stayed a few hours, seeming to begrudge even that. He told them what they had seen in their travels.

Oceanus was a terrible place, frozen and forbidding. They had crossed it as quickly as possible. There was a humanoid race down there, but Whistlestop would not go down for a close look. They had thrown rocks from a wooden catapult even when the blimp was a kilometer above them. Calvin described them as human in shape, covered with long white hair. They shot first and asked questions later. He called them Yeti.

"Mnemosyne is a desert," he said. "It looks odd, because the dunes stack up a lot higher than on Earth, from the low gravity, I guess. There's plant life down there. I saw some small animals when we went down low, and what looked like a ruined city and a few small towns.

Places that might have been castles a thousand years ago perched up on vertical rock spires, crumbling apart. It would have taken a thousand years of coolie labor to build them, or some pretty good helicopters.

"I think something has gone badly wrong in here. It's all going to dust. Mnemosyne might have looked like this place once, right down to the empty river bed and the corpses of huge trees being eaten away by sandstorms. Something changed the climate, or got away from the builders.

"It was probably this worm we saw. There's only one of them, Whistlestop says. Mnemosyne is only big enough for one. If there were two, they fought it out long ago and only this granddaddy worm is left. It's big enough to eat Whistlestop like an olive."

Both Cirocco and Bill looked up at Calvin's mention of giant worms.

"I never did see the whole thing, but I wouldn't be surprised if it's twenty kilometers long. It's just a big, long tube, with a hole at both ends as wide as the whole damn worm. It's segmented, and the body looks hard, like an armadillo shell. It's got a mouth like a buzz saw, teeth on the inside and the outside both. It spends its time under the sand, but sometimes it isn't deep enough and it has to come to the surface. We watched it one of those times."

"There was a worm like that in a book," Bill said.

"A movie, too," Cirocco said. "It was called *Dune*."

Calvin seemed annoyed at the interruption, and glanced up to see if the blimp was still close.

"Anyway," he said, "I wondered if that worm might be what's giving Mnemosyne such a bad time. Can you imagine what it'd do to tree roots? It could wreck the whole area in a couple years. The trees die, pretty soon the soil is going bad, can't hold water anymore, and right after that the rivers go underground. They must, you know; Ophion goes through Mnemosyne. You can see where it disappeared and where it comes up again. The flow isn't broken, but it doesn't do Mnemosyne any good.

"So then I thought that nobody who was planning this place would have put a worm like that in it. It must not like the dark, or else it would go right through Oceanus and wreck the whole place. I think it's just luck that didn't happen, if this place is getting by on luck, it can't have too long to go. That worm's got to be a bad mutation, and that means there's nobody around with enough power to kill it and get things back on the track. I'm afraid I think the builders either died out or reverted to savagery, like those stories you were telling us, Bill."

"It's a possibility," Bill agreed.

Cirocco snorted. "Sure it is. It's also possible you're reading too much into that worm. Maybe the people here *like* worms and couldn't bear to leave this one behind. Then he grew until he needed a bigger house, and they gave him Mnemosyne. Anyhow, we've still got to try to get to the hub."

"You do that," Calvin agreed. "I'm going to sail around the rim and see who's still alive down there. The builders could have taken a tumble, and still have enough technology to make a radio. If they do, I'll come tell you, and you folks are home free."

"'You folks'?" Cirocco said. "Come on, Calvin. We're all in this together. Just because you won't stick with us doesn't mean we'd abandon you here."

Calvin frowned, and would say no more.

Before Whistlestop got underway, Calvin tossed out a few smilers attached to parachutes. He was using them as weights to draw chutes out of the dispenser, because the bluish silk and the shrouds were the most useful items they had yet found.

Gaby folded the chutes and stowed them carefully, vowing that she would dress Cirocco like a queen. Cirocco resigned herself to it. It was a small price to pay to keep Gaby happy.

And once again *Titanic* was launched, this time with a new sense of urgency. They had to contact a race advanced enough to help with antiseptic surgery or find a way to build a fire, and it had to be soon. The thing in her belly would not wait.

She thought about it a lot in the following days. Her

revulsion was like a tight fist inside her. Most of it stemmed from the unknown nature of the beast that had planted its seed in her.

And yet abortion would have been her course even if she had been sure she was nurturing a human fetus. It had nothing to do with the idea of motherhood itself; she planned to become a mother when she retired from NASA, probably at age forty or forty-five. She had a dozen cells in cryogenic suspension at O'Neil One, ready to be fertilized and implanted when she felt ready to give birth. It was a common precaution among astronauts, and even the Lunar and L5 colonists: a hedge against radiation damage to reproductive tissue. She planned to raise a boy and a girl while old enough to be their grandmother.

But she would choose the time. Whether the father was a human and a lover, or a shapeless monstrosity in the bowels of Gaea, she would control her own reproductive organs. She was not ready, not by many years. Notwithstanding that Gaea was no place to be burdened with an infant, she had many things yet to do, endeavors where a child would be as great a problem as it would be here. And she fully intended to get out and do those things.

Chapter Eleven

The support cables came in rows of five organized into groups of fifteen, and rows of three standing alone.

Each night region had fifteen cables associated with it. There was a row of five vertical cables that went straight up the hollow horn in the roof that was the inside of one of the spokes of Gaea's wheel. Two of these came to the ground in the highlands and were virtually a part of the wall, one north and the other south. One emerged from a point midway between the outermost cables, and the other two were spaced evenly between the center and the edge cables.

In addition to these central cables, the night regions had two more rows of five that radiated from the spokes but attached in daylight areas, one row twenty degrees east and the other twenty degrees west of the central row. The spoke above Oceanus, for example, sent cables into Mnemosyne and Hyperion. The set of fifteen cables supported the ground under a region equal to over forty degrees of Gaea's circumference.

The cables that went from daylight through a twilight zone and into a night did so at a sharp angle to the ground, an angle that increased with altitude until approached sixty degrees at the point of juncture with the roof.

Then there were rows of three cables, associated solely with daylight areas. These cables were vertical, rising straight from the ground until they pierced the roof and emerged into space. It was the middle of Hyperion's row of three that *Titanic* and her crew now approached.

It grew more magnificent and more intimidating with each passing day. Even from Bill's camp it had seemed to lean over them. The lean was no more pronounced now, but the thing had grown in size. It hurt to look up at it. Knowing that a vertical column is five kilometers in diameter and 120 kilometers high is one thing. Seeing it is something else.

Ophion made a wide loop around the cable's base, starting at the south and going north before resuming its general eastward direction. It was a feature they had seen while still distant from the cable. The annoying thing about traveling in Gaea was that the landscape could be seen easily while they were far from it. The closer they approached the more foreshortened the view became, until surface features were flattened beyond interpretation. The land they traveled through always looked as flat as the Earth. It was only far away that it began to curve.

"You want to tell me again why we're doing this?" Gaby shouted ahead to Cirocco. "I don't think I got it."

The trip to the spoke was harder than they had expected. Before, they had followed the river when traveling through the jungle. It had made a natural highway. Now Cirocco knew the true meaning of impenetrable. The land was covered with an almost solid wall of vegetation, and their only cutting tools had been fashioned from their helmet rings. To make it worse, the ground rose steadily as they approached the cable.

"I could do with a little less griping," she called back. "You know we have to do this. It should get easier soon."

They had already learned some useful information. Most important so far was the fact that it really was a cable, composed of wound strands. There were over a hundred of the strands, each a good 200 meters in diameter.

The strands were tightly wound for most of their length, but half a kilometer from the ground they began to diverge, meeting the ground as separate entities. The base of the cable became a forest of huge towers, rather than a single gigantic one.

Most interesting of all, several of the strands were broken. They could see the twisted ends of two far above, curling like split ends in a shampoo ad.

As she broke through to clear land, Cirocco saw that whatever was under the soil, the rubbery substance the cables attached to, had stretched. Each strand had pulled out a cone of it, and the cones were heaped with sand. It was possible to see between the outer strands to a forest of them diminishing to blackness.

The land between them and the cable was sandy, with huge boulders scattered through it. The sand was reddish-yellow, and the rocks were sharp-edged, showing few signs of erosion. They looked as if they had been ripped violently from the ground.

Bill tipped his head back, following the cable to the glare of the translucent roof.

"My God, what a sight," he said.

"Think of how the natives must see it," Gaby said. "The cables from heaven that hold up the world."

Cirocco shielded her eyes. "It's no wonder they think of God as living up there," she said. "Think of the puppet master who would use these strings."

The ground was firm as they started up the slope, but the higher they went the more it began to slip. Nothing grew there to hold the soil together. It was sand, wet on top but dry underneath. It formed a crust which their feet broke into unstable, shifting plates that skittered down behind them.

Cirocco forged ahead, determined to get to the strand itself, but before long she was sliding back as far as she struggled up, still 200 meters from the top. Bill and Gaby hung back and watched her try to get a grip in the unstable ground. It was no use. She went down on her face and rolled back, sat up and glared at the cable, so tantalizingly close.

"Why me?" she asked, and slammed her fist on the

ground. She wiped the sand from her mouth.

She stood, but her feet slipped again. Gaby reached for her arm and Bill nearly went down on top of them when he tried to help. They had lost another meter.

"So much for that," Cirocco said, tiredly. "I still want to look around here, though. Anybody coming with me?"

No one was too enthusiastic, but they followed her down the slope and started into the forest of cable strands.

Each strand had its own pile of sand heaped around it. They were forced to follow a winding path between them. Tough, brittle weeds grew in the hard-packed soil at the bottoms of the giant molehills.

It grew dark as they worked their way in—dark, and much quieter than it had been in their weeks on the river. There was a far-away howling like wind through long, abandoned hallways, and far above, the tinkling of wind chimes. They heard their own footsteps, and the sound of each other's breathing.

The sense of being in a cathedral was impossible to escape. Cirocco has seen a place like it before, among the giant Sequoias of California. It was greener there and not as quiet, but the stillness and the feeling of being lost among vast and indifferent beings was the same. If she saw a cobweb, she knew she would not stop running until she reached daylight.

They began to notice hanging shapes above them, like torn tapestries. They were motionless in the dead air, insubstantial shapes in the shadows high overhead. Fine dust drifted around them, eddied by the slightest breeze.

Gaby touched Cirocco's arm lightly. She jumped, then looked up where Gaby was pointing.

Something clung to the side of one of the strands, fifty meters above the top of the sandhill. She thought it was sitting on a ledge, then wondered if it might be a growth of some kind.

"Like a barnacle," Bill said.

"Or a colony of them." Gaby whispered, then coughed nervously and repeated herself. Cirocco knew how she felt; it seemed like they *ought* to be whispering.

Cirocco shook her head. "I'm reminded of the cliff dwellings in Arizona."

In a few minutes they spotted more of them, most far higher and less distinct than the one Gaby had found. Were they dwellings, or parasites? There was no way to tell.

Cirocco took a last look around and thought she saw something in the distance, right on the edge of total darkness.

It was a building. Shortly after she realized that, she knew it was a ruin. Fine sand was heaped around it.

It was almost refreshing to find something built on a human scale. The building was the size of some of the smallest pueblos of Colorado, and in fact looked a bit like them. There were three layers of hexagonal chambers with no apparent doorways. Each layer was made of rooms slightly larger than the ones below. She moved closer and touched one wall. It was cool stone, cut and dressed and fitted together without motar, in the Incan fashion.

Looking closer, she saw there were actually five layers of chambers, but the two lowest were much smaller than the three she had seen from a distance, and made from smaller stones. Brushing away the sand at the base of the wall, she found a sixth layer, then a seventh, each tinier than the one above.

"What do you make out of that?" she asked Bill, who had knelt beside her while she dug.

"It's an odd way to build."

Cirocco dug deeper but was soon defeated by sand sliding back as fast as she could scoop it out. The lowest layer she had found was made of chambers no more than half a meter high and about as broad, built from stones the size of masonry bricks.

They circled the structure and found a place where it had crumbled. Massive stones from the top had crushed most of the smaller ones below. There was one chamber intact but for a missing wall. They saw no interior doors, and no place to enter the structure from outside.

"Why build a place with no doors?"

"Maybe they got in from below," Gaby suggested.

"Without a bulldozer, we'll never know." Cirocco was thinking of the equipment they had brought for use with the satellite lander, and winced when the thought led her back to the debris of her ship broken and tumbling in space.

"I was wondering what connection this has to the cable," Bill said. "Was it built for maintenance workers or put up later, after things broke down?"

Cirocco raised an eyebrow. "We're assuming that things have broken down?"

He spread his hands. "There's structural damage that hasn't been repaired. You saw those broken strands."

She knew he had a point. The whole dark miasma beneath the cable reeked of disuse, abandonment. It was a musty grave, or the bones of something that had once been mighty.

But even in decline Gaea was magnificent. The air was fresh, the water clean. It was true that large areas were now desert or frozen wasteland, and it was hard to believe it had been planned that way. And yet she felt the ecological systems would have deteriorated even further if there weren't someone up there with some degree of control.

"Gaea is not unguided," Gaby said, echoing Cirocco's thoughts without knowing it. "This building looks old to me. Thousands of years would probably not be too far off."

"It sure *feels* that old," Bill agreed.

"I know something of the complexities involved in maintaining a biosystem," Gaby went on. "Gaea is larger than O'Neil One, and that makes her more flexible. But in a few centuries things would break down without control. Things have not broken down completely."

"It could be robots," Bill said.

"That's fine with me," Cirocco said. "As long as there's some intelligence behind this, I plan to contact it and ask for help. Computers might be easier to deal with."

Bill, who had read a great deal of science fiction, could make a dozen theories about any aspect of Gaea. He was partial to the ever-reliable plague mutation: something that came out of nowhere and killed enough builders to leave Gaea in the hands of automatic safety devices.

"She's a derelict, I'll bet on it," he told them. "Just like the ship from Heinlein's *Orphans of the Sky*. A lot of people set out in Gaea thousands of years ago and lost control on the way. The ship's computer put it in orbit around Saturn, shut down the engines, and is still up there keeping the air pumping and waiting for more orders."

They took a different route out, partly because it was impossible to tell how they had come in. Cirocco did not worry because as long as they went toward the light they were all right.

They reached the sunlight at a point far to the north of where they had gone in, and now could see something that had been concealed at their point of entry by the cable itself. It was a broken strand, but this one was on the ground.

Cirocco's first thought was of the giant sandworm Calvin had described. The strand looked like a living thing, shining in the yellow light. Then she recalled the Brazilian pipelines she had seen on survival training: great silver tubes that knifed through the rain forest as if it were a contemptible obstacle.

The strand had cleared its own path when it fell, bringing down the tallest trees, crashing inexorably to the ground. The jungle had closed over it since that time, but the great mass still looked as if it could rise at any moment and shake off the encroaching vines, turning the trees into matchsticks.

Five hundred meters above, the severed upper end of the strand curled away from the body of the cable. It was ragged, and the inside revealed by the break glistened and threw back reflections of red and blue-green and tarnished copper. Gray discolorations like bread mold grew in the stump, and from the bottom a waterfall went straight down to a clump of vegetation widely separated from the forest. The volume of water was substantial and noisy, but issuing from the huge and twisted strand it looked like nothing more than a drip from a broken pipe.

They approached the fallen strand, found it to be composed of an array of hexagonal facets only a few millimeters across, cloudy with swirls of gold just beneath the surface. It threw back dull, broken reflections, as if they were using the eye of a giant insect for a mirror.

They followed it down the hill and into the jungle, where the broken end turned out to be hollow but so clogged with brush and vines that entering it was impossible.

"Whatever was inside, the plants like it," Gaby said.

Cirocco said nothing. The advanced state of decay was depressing. The strand's open end was big enough to have flown *Ringmaster* right through it. It was a small thing on the scale of Gaea, only one of 200 strands in this cable alone. And yet it was such a towering wreck, going so quickly to rot and dissolution. When it parted, the whole surface of Gaea must have twanged in sympathy.

And no one had done anything about it.

She said nothing, but it was hard to look at the remains and feel there was someone still watching the machines.

Chapter Twelve

Two days after their exploration of the cable interior, the crew of *Titanic* found themselves leaving the tropical forest. The land had never been hilly except in the neighborhood of the cable; now it turned flat as a billiard table and Ophion sprawled for kilometers in every direction. There was no longer a shoreline as such. The only things to mark the end of the river and the beginning of the marshlands were strands of tall grass rooted in the bottom and the occasional meter-high mud bank. A sheet of water stretched over everything, seldom more than ten centimeters deep except in the winding mazes of sloughs, bayous, inlets, and backwaters. These were kept clear and gouged deeper by big eels and one-eyed mudfish the size of hippos.

The trees in the region came in three varieties, growing in widely scattered clumps. The kind that appealed to Cirocco looked like glass sculpture, with straight, transparent trunks and regular branches in a crystalline arrangement. The smallest branches were filaments that could have been used in fiber optics. When the wind blew, the weakest branches broke off. Recovered and wrapped with chute cloth on one end, they made excellent knives. From the flashing effect when the filaments moved, Gaby named them Xmas trees, pronouncing it "exmas."

The other major vegetation was not so much to Cirocco's liking. One plant—it seemed wrong to call it a tree, though it was large enough—resembled a pile of what can be seen on the ground at any cattle ranch. Bill named them dung trees. On their closest approach to one they could see that there was an internal structure, but no one wanted to get too near because they smelled all too much like what they appeared to be.

Then there were trees that did a better job of looking the part. They had something of the cypress and a little of the willow in them, growing in untidy tangles festooned with creepers that struggled to pull them down.

It was alien in a much more unpleasant way than the highlands had been. The jungle they had left behind was not too different from the Amazon or the Congo. Here, nothing looked familiar, everything was misshapen and threatening.

Camping was impossible. They began tying the boat to trees and sleeping in it. It rained every ten to twelve hours. They rigged chutecloth tents over the bow, but water always leaked in and pooled in the bottom. The weather was hot but the humidity was so high that nothing ever dried out.

With the mud, the heat and dampness and sweat, they grew irritable. They were short on sleep, often managing no more than a fitful doze while off duty, doing even worse when all three tried to sleep and ended up competing for the limited space on *Titanic*'s sloping bottom.

Cirocco awoke from a nightmare of being unable to breathe. She sat up, feeling the cloth of her robe peel away from her skin. She felt sticky between her fingers and toes, under her neck, and in her lap.

Gaby nodded to her as she stood up, then turned her attention back to the river.

"Rocky," Bill said. "There's something you'll want to—"

"No," she said, holding her hands up. "Dammit, I want coffee. I'd *kill* for coffee."

Gaby smiled dutifully, but it looked like an effort. They knew by now that Cirocco was a slow starter.

"Not funny. Right." She stared bleakly out at the land that looked as decayed and rotten as she felt. "Just give me a minute before you start asking me things," she said. She struggled out of her clinging clothes and jumped in the river.

It was better, but not much.

She bobbed, treading water and holding the side of the boat and thinking about soap until her foot touched something slippery. She didn't wait to find out what it was, but pulled herself over the edge and stood with water pooling at her feet.

"Now. What is it you wanted?"

Bill pointed toward the north shore. "We've been seeing smoke over that way. You can see some of it now, just to the left of that bunch of trees."

Cirocco leaned over the edge of the boat and saw it: a thin line of gray sketched against the backdrop of the distant north wall.

"Let's beach this thing and take a look."

It was a long, grueling slog through knee-deep mud and stagnant water. Bill led the way. They began to get excited as they came around the big dung tree that had obscured their vision. Cirocco caught a whiff of smoke over the stronger stench of the tree, and hurried over the slippery ground.

It began to rain just as they arrived at the fire. It was not a hard rain, but it wasn't much of a fire, either. It looked as if all they would get out of it would be black soot on their legs.

The fire was an irregular smudge covering a square hektometer, smoldering fitfully at the edges. As they watched, the gray smoke began to turn white as the rain fell. Then a tongue of flame licked the bottom of a bush a few meters away.

"Get something that's dry," Cirocco ordered. "Anything at all. Some of that marsh grass, and some sticks. Hurry, we're losing it." Bill and Gaby ran off in different directions as Cirocco knelt by the bush and blew on it. She ignored the smoke in her eyes and kept blowing until she felt dizzy.

Soon she was piling on reasonably dry wood. Finally she could sit back and feel sure it would keep burning. Gaby shouted and threw a stick so high it was nearly invisible before it started to come down. Cirocco grinned when Bill slapped her on the back. It was a small victory, but it could be an important one. She felt great.

When the rain stopped, the fire was still going.

The problem was how to keep it going.

They discussed it for hours, tried and discarded several solutions.

It took the rest of the day and most of the next to make their plan work. They made two bowls from the swamp clay, fired them carefully, then dried a large quantity of the wood which burned most slowly. When that was done, they made small fires in both of the bowls. It seemed wise to have a spare. The scheme would require someone to tend the fire at all times, but they were willing to do that until they found a better solution.

When they were through, it was nearing time for a sleep period. Cirocco wanted to see if they could make it to dry ground, not really trusting their arrangements for the fire, but Bill suggested they make a kill first.

"I'm getting pretty tired of those melons," he said. "The last one I had tasted rancid."

"Yeah, but there's no smilers. I haven't seen one in days."

"Then we'll knock over something else. We need some meat."

It was true they had not been eating well. The marsh had nothing like the profusion of fruit-bearing plants they had found in the forest. The one native plant they had tried tasted like a mango and gave them diarrhea. On the boat that was comparable to an inner circle of hell. Since then they had relied on stored provisions.

They decided the big mudfish were the most obvious prey. Like all the other animals they had encountered, the fish took little notice of them. Everything else was too small and quick, or, like the giant eels, too big.

The mudfish liked to sit in the ooze with their snouts buried, moving by flipping their tails.

She and Gaby and Bill soon had one surrounded. It was their first close look at one. Cirocco had never seen a creature so ugly. It was three meters long, flat on the bottom, and bulged in the middle from its blunt snout to a wicked-looking horizontal tail fluke. There was a long gray ridge along its back, soft and loose like a rooster's comb, but slimy. It swelled and deflated rhythmically.

"Are you sure you want to eat that?"

"If it'll hold still long enough."

Cirocco was stationed four meters in front of the mudfish while Gaby and Bill approached from the sides. All three carried swords made from broken Xmas-tree branches.

The mudfish had one eye the size of a pie plate. One edge of the eye elevated until it was looking at Bill. He froze. The fish made a snuffling sound.

"Bill, I don't like this."

"Don't worry. It's blinking, see?" A stream of liquid spurted from a hole above the eye, producing the snuffling she had heard. "It's keeping its eye wet. No eyelids."

"If you say so." She flapped her arms, and the fish obligingly looked away from Bill and toward her. She wasn't sure that was an improvement, but took a step forward on the balls of her feet. The fish looked away, bored by it all.

Bill moved in, braced himself, and put his sword through the flesh just behind the eye, leaning on it. The fish jerked as Bill released the sword and danced back.

Nothing happened. The eye did not move, and the organs on its back no longer swelled in and out. Cirocco relaxed, and saw Bill grinning.

"Too easy," he said. "When is this place going to give us a challenge?" He took the hilt of his sword and pulled it out. Dark blood spurted over his hand. The fish bent, touching its snout with its tail, then swung the tail sideways and down on Bill's head. It scooped deftly under his motionless body and hurled him into the air.

Cirocco did not even see where he came down. The fish arched again, this time balancing on its belly with both snout and tail in the air. She saw its mouth for the first time. It was round, lamprey-like, with a double row of teeth that counter-rotated and clattered. The tail hit the mud and the fish jumped at her.

She dived flat to the ground, ploughing up a wake of mud with her chin. The fish plopped behind her, arched, and flipped fifty kilos of mud into the air as it lashed madly with its tail. The sharp fin sliced the ground in front of her face, then rose for another try. She scurried on her hands and knees, slipping every time she tried to stand.

"Rocky! Jump!"

She did, and narrowly missed having her arm taken off as the fish's tail hit the ground again.

"Go, go! It's coming after you!"

A glance behind showed only rotating teeth. All she could hear was their terrible buzz. It meant to eat her.

She was in mire up to her knees and heading toward deeper water, which did not seem like a good idea, but every time she tried to turn the tail flashed out of the mud. Soon she was blind from the constant barrage of filthy water. She slipped, and before she could get up the tail hit the side of her head. She was conscious but her ears were ringing as she turned over and groped for her sword. The mud had swallowed it. The fish was a meter away, curling for a leap that would crush her, when Gaby came running past it. Her feet scarcely touched the ground. She hit Cirocco with a flying tackle hard enough to loosen teeth, the fish leaped, and all three of them skidded three meters through the mud.

Cirocco was dimly aware of a slimy wet wall under one foot. She kicked. The fish lashed at them again as Gaby pulled Cirocco along, swimming through the mud. Then she let go, and Cirocco lifted her head out of the water, gasping.

She saw Gaby's back as she stood facing the creature. The tail came slashing around at the level of Gaby's neck, deadly as a scythe, but she ducked and held up her sword. It broke close to the hilt, but the sharp edge cut a big flap in the fin. The fish didn't seem to like it. Gaby leaped again, straight for the hideous jaws, and landed on the creature's back. She stabbed her sword hilt into the eye, slashing down instead of thrusting as Bill had done. The fish threw her off, but now the tail had no direction. It beat the ground furiously as Gaby looked for a chance to cut again.

"Gaby!" Cirocco shouted. "Let it go. Don't get yourself killed."

Gaby glanced back, then hurried to Cirocco.

"Let's get out of here. Can you walk?"

"Sure, I . . ." The ground whirled. She clutched Gaby's sleeve to steady herself.

"Hang on. That's thing's getting closer."

Cirocco didn't have a chance to see what she meant, because Gaby lifted her before she knew what was happening. She was too weak and confused to fight it as Gaby brought her out of the bog, slung over her shoulder in a fireman's carry.

She was put down gently on a patch of grass, and then she saw Gaby's face hovering over her. Tears were running down her cheeks as she gently probed Cirocco's head, then moved down to her chest.

"Ow!" Cirocco winced and curled around the pain. "I think you broke a rib."

"Oh, my God. When I picked you up? I'm sorry, Rocky, I—"

Cirocco touched her cheek. "No, dummy, when you hit me like the front line of the Giants. And I'm glad you did."

"I want to check your eyes. I thought you—"

"No time. Help me up. Got to see about Bill."

"You first. Just lie back. You shouldn't—"

Cirocco slapped her hand away and rose as far as her knees before doubling over and vomiting.

"See what I mean? You've got to stay here."

"All right," she choked. "Go find him, Gaby. Take care

of him. Bring him back here, alive."

"Just let me check your—"

"Go!"

Gaby bit her lip, glanced at the fish still thrashing in the distance, and looked tortured. Then she leaped to her feet and ran in what Cirocco hoped was the right direction.

She sat there holding her belly and cursing softly until Gaby returned.

"He's alive," she said. "Out cold, and I think he's hurt."

"How bad?"

"There's blood on his leg and his hands and all over his front. Some of it's fish blood."

"I told you to bring him here," Cirocco growled, trying to hold back another fit of nausea.

"Sssh," Gaby soothed, rubbing her hand lightly over Cirocco's forehead. "I can't move him until I can make a litter. First, I'm going to get you back to the boat and bedded down. Hush! If I have to fight you, I will. You wouldn't want a punch in the jaw, would you?"

Cirocco felt like throwing a punch herself, but the nausea overcame the urge. She settled to the ground and Gaby scooped her up.

She remembered thinking how ridiculous they must look: Gaby was 150 centimeters tall while Cirocco was 185. In the low gravity Gaby had to move cautiously, but the weight was no problem.

Things didn't spin so badly when she closed her eyes. She put her head on Gaby's shoulder.

"Thanks for saving my life," she said, and passed out.

She woke to the sound of a man screaming. It was not a sound she ever cared to hear again.

Bill was semi-conscious. Cirocco sat up and cautiously touched the side of her head. It hurt, but the dizziness was gone.

"Come here and give me a hand," Gaby said. "We've got to hold him down or he'll hurt himself."

She hurried to Gaby's side. "How bad is he?"

"Real bad. His leg's broken. Probably some ribs, too, but he hasn't coughed up any blood."

"Where's the break?"

"Tibia or fibula. I don't which is which. I thought it was a laceration until I put him on the litter. He started fighting and the bone stuck out."

"Jesus."

"At least he's not losing much blood."

Cirocco felt another quiver in her stomach as she examined the ragged gash in Bill's leg. Gaby was washing it with boiled chutecloth rags. Every time she touched it, he screamed hoarsely.

"What are you going to do?" Cirocco asked, vaguely aware that she should be telling her what to do, not asking.

Gaby looked agonized. "I think you should call Calvin."

"What's the use of that? Oh, yeah, I'll call the son-of-a-bitch, but you saw how long it took the last time. If Bill's dead when he gets here, I'll kill him."

"Then we have to set it."

"You know how to do it?"

"I saw it done, once," said Gaby. "With anesthetic."

"What we've got is a lot of rags that I hope are clean. I'll hold his arms. Wait a minute." She moved to Bill's side and looked down at him. He stared at nothing, and his forehead was hot when she touched it.

"Bill? Listen to me. You're hurt, Bill."

"Rocky?"

"It's me. It's going to be all right, but your leg is broken. Do you understand?"

"I understand," he whispered, and closed his eyes.

"Bill, wake up. I'll need your help. You can't fight us. Can you hear me?"

He lifted his head and looked down at his leg. "Yeah," he said, wiping his face with a dirty hand. "I'll be good. Get it over with, will you?"

Cirocco nodded to Gaby, who grimaced and pulled.

It took three tries, and left both women shaken. On the second pull the bone end protruded with a wet sound that made Cirocco throw up again. Bill bore it well, his breath whistling and his neck muscles standing out like cords, but he no longer screamed.

"I wish I knew how good a job that is," Gaby said. Then she began to cry. Cirocco let her alone and worked on binding the splint to Bill's leg. He was unconscious by the time she was through. She stood and held her bloody hands up in front of her.

"We'll have to move on," she said. "It's no good here. We have to find a place where it's dry and set up a camp and wait for him to get better."

"He probably shouldn't be moved."

"No," she sighed. "But he has to be. Another day ought to bring us to that high country we saw earlier. Let's go."

Chapter Thirteen

It took two days instead of one, and they were terrible days.

They stopped frequently to sterilize Bill's bandages. The bowl they used to heat the water was nothing so fine as a ceramic pot; it flaked and wanted to melt, and left the water clouded. The water took the better part of an hour to boil because the pressure in Gaea was higher than one atmosphere.

Gaby and Cirocco snatched a few hours sleep, one at a time, when the river was quiet and wide. But when they came to a hazardous stretch it took both of them to keep the boat from going aground. It continued to rain regularly.

Bill slept, and woke after the first twenty-four hours looking five years older. His face was gray. When Gaby changed the bandage his wound did not look good. The lower leg and most of his foot was nearly twice their normal size.

By the time they left the swamp he was delirious. He sweated profusely, and ran a high fever.

Cirocco contacted a passing blimp early on the second

day, getting back the high, rising whistle that Calvin had told her meant, "Okay, I'll tell him," but she was already starting to fear it was too late. She watched the blimp sail serenely toward the frozen sea, and asked herself why she had insisted they leave the forest. And if they must, why not go on Whistlestop, sailing over it all, far from terrible things like mudfish that refused to die?

Her reasons were as valid now as they had been then, but it didn't stop her from blaming herself. Gaby could not ride in the blimps, and they had to find a way out. But she thought there must be easier, more satisfying things than taking the responsibility for other lives, and she was sick of her own life. She wanted out, she wanted someone else to take the burden. How had she ever thought she could be a Captain? What had she done right since taking command of *Ringmaster*?

What she really wanted was simple, but so hard to find. She wanted love, just like everyone else. Bill had said he loved her; why couldn't she say it back to him? She had thought she might be able to say it, someday, but now it looked like he was going to die, and he was her responsibility.

She also wanted adventure. It had driven her all through her life, from the first comic book she opened, the first space documentary she had watched as a wide-eyed child, the first old black and white flat-screen swashbucklers and full-color westerns she saw. The thirst to do something outrageous and heroic had never left her. It had pushed her away from the singing career her mother wanted, and the housewife role everyone else thrust at her. She wanted to swoop down on the base of the space pirates, lasers blazing, to slink through the jungle with a band of fierce revolutionaries for a night raid on the enemy stronghold, to search for the Holy Grail or destroy the Death Star. She had found other reasons, as an adult, to slog her way through college and train herself to be the best there was so that when the chance came, they could choose no other for the Saturn mission. Beneath it all, nevertheless, it was the itch to travel and see strange places and do things no one else had done that landed her on the decks of *Ringmaster*.

Now she had her adventure. She was floating down a river in a cockleshell boat inside the most titanic structure ever seen by a human eye, and a man who loved her was dying.

East Hyperion was a land of gently rolling hills and long stretches of plains, dotted with wind-blown trees like an African savanna. Ophion grew narrower and began to rush along, at the same time becoming mysteriously cooler.

They drifted for five or six kilometers at the mercy of the river, past low cliffs that dropped abruptly at the water's edge. *Titanic* was unsteerable when she moved fast. Cirocco watched for a widening in the river and a place to land.

She saw it, and they spent two hours fighting the current with poles and paddles to bring the boat to the rocky shore. Both of them were on their last reserves of strength. More ominously, there was no food in the boat and East Hyperion did not look fertile.

They dragged *Titanic* up the shore, feet sliding over rocks tumbled smooth by the water, until they were sure it was out of danger. Bill was not aware of the movement. He had not spoken in a long time.

Cirocco sat up with Bill while Gaby fell into a death-like sleep. She kept herself awake by exploring the area within a hundred meters of the campsite.

There was a low bank twenty meters from the river's edge. She scrambled to the top.

East Hyperion looked like a great place for a farmer. Wide stretches of the land looked like a yellow Kansas wheat field. That illusion was spoiled by other areas that were rust red, and still others of a pale blue mixed with orange. It all rippled in the wind like tall grass. Dark shadows drifted by, some of the clouds so low they formed fogbands in the creek beds, even in sunlight.

To the east, hills marched to the twilight zone of west Rhea, gradually gaining a green coloring that must have been forest, then losing it in the darkness to become stark rocky mountains. In the west the land flattened out, with the shallow lakes and bogs of the mudfish marsh glittering as they caught the sunlight. Beyond that was the darker green of the tropical forest, and higher up the curve were more plains that vanished into the twilight of Oceanus, with its frozen sea.

Scanning the distant hills, she saw a group of animals: black dots against the yellow background. Perhaps two or three of the dots were larger than the others.

She was about to return to the tent when she heard the music. It was so faint and distant that she realized she had been hearing it for some time without recognizing it for what it was. There would be a rapid cluster of tones, then a sustained note, wrenchingly sweet and clear. It spoke of quiet places and an ease she thought she might never see again, and was as familiar as a song heard in the cradle.

She found herself crying quietly, being as still as she could, willing the wind to be still with her. But the song was gone.

The Titanide found them while they were taking down the tent prior to moving Bill. It stood on the top of the bluff where Cirocco had been the day before. Cirocco waited for it to make the first move, but it seemed to have the same idea.

The most obvious word for the thing was centaur. It had a lower part shaped like a horse, and an upper half so human it was frightening. Cirocco was not quite sure she believed in it.

It was not as Disney had envisioned centaurs, nor did it have much to do with the classical Greek model. It had a lot of hair, yet its dominant feature was pale naked skin. There were great multi-colored cascades of hair on the head and tail, on the lower parts of all four legs, and on the creature's forearms. Oddest of all, there was hair between the two front legs, in the place where a decent horse—which Cirocco's mind kept trying to see—had nothing but smooth hide. It carried a shepherd's crook, and but for a few small ornaments, wore no clothing.

Cirocco was sure this was one of the Titanides Calvin had mentioned, though he had made a mistake in translation. It—*she*, Calvin had said they were all female—she was not six-legged, but six-limbed.

Cirocco took a step forward, and the Titanide put a hand to her mouth, then held it out in a quick gesture.

"Look out!" she called. "Please be cautious."

For a split second Cirocco wondered what the Titanide was talking about, but that was quickly buried in astonishment. The Titanide had not spoken English, Russian, or French, which until that moment had been the only languages Cirocco knew.

"What's the..." She stopped, clearing her throat. Some of the words were pitched quite high. "What's the matter? Are we in danger?" Questions were hard, requiring a complex appoggiatura.

"I perceived you to be," the Titanide sang. "I felt you must surely fall. But you must know what is right for your own kind."

Gaby was looking at Cirocco strangely.

"What the hell's going on?" she asked.

"I can understand her," Cirocco said, not wanting to get into it any deeper. "She told us to be careful."

"Careful of... *how*?"

"How did Calvin understand the blimp? Something's been messing with our minds, honey. It's coming in handy right now, so shut up." She hurried on before other questions could be voiced, because she knew none of the answers.

"Are you the people of the marshes?" the Titanide asked. "Or do you come from the frozen sea?"

"Neither," Cirocco trilled. "We have traveled through the marsh on our way to the... to the sea of evil, but one of us is hurt. We mean you no harm."

"You will do me little harm if you go to the sea of evil, for you will be dead. You are too large to be angels who have lost their wings, and too fair for creatures of the sea. I confess I have not seen your like before."

"We... could you join us on the beach? My song is weak; the wind does not lift it."

"I'll be there in two shakes of your tail."

"Rocky!" Gaby hissed. "Look out, she's going to come down!" She moved in front of Cirocco and stood with her glass sword held ready.

"I *know* she is," Cirocco said, grappling with Gaby's sword arm. "I asked her to. Put that away before she gets the wrong idea, and stay back. I'll yell if there's trouble."

The Titanide came down the cliff forelegs-first, her arms out for balance. She danced nimbly, riding the small avalanche she had created, then she was trotting toward them. Her feet made a familiar clopping sound on the rocks.

She was thirty centimeters taller than Cirocco, who found herself taking a step backward as the Titanide drew closer. Seldom in her life had she met a taller woman, but this female creature would have towered over anyone but a professional basketball player. Seen close, she was more alien than ever, precisely because parts of her were so human.

A series of red, orange, and blue stripes that Cirocco had thought were natural markings turned out to be paint. They were arranged in patterns, confined mostly to her face and chest. Four chevron stripes adorned her belly, just above where her navel would have been if she had possessed one.

Her face was wide enough to make the broad nose and mouth look appropriate. Her eyes were huge, with a lot of space between them. The irises were brilliant yellow, with radial streaks of green surrounding wide pupils.

The eyes were so astonishing that Cirocco almost failed to notice the most non-human feature of her face. She had thought they were an odd kind of flower tucked behind each ear, but they turned out to be the ears themselves. The pointed tips reached over the crown of her head.

"I am called C Sharp..." she sang. It was a series of musical notes in the key of C Sharp.

"What did she say?" Gaby whispered.

"She said her name was..." She sang the name, and the Titanide's ears perked up.

"I can't call her that," Gaby protested.

"Call her C Sharp. Will you shut up and let me do the talking?" She turned back to the Titanide.

"My name is Cirocco, or Captain Jones," she sang. "This is my friend, Gaby."

The ears drooped to her shoulders, and Cirocco nearly laughed. Her expression had not changed, but the ears had spoken volumes.

"Just 'sheer-ah-ko-or-cap-ten-jonz'?" she changed in an imitation of Cirocco's monotone. When she sighed her nostrils flared with the force of it, but her chest did not move. "It is a long name, but not a windy one, begging your pardon. Do you folk feel no joy, to name yourselves so dourly?"

"Our names are chosen for us," Cirocco sang, feeling unaccountably embarrassed. It was a dull moniker to give the Titanide after she had handed Cirocco such a sprightly air. "Our speech is not as yours, nor our pipes so deep."

C Sharp laughed, and it was an entirely human laugh. "You speak with the voice of a thin reed, indeed, but I like you. I would take you home to my hindmother for a feast, if you were agreeable."

"We would accept your invitation, but one of us is badly injured. We need help."

"Which of you is it?" she sang, ears flapping in consternation.

"It is neither of us, but another. He has broken the bone in one of his legs." She noted in passing that the Titanide language included pronoun constructions for male and female. Song fragments meaning male-mother and female-mother and even less likely concepts flitted through her head.

"A bone in his leg," C Sharp sang, her ears doing a complicated semaphore. "Unless I miss my guess, this is quite serious for folk such as you, who cannot spare one. I will call the healer at once." She raised her staff and sang briefly into a small green lump at the end.

Gaby's eyes widened.

"They have radio? Rocky, tell me what's going on."

"She said she'd call a doctor. And that I have a dull name."

"Bill could use the doctor, but he ain't gonna be a member of the AMA."

"Don't you think I know that?" she hissed, angry.

"Bill's looking very bad, dammit. Even if this doctor has nothing but horse pills and ju-ju, it won't hurt for him to take a look."

"Was that your speech?" C Sharp asked. "Or are you in respiratory distress?"

"It's the way we talk. I—"

"Please forgive me. My hindmother says I must learn tact. I am merely—" she sang the number twenty-seven and a time word that Cirocco could not convert, "—and have much to be taught beyond womb knowledge."

"I understand," sang Cirocco, who did not. "We must be strange to you. You certainly are to us."

"Am I?" The key of her song betrayed that it was a new thought to C Sharp.

"To one who has never seen your kind."

"It must be as you say. But if you have never seen a Titanide, from whence do you come in the great wheel of the world?"

Cirocco had been puzzled by the way her mind translated C Sharp's song. It was when she heard the notes "whence" that she realized, by calling to mind alternate interpretations of the two-note word, that C Sharp was speaking in polite, formal modality, using the microtone flattening of pitch reserved for the young speaking to elders. She switched to the chromatic tone rows of instructional mode.

"Not from the wheel at all. Beyond the walls of the world is a bigger place that you can't see—"

"Oh! You're from *Earth*!"

She had not said Earth, any more than she had called herself a Titanide. But the impact of the word for the third planet from the sun surprised Cirocco as much as if she had. C Sharp went on, her attitude and posture having shifted with her switch—following Cirocco's lead—to teaching speech. She became animated, and if her ears had been the tiniest bit wider she would have flapped into the air.

"I'm confused," she sang. "I thought Earth was a fable for the young, spun out around campfires. And I thought Earth beings to be like Titanides."

Cirocco's newly tuned ear strained at the last word, wondering if it should be translated as people. As in "we people, you barbarians." But the chauvinistic overtones were not there. She spoke of her species as one among many in Gaea.

"We are the first to come," Cirocco sang. "I'm surprised you know of us, as we knew nothing of you until this moment."

"You don't sing of our great deeds, as we sing of yours?"

"I'm afraid not."

C Sharp glanced over her shoulder. Another Titanide stood atop the bluff now. She looked much like C Sharp, but with a disturbing difference.

"That's B Flat..." she sang, then, looking guilty, shifted back to formal mode.

"Before his arrival, there is a question I would ask that has been burning my soul since first I saw you."

"You don't have to treat me as an elder," Cirocco sang. "You might be older than I am."

"Oh, no. I am three by the reckoning of Earth. What I wish to know, hoping the inquiry is not an impudent one, is how you stand for so very long without toppling over?"

Chapter Fourteen

When the other Titanide joined them, the disturbing difference Cirocco noted earlier was abundantly clear, and even more disturbing. Between the front legs, where C Sharp had a patch of hair, B Flat had a completely human penis.

"Holy God," Gaby whispered, nudging Cirocco's elbow.

"Will you be quiet?" Cirocco said. "This makes me very nervous."

"You, nervous? What about me? I can't understand a note you're singing. But it's pretty, Rocky. You sing real nice."

Other than the male genitals in front, B Flat was almost identical to C Sharp. Both had high, conical breasts and hairless, pale skin. Their faces were both vaguely feminine, wide-mouthed and beardless. B Flat had more paint on his body, more flowers in his hair. Aside from that and the penis the two would have been hard to tell apart.

One end of a wooden flute protruded from a fold of

skin at the level of his missing navel. Apparently it was a pouch.

B Flat stepped forward and extended his hand. Cirocco stepped back and B Flat moved swiftly, putting a hand on each of her shoulders. She was frightened for only a moment, then realized he shared C Sharp's apprehension. He had thought she was falling backwards, and meant only to steady her.

"I'm fine," she sang, nervously. "I can stand on my own." His hands were large, but perfectly human. It felt very strange to be touching him. Seeing an impossible creature was quite different from feeling its body heat. It brought home forcefully the fact that she was making humanity's first contact with an intelligent alien. He smelled of cinnamon and apples.

"The healer will arrive soon." He sang the song of equals with her, though scored in a formal mode. "In the meantime, have you eaten?"

"We would offer you food ourselves," Cirocco sang, "but in truth, we have run out of provisions."

"And my fore-sister offered you none?" B Flat gave C Sharp a reproving look, and she hung her head. "She is curious and impulsive, but not thoughtful. Please forgive her." The words he used to describe his relationship to C Sharp were complex. Cirocco had the vocabulary, but not all the referrents.

"She has been most kind."

"Her hindmother will be pleased to hear it. Will you join us? I do not know what manner of food you prefer, but if we have anything to your liking, it is yours."

He reached into his pouch—a leather one strapped around his waist, not the one that was part of his body—and came up with something large and reddish-brown, like a smoked ham. He handled it like a turkey drumstick. The Titanides sat, folding their legs neatly and easily, so Cirocco and Gaby sat, too, an operation the Titanides watched with frank interest.

The joint of meat was passed around. C Sharp brought out several dozen green apples. The Titanides simply put them into their mouths whole. There was a crunch, and they were gone.

Gaby was frowning at the fruit. She raised an eyebrow as Cirocco took a bite of one. It tasted like a green apple. It was white and juicy inside, and had small brown seeds.

"Maybe we'll figure all this out later," Cirocco said.

"I wouldn't mind a few answers right *now*," Gaby retorted. "Nobody's going to believe we sat around eating goddam green pippin *apples* with flesh-colored *centaurs*."

C Sharp laughed. "The one named Ga-*bee* sings a rousing song."

"Is she talking to me?"

"She likes your song."

Gaby smiled sheepishly. "It was nothing like the Wagner that's been coming from your direction. How do you understand them? What about the way they look? I've heard of parallel evolution, but from *the waist up*? Humanoids I could believe. I was ready for anything from big blobs of jello to giant spiders. But they look *too* much like us."

"Yet most of them look nothing like us."

"Right!" Gaby said, shouting again. "But look at that face. Take away the donkey ears. The mouth is wide and the eyes are big and the nose looks like he got hit in the face with a shovel, but it's in the range of what you can find on Earth. Look lower, if you dare." She shuddered. "Look *only* at that, and I defy you to tell me it's not a human penis."

"Ask her if we can join in," B Flat sang, heartily. "We don't know the words, but can improvise an accompaniment."

Cirocco sang that she had to speak to her friend a little longer, and would translate later. He nodded, but followed the conversation attentively.

"Gaby, please don't shout at me."

"I'm sorry." She looked at her lap and made an effort to calm down. "I like things to make sense. A human penis on an alien creature doesn't. Did you see their hands? They have fingerprints, I saw them. The FBI would file them with no questions asked."

"I saw that."

"If you could tell me how you talk to them..."

Cirocco spread her hands. "I don't know. It's as if the

language was always in my mind. Singing is harder than listening, but only because my throat's not up to it. It scared me at first, but now it doesn't. I trust them."

"Just like Calvin trusts the blimps."

"It's clear that something toyed with us while we were asleep. Somebody gave me the language—I don't know how or why—and that somebody gave me something else. It's a feeling that the purpose behind the gift was not evil. And the more I talk to the Titanides, the more I like them."

"Calvin said pretty much the same things about the goddam blimps," Gaby said darkly. "You nearly arrested him."

"I think I understand him a little better now."

The Titanide healer—a female whose name was also in the key of B Flat—entered their tent and spent some time examining Bill's leg under Cirocco's watchful eye. The edges of the wound were yellow and blue-black. Fluid bubbled out when the healer pressed around it.

The healer was aware of Cirocco's concern. She twisted her human torso and rummaged in a leather satchel held to her equine back by a cinch strap, came up with a clear round flask filled with brown fluid.

"A strong disinfectant," she sang, and waited.

"What is his condition, healer?"

"Very grave. Without treatment, he will be with Gaea in a few tens of revolutions." Cirocco translated it that way at first, but there had been one word used for the time period. Applying metric prefixes, she thought of it as a decarev. One revolution of Gaea took nearly one hour.

The meaning of "be with Gaea" was clear, though she did not use the word *Gaea*. She referred at once to her world, to the Goddess who was the world, and to the concept of returning to the soil. There was no connotation of immortality.

"Perhaps you would prefer to await the arrival of a healer of your own kind," the Titanide sang.

"Bill may never see him."

"This is so. My remedies should remove the infestations of small parasites. I don't know if they will inhibit the workings of his metabolism. I could not promise you, for instance, that my treatment would not harm the pump which propels his vital fluids, as I don't know where this pump is located in your kind."

"It's right here," Cirocco sang, thumping her chest.

The Titanide's ears jumped up and down. She pressed one ear to Bill's chest.

"No fooling," she sang. "Well, Gaea is wise, and says not why she spins."

Cirocco was in an agony of indecision. The concepts of metabolism and of germs were not things a witch doctor would know about. Those words had translated exactly that way. Yet even the healer was aware that her medicine might harm a human body.

But Calvin was gone, and Bill was dying.

"Pray, what are these used for?" the healer sang. She was holding Bill's foot. Her fingers gently bent the toes.

"Uh, they're..." she groped, but could not find the words for atrophied evolutionary vestiges. There was a word for evolution, but not as applied to living things. "They're useful in keeping one's balance, but not indispensible. They are oversights, or imperfections of design."

"Ah," the healer crooned. "Gaea makes mistakes, it is well known. Take, for instance, the one with whom I was first hindsexed, many myriarevs ago." Cirocco wanted to translate the object of the last sentence as "my husband," but that didn't fit; it could as easily have been "my wife," though that was off the mark, too. There was not an English equivalent, she realized, then remembered her problem.

"Do what you can for my friend," she sang. "I commend him into your hands."

The healer nodded, and got to work.

She first bathed the wound with the brown liquid. She packed it with a yellow jelly and put a large leaf next to the skin, "to lure out the small eaters of his flesh." Cirocco's hopes rose and fell as she watched. She didn't care for the leaf, nor for the reference to luring. It looked too primitive. But when the healer dressed the wound, she used bandages taken from sealed packets that she said had been "cleansed of parasites."

As she worked, she examined Bill's body with great interest, sometimes humming a little ditty of astonishment.

"Now who would have thought of that ... ? ... a muscle *here*? Attached *so*? Like walking on broken feet ... no, I don't believe it." She described Gaea variously as wise, endlessly inventive, needlessly elaborate, and a silly fool. She also observed that Gaea enjoyed the occasional joke as well as the next deity—this while staring in astonishment at Bill's buttocks.

Cirocco was covered in sweat when the healer was through. At least she had not produced rattles or voodoo dolls, nor drawn magical marks in the sand. When she had tied the last knot in the bandages, she began to sing a song of healing. Cirocco couldn't see that it would hurt anything.

The healer bent over Bill and put her arms around and under him, lifted him gently from the waist and held him close to her body. She placed his head on her shoulder and bent her own head down until her lips were close to his ear. She rocked back and forth, crooning a lullaby without words.

Bill gradually stopped shivering. Color began to return to his face, which became more peaceful than it had been since the injury.

In a few minutes, Cirocco would have sworn he was smiling.

Chapter Fifteen

_____

Cirocco found she had some preconceptions that had to be discarded.

The first was the most obvious. When B Flat arrived and looked much like C Sharp except for his sexual organs, she had assumed Titanides were going to be hard to tell apart.

The group that showed up in response to C Sharp's call looked like escapees from a merry-go-round.

The healer had emerald green head and tail hair. The rest of her body was covered in thick, snow-white fur. There was another hairy one: a strawberry blonde with a dappling of violet. There was a brown and white pinto, and one without any hair at all except on his tail. His skin was pale blue.

The last of the group looked naked but was not; she had the pelt of a horse not only on the part of her where it would have looked reasonable, but on her human upper-half, too. She was zebra-striped in bright yellow and searing orange, and had lavender head and tail hair. Looking away from her did no good; the image burned itself into the retina.

Not satisfied with the carnival atmosphere, the Titanides painted their bare skins and stained patches of their hair. They wore necklaces and bracelets, stuck baubles in holes pierced through noses and ears, tied chains of brass links and colored stones or ropes of flowers around their legs. Each had a musical instrument slung over the shoulder or protruding from the pouch, made of wood or animal horn or seashell or brass.

The second preconception—which was actually the first, since Calvin had told them about it—was that Titanides were all female. A tactful question to the healer brought a straightforward answer and an awesome demonstration. The Titanides each had three sex organs.

She knew about the frontal, human-sized male or female genitalia. These determined the pronoun gender for reasons that must have made sense to a Titanide.

In addition, each had a large vaginal opening under the tail, just like a female horse.

It was the one in the middle that shocked Gaby and Cirocco. In the soft belly between the healer's hind legs was a thick, fleshy sheath, and out of it came a penis that was human in every detail but for the fact that it was as long and thick as Cirocco's arm.

Cirocco had thought herself sophisticated. She had seen many naked men, and it had been years since any of them had anything new to show her. She liked men and she liked intercourse, but that thing made her think about becoming a nun. Her strong reaction disturbed her. She knew it was the same feeling Gaby had expressed, that of being more upset by close parallels than by something utterly alien.

The third thing Cirocco had to re-think was triggered by the realization that, though she knew the language and could now use the nouns for each of the Titanide sex organs, she had not known of the rear ones until told about them. She still did not know why there were three, and could not find the knowledge in her mind.

What she had were word lists and grammatical rules of composition. It worked well for nouns; she had only to think of an object to know the word. It began to fail with

some of the verbs. Running and jumping and swimming and breathing were clear enough. Verbs for things Titanides did and humans didn't were not so neat.

Where the system fell apart was in describing familial relationships, codes of behavior, mores, and a host of other things where Titanides and humans shared little common ground. These concepts became null notes in the Titanide songs. She sometimes translated them to herself or to Gaby with complex hyphenates such as she-who-is-my-hindmother's-frontal-ortho-sibling, or the sense-of-righteous-loathing-for-angels. These phrases were each one word in Titanide song.

It came down to the fact that an alien thought in her head was still an alien thought. She could not deal with it until it was explained to her; she had no referrents.

The last complication caused by the arrival of the healer's group was in the matter of names: There were too many names in the same key signatures, so her original system fell apart. Gaby couldn't sing them, so Cirocco had to find English words to use.

She had started off in a musical vein, and decided to continue it. The first one they met she now dubbed C-Sharp Hornpipe because the name sounded like a sailor's hornpipe. B Flat became B Flat Banjo. The healer was B Lullaby, the strawberry blonde was G-minor Valse, the pinto B Clarino, and the blue Titanide now bore the name of G Foxtrot. She called the yellow and orange zebra D-minor Hurdy-gurdy.

Gaby promptly dropped the key signatures, as someone who was always being called Rocky should have known she would.

The ambulance was a long wooden wagon with four rubber-tired wheels, pulled by two Titanides in loose harness. It had a pneumatic suspension and friction brakes operated by the team of pullers. The wood was bright yellow, like new pine, milled wondrously smooth and fitted together with no nails.

Cirocco and Gaby put Bill on a huge bed in the center of the wagon and climbed in after him, along with

Lullaby, the Titanide healer. She took her station at his bedside, legs folded beneath her, singing to him and wiping his brow with a wet cloth. The other Titanides walked alongside, except for Hornpipe and Banjo, who remained behind with their flocks. They had around 200 animals the size of cows, each with four legs and a thin, supple neck three meters long. The necks had digging claws and puckered mouths at the end. They fed by forcing their mouths into the ground and sucking milk from the backs of sludgeworms. They had one eye at the base of the neck. With their heads in the ground they could still see what was happening above.

Gaby looked at one with a faintly scandalized expression on her face, reluctant to admit that such a thing could exist.

"'Gaea has her good days and her bad days,'" she concluded, quoting a Titanide aphorism Cirocco had translated. "She must have come off a nine-day binge when she thought *that* one up. What about those radios, Rocky? Can we get a look at them?"

"I'll see." She sang to Clarino, the pinto, asking if they might look at his speakerplant, then stopped as soon as she had the word out.

"They don't build them," she said. "They grow them."

"Why didn't you say so before?"

"Because I just now realized it. Bear with me, Gaby. The word for them means 'the seed of the plant that carries song.' Take a look."

The item strapped to the end of Clarino's staff was an oblong yellow seed, smooth and featureless but for a soft brown spot.

"It listens here," Clarino sang, indicating the spot. "Do not touch it, as it will go deaf. It sings your song to its mother, and if she is pleased she sings it to the world."

"I fear I do not entirely understand."

Clarino pointed over Gaby's shoulder. "There is one who still has her children."

He trotted to a clump of bushes growing in a hollow. A bellshaped growth emerged from the ground beside each bush. Grasping the bell, he wrenched a plant free and carried it, roots and all, back to the wagon.

"One sings to the seeds," he explained. He took his brass horn from his shoulder and played several bars of a dance in five-four time. "Bend your ears now..." He stopped, embarrassed. "That is, do what your kind does to enhance your hearing."

After half a minute, they heard the horn notes, reedy as an old Edison cylinder, but quite distinct. Clarino sang a harmonic, which was quickly repeated. There was a pause, then the two themes were played simultaneously.

"She hears my song and likes it, you see?" Clarino sang, with a big smile on his face.

"Like the request line of a radio station," Gaby said. "What if the disc jockey doesn't want to play that song?"

Cirocco translated Gaby's question as best she could.

"It takes practice to sing pleasingly," Clarino acknowledged. "But they are of good faith. The mother can speak more swiftly than four feet can fly."

Cirocco translated but Clarino interrupted her.

"The seeds are also useful in building the eyes that see in darkness," he sang. "With them we scan the well of wind for the approach of angels."

"That sounded like radar," Cirocco said.

Gaby eyed her dubiously. "You going to believe everything these over-educated polo ponies tell you?"

"You tell me how those seeds work if it isn't electronically. Would you prefer mental telepathy?"

"Magic might be easier to swallow."

"Call it magic, then. I think there's crystals and circuits in those seeds. And if you can grow an organic radio, why not radar?"

"Maybe radio. Only because I've seen it with my own eyes, *not* because I want to have anything to do with it. But not radar."

The Titanide radar installation was under a tent in the front of the ambulance. It would have baffled Rube Goldberg. There were nuts and leaves attached to a pot of soil with thick coppervines leading into it. Lullaby said the soil contained a worm which generated "essence of power." There was a rack of radio seeds connected with snarls of needle-tipped vines, apparently inserted with some precision since each seed had a tight cluster of oozing pinpricks around the spot where contact had finally been made. There were other things, all of a vegetable nature, including a leaf that glowed when struck by a beam of light from yet another plant.

"It's easy to read," Lullaby sång, cheerfully. "This dot of false fire represents the sky giant you see over there, toward Rhea." She indicated a spot on the screen with her finger. "See how it loses life...there! Now it shines brightly, but shifted."

Cirocco began a translation, but Gaby interrupted her.

"I know how radar works," she grumbled. "The whole set-up offends me."

"We have little need of it now," Clarino assured them. "This is not the season for angels. They come when Gaea breathes from the east, and torment us until she sucks them back to her breast."

Cirocco wondered if she heard that right; did she sing "sucks them *at* her breast"? She didn't pursue it because Bill groaned and opened his eyes.

"Hello," Lullaby sang. "So glad you could come back."

Bill yelped, then screamed when he put pressure on his leg.

Cirocco put herself between Bill and Lullaby. He saw her, and sighed in relief.

"*Very* bad dream, Rocky," he said.

She rubbed his forehead. "It wasn't all a dream, probably."

"Huh? Oh, you mean the centaurs. No, I remember when the white one was rocking me and singing."

"Well, how are you feeling, then?"

"Weak. My leg doesn't hurt so bad. Is that a good sign, or is it dead?"

"I think you're getting better."

"What about...uh, you know. Gangrene." He looked away from her.

"I don't think so. It looked a lot better after the healer treated you."

"Healer? The centaur?"

"It was all there was left to do," Cirocco said, doubts overwhelming her again. "Calvin hasn't arrived. I watched her, and she seemed to know what she was doing."

She thought he had gone back to sleep. After a long time his eyes opened and he smiled faintly.

"It's not a decision I'd have wanted to make."

"It was terrible, Bill. She said you were dying, and I believed her. It was either do nothing until Calvin got here—and I don't know what *he* could do without any medicine—and *she* said she could kill the germs, which made sense because—"

He touched her knee. His hand was cold, but steady.

"You did the right thing," he said. "Watch me. I'm going to be walking in another week."

It was late afternoon—always, monotonously, late afternoon—and someone was shaking her shoulder. She blinked rapidly.

"Your friends have arrived," Foxtrot sang.

"It was the sky giant we saw earlier," Lullaby added. "They were aboard all the time."

"Friends?"

"Yes, your healer, and two others."

"Two..." She got to her feet. "Those others. Do you have news of them? One is known to me. Is the second like her, or male like my friend Bill?"

The healer frowned. "Your pronouns confuse me. I frankly do not know which of you is male and which female, since you hide behind strips of cloth."

"Bill's male, me and Gaby are female. I'll explain it to you later, but which one is on the sky giant?"

Lullaby shrugged. "The giant did not say. He is as bemused as I."

Whistlestop hovered over the column of Titanides and the wagon, which had halted to wait for the drop. A chute blossomed with a tiny black figure on the end of it. Calvin, no doubt about it.

While he drifted down another chute appeared, and Cirocco strained to see who it might be. The figure looked too big, somehow. Then a third chute opened, and a fourth.

There were a dozen parachutes in the air before she spotted Gene. The rest, incredibly, were Titanides.

"Hey, it's Gene!" Gaby yelled. She was standing a short distance away with Foxtrot and Clarino. Cirocco had stayed with the wagon. "I wonder if April is—"

"*Angels*! Angels attacking! Form up!"

The voice was a screech: a Titanide voice that had lost all its music, choked with hate. Cirocco was dumbfounded to see Lullaby hunched over the radar set, shouting orders. Her face was contorted, all thought of Bill forgotten.

"What's going on?" she began, then ducked as Lullaby vaulted over her.

"Get down, two-legs! Stay out of this."

Cirocco looked up, and the sky was filled with wings. They were dropping around the sides of the blimp, wings tucked to gain speed, attacking the falling Titanides who hung helplessly from their shrouds. There were dozens of them.

She was thrown to the floor of the wagon when it jerked forward to the sound of snapping harness leather. She just missed falling out the open tailgate, struggled to her hands and knees in time to see Gaby leap and catch the sides of the wagon with her hands. Cirocco helped her in.

"What the hell's going on?" Gaby held a bronze sword Cirocco had not seen before.

"Watch out!" Bill was tossed from his bed. Cirocco crawled to him and tried to get him back in, but the wagon kept crashing over rocks and crevices.

"Stop this thing, goddam it!" Cirocco yelled, then sang it in Titanide. It made no difference. The two hitched in front were heading for the battle and nothing would stop them. One held a sword which she brandished above her, shrieking like a demon.

Cirocco slapped one of them on the rump and almost lost her scalp as the sword flashed at her. Keeping her head low, she looked down at the knots hitching the Titanides to the wagon.

"Gaby, give me that thing, quick." The sword came

through the air hilt-first and landed at her feet. She hacked at the leather harnesses. One came free, then the other.

The Titanides did not notice the loss. They quickly outdistanced the wagon, which then slammed to a halt against a boulder.

"What was that all—"

"I don't know. All anyone told me is to stay low. Give me a hand with Bill, will you?"

He was awake, and did not seem to be hurt. He watched the sky as they put him back on the pallet.

"Holy Christ!" he said, just loud enough to be heard over the screech of the Titanides. "They're getting murdered up there."

Cirocco looked up in time to see one of the flying creatures slash three parachute shrouds above one of the descending Titanides. The chute folded. With sickening speed the Titanide vanished behind a low hill to the west.

"Those are angels?" Bill wondered.

To Titanides, they were angels of death. Human in shape, with feathered wings that measured seven meters from tip to tip, the angels turned the peaceful air over Hyperion into a slaughterhouse. All the parachutes were soon cleared from the sky.

The battle went on behind the hill, out of their sight. Titanides screeched like fingernails on a blackboard, and high above was an eerie wail that had to be the angels.

"Behind you," Gaby warned. Cirocco turned quickly.

An angel approached silently from the east. It skimmed the ground, great wings motionless, growing larger with impossible speed. She saw the sword in its left hand, the human face twisted with bloodlust, tears streaking from the corners of the eyes, the muscles knotting in the arm as it brought the sword back . . .

It passed over them, beating its wings to rise over the low hill. The tips touched the ground and stirred gouts of dust.

"Missed me," Gaby said.

"Sit down," Cirocco told her. "You make a great target standing up like that. And it did *not* miss you. It changed

its mind at the last moment; I saw it stop the swing."

"Why did it do that?" She crouched beside Cirocco and scanned the horizon.

"I don't know. Most likely because you don't have four legs. But the next one might not be so observant."

They watched another angel approach from a slightly different angle. It sliced through the air, legs together, some kind of tail surface extending behind its feet, arms at its sides, wings twitching just enough to maintain speed. In grace and economy of motion, Cirocco had never seen its equal.

They saw another build speed by flying straight at the ground. It pulled out at the last possible instant, kissing the ground until it vanished over the brow of the hill. Any crop duster in the world would have been hollow-eyed and white-faced.

"They're very good," Gaby whispered.

"I wouldn't want to get in a dogfight with them," Cirocco agreed. "They'd fly the pants off me."

A chilly wind blew up from the east, raising dust from the dry ground.

Then the Titanides came charging around the hill, followed by a flock of angels. Cirocco recognized Lullaby and Clarino and Foxtrot. Clarino's left foreleg was red with blood. The Titanides carried wooden lances tipped with brass, and bronze swords.

They were no longer giving voice to their battle song, but the frenzy was still in their eyes. Steam puffed from their nostrils and the ones with bare skin glistened. They thundered by, then wheeled to face the angels.

"They're using the wagon for cover!" Gaby shouted. "We're going to be caught in the middle. Get off, quick!"

"What about Bill?" Cirocco yelled.

Gaby's eyes locked with hers for an instant. She seemed about to speak, then growled something unintelligible and took her sword from Cirocco. With a lot more courage than common sense, she stood at the back of the wagon and faced the oncoming angels. Once again, all Cirocco could see was her back as she stood between her love and approaching danger.

The angels ignored her.

She stood with her sword ready, but they went around the sides of the wagon to reach the Titanides who were making a stand behind it.

The noise was beyond belief. The wail of the angels mixed with the shriek of the Titanides while scores of giant wings tore the air.

A monstrous shape loomed out of the dust cloud, a nightmare painted in shades of brown and black, wings moving like shadows come to life. It was blind, sword and lance jabbing aimlessly as the angel tried to get its bearings in the miasma. It seemed no larger than a child of ten. Dark blood ran from a wound in its side.

It was above them when it hurled its lance. The brass tip passed through the sleeve of Gaby's robe and bit into the floor of the wagon, twanging like a bowstring. Then the angel was past them, and a wooden spear was growing from its neck. It fell, and Cirocco could see nothing more.

As quickly as the battle had come to them, it was gone. The wailing took on a different note and the angels rose, dwindled, became nothing but flapping shapes high in the air, headed east.

There was a commotion on the ground beside the wagon. The three Titanides were trampling the body of the fallen angel. It was hard to tell that the body had ever looked human. Cirocco looked away, sickened by the blood and the murderous rage on the faces of the Titanides.

"What do you think made them go away?" Gaby asked. "Just a couple more minutes and they'd have wrapped it up."

"They must know something we don't," Cirocco said.

Bill was looking to the west.

"There," he said, pointing. "Somebody's coming."

Cirocco saw two familiar figures. It was Hornpipe and Banjo, the shepherds, approaching at full gallop.

Gaby laughed, bitterly. "You'll have to show me something better than that. One of those kids is only three years old, Rocky said."

"There," Bill said again, pointing the other way.

Over the hill came a wave of Titanides, like a motley cavalry.

Chapter Sixteen

It was six days after the angel attack, the sixty-first day of their emergence in Gaea. Cirocco was prone on a low table with her feet in improvised stirrups. Calvin was down there somewhere, but she refused to watch him. Lullaby, the white-haired Titanide healer, watched and sang as the operation progressed. Her songs were soothing, but nothing helped a great deal.

"The cervix is dilated," Calvin said.

"I'd just as soon not hear about it."

"Sorry." He straightened briefly, and Cirocco saw his eyes and forehead above the surgical mask. He was sweating profusely. Lullaby wiped it away and his eyes showed his gratitude. "Can you move that lamp closer?"

Gaby positioned the flickering lamp. It threw huge shadows of her legs onto the walls. Cirocco heard the metallic click of instruments taken from the sterilizing bath, then felt the curette rattle through the speculum.

Calvin had wanted stainless steel instruments, but the Titanides could not make them. He and Lullaby had worked with the best artisans until he had brass tools he felt he could use.

"It hurts," Cirocco gritted.

"You're hurting her," Gaby explained, as if Calvin could not understand English.

"Gaby, you'll either be quiet or I'll find someone else to hold the lamp." Cirocco had never heard Calvin speak so harshly. He paused, wiped his brow on his sleeve.

The pain was not intense, but persistent and hard to place, like an ache of the inner ear. She could hear and feel the scraping, and it set her teeth on edge.

"I've got it," Calvin said softly.

"Got what? You can see it?"

"Yeah. You're further along than I thought. It's a good thing you insisted we get it done." He resumed his scraping, pausing from time to time to clean the curette.

Gaby turned away to examine something in the palm of her hand. "It's got four legs," she whispered, and started to come to Cirocco's side.

"I don't want to see it. Get it *away* from me."

"May this one look?" Lullaby sang.

"No!" She was fighting nausea, and could not sing the answer to the Titanide, but shook her head violently. "Gaby, *destroy* it. Right now, do you hear me?"

"It's done, Rocky."

Cirocco let out a deep breath that turned into a sob. "I didn't mean to yell at you. Lullaby said she wanted to see it. I probably should have let her. Maybe she'd know what to make of it."

Cirocco protested that she could walk, but Titanide ideas of medicine included much cuddling, body warmth, and songs of reassurance. Lullaby carried her across the dirt street to the quarters the Titanides had given them. She sang the song of support in times of mental anguish while lowering her into a bed. There were two empty ones beside it.

"Welcome to the veterinary hospital," Bill greeted her. She managed a weak smile as Lullaby arranged the covers.

"Your humorous friend cracks jokes again?" Lullaby sang.

"Yes, he calls this the place-of-healing-for-animals."

"He should be ashamed. Healing is healing. Drink this, and you will relax."

Cirocco took the wineskin and drank deeply. It burned all the way down and warmth spread through her. The Titanides drank fermented beverages for the same reasons humans did, one of the more pleasant discoveries of the last six days.

"I've got a feeling my wrists were just slapped," Bill said. "I know that tone of voice by now."

"She loves you, Bill, even when you're naughty."

"I was hoping to cheer you up."

"It was an interesting try. Bill, it had four legs."

"Ouch. And me making jokes about animals." He reached across and took her hand.

"It's okay. It's over now, and all I'd like to do is sleep." She took two more deep pulls on the wineskin, and did just that.

Gaby spent the first hour after her operation telling everyone she felt fine, then she threw up and was feverish for two days. August came through with no ill effects at all. Cirocco was sore but healthy.

Bill was doing well in that he was healing, but Calvin said the bone had not been set properly.

"So how much longer will it be?" Bill asked. He had asked the question before. There was nothing to read, no television to watch; nothing but the window looking out over a dark street in Titantown. He could not speak to his nurses except in pidgin ditties. Lullaby was learning English, but very slowly.

"At least two more weeks," Calvin said.

"I feel like I could walk on it now."

"You probably could, and that's the danger. It'd pop like a dry stick. No, I won't let you up, even on crutches, for another two weeks."

"What about taking him outside?" Cirocco asked.

"Would you like to go outside, Bill?"

They took Bill and his bed out the door and a short distance along the street before putting him down beneath

one of the canopied trees that made Titantown invisible
from the air, and provided the nearest approach to night
they had seen since their exploration of the cable base.
The Titanides kept their homes and streets lighted all the
time.

"Have you seen Gene today?" Cirocco asked.

"Depends on what you mean by today," Calvin asked,
with a yawn. "You still have my watch."

"But you haven't seen him?"

Calvin shook his head. "Not for a while."

"I wonder what he's been up to."

Calvin had found Gene following the Ophion through
steep terrain as it wound its way among the Nemisis
Mountains of Crius, the day region just west of Rhea. He
said he had emerged in the twilight zone, and had been
walking ever since, trying to hook up with the others.

When asked what he'd been doing, all he would say was
"surviving." Cirocco didn't doubt that, but wondered just
what he meant by it. He brushed off his own experiences
in sensory deprivation, saying he had been worried at first
but calmed down when he understood the situation.

Cirocco wasn't sure she knew what he meant by that,
either.

At first she was happy to have someone who seemed as
minimally affected as she had been. Gaby still moaned in
her sleep. Bill had gaps in his memory, though it was
returning slowly. August was chronically depressed and
verging on the suicidal. Calvin was happy but wanted to
be alone. Only she and Gene seemed relatively un-
changed.

But she knew she had been touched by mystery during
her stay in darkness. She could sing to the Titanides. She
felt more had happened to Gene than he was talking
about, and she began to look for signs of it.

He smiled a lot. He kept assuring everyone he was
okay, even when no one asked. He was friendly.
Sometimes it was too hearty, but other than that he
seemed fine.

She decided to find him and try once more to talk
about the missing two months.

• • •

She liked Titantown.

It was warm under the trees. Since the heat in Gaea came from the ground up, the high vault acted to trap it. It was a dry heat; by wearing a light shirt and no shoes, Cirocco found her body cooled itself at peak efficiency. The streets were pleasantly lighted with paper lanterns that reminded her of the Japanese. The ground was hard-packed earth, moistened by things called sprinkler-plants that sprayed mist once per revolution. When that happened it smelled like a summer night's light rainfall. Hedges were so crusted with flowers that petals fell from them in a steady rain. They grew quite well in perpetual darkness.

The Titanides had never heard of urban planning. Dwellings were scattered haphazardly on the ground, under the ground, and even in the trees. Roads were informally defined by traffic. There were no signs or named streets, and a map of the town would soon have been covered with corrections as new homes were grown in the middle of the road and pedestrians trampled their way through hedges until a new equilibrium was established.

Everyone had a cheery song of greeting for her.

"Hello, Earth monster! Still balanced, I see."

"Oh, look, it's the two-legged oddity. Come and feast with us, Sheer-ah-ko."

"Sorry folks," she sang. "Got business. Have you seen C-sharp Meistersinger?"

It amused her to translate their songs that way, though in Titanide, monster and oddity held no insult.

But the invitation to feast was a hard one to turn down. After two months of raw meat and bland fruit, the Titanides' food was too good to be true. Their cuisine was their greatest art form, and with a few minor exceptions the humans could eat anything the Titanides could eat.

She found the building she called City Hall more by luck than design, stopping frequently to ask directions. (First left, second right, then around the . . . no, that was

blocked last kilorev, wasn't it?) The Titanides understood
the layout, but she didn't think she ever would.

It was City Hall simply because Meistersinger lived
there, and he was the Titanides' closest approach to
leadership. Actually, he was a warlord, but even that was
limited. It was Meistersinger who led the reinforcements
on the day of the battle with the angels. Since then, he had
behaved like everyone else.

Cirocco had meant to ask if he knew where Gene might
be found, but it was not necessary. Gene was already
there.

"Rocky, so glad you could drop by," he said, getting up
and putting his arm over her shoulder. He kissed her
lightly on the cheek, which annoyed her.

"Me and Meistersinger were just talking over a couple
things you might be interested in."

"You were...you can speak to them?"

"His phrasing is atrocious," Meistersinger sang, in the
difficult aeolian mode, "in the manner of the Crian
peoples. His voice will not settle decently, and his ear is
more suited to the...shall we say unmodulated words of
your own pipes. But we can sing together, after a fashion."

"I heard some of that," Gene sang, laughing. "Thinks
he can talk over my head, like spelling words in front of a
baby."

"Why didn't you tell me this before, Gene?" she asked,
searching his eyes.

"I didn't think it was important," he said, waving it off.
"I got a dose of what you got, but it didn't take so well."

"I just wish you'd told me, that's all."

"I'm sorry, okay?" He seemed irritated, and she
wondered if he had meant her to know. Surely he didn't
think he could have concealed it much longer.

"Gene has been telling me many interesting things,"
Meistersinger sang. "He has made lines all over my table,
but they make little sense to me. I would understand, and
pray that your superior song might clear away the
darkness."

"Yeah, Rocky, you take a shot. I can't get this dumb
son-of-a-donkey to see it."

Cirocco glanced sharply at him, relaxed when she recalled Meistersinger knew no English. She still thought it bad mannered and childish. The Titanide was anything but stupid.

Meistersinger was kneeling beside one of the low tables the Titanides preferred. He had dull orange fur a few centimeters long, with only his face bare. The skin was chocolate brown. His eyes were light gray, set in a face that had at first seemed identical for Titanides, but now seemed to Cirocco to have as many variations as human faces. She could now tell one from another without reference to coloring.

But the face was still a female one. She could not shake that cultural conditioning, even when the penis was visible.

Gene had used skin paint to draw a map on Meistersinger's table. Two parallel lines ran east and west, and other lines cut the space between into rectangles. It was the inner rim of Gaea, spread out and seen from above.

"Here's Hyperion," he said, jabbing with a paint-reddened finger. "On the west, Oceanus, on the east . . . what did you call it?"

"Rhea."

"Right. Then comes Crius. There's support cables running here, here, and here. Titanides live in east Hyperion, and west Crius. But there are no angels in Rhea. Do you know why, Rocky? Because they live in the spokes."

"What's this about, anyway?"

"Bear with me. Make him understand, will you?"

She did her best. After several attempts, he looked interested and put one orange-nailed finger near a dot in west Hyperion.

"This, then, would be the great stairway to heaven near the village?"

"Yes, and Titantown is next to it."

Meistersinger frowned. "Why do I see it not?"

"I got that," Gene said, in English. "'Cause I've drawed it not," he sang. With a flourish, he made another dot beside the larger one.

"How will these lines kill all of the angels?" Meistersinger asked.

Gene turned to Cirocco. "Did he ask why I'm drawing all this?"

"No, he asked what this has to do with killing angels, and I'd like to add a question of my own, which is, *what in hell are you doing*? I forbid you to go on with this discussion. We can't aid either side of two warring nations. Didn't you read the Geneva Contact Protocols?"

Gene was silent for a moment, looking away from her. When he looked back, he spoke quietly.

"Don't you remember that slaughter, or did you really miss it all? They got wiped out, Rocky. Fifteen of these jackasses jumped. All but one died, and so did two more that were with you. The angels lost two, plus one wounded."

"Three. You didn't see what happened to the third." It still made her sick to think of it.

"Whatever. The thing is, it was a new tactic. The angels hitched a ride on top of the blimp. At first we thought the angels had made an alliance with the blimps, but it turns out the blimps are upset, too. They're neutrals. The angels got aboard during a storm, so the blimp thought the extra weight was just water. He gains a couple tons when it rains."

"What's all this 'we' stuff? Are you making an alliance? You don't have that power. *I* do, as ship's Captain."

"Maybe I should point out that your ship is gone."

If he had meant to wound her, his aim could not have been better. She cleared her throat, and went on. "Gene, we're not here as military advisors."

"Hell, I just thought I'd show them a few things. Like this map. You can't plan strategy without a map. They'll need some new tactics, too, but—"

Meistersinger made the high whistle that served as a throat-clearing sound. Cirocco realized they had been ignoring him.

"Pardon me," he sang. "This drawing is a fine thing indeed. I will have it painted on my chest at the next tri-city jamboree. But we were speaking of ways to kill angels. I would be pleased to hear more of the gray powder of violence you mentioned earlier."

"*Je*-zus, Gene!" Cirocco exploded, then controlled her voice. "Meistersinger. My friend, whose command of your songs is poor, must have expressed himself badly. I know of no such powder."

Meistersinger's eyes were bland pools. "If not the gray powder, then speak to me of the device for hurling spears into the air farther than the hand can throw."

"Again, you must have misunderstood. Bear with me for a moment longer, please." She turned to Gene, trying for a calm front. "Gene, get out. I'll talk to you later."

"Rocky, all I want to do is—"

"That's an order, Gene."

He hesitated. She was trained in hand combat and had the longer reach, but he was trained, too, and had more strength. She was far from sure she could beat him, but got ready to try.

The moment passed. Gene relaxed, then slammed his palm on the table and stalked from the room. Meistersinger had followed it with eyes that missed nothing.

"I'm sorry if I caused bad feeling to flow between you and your friend," the Titanide sang.

"It was not your fault." Her hands were cold now that the confrontation was over. "I . . . see here, Meistersinger," she sang in equals mode. "Which did you believe? Me, or Gene?"

"Face it, Rah-kee, you looked like you had something to hide."

Cirocco chewed a knuckle while wondering what to do. The Titanide was sure she was lying, but how much did he already know?

"You're right," she sang at last. "We have a powder of violence, strong enough to destroy this entire town. We know secrets of destruction that I am ashamed to even hint at; things that could blow a hole in your world and leak the air you breathe into cold space."

"We need nothing like that," Meistersinger sang, looking interested. "The powder will do nicely."

"I can't give it to you. We brought none with us."

The Titanide had obviously considered his song

carefully when he finally sang again.

"Your friend Gene thought it possible to make these things. We are clever with wood, and the chemistry of living things."

Cirocco sighed. "He's probably right. But we cannot give you the secrets."

Meistersinger was silent.

"My own personal feelings have little to do with the matter," she explained. "Those who are above me, the wise ones of my kind, have said this should be so."

Meistersinger shrugged. "If your elders command it, you have little choice."

"I'm glad you see it that way."

"Yes." He paused, again choosing his song carefully.

"Your friend Gene is not so respectful of his elders. If I asked him again, he might tell me things that I need for victory."

Her heart sank, but she tried not to let him see.

"Gene was forgetful. He had a difficult time in his journey; his thoughts wandered, but now I have reminded him of his duty."

"I see." He pondered again, offering her a glass of wine, which she drank gratefully.

"I believe I myself could construct a launcher of spears. A flexible stick, ends tied together with a thong."

"Frankly, I'm surprised you don't have it already. You have much more complex things."

"We do have something like it which children use for games."

"The nature of your war with the angels puzzles me. Why do you fight?"

Meistersinger frowned. "Because they are angels."

"There's no other reason? I had been impressed with your tolerance of other races. You feel no animosity for me and my friends, or the blimps, or the yeti in Oceanus."

"They are *angels*," he repeated.

"You don't wish to live in the same land?"

"Angels would be unable to suckle their young at Gaea's breast if they left the great towers. And we could not live clinging to the walls."

"So you don't compete for land or food. Could the reason be religious? Do they worship another God?"

He laughed. "Worship? You put your song together oddly. There is only one Goddess, even to the angels. Gaea is known to all races within her."

"Then I just don't understand. Could you make me see? Why do you fight?"

Meistersinger the warlord thought for a long time. When he at last sang, it was in a mournful minor key.

"Of all the things in this life, that is the one I would most like to ask Gaea. That we must all die and return to mud—I have no objections, no bitterness. That the world is a circle and winds blow when Gaea breathes—these are things I understand. That there are times when one must go hungry, or when the mighty Ophion is swallowed in dust, or the cold wind from the west freezes us—these things I accept, as I doubt I could do a better job with these matters. Gaea has many lands to tend, and at times must turn her gaze elsewhere.

"When the great pillars of the sky snap, such that the ground trembles and one fears the world will come apart and fling herself into the void, I do not complain.

"But at the time of Gaea's breath, when the hate is upon me, I reason no more. I lead my people into battle, knowing not that my own hinddaughter falls at my side. *I knew it not.* She was a stranger to me because the sky was filled with angels and it was time to fight. It is only later when the rage lifts from us that we count the cost. It is then the mother finds her child slain on the field. It was then I found the daughter of my flesh wounded by angels but trampled by the feet of her own people.

"This was five breaths ago. My heart grew sick, and I fear it will never heal."

Cirocco dared not break the silence as Meistersinger turned from her. He stood and walked to the door, faced the darkness while Cirocco watched the candle flicker on the table. He made sounds that were certainly the sounds of weeping, though they did not sound like human weeping. After a time, he came back to her and sat, looking very tired.

"We fight when the rage takes us. We do not stop fighting until the angels are all dead or gone back to their home."

"You speak of Gaea's breath. I am a stranger to it."

"You have heard it wailing. It is a raging gale from the heavenly towers; cold from the west and hot from the east."

"Have you ever tried to talk to the angels? Will they not listen to your song?"

He shrugged again. "Who can sing to an angel, and what angel would listen?"

"I'm still bothered that no one has tried . . . to negotiate with them." That word was difficult. The one she finally settled on meant "surrender," or "turn tail" in a literal sense. "If you could sit down and hear each other's songs, perhaps you could have peace."

His brow wrinkled. "How can there be the feeling-of-harmony-among siblings when they are angels?" The word he used was the same one Cirocco had picked as the best of an inadequate lot. "Peace" among Titanides was a universal condition, hardly worth comment. Between Titanides and angels, peace was a concept the language could not embrace.

"My people have no enemies of other races, but fight among ourselves," Cirocco said. "We have evolved ways of resolving these conflicts."

"This is not a problem for us. We deal well with hostility among our own kind."

"Maybe you could teach us about that. But for my part, I could wish that I might show you the ways we have learned. Sometimes both parties are too hostile to sit down and talk. In that case, we use a third party to sit between the enemies."

He raised one eyebrow, then lowered them both suspiciously. "If this works, why do you have need of so many weapons?"

She had to smile. It was not easy to put something over on the Titanides.

"Because it doesn't always work. Then our warriors try to destroy each other. But our weapons have grown so fearsome that no one has used them in a long time. We have become better at peace, and I offer as proof that while having been able to destroy our entire planet for at least ... make it sixty myriarevs, we have not done so."

"That is the blink of an eye as Gaea turns," he sang.

"I'm not bragging. It is a terrible thing to live with the knowledge that not only your ... your hindmother and friends and neighbors can be wiped out, but every one of your kind down to the smallest stripling."

Meistersinger nodded gravely, looking impressed.

"It is up to you. Our kind can offer you more war, or the possibility of peace."

"I see that," he sang, preoccupied. "It is a grave decision to make."

Cirocco decided to shut up. Meistersinger knew it was within his power to learn of the weaponry Gene offered to give.

The candle in the wall holder guttered to darkness; only the one between them survived to cast dancing light across his feminine features.

"Where could I find this one to stand in the middle? It seems to me that such a one would be hit by spears thrown from both sides."

Cirocco spread her hands. "I am willing to offer my services as an authorized representative of the United Nations."

Meistersinger studied her. "Meaning no disrespect to the you-nigh-ted-naish-uns, we have never heard of them. Why would they be interested in our wars?"

"The United Nations is always interested in wars. Frankly, they are no better than we are as a whole, which is to say far from perfect."

He shrugged, as if he had assumed that from the start. "Why would you do this for us?"

"I'm going through the territory of the angels anyway, on my way to see Gaea. And I hate war."

For the first time Meistersinger looked impressed. It was plain that his opinion of her had gone up significantly.

"You did not say you were a pilgrim. This puts a new

light on matters. I fear you are a fool but it is a holy foolishness." He reached across the table and took her head in his big hands, leaned over, and kissed her forehead. It was the most ritualistic thing she had seen a Titanide do, and it touched her.

"Go, then," he said. "I will think no more of new weapons. Things are fearsome enough, without taking a road that must lead to destruction."

He paused, seeming to draw in on himself.

"If by some happenstance you should actually see Gaea, I wish you would ask her for me why my hinddaughter had to die. If she will not answer you, slap her face and tell her it's from Meistersinger."

"I'll do that." She got up, strangely exhilarated, somehow less worried about the future than she had been in two months. She started to leave, but was curious about something.

"What was the kiss for?" she asked.

He looked up.

"It was the kiss for the dead. When you leave, I will never see you again."

Chapter Seventeen

Hornpipe had assumed the role of guide and source of information for the human party. She said her hind-mother approved, and felt it would be a good learning experience. The humans were the most exciting things to happen in Titantown for many a myriarev.

When Cirocco expressed a desire to see the place of winds outside town, Hornpipe packed a picnic lunch and two full wineskins. Calvin and Gaby volunteered to go, but August just sat looking out the window, something she did often. Gene could not be found. Cirocco reminded Calvin he had pledged to stay with Bill.

Bill told her to wait until he was healed. She was forced to remind him that she was still in charge. He had been forgetting that as confinement made him peevish and petty. Cirocco understood, but liked him least when he turned protective.

"Nice day for a picnic," Hornpipe sang as Cirocco and Gaby joined her on the edge of town. "The ground is dry. We should make it there and back in four or five revs."

Cirocco knelt and tied the shoelaces of the soft leather mocassins that Titanides had made for her, then stood and looked out over the brown land to where the west central Rhea cable—the place of winds—loomed in the clear air.

"I hate to disappoint you," she sang, "but it will take me and my friend a decarev to get there, and the same coming back. We plan to camp at the base and take the false death."

Hornpipe shivered. "I wish you would not do that. It frightens me. How do the worms know not to eat you?"

Cirocco laughed. The Titanides did not sleep, ever. They found it even more disturbing than the odd knack of balancing forever on two legs.

"There's an alternative. I hesitate to suggest it for fear of offending you. On Earth we have animals—not people—that are built something like you. We ride upon their backs."

"On their backs?" She looked puzzled, then her face lit up as she made the connection. "You mean with one of your legs on each...of course, I see! Do you think it would work?"

"I'm willing to try it if you are. Hold out your hand. No, turn it...that's it. I'm going to put my foot on it..." She did so, grabbed Hornpipe's shoulder, and swung herself up and over. She sat on the broad back with a cinch strap under her and a saddlebag behind each leg. "Is that comfortable?"

"I hardly know you're there. But how will you stay on?"

"That's what we'll have to see. I thought I'd—" She broke off with a high-pitched yelp. Hornpipe had turned her head all the way around.

"What's wrong?"

"Nothing. We're not so limber as that. I can hardly believe you're doing it. Never mind. Turn around and watch where you're going, and start out slow."

"What gait would you prefer?"

"Huh? Oh. I don't know anything about it."

"All right. I'll trot first, and work up to a slow gallop."

"Do you mind if I put my arms around you?"

"Not at all."

Hornpipe made a wide circle, gradually increasing her

speed. They raced by Gaby, who cheered and shouted.
When Hornpipe trotted to a stop she was scarcely
breathing hard.

"Will it work, do you think?" Cirocco asked.

"I should think so. Let's try it with both of you."

"I'd like something to cover this strap," Cirocco said.
"As for Gaby, why don't we find someone else for her?"

Within ten minutes Hornpipe had two cushions and
another volunteer. This one was male, and covered in
lavender fur, with white head and tail hair.

"Hey, Rocky. I've got a fancier mount than you."

"Depends on how you look at it. Gaby, I'd like you to
meet—" she sang the name, reversed the introduction,
then whispered an aside to Gaby. "Call him Panpipe."

"What's wrong with Leo or George?" she groused, but
shook hands with him and easily leaped astride.

They set out, the Titanides singing a traveling song that
the women joined as best they could. When that one
ended they learned another. Then Cirocco eased into
"The Wonderful Wizard of Oz," following it up with "The
Caissons Go Rolling Along," and "Off We Go Into the
Wild Blue Yonder." The Titanides were delighted, they
had not known the humans had songs.

Cirocco had been on a raft trip down the Colorado
River, and in a nutshell boat on the Ophion. She'd flown
over the south pole and hopped across the United States
in a biplane. She had traveled by snowmobile and bicycle,
cable car and gravity train, and once took a short trip on a
camel. None of them were anything like riding a Titanide
under the vault of Gaea, in that long afternoon forever on
the verge of sunset. Ahead of her a stairway to heaven
sprang from the ground and retreated into night.

She threw her head back and sang.

"It's a long way to Tipperary, it's a long way to go . . ."

The place of winds was hard rock and tortured earth.

Ridges like gnarled knuckles began to wrinkle the
brown land, and between them deep chasms opened. The
ridges splayed out and became fingers that gripped the
land and crumpled it like a sheet of paper. The fingers

soon joined a weathered hand and then a long shaggy arm reaching out of the night.

The air was never still. Sudden gusts from every direction generated a thousand dust devils to dance erratically in their path.

Soon they heard the howling. It was a hollow sound, not pleasant, but with none of the terrible sadness of the great wind from Oceanus known as Gaea's Lament.

Hornpipe had given them some idea of what to expect. The ridges they were climbing were cable strands emerging at a thirty-degree angle to the ground, and covered with soil. The wind had eroded the land into gullies that all ran toward the source of the sound.

They began to pass suction holes in the ground, some no bigger than half a meter across, others large enough to swallow a Titanide. Each had its own distinctive whistling note. It was a non-harmonic, non-quantized music, like some of the more opaque experiments from the turn of the century. Behind it all was a continuous organ note.

The Titanides picked their way up the last, long ridge. It was hard, rocky ground, long since scoured of loose dirt, but the spine of the ridge was narrow and the chasms were wide and deep. Cirocco hoped they would know when it was best to stop. Already the wind whipped tears from her eyes.

"This is the place of winds," Hornpipe sang. "We dare not approach any closer, as the winds become strong enough to carry you away. But you can see the Great Howler if you go down the slope. Would you like me to carry you there?"

"Thanks, I'll walk," Cirocco said, and swung to the ground.

"I'll show the way." Hornpipe started down the slope, taking short, mincing steps and looking unstable, but apparently having no trouble.

The Titanides came to a vertical drop and followed it to the east. When Gaby and Cirocco reached it they felt an increase in both the wind and the noise.

"If it gets much worse than this," Cirocco shouted, "I think we'd better give it up!"

"I'm with you."

But when they reached the place the Titanides had stopped, they saw it was as far as they would need to go.

There were seven visible suction holes, all of them at the ends of long, steep ravines. Six were from fifty to 200 meters across. The Great Howler could have swallowed them all.

Cirocco guessed it was a kilometer from the base of the opening to its top, and half that across its widest point. The oval shape was enforced by its position between two cable strands that made a sharp vee as they emerged from the brown land. Where they met, the great mouth of bare stone gaped open.

The sides of the opening were so smooth they flashed in the sunlight, like contorted mirrors. They had been polished by a thousand years of wind and the abrasive sand it carried. Veins of lighter ore in the dark stone gave it a mother-of-pearl sheen.

Hornpipe leaned over and sang close to Cirocco's ear.

"I can see why," Cirocco bellowed back.

"What did she say?" Gaby wanted to know.

"She said they call this place the fore-crotch of Gaea."

"I can see why. We're on one of her legs."

"That's the idea."

Cirocco touched Hornpipe's rump and gestured back to the top of the ridge. She wondered what they thought of this place. Awe? Not likely. It was just outside of town. Were the Swiss awed by mountains?

It was good to get back to relative quiet. She stood beside Hornpipe and surveyed her surroundings.

If the cable base was a giant hand, as she had seen it earlier, they had made it to the second knuckle of one of the fingers. The Howler was down in the webbing between two fingers.

"Is there another way up?" Cirocco sang. "A way to reach the broad plain up there, without being sucked up to Gaea?"

Panpipe, who was a little older than Hornpipe, nodded.

"Yes, many. This great mother of holes is the largest.

Any of the other ridges will allow you to reach the
plateau."

"Then why didn't you take me up there?"

Hornpipe looked surprised. "You said you wished to
see the place of winds, not climb up to meet Gaea."

"My fault," she acknowledged. "But what is the best
way to the top?"

"The very top?" Hornpipe sang, wide-eyed. "I was
merely joking. Surely you will not go there?"

"I'm going to try."

Hornpipe pointed to the next ridge to the south.
Cirocco studied the land across the chasm. It looked no
more difficult than the ridge they had climbed. That had
taken the Titanides an hour and a half, so she should be
able to walk it in six to eight hours. There was another six
hours of uphill terrain until the plateau was reached, and
beyond that . . .

From this vantage point the slanted cable was a
preposterous mountain. It sloped away from her for
approximately fifty kilometers, to the darkness above the
Rhea border. For three of these kilometers nothing grew;
it was chocolate-brown dirt and gray rock. For a similar
distance there were only twisted, leafless trees. Beyond
that, the persistent life of Gaea had found a foothold. She
could not tell if it was grass or woodlands, but the
five-kilometer diameter barrel of the cable was crusted in
green—the corroded anchor chain of a sea-going vessel.

The green extended to the Rhea twilight zone. The
zone was not a sharp-edged thing; it began gradually as
the color was washed away by darkness. Green faded to
bronze, deepened to dark gold, to silver over blood red,
and finally to the color of clouds with the moon behind
them. By then the cable was all but invisible. The eye
followed the impossible curve as it dwindled to a rope, a
string, a thread, before joining the looming darkness of
the roof and vanishing into the spoke opening. The spoke
could be seen to constrict gradually, but it was too dark to
see much beyond that.

"It can be done," she said to Gaby. "To the roof, at

least. I was hoping there would be some sort of mechanical lift here at the bottom. There might still be, I guess, but if we searched for it . . ." She waved her hand at the corrugated land. "It could take months."

Gaby studied the slope of the cable, sighed, and shook her head slowly.

"I go where you go, but you're crazy, you know? We'll never get past the roof. Take a look, will you? From there on in, we'd be climbing on the *bottom* of a forty-five-degree slope."

"Mountaineers do it all the time. You did it, in training."

"Sure. For ten meters. We'll have to do it for fifty or sixty kilometers. And then—here's the good news—*then* we only have to go straight up. For 400 kilometers."

"It won't be easy. We've got to try."

"Madre de Dios." Gaby hit her forehead with the heel of her hand, and rolled her eyes.

Hornpipe had watched Cirocco's gestures as she outlined the problem. Now she sang, *largo*.

"You will climb the great stairs?"

"I must."

Hornpipe nodded, then bent and kissed Cirocco's forehead.

"I wish you folks would stop doing that," Cirocco said, in English.

"What was it for?" Gaby asked.

"Never mind. Let's get back to town."

They stopped after leaving the zone of wind. Hornpipe put out a groundcloth and they sat down to a picnic. The food was hot, stored in nutshell thermos bottles. Cirocco and Gaby ate perhaps a tenth of it between them, and the Titanides wolfed down the rest.

They were still five kilometers from Titantown when Hornpipe looked over her shoulder, the expression on her face a mixture of mournfulness and anticipation. She gazed at the dark roof.

"Gaea breathes," she sang, sadly.

"What? Are you sure? I thought it would be noisy, and we'd have plenty of time to—does that mean there'll be angels?"

"Noisy from the *west*," Hornpipe corrected her. "The breath of Gaea is silent from the east. I fancy I can hear them already." She missed a step, nearly throwing Cirocco.

"Well, hurry, damn it! If you're trapped out here alone you won't have a chance."

"It's too late," Hornpipe sang, and now her eyes yearned, her lips drew back to bare bright teeth.

"Move!" Cirocco had practiced that tone of command for years, and somehow managed to put it in a Titanide song. Hornpipe leaped to a gallop, and Panpipe followed close behind.

Soon even Cirocco could hear the wail of angels. Hornpipe's gait wavered; she wanted very badly to turn back and do battle.

They were approaching a lone tree, and Cirocco made a snap decision.

"Pull up. Hurry, we don't have much time."

They halted under the spreading branches and Cirocco jumped down. Hornpipe tried to bolt but Cirocco slapped the Titanide's face, which seemed to calm her temporarily.

"Gaby, cut off those saddlebags. Panpipe! Stop that! Come back here at once."

Panpipe looked undecided, but came back to them. Gaby and Cirocco worked frantically, tearing their clothes into strips, each making three strong ropes.

"My friends," Cirocco sang, when she had the tethers, "I don't have time to explain. I ask you to trust me and do as I say." She put every ounce of determination she possessed into the song, scoring it in the mode used from the old and wise to the young and foolish. It worked, but just barely. Both Titanides kept looking to the east.

She had them lie on their sides.

"That hurts," Hornpipe complained when Cirocco tied her hind legs together.

"I'm sorry. It's for your own good." She quickly bound

her forelegs and arms, then tossed a wineskin to Gaby. "Get as much of this down him as you can. I want him too stinking drunk to move."

"Gotcha."

"My child, I want you to drink this," she sang. "You too, over there. Drink *lots* of it." She held the nipple to Hornpipe's lips. The sound of the angels was louder now. Hornpipe's ears twitched up and down rapidly.

"Cotton, cotton," she muttered. She tore strips from her already frayed tunic and rolled them into tight balls. "It worked for Odysseus, maybe it'll work for me. Gaby, the ears. Plug his ears."

"That *hurts!*" Hornpipe howled. "Let me *up,* Earth monster. I don't *like* this game." She began to moan, the notes only occasionally resolving into words of hate.

"Have some more wine," Cirocco crooned. The Titanide choked as she poured it down her throat. The cries of the angels were very loud now. Hornpipe began to screech in reply. Cirocco grabbed the Titanide's ears and squeezed them, then cradled the big head in her lap. She put her lips to one ear and sang a Titanide lullaby.

"Rocky, help!" Gaby yelled. "I don't know any of those songs. Sing louder!" Panpipe was struggling, shrieking as Gaby tried to hold him by the ears. He lashed out with his bound hands and threw her away from him.

"Grab him! Don't let him get away."

"I'm *trying.*" She ran behind him and tried to pin his arms to his sides, but he was much too strong for her. She tumbled away again, got up with a cut over her right eye.

Panpipe was gnawing at the bonds that held his wrists together. The cloth tore and he was clawing at his ears.

"What now, Rocky?" Gaby screamed, desperately.

"Come help me," she said. "He'll kill you if you get in his way." It was far too late to stop Panpipe. His front legs were free and he was contorted like a snake, tearing at the strap that bound the other two.

Without a glance at the women and Hornpipe, he charged toward Titantown. Soon he was gone over the top of a low hill.

Gaby did not seem aware that she was crying as she

knelt beside Cirocco, nor did she do anything about the trickle of blood down the side of her face.

"How can I help?"

"I don't *know*. Touch her, sooth her, do anything you can think of to keep her mind off angels."

Hornpipe was thrashing now, her teeth clenched, face bloodless. Cirocco held on, getting as close as she dared while Gaby slipped a rope around the Titanide's chest, pinioning her arms at her side.

"Hush, hush," Cirocco whispered. "There's nothing to be afraid of. I'll watch over you until your hindmother returns. I'll sing you her songs."

Hornpipe gradually quieted, her eyes regaining the intelligence Cirocco had seen on the first day they met. It was infinitely better than the fearsome animal she had become.

It was ten more minutes before the last of the angels went by overhead. Hornpipe was drenched in sweat, like someone kicking a heroin or alcohol addiction.

She began to giggle as they waited for the angels to return. Cirocco reclined on her side, facing Hornpipe, holding her head close and was startled when the Titanide began to move. It was not a testing of the bonds, as her earlier movements had been. It was frankly sexual. She gave Cirocco a wet kiss. Her mouth was so large and warm it was unnerving.

"Would that I were a boy," she crooned, drunkenly. Cirocco glanced down.

"Jesus," Gaby breathed. The Titanide's huge penis was out of its sheath, its tip pulsing on the dust.

"You may be a girl to you," Cirocco sang, "but you're too much of a boy for me."

Hornpipe thought that was hilarious. She roared, and tried to kiss Cirocco again but gave it up amiably enough when Cirocco drew back.

"I would do you great harm," she chortled. "Alas, that is for *rear* holes, of which you have none. Would that I were a boy, and had a member fit for you."

Cirocco smiled and let her rave on, but her eyes were

not smiling. She looked over Hornpipe's shoulder at
Gaby.

"Last resort," she said, quietly, in English. "If it looks
like she's going to get free, take that rock and hit her over
the head. If she gets away, she's dead."

"Gotcha. What's she talking about?"

"She wants to make love to me."

"With *that*? Maybe I'd better bean her now."

"Don't be silly. We're in no danger from her. If she gets
loose, she won't even see us. Do you hear them coming
back?"

"I think so."

It turned out to be not nearly so difficult the second
time. They never gave Hornpipe a chance to hear the
angels, and while she sweated and shook as if she could
somehow feel them, she never struggled very hard.

And then they were gone, back to the eternal darkness
of the spoke high above Rhea.

She cried when they released her; the helpless sobs of a
child who doesn't understand what has happened to her.
That turned into petulance and complaints, chiefly about
her sore legs and ears. Gaby and Cirocco rubbed her legs
where the ropes had chafed. Her cloven hooves were as
clear and red as cherry jello.

She seemed confused as to the whereabouts of
Panpipe, but not distressed when she understood he had
gone into battle. She gave them sloppy kisses and pressed
herself against them amorously, causing Gaby some
concern even when Cirocco explained the Titanides
rigidly divided frontal and rear intercourse. The frontal
organs were for the production of semi-fertilized eggs,
which were then manually implanted in a rear vagina and
brought to fecundity by a rear penis.

When she got to her feet she was too drunk to carry
them. They walked her in circles and finally headed her
back toward town. In a few hours they could get on her
back again.

Titantown was in sight before they found Panpipe.

The blood had already dried in his pretty blue fur. A lance stuck out from his side, pointed at the sky. He had been mutilated.

Hornpipe knelt at his side and wept while Gaby and Cirocco hung back. There was bitterness in Cirocco's mouth. Did Hornpipe blame her? Would she have preferred to have died with him, or was that a hopelessly Earthling notion? The Titanides didn't seem to understand the glory of battle; it was something they did because they couldn't help it. Cirocco admired them for the first pitied them for the second.

Do you rejoice for the one you saved, or weep for the one you lost? She could not do both, so she wept.

Hornpipe struggled to her feet, much heavier than she had been. Three years old, Cirocco thought. It meant nothing. She had some of the innocence of a human of the same age, but she was a Titanide adult.

She picked up the severed head and kissed it once, then set it down by the body. She sang nothing; the Titanides had no song for this moment.

Gaby and Cirocco got on her back again, and Hornpipe set out for town at a slow trot.

"Tomorrow," Cirocco said. "We leave for the hub tomorrow."

Chapter Eighteen

Five days later, Cirocco was still preparing to depart. There was the problem of who and what to take.

Bill was out, though he had other opinions. So was August. She spoke seldom now, spending her time on the edge of town, answering questions in monosyllables. Calvin could not say if the best therapy would be to leave her or to take her with them. Cirocco had to decide in favor of the mission, which would be in trouble if August suffered a breakdown.

Calvin was out because he had promised to stay in Titantown until Bill was well enough to care for himself; after that, he was on his own.

Gene was in. Cirocco wanted him where she could keep an eye on him, far from Titanides.

That left Gaby.

"You can't leave me," she said, not pleading, merely stating a fact of life. "I'll follow you."

"I won't try to. You're a pest with this fixation you have on me that I don't deserve. But you saved my life, which I've never really thanked you for, and I want you to know I'll never forget it."

"I don't want your thanks," Gaby said. "I want your love."

"I can't give it to you. I *like* you, Gaby. Hell, we've been side by side since this thing started. But we're doing the first fifty kilometers in Whistlestop. I won't force you to get on."

Gaby paled, but spoke up bravely. "You won't have to."

Cirocco nodded. "As I say, it's up to you. Calvin says we can get to the level of the twilight zone. The blimps don't go any higher than that, because the angels don't like it."

"So it's you and me and Gene?"

"Yeah." Cirocco frowned. "I'm glad you're going."

They needed many things and Cirocco did not know how to obtain them. The Titanides had a system of exchange, but prices were established by a complex formula involving degrees of relationship, standing in the community, and need. No one went hungry, but low-status individuals like Hornpipe had little but meals, shelter, and the bare necessities of body ornamentation. The Titanides viewed these as only slightly less vital than food.

There was a credit system, and Meistersinger used some of his, but relied mostly on pegging Cirocco's status arbitrarily high, claiming her as his spiritual hinddaughter and making a case that she should be adopted as such by the community because of the nature of her mission.

Most of the Titanide artisans bought the idea, and were almost too helpful in outfitting the party. Backpacks were made with straps arranged for human bodies. Then everyone came offering his or her finest wares.

Cirocco had decided each of them could carry around fifty kilos of mass. It bulked large, but weighed only twelve kilos and would get lighter as they climbed toward the hub. Gaby said the centripetal acceleration there would be one fortieth of a gravity.

Rope was the first consideration. The Titanides had a plant that grew fine rope, strong, thin, and supple. Each human could carry a hundred-meter coil of it.

The Titanides were good climbers, though they largely confined their efforts to trees. Cirocco discussed pitons with the ironworkers, who came back with their best efforts. Unfortunately, steel was news to the Titanides. Gene looked at the pitons and shook his head.

"It's the best they can do," Cirocco said. "They tempered it, like I told them."

"It's still not enough. But don't worry. Whatever the insides of the spoke is, it won't be rock. Rock could never stand up to the pressures trying to tear this place apart. In fact, I don't know of anything strong enough."

"Which just means the people who built Gaea knew things we don't know."

Cirocco was not too disturbed. The angels lived in the spokes. Unless they existed by flying all their lives, they had to perch somewhere. If they could perch on something, she could cling to it.

They brought hammers to drive the pitons, the lightest and hardest the Titanides could make. The metalworkers provided them with hatchets and knives, and whetstones to sharpen them. They each packed a parachute, courtesy of Whistlestop.

"Clothes," Cirocco said. "What kind of clothes should we bring?"

Meistersinger looked helpless.

"I have no need of them, as you can see," he sang. "Some of our people who are naked-skinned, as you are, wear them in the cold times. We can make what you want."

So they were outfitted in the finest patterned silks from head to toe. It was not actually silk, but felt like it. Over that were felt shirts and pants, two sets for each of them, and woven sweaters for upper and lower parts of the body. Fur coats and pants were made, and fur-lined gloves and hard-soled moccasins. They had to go prepared for anything, and though the clothing took a lot of space, Cirocco didn't begrudge it.

They packed silk hammocks and sleeping bags. The Titanides had matches, and oil-burning lamps. They took one each, and a small supply of fuel. There was no way it would stretch for the whole journey, but neither would their food or water.

"Water," Cirocco fretted. "That could be a big problem."

"Well, like you said, the angels live up there." Gaby was helping with the packing on the fifth day of preparations. "They must drink something."

"That doesn't mean waterholes will be easy to find."

"If you're going to be all the time worrying, we might as well not go."

They took waterskins good for about nine or ten days, and then filled out the mass limit with as much dried food as would fit. They planned to eat what the angels ate, if that was possible.

On the sixth day everything was ready, and she still had to face Bill. She was glum about the possibility of having to use her authority to end the argument, but knew she would do so if it came to it.

"You're all crazy," Bill said, hitting his palm on the bed. "You have no idea what you'll find up there. Do you seriously think you can climb up a chimney *400 kilometers high?*"

"We're going to see if it's possible."

"You're gonna get yourselves killed. You ought to be doing a thousand klicks when you hit."

"I figure terminal velocity in this air couldn't be much over 200. Bill, if you're trying to cheer me up, you're doing a lousy job." She had never seen him like this, and she hated it.

"We should all stick together, and you know it. You're still overcompensating because you lost *Ringmaster,* trying to act the hero."

If there hadn't been a grain of truth in what he said, it couldn't have hurt so much. She had thought about it for long hours while trying to sleep.

"Air! What if there's no air up there?"

"We're not going to commit suicide. If it's impossible, we'll accept it. You're manufacturing arguments."

His eyes pleaded with her.

"I'm asking you, Rocky. Wait for me. I have never asked anything before, but I'm asking for this now."

She sighed, and gestured for Gaby and Gene to leave the room. When they were gone she sat on the edge of his bed and reached for his hand. He moved it away. She stood up quickly, furious at herself for trying to reach him that way, and at him for rejecting her.

"I don't seem to know you, Bill," she said, quietly. "I thought I did. You've been a comfort to me when I was lonely, and I thought I might love you in time. I don't fall in love easily. Maybe I'm too suspicious; I don't know. Sooner or later everybody demands that I be what they want me to be, and now you're doing it."

He said nothing, did not even look at her.

"What you're doing is so unfair I could scream."

"I wish you would."

"Why? So I'd fit your picture of what a woman's supposed to do? Damn it, I was a Captain when you met me; I didn't think that was so important to you."

"I don't know what you're talking about."

"I'm talking about the fact that if I leave here now, it's all over between us. Because I won't wait for you to come along to keep me safe."

"I don't know what you're—"

She did scream then, and it felt good. She could even manage a bitter laugh when it was over. It had startled Bill. Gaby stuck her head in the door, then vanished when Cirocco did not acknowledge her presence.

"Okay, okay," she said. "I'm over-reacting. It's because I lost my ship and have to make up for it by covering myself with glory. I'm frustrated because I haven't been able to put this crew back together and get it functioning, even to the extent of having the one man I thought I could depend on respect my decisions, shut up, and do what he's told. I am one odd critter; I know that. Maybe I'm too aware of things that would be different if I was a man. You *get* sensitive when you see it happen over and over on your way up, and you have to be twice as good to get the job.

"You disagree with my decision to go up. You have stated your objections. You said you loved me. I don't think you do any more, and I'm very sorry things turned out this way. But I order you to wait here until I return, and say no more to me about it."

His mouth was set in an uncompromising line.

"It's because I love you that I don't want you to go."

"My God, Bill, I don't want that kind of love. 'I love you, so hold still while I tie you down.' What hurts is that it's you doing it. If you can't have me as my own woman, able to make my own decisions and take care of myself, you can't have me at all."

"What kind of love is that?"

She felt like crying, but knew she didn't care.

"I wish I knew. Maybe there's no such thing. Maybe one has to be taken care of by the other, which means I'd better start looking for a man who'll be dependent on me because I won't have it the other way. Can't we just care for each other? I mean when you're weak I help out, and when I'm weak you support me."

"It looks like you're never weak. You just said you can take care of yourself."

"Any human being should. But if you think I'm not weak, you don't know me. I'm like a little baby right now, wondering if you're going to let me leave here without a kiss, without even wishing me good luck."

Damn it, there went a tear. She wiped at it quickly, not wanting him to accuse her of using tears as a weapon. How do I get in these no-win situations? she wondered. Strong or weak, she would always be on the defensive about it.

He relented enough for a kiss. There seemed little to say when they moved apart. Cirocco could not tell what his reaction was to her dry eyes. She knew he was hurt, but did that hurt him more?

"You come back as soon as you can."

"I will. Don't worry too much about me. I'm too mean to kill."

"Don't I know it."

"Two hours, Gaby. Tops."

"I know, I know. Don't talk about it, okay?"

Whistlestop looked even larger than before, sitting on

the flat plain to the east of Titantown. Ordinarily the blimp never came lower than treetop level. It had been necessary for all the fires in town to be extinguished to persuade him to come to ground.

Cirocco looked back at Bill, standing on his crutches beside the pallet the Titanides had used to carry him out. He waved, and she waved back.

"I take it back, Rocky," Gaby said, teeth chattering. "Talk to me."

"Easy, girl, easy. Open your eyes, will you? Watch where you're going. Oops!"

A dozen animals had queued up inside the blimp's stomach, like subway passengers impatient to get home. They tumbled over each other getting out. Gaby was knocked down.

"Help me, Rocky?" She said it desperately, risking only one quick glance up at Cirocco.

"Sure." She tossed her pack to Calvin, who was already inside with Gene, and lifted the other woman. Gaby was so tiny, and so cold.

"Two hours."

"Two hours," Gaby repeated, dully.

There was a quick pounding of hooves, and Hornpipe appeared at the open sphincter. She grabbed Gaby's arm.

"Here, small one," she sang. "This will help you through your troubles." She pressed a wineskin into Gaby's hand.

"How did you know..." Cirocco began.

"I saw the fear in her eye and remembered the service she did me. Did I do right?"

"You did marvelously, my child. I thank you for her." She didn't tell Hornpipe about the wineskin in her own pack, brought along for just that purpose.

"I will not kiss you again, since you say you will return. Good fortune to you, and may Gaea spin you back to us."

"Good fortune." The opening closed silently.

"What did she say?"

"She wants you to get blasted."

"I already had a drink or ten. But now that you mention it..."

Cirocco stayed with her as she succumbed to a

screaming fit, feeding her wine until she was on the verge of unconsciousness. When she was sure Gaby would be all right, she joined the men at the front of the gondola.

They were already in the air. Water ballast was still spilling from a hole near Whistlestop's nose.

Soon they were skimming the upper surface of the cable. Looking down, Cirocco saw trees and areas of grass. Parts of the cable were completely overgrown. The thing was so large that it looked almost like a flat strip of land. There would be no danger of falling until they reached the roof.

The light slowly began to fail. In ten minutes they were in orange-tinted dusk, heading for eternal night. Cirocco was sad to see the light go. She had cursed it for being so unvarying, but at least it was light. She would not see it again for some time.

She might not ever see it again.

"This is the end of the line," Calvin said. "He'll bring you in a little lower and put you down by cable. Good luck, you crazy fools. I'll be waiting for you."

Gene helped Cirocco get Gaby into her harness, then went first to hold her when she reached the ground. Cirocco watched from above until it was done, then got a kiss for luck from Calvin. She settled her own harness around her hips and let her feet drop over the edge.

She descended into the twilight zone.

Chapter Nineteen

They felt lighter when they landed on the cable, being
about one hundred kilometers nearer the center of
Gaea—and one hundred long kilometers from her floor.
The gravity had dropped from almost one quarter gee to
less than a fifth. Cirocco's pack weighed nearly two kilos
less, and her body weight had decreased by two and a half.

"It's a hundred kilometers to where the cable joins the
roof," Cirocco said. "I'd say it's a thirty-five-degree slope
here. It should be easy enough for now."

Gene looked skeptical.

"More like forty degrees, I'd say. Closer to forty-five.
And it gets steeper. Say sixty degrees before we reach the
level of the roof."

"But in this gravity—"

"Don't laugh at a forty-degree slope," Gaby said. She
was sitting on the ground, looking green but cheerful. She
had thrown up, but said anything was better than being in
the blimp. "I've done some climbing on Earth with a
telescope strapped to my back. You've got to be in good
shape, and we're not."

"She's right," Gene said. "I've lost weight. Low gravity makes you lazy."

"You people are defeatists."

Gene shook his head. "Just don't think we're going to get a five to one advantage. And don't forget that pack masses almost as much as you do. Be careful with it."

"Hell, we set out on the longest mountain climb ever attempted by human beings; do I hear singing? No, nothing but grousing."

"If there's songs to be sung," Gaby said, "we'd better sing 'em now. We ain't gonna feel like it later."

Well, Cirocco thought, I tried. She was aware the trip was going to be hard, but felt the hard part would not begin until they reached the roof, which she thought they could do in five days.

They were in a dim forest. Trees of cloudy glass loomed over them, further filtering what light reached the twilight zone, giving everything a bronze hue. Shadows were conical and impenetrable, pointing the way east, toward night. A canopy of pink, orange, blue-green, and gold cellophane leaves arched overhead: an extravagant sunset late in a summer evening.

The ground vibrated softly beneath their feet. Cirocco thought about the huge volumes of air rushing through the cable on its way to the hub, and wished there was some way of putting that immense power to use.

It was not difficult climbing. The ground was hard, smooth, packed dirt. The shape of the land was dictated by the winding of the strands under the thin layer of soil. It humped in long ridges that, after a few hundred meters, could be seen angling toward the sloping sides of the cable.

The vegetation grew most thickly where the dirt was deepest, between the strands. They adopted the tactic of following a ridge until it began to curl under the cable, then crossing a shallow gully to the next strand to the south. That would be good for another half kilometer, then they would cross again.

Each gully had a small stream at the bottom. None held more than a trickle, but the water flowed swiftly and cut deep channels in the dirt, all the way down to the cable.

Cirocco guessed the streams must fall right off the cable somewhere to the southwest.

Gaea was as prolific up here as she was on the ground. Many of the trees bore fruit, and they were alive with arboreal animals. Cirocco recognized a sluggish, rabbit-sized creature that was edible and easy to kill.

By the end of the second hour Cirocco realized the others had been right. She knew it when a cramp seized her calf and sent her sprawling on the warm ground.

"Don't say it, damnit."

Gaby grinned. She was sympathetic, but still pleased with herself.

"It's the slope. It doesn't feel all that hard to go up it; you're right about the weight. But it's so steep you have to do it on your toes."

Gene sat beside them, his back to the slope. Through a rift in the trees, they could just see a patch of Hyperion, shining bright and attractive.

"The mass is a problem, too," he said. "I've had to walk with my nose just about touching the ground to get moving at all."

"My arches hurt," Gaby confirmed.

"Me, too," Cirocco said, miserably. The pain was going away now as she massaged her leg, but it would be back.

"It's damn deceptive," Gene said. "Maybe we'd do better on all fours. We're making our thighs and the backs of our legs do too much of the work. We should spread it out some."

"He's got a point. And it would help us get in shape for the straight-up part. That's going to be mostly arm work."

"You're both right," Cirocco said. "I was pushing too hard. We're going to have to stop more often. Gene, would you get that medical kit out of my pack?"

There were various remedies for sniffles and fevers, vials of disinfectant, bandages, a supply of the topical anaesthetic Calvin had used for the abortions—even a bag of berries that worked as a stimulant. Cirocco had tried them. There was a first-aid booklet Calvin had written that told how to deal with problems from a bloody nose to an amputation. And there was a round jar of violet salve Meistersinger had given her for "the pains of the road." She rolled up her pants leg and rubbed some on, hoping it would work as well for humans as it did for Titanides.

"Ready?" Gene was up, adjusting his pack.

"I think so. You take the lead. Don't go as fast as I was; I'll tell you if you're going too fast for me. We're going to stop in twenty minutes, rest for ten."

"You got it."

Fifteen minutes later Gene was in pain. He howled, ripped off his boot, and massaged his bare foot.

Cirocco was glad for the chance to rest. She stretched out and dug into a pocket for the jar of ointment, then rolled over on her back and handed it up-slope to Gene. With the pack under her she sat almost erect, but with her legs trailing down the slope. Beside her, Gaby had not bothered to turn over.

"Fifteen minutes up, and fifteen minutes resting."

"Anything you say, boss lady," Gaby sighed. "I'll flay myself alive for you, I'll climb till my hands and feet are bloody wrecks. And when I die, just write on my tombstone that I died like a soldier. Kick me when you're ready to go." She began snoring loudly, and Cirocco laughed. Gaby opened one eye suspiciously, then laughed, too.

"How about 'Here lies a spacewoman'?" Cirocco suggested.

"'She done her duty,'" Gene said.

"Honestly," Gaby sniffed. "Where's the romance in life? Tell somebody your epitaph and what do you get? Jokes."

Cirocco's next cramp came during the following rest period. Cramps, actually, as both legs were involved this time. There was nothing funny about it.

"Hey, Rocky," Gaby said, touching her shoulder hesitantly. "There's no sense killing ourselves. Let's take an hour this time."

"This is *ridiculous*," Cirocco managed to grunt. "I'm barely winded. It just doesn't feel right to sit on my butt." She looked at Gaby suspiciously. "How come *you* don't get cramps?"

"I'm slacking," Gaby admitted, with a straight face. "I hitch a rope to that butt you don't want to sit on, and let you do the donkey work."

Cirocco had to laugh, though weakly.

"I'll just have to live with it," she said. "Sooner or later I'll be in better shape. Cramps won't kill me."

"No. I just hate to see you hurt."

"How about ten up, twenty down?" Gene suggested. "Just until we start to work ourselves into something more."

"No. We go up for fifteen minutes, or until one of us can't go on, whichever is sooner. Then we rest the same time, or until we're all able to climb. We do that for eight hours..." She checked her watch. "That's a little more than five hours from now. Then we make camp."

Gaby sighed. "Lead on, Rocky. That's what you're good at."

It was gruesome. Cirocco continued to have the greatest share of pains, though Gaby began to experience them, too.

The Titanide salve helped, but they had to use it sparingly. Each of them packed a medical kit, and they had already gone through Cirocco's supply. She hoped they would not be needing it past the first few days of the journey, but wanted to retain at least one jar for the climb up the inside of the spoke. After all, it was not unbearable pain. When it grabbed her she was likely to yelp, then sit down and wait for it to pass.

At the end of the seventh hour she relented, feeling a little chagrined at her own stubbornness. It was almost as if she had been trying to prove Bill was right, forcing herself to be tough, to go to the limits of her endurance and then a little beyond.

They made camp at the bottom of a gully, gathering wood for a fire but not bothering to set up their tents. The air was hot and muggy, but the fire was a welcome light in the increasing gloom. They sat around it at a comfortable distance, stripped down to their gaudy silken under-clothes.

"You look like a peacock," Gene said, taking a drink from his wineskin.

"A very tired peacock," Cirocco sighed.

"How far do you think we've come, Rocky?" Gaby asked.

"It's hard to say. Fifteen kilometers?"

"I'll go along with that," Gene said, nodding. "I counted steps along a couple ridges and averaged it. Then I kept track of the number of ridges we crossed."

"Great minds think alike," Cirocco said. "Fifteen today, twenty tomorrow. We'll be at the roof in five days." She stretched out and watched the shifting colors of the leaves overhead.

"Gaby, you're elected. Dig into that sack and rustle us up some grub. I could eat a Titanide."

They did not make twenty kilometers the next day; they did not make ten.

They woke with sore legs. Cirocco was so stiff she could not bend her knees without wincing. They stumbled around fixing breakfast and breaking camp, moving like octogenarians, then forced themselves through a series of kneebends and isometrics.

"I know this pack is a few grams lighter," Gaby moaned, as she slung it on her back. "I ate two meals out of it."

"Mine's gained twenty kilos," Gene said.

"Bitch, bitch, bitch. C'mon, you apes. You wanna live forever?"

"Live? This is living?"

The second night came only five hours after the first because Cirocco decided it had to.

"Thank you, o Great Mistress of Time," Gaby sighed, as she stretched out on her sleeping bag. "If we try, maybe we can set a new record. A two-hour day!"

Gene let himself down beside her.

"When you get the fire going, Rocky, I'll take about five of those steakplant fillets. In the meantime, walk softly, will you? When your knees crack you wake me up."

Cirocco put her hands on her hips and glared at them.

"So that's how it's going to be, huh? I've got news for you two. I outrank you."

"Did she say something, Gene?"

"Didn't hear a word."

Cirocco limped around until she had gathered enough wood for a fire. Kneeling to start it turned out to be a very complex problem, one she was not sure she could solve. It involved wrenching abused joints through angles they just did not want to take.

But after a time the steakplants were snapping in the grease, and Gene and Gaby followed their noses to the source of the heavenly aroma.

Cirocco had just enough strength to kick dirt over the coals and unroll her sleeping bag. She was asleep on her way to it.

The third day was not as bad as the second, in the same way the Chicago Fire was not as bad as the San Francisco Earthquake.

They made ten kilometers over gradually steepening ground in just under eight hours. Gaby remarked at the end of it that she no longer felt eighty years old. She now felt seventy-eight.

It became necessary to use a new climbing tactic. The increasing slope of the ground made walking, even on all fours, more difficult. Their feet would slip and they would go down on their stomachs with arms and legs spread to prevent a backward slide.

Gene suggested they alternately take one end of the rope and crawl up as far as it would reach, then tie the end to a tree. The other two, waiting at the bottom, then had an easy hand-over-hand pull and walk. The one who went ahead worked hard for ten minutes while the other two rested, then could rest for two turns before going again. They made 300 meters at a time.

Cirocco looked at the stream near their third campsite and thought about taking a bath, then decided against it. Food was what she wanted. Gene, with some grumbling, took his turn at the frying pan.

She actually felt good enough to look through her pack and check the level of stored provisions before collapsing.

The fourth day they made twenty kilometers in ten hours, and at the end of the day Gene grabbed Cirocco.

They had pitched camp where the stream they were following was wide enough for a bath, and Cirocco had taken off her clothes and lowered herself in without even thinking about it. Soap would have been nice, but there was fine sand on the bottom and she could scour herself with that. Soon Gaby and Gene joined her. Later, Gaby went off on Cirocco's instructions to find fresh fruit. There were no towels, so she was squatting naked by the fire when Gene put his arms around her.

She jumped, scattering burning twigs, and pushed his hands away from her breasts.

"Hey, stop that." She struggled, and broke away.

He was not at all abashed.

"Come on, Rocky, it's not like we've never touched each other before."

"Yeah? Well, I don't like people sneaking up on me. Keep your hands to yourself."

He looked exasperated. "Is it going to be like that? What am I supposed to do with two naked women running around?"

Cirocco reached for her clothes.

"I didn't know the sight of naked women made you lose control of yourself. I'll bear it in mind."

"Now you're angry."

"No, I'm not angry. We're going to have to live close for some time, and it wouldn't do to get angry." She pressed the fasteners of her shirt and eyed him warily for a moment, then repaired the fire, careful to sit facing him.

"You're angry anyway. I didn't mean anything by it."

"Just don't grab me, is all."

"I'd send you roses and candy, but it's a little impractical."

She smiled, and relaxed a little. It sounded more like the old Gene, which was an improvement over what she had seen in his eyes a moment ago.

"Listen, Gene. We didn't make the greatest pair back on the ship, and you know it. I'm tired, I'm hungry, and I still feel dirty. All I can say is, if I feel ready for anything, I'll let you know."

"Fair enough."

Neither of them said anything as Cirocco built the fire bigger, carefully keeping it on the little shelf they had dug into the dirt.

"Are you . . . do you and Gaby have something going?"

She flushed, hoping it wasn't visible in the firelight.

"That's none of your business."

"I always thought she was gay underneath," he said, nodding. "I didn't think you were."

She took a deep breath and looked at him narrowly. The darting shadows revealed nothing on his blond-bearded face.

"Are you deliberately needling me? I said it was none of your business."

"If you weren't queer for her, you'd have just said no."

What was the matter with her? she wondered. Why was he making her skin crawl? Gene had always operated by his own bonehead logic when it came to people. His bigotry was carefully suppressed and socially acceptable, or he would never have been chosen for the trip to Saturn. He blundered cheerfully through his relationships, genuinely surprised when people took offense at his tactlessness. It was a common-enough personality, so well controlled, according to his psychological profile, as to barely qualify as an eccentricity.

So why did she feel so uncomfortable when he looked at her?

"I'd better set you straight so you don't hurt Gaby. She's fallen in love with me. It has something to do with the isolation; I was the first person she saw afterward, and she developed this fixation. I think she'll grow out of it because she's never been significantly homosexual before. Nor heterosexual, for that matter."

"She covered it up," he suggested.

"What year is this? Nineteen-fifty? You astonish me, Gene. You don't hide anything from those NASA tests. She had a homosexual affair, sure. I had one, and so did you. I read your dossier. You want me to tell you how old you were when it happened?"

"I was just a kid. The point is, I could tell about her when we made love. No reaction, you know? I'll bet it's not like that when you two make it."

"We don't—" She stopped herself, wondering how she had been drawn in as far as she was.

"This conversation is over. I don't want to talk about it, and besides, Gaby's coming back."

Gaby approached the fire and dropped a net full of fruit at Cirocco's side. She squatted, looked thoughtfully back and forth between the two of them, then stood up and put on her clothes.

"Are my ears burning, or is it my imagination?"

Neither Gene nor Cirocco spoke, and Gaby sighed.

"Here we go again. I think I'm starting to agree with the folks who say manned space missions cost more than they're worth."

The fifth day took them irrevocably into night. There was now only the ghostly light reflected by the day areas curving up on each side. It was not much, but it was enough.

The ground was noticeably steeper, with a thinner layer of dirt. Often they walked on the warm, bare strands, which provided surer traction. They began tying themselves together, and were careful to see that two were always hanging on while the other climbed.

Even here the plant life of Gaea had not given up. Massive trees splayed roots flat to the cable, sending out runners that scrambled into the surface and hung on tenaciously. The effort of wresting a living from such uninviting terrain had robbed them of beauty. They were gaunt and lonely, their trunks translucent with a pale inner light, their leaves the merest wisps of nothing. In places, the roots could be used as ladders.

At the end of the day they had come seventy kilometers

in a straight line, and were fifty kilometers nearer the hub. The trees had thinned enough for them to see they had climbed above the level of the roof, well on their way into the narrowing wedge of space between the cable and the bell-shaped mouth of the Rhea spoke. They could look back and see Hyperion spread out below, as though they rode on a kite tied to a monster string tethered in the rocky knot called the place of winds.

They saw the glitter of the glass castle early on the sixth day. Cirocco and Gaby crouched in a tangle of tree roots and scanned it as Gene carried the rope to the foot of the structure.

"Maybe that's the place," Cirocco said.

"You mean your elevator lobby?" Gaby snorted. "If that's it, I'd as soon ride a roller coaster with paper rails."

It looked something like an Italian hill town, but made of spun sugar, a million years old, and half melted. Domes and balconies, arches, flying buttresses, battlements, and terraced roofs perched on a jutting shelf and dripped over the edge like syrup poured over a waffle and quick-frozen. Tall towers jutted at all angles: pencils in a cup. They were tall and spindly. In the corners, drifts of snow or pastel confectioner's sugar sparkled.

"It's a hulk, Rocky."

"I can see that. Let me have my fantasy, will you?"

The castle fought a silent battle with wispy white vines. It looked like a stand-off; the castle had taken mortal damage, but when they joined Gene, Cirocco and Gaby heard the vines giving off the dry rustle of death.

"Like Spanish moss," Gaby observed, tugging a handful free of the entangling mass.

"But bigger."

Gaby shrugged. "If Gaea can't build it in the large economy size, she doesn't bother."

"There's a door up here," Gene called back. "You want to go in?"

"You bet."

There was five meters of level space between the edge of the shelf and the castle wall. Not far from them was a

rounded arch, not much taller than the top of Cirocco's head.

"Whew!" Gaby breathed, leaning against the wall. "Walking on level ground is almost enough to make you dizzy. I'd forgotten how."

Cirocco lit a lamp and followed Gene through the arch and into a hall of glass.

"We'd better stick together," she said.

There seemed good reason for the caution. While none of the surfaces were completely reflective, the place had a lot in common with the mirror houses at carnivals. They could see through the walls to rooms on all sides of them, which also had glass walls leading to more rooms.

"How do we get out, once we're in?" Gaby asked.

Cirocco pointed down. "Follow our footprints."

"Ah. How silly of me." Gaby bent and looked at the fine powder coating the floor. There were larger, flat sheets scattered through it.

"Ground glass," she said. "Don't fall down."

Gene shook his head. "I thought so at first, too, but it's not glass. It's thin as a soap bubble, and it won't hold an edge." He picked a wall and pressed it gently with the palm of his hand. It shattered with a soft tinkling sound. He caught one of the pieces that drifted down around him and crushed it in his hand.

"How many of those walls could you break before the second floor falls on us?" Gaby asked, pointing at the room above them.

"A lot, I think. Look, this place is a maze, but it wasn't originally. We walk through some of the walls because something broke them already. But this was a stack of cubes, with no way in or out of any of them."

Gaby and Cirocco looked at each other.

"Like the building we looked at under the cable," Cirocco said, for both of them. She described it to Gene.

"Who makes buildings with rooms you can't get in or out of?" Gaby asked.

"The chambered nautilus does," Gene said.

"Say again?"

"The nautilus. It makes its shell in a spiral. When the

shell gets too small, it moves up and seals off part of the shell in back. You cut them in half, they're very pretty. It sounds a lot like the building you saw; little rooms on the bottom, big ones on top."

Cirocco frowned. "But all these rooms look about the same size."

Gene shook his head. "The difference isn't great. This room is a little taller than the one over there. There'll be smaller rooms somewhere else. These things built sideways."

The picture that emerged of the creatures that built the glass castle was of something that worked like sea corals. The colony abandoned houses as they outgrew them, building on the remains. Parts of the castle towered ten levels or more. Structural strength came from the tissue-thin walls but from the interstices that made up the edges. They were like clear lucite bars, thick as Cirocco's wrist, very hard and strong. If all the walls in the castle had been broken out, the outline would have remained, like the steel underpinnings of a skyscraper.

"Whoever built it wasn't the last to use it," Gaby suggested. "Somebody moved in and made a lot of modifications, unless these creatures were considerably more sophisticated than what we decided. But either way, everybody's long gone."

Cirocco tried not to be disappointed, but it didn't do any good. It was a letdown. They were still far from the top, and it looked like they would have to climb every meter.

"Don't be angry."

"What's that?" Cirocco came awake slowly. Hard to believe it's been eight hours already, she thought.

But how did he know? She had the watch.

"Don't look at it." It was said in the same even tone, but Cirocco froze with her arm half raised. She saw Gene's face, orange in the dying firelight. He was kneeling over her.

"Why... what is it, Gene? Is something wrong?"

"Just don't be angry. I didn't mean to hurt her, but I

couldn't very well let her watch, could I?"

"Gaby?" She started to rise, and he let her see the knife. In the heightened awareness of the moment, she saw several things: Gene was naked; Gaby was lying face down, nude, and did not seem to be breathing; Gene had an erection. There was blood on his hands. Her senses sharpened to a keen edge. She could hear his even breathing, smell blood and violence.

"Don't be angry," he said, reasonably. "I didn't want to do it this way, but you forced me."

"All I said was—"

"You're angry, I can tell." He sighed at the unfairness of it all and produced a second knife—Gaby's—in his left hand. "If you think about it, you have yourself to blame. What do you think I'm made of? You women. Do your mothers tell you to be selfish? Is that it?"

Cirocco tried to think of a safe answer, but he apparently didn't want one. He moved over her and put the tip of a knife under her chin. She flinched; the tip bit into the soft flesh. It was colder than his eyes.

"I don't understand why you're doing this."

He hesitated. The second knife had been moving in the direction of her belly; now he stopped with it just out of her sight. She licked her lips and wished she could see it again.

"That's a fair question. I've always thought about it—what man doesn't?" He searched her eyes for understanding, looked forlorn when he did not find it. "Ah, what's the use? You're a girl."

"Try." The knife was moving again. She felt it press flat against the inside of her thigh. Sweat broke out on her forehead. "You don't have to do it this way. Put the knife down, and I'll give you anything you want."

"Ah-ah." There was the knife again, waggling back and forth like a mother's admonishing finger. "I'm not a stupid man. I know how you women work."

"I swear. It doesn't have to be this way."

"It does. I've killed Gaby, and you won't forgive that. It never was fair, you know. You tantalize us all the time. We're always horny, and you're always saying no." He was sneering, but the expression quickly vanished to be replaced once again by calmness. She had liked the sneer better.

"I'm just evening things out. Back when you people left me alone in the dark I decided I'd do what I please. I made friends in Rhea. You're not going to like them much. I'm the Captain from now on, like I should have been in the first place. You'll do what I say. Now don't do anything stupid."

She gasped as the sharp point of the knife tore her pants. She thought she knew what he was about to use the knife for, and wondered if she'd rather be stupid and dead than alive and mutilated. But once the pants were gone he cut no further. Her attention returned to the knife under her chin.

He entered her. She turned her face away and the knife point followed. It hurt like hell, but that was not important. What mattered was the twitch in Gaby's cheek, the trail her hand had made through the dust while moving closer to the hatchet, her half-open eye and the gleam in it.

Cirocco looked up at Gene and had no trouble putting fear into her voice.

"Don't! Oh, please, don't, I'm not ready. You'll kill me!"

"You're ready when I say you are." He lowered his head and Cirocco risked a glance at Gaby, who seemed to understand. Her eye closed.

It all happened far away. She had no body, that was someone else who was hurting so badly. Only the knife point at her chin had meaning, until he began to tire.

What would the price of his failure be? she wondered. Right. Then he can't fail. A moment would come when his attention would waver, but she had to insure that moment arrived. She began to move under him. It was the most disgusting thing she had ever done.

"Now we see the truth," he said, with a dreamy smile.

"Don't talk, Gene."

"You got it. See how much better it is when you don't fight?"

Was it her imagination, or was her skin not quite so taut under the knife? Had it pulled back? She tasted the thought, careful not to fool herself, and decided it was true. She had acquired an exquisite sensitivity. The slight easing of pressure was like the lifting of a great weight.

He would have to close his eyes. Didn't they always close their eyes?

He closed them and she almost moved, but he opened them again, quickly. Testing her, damn it. But he saw no deception. Normally she was a lousy actress, but the knife had inspired her.

His back arched. His eyes closed. The knife pressure was gone.

Nothing went right.

She slapped his arm one way, turned her head the other; the knife cut the side of her cheek. She punched at his throat, meaning to crush it, but he moved just enough. She twisted, kicked, felt the knife slash her shoulder blade. Then she was up—

—but not running. Her feet did not touch the ground for agonizing seconds while she waited for the knife to bite.

It did not, and she got enough of a toehold to bound into the air again and start away from him. She glanced over her shoulder while in the air and realized her kick had been stronger than she imagined. It had lifted him from the ground and he was only now touching again. Gaby was still in the air. Adrenalin was causing Earth muscles to behave madly in the low gravity.

The chase took forever to get going, but picked up speed rapidly.

She didn't think he knew Gaby was behind him. He would never have pursued Cirocco so single-mindedly if he had seen seen Gaby's face.

They had camped in the castle's central plaza, a level area the builders had never subdivided. The fire was twenty meters from the first gallery of rooms. Cirocco was still accelerating when she hit the first wall. She never broke stride, smashing a dozen of them before reaching up to grab one of the girders. She swung through a ninety-degree turn and rose, tumbling, through three ceilings before stopping in the air. She heard crashes as Gene blundered on, not understanding her maneuver.

She put her feet on a girder and pushed up again. She rose, a cloud of glass shards ascending with her, twisting and turning in dreamy slow motion. She leaped to the side and went through three walls before stopping. She broke through to her left, went up another floor, then over and down through two more.

She stopped, crouching on a girder, and listened.

There was the far-off tinkle of breaking glass. It was dark. She was in the middle of a chambered maze that stretched to infinity in all directions: up, down, and sideways. She didn't know where she was, but neither did he, and that was the way she wanted it.

The crashing grew louder and she saw Gene sail up through the room to her left. She dived right and down, catching a girder two floors below and diverting her momentum to the right again. She came to rest, her bare feet on another girder. Around her, broken glass settled slowly.

She would not have known he was so close if the shower of glass had not preceded him. He had been walking along the girders, but the weight of part of his foot was too much for an unbroken pane that already supported debris from Cirocco's passage. It shattered, and the glass came down like snowflakes. She swung around the girder and pushed downward with her feet.

She hit hard, and turned, dazed, to see him land on his feet, as she would have done if she had any damn sense and counted floors. She remembered thinking that as he stood over her, then she saw the hatchet hit his head, and she passed out.

She came to her senses suddenly, screaming, which was something she had never done before. She did not know where she was, but she had been back in the belly of the beast, and not alone. Gene was there, explaining calmly why he intended to rape her.

Had raped her. She stopped screaming.

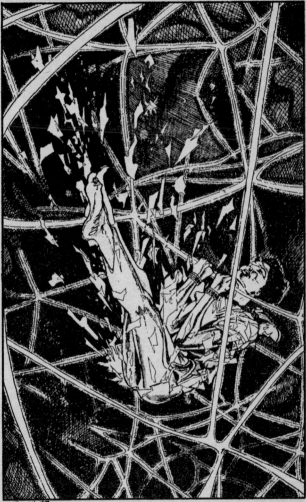

She was not in the glass castle. There was a rope around her waist. The ground sloped down in front of her. Far below was the dark silver sea of Rhea.

Gaby was beside her, but she was quite busy. She had two ropes around her waist. One went up the slope to the same tree Cirocco was attached to. The other hung taut over darkness. Tears had washed a channel through the dried blood on her face. She was using a knife to saw through one of the ropes.

"Is that Gene's pack there, Gaby?"

"Yeah. He won't be needing it. How are you feeling?"

"I've been better. Bring him up, Gaby."

She looked up, her mouth hanging open.

"I don't want to lose the rope."

His face was a bloody wreck. One eye was swollen shut, the other merely a slit. His nose was broken and three of his front teeth were gone.

"Quite a fall he took," Cirocco observed.

"Nothing to what I had in mind."

"Open his pack and bandage that ear. He's still losing blood."

Gaby was building toward an explosion, but Cirocco cut her off with an unwavering stare.

"I'm not going to kill him, so don't suggest it."

His ear had been severed by Gaby's hatchet throw. That had been unintentional on her part; she had meant to plant it in the side of his head, but it had turned in the air and hit him a glancing blow powerful enough to knock him out. He moaned while Gaby bandaged him.

Cirocco began rummaging through his pack, taking things they could use. She kept the provisions and the weapons, threw everything else over the side.

"If we let him live, he's going to follow us, you know that."

"He might, and I could definitely do without it. He'll have to go over the edge."

"Then why the hell am I—"

"With his chute. Untie his legs."

She fitted the harness around his crotch. He moaned

again, and she looked away from what Gaby had done to him there.

"He thought he killed me," she was saying, tying the last knot on the bandages. "He meant to, but I turned my head."

"How bad is it?"

"Not deep, but bloody as hell. I was stunned, and it's lucky I was too weak to move after what he ... after ..." Her nose was running, and she wiped it on the back of her hand. "I passed out pretty quick. The next thing I knew he was bending over you."

"I'm glad you woke up when you did. I made a mess of my escape. And thank you for saving my ass again."

Gaby looked at her bleakly, and Cirocco was immediately sorry about her choice of words. Gaby seemed to feel personally responsible for what had happened. It couldn't be easy, Cirocco thought to lie still while someone you love is being violated.

"Why are you letting him live?"

Cirocco looked down at him, and fought through a sudden burning rage until she felt in control again.

"I ... you know he was never like this before."

"I do *not* know it. He was always a fucking animal underneath, or how could he have done it?"

"We all are. We suppress it, but he can't anymore. He talked to me like a little boy who's hurt—not angry, just hurt—because he's not been getting his way. Something happened to him after the crash, just like something happened to me. And you."

"But we didn't try to kill anyone. Listen, let him parachute down. That's okay. But I think he ought to leave his balls up here." She hefted the knife, but Cirocco shook her head.

"No. I never liked him much, but we got along. He was a good crewman, and now he's insane, and ..." She was going to say it was partly her responsibility, that he would never have gone insane if she had kept her ship in one piece, but she could not get it out.

"I'm giving him a chance because of what he was. He said he had friends down there. Maybe he was just raving, or maybe they'll take him in. Cut his hands free."

Gaby did, and Cirocco gritted her teeth and pushed him with her foot. He began to slide, and seemed to become aware of his surroundings. He screamed as the parachute trailed out behind him, then vanished around the curve of the cable.

They never saw if it opened.

The two women sat there for a long time. Cirocco was afraid to say anything. There was the possibility she would start crying and be unable to stop, and there was no time for it. There were wounds to care for, and a trip to finish.

Gaby's head was not bad. It should have had stitches, but the disinfectant and a bandage was all they could do. She would have a scar on her forehead.

So would Cirocco, from her impact with the castle floor. There would also be one from the point of her chin to her left ear, and another across her back. None of the cuts were serious enough to worry her.

They tended each other and loaded their packs, and Cirocco looked up at the long stretch of the cable yet to climb before they reached the spoke.

"I think we should go back to the castle and rest before we tackle it," she said. "A couple days. Get our strength."

Gaby looked up.

"Oh, sure. But the next part's going to be easier. Bringing you two down here, I found a stairway."

Chapter Twenty

The stairway emerged from a heap of sand at the uppermost border of the glass castle and went straight as an arrow until it could no longer be seen. Each step was a meter and a half wide and forty centimeters high, and appeared to have been carved into the face of the cable.

After Cirocco and Gaby had followed it for a time, they began to think it might actually do them little good. It was curving to the south, toward the drop-off. Before long it would surely be impassable.

But the steps remained perfectly level. Soon they were walking on a terraced shelf with a huge wall rising on one side and a sheer drop on the other. There was no handrail, no protection at all. They pressed close to the wall, and trembled with every gust of wind.

Then the shelf began to turn into a tunnel.

It was a gradual thing. There was still open space on the right, but the wall had begun to curl over their heads. The path was curving under the cable.

Cirocco tried to visualize it: always rising, but corkscrewing around the outside of the cable.

After another 2000 steps, they were in pitch blackness.

"Stairs," Gaby muttered. "They build a thing like this, and they put in stairs." They had stopped to get out their lamps. Gaby filled hers and trimmed the wick. They would burn one at a time and hope there was enough oil to get them out the other side.

"Maybe they were health nuts," Cirocco suggested. She struck a match and held it to the wick. "More likely this was an emergency measure, for a loss of power."

"Well, I'm glad they're here," Gaby admitted.

"They were probably here all the way but down lower they're covered with dirt. It means this place has been unattended for a long time. The trees up here must be new mutations."

"Whatever you say." Gaby held the lamp high and looked ahead, then back where she could still see a wedge of light. Her eyes narrowed.

"Look, it's like we're at an angle in the road. It curves along the outside, then it cuts to the left and goes straight in."

Cirocco studied it, and thought Gaby was right.

"It looks like we might be cutting right through the center."

"Oh, yeah? Remember the place of winds? All that air is going through here, someplace."

"If this tunnel led to it, we'd know it already. It would have blown us right off the side."

Gaby looked at the ascending staircase in the flickering lamplight. She sniffed the air.

"It's pretty warm in here. I wonder if it gets hotter?"

"No way to know but by going in."

"Uh-huh." Gaby swayed and the lamp threatened to fall from her fingers. Cirocco put a hand on her shoulder.

"You all right?"

"Yeah, I'm...no, dammit, I'm not." She leaned against the warm corridor wall. "I'm dizzy, and my knees are weak." She held out her free hand and looked at it; it trembled slightly.

"Maybe a day of rest wasn't enough." Cirocco studied her watch, gazed up the corridor, and frowned. "I'd hoped to be out on the other side and back on the top of the cable again before we rested."

"I can make it."

"No," Cirocco decided. "I don't feel so hot myself. The question is do we camp here in the corridor where it's so hot, or go outside?"

Gaby looked back at the drop-off many steps behind them.

"I don't mind a little sweat."

There was something about having a fire, even when the weather was unbearably hot. They did not discuss it; Cirocco took small twigs and moss from Gene's pack and started to build one. Soon she had a small blaze crackling. She fed it like a miser as they went about the mechanical business of setting a meager camp. Sleeping bags were unrolled, pans and knives brought out, provisions searched for the night's food.

We're a good team, Cirocco thought, hunkered down while she watched Gaby dice vegetables into the bubbling remains of last night's stew. Her hands were small and deft, with brown dirt ground into the palms. They could no longer spare water for washing.

Gaby wiped her brow with the back of her hand and glanced up at Cirocco. She smiled—a flickering, tentative thing that broadened when Cirocco smiled back. One eye was nearly covered by a bandage. She dipped the spoon into the stew and slurped noisily.

"Those radish dinguses are best left crunchy," she said. "Give me your plate."

She ladled a generous helping and the two of them sat back, side by side but at arm's length, and ate.

It was delicious. Listening to the small sounds, the pop of the fire and the scraping of spoons on wooden plates, Cirocco was grateful to relax and think of nothing.

"Do you have any more salt?"

Cirocco dug in her pack and found the sack, and also two forgotten sweets, wrapped in yellow leaves. She pressed one into Gaby's hand and laughed when her eyes lit up. She put her own plate down and unwrapped the

chewy, bite-sized confection, held it under her nose and
sniffed. It smelled too good to eat all at once. She bit it in
half, and the flavor of sugared apricots and sweet cream
burst through her mouth.

Gaby was just short of hysterical at Cirocco's
expression of delight. She ate the other half, then began
casting covetous glances at the sweet Gaby had put at her
side, while Gaby tried to keep a straight face.

"If you're keeping that for breakfast, you're going to
have to stay awake all night."

"Oh, don't worry. I just have enough manners to know
dessert is for *after* dinner."

She made the unwrapping last five minutes, then
examined it critically for another five, sputtering
helplessly at Cirocco's antics. Cirocco did a passable
imitation of a cocker spaniel at the dinner table and a
homeless waif looking in the window of the bakery, and
gasped when Gaby finally put it in her mouth.

She was having so much fun that it hurt when she
wondered—while sniffing eagerly with her face close to
Gaby's—if the silliness was wise. Gaby was obviously in
heaven with all the attention; her face was flushed with
laughter and excitement, her eyes sparkled.

Why couldn't she just relax and enjoy it?

She must have let some of her worry show, because
Gaby was immediately serious. She touched Cirocco's
hand and looked at her urgently, then slowly shook her
head. Neither of them dared speak, but Gaby had told her
more plainly than any words she might have said, "You
have nothing to fear from me."

Cirocco smiled, and so did Gaby. They spooned up the
last of the stew, holding the plates close to their mouths
and not worrying about table manners.

But it was not quite the same. Gaby was silent. Soon
her hands began to tremble, and the plate clattered to the
steps. She sat up, gasping and sobbing, and Cirocco's
hand on her shoulder brought her groping blindly. She
drew her knees up and clenched her fists under her chin,
buried her face under Cirocco's neck and wept.

"Oh, I hurt, I hurt so much."

"Then let it out. Cry." She put her cheek on the short,

black hair, very fine and beginning to look tousled, then lifted Gaby's chin and looked for a place to kiss that wasn't covered by bandage. She was going for the cheek but at the last moment, not sure why she did it, she kissed her lips. They were moist, and very warm.

Gaby looked at her for a long moment, sniffed loudly, and put her face back on Cirocco's shoulder. She burrowed into the hollow of her neck, then was still. No shakes, no sobs.

"How are you so strong?" she asked, her voice muffled but very close.

"How are you so brave? You keep saving my life."

Gaby shook her head. "No, I mean it. If I didn't have you to lean on right now, I'd go crazy. And you don't even cry."

"I don't cry easily."

"Rape is easy?" She searched Cirocco's eyes again. "God, I hurt so bad. I hurt from Gene, and I hurt for you. I don't know which is worse."

"Gaby, I'd be willing to make love to you if that would help stop the pain, but I hurt, too. Physically."

Gaby shook her head.

"That's not what I want from you, even if you were feeling great. If you're 'willing,' that's no good. I'm not Gene, and I'd rather keep the hurt than have you like that. It's enough to love you."

What to say, what to say? Stick to the truth, she told herself.

"I don't know if I'll ever love you back. Not that way. But so help me," she hugged Gaby and wiped quickly at her nose, "so help me, you're the best friend I ever had."

Gaby let out her breath with a soft sigh.

"That will have to do, for now." Cirocco thought Gaby was going to cry again, but she didn't. She hugged Cirocco once, briefly, and kissed her neck.

"Life is very hard, isn't it?" she asked in a small voice.

"It is that. Let's get to bed."

They started out on three steps; Gaby stretched on the highest, Cirocco tossing and turning on the next, and the embers of the fire on the step below her.

But Cirocco cried out in the night and woke in utter darkness. Sweat was pouring from her body as she waited for Gene's knife to slash. Gaby pulled her down and held her until the nightmare had passed.

"How long have you been here?" Cirocco asked.

"Since I started to cry again. Thanks for letting me join you."

Liar. But she smiled when she thought it.

It grew hotter for a thousand steps, so hot that the walls could not be touched and the soles of their boots were burning. Cirocco tasted defeat, knowing there had to be at least several thousand more steps before they were in the middle, from which point they might expect it to cool again.

"One thousand more steps," she said. "If we can make it that far. If it's not cooler, we go back and try it on the outside." But she knew the cable was too steep now. The trees had become inconveniently far apart even before they entered the tunnel. The tilt of the cable would reach eighty degrees before they arrived at the spoke. She would be faced with her hypothetical glass mountain, the worst possibility she had imagined when preparing for the trip.

"Whatever you say. Just a minute, I want to take off this shirt. I'm smothering."

Cirocco stripped down, too, and they continued to hike through the furnace.

Five hundred steps later, they put their clothes back on. Three hundred steps beyond that, they opened their packs and got out their coats.

Ice began to form on the walls, and snow crunched underfoot. They donned gloves and pulled up the hoods on their parkas, then stood in lamplight which had become amazingly bright with the white walls to reflect it, watching ice crystals condense from their breaths and looking forward at a corridor that was unquestionably narrowing.

"A thousand more steps?" Gaby suggested.

"You must have read my mind."

The ice soon forced Cirocco to bend her head, then get

on her hands and knees. It quickly grew dark again as
Gaby led with the lamp in front of her. Cirocco paused
and blew on her stiff hands, then got on her belly and
crawled.

"Hey! I'm stuck!" She was pleased to hear no panic in
her voice. It was frightening, but she knew she could get
free if she backed up.

The scrabbling sounds in front of her stopped.

"Okay. I can't turn around here, but it's getting wider.
I'll go ahead and see what it's like. Twenty meters. Okay?"

"Right." She listened to the sounds getting farther
away. The darkness closed in and she had just enough
time to work up a very cold sweat before the light dazzled
her. In a moment Gaby was back. There were ice crystals
on her eyebrows.

"This is the worst spot, right here."

"Then I'll get through. I didn't come this far to end up
like a cork in a bottle."

"It's what you get for eating all those sweets, fatty."

Gaby could not pull her through, so she backed up and
managed to get the brass pick from her pack. They
chipped at the ice and tried it again.

"Breathe *out*," Gaby suggested, and tugged on her
hands. She came through.

Behind them, a flat chunk of ice about a meter long fell
from the roof and skidded noisily toward daylight.

"That must be why this passage is open," Gaby said.
"The cable is flexible. It bends and the ice cracks."

"That and the warm air from behind us. Let's stop
plugging it up, okay? Get moving."

Soon they could stand, and shortly afterward the ice
was just a memory. They took off their coats and
wondered what was next.

The rumbling began 400 steps farther on. It grew
louder until it was easy to imagine huge machines
thrumming just beyond the walls of the tunnel. One of the
walls was hot, but not anything like what they had already
traveled through.

They felt sure it was the sound of the air being sucked
from the place of winds toward some unknown

destination high above. Two thousand more steps brought them beyond it and into another hot region. They hurried through it, not bothering to strip as they knew they were close to the far end of the tunnel. As expected, the heat diminished after reaching a sauna-bath peak that Cirocco estimated at seventy-five degrees.

Gaby was still in the lead, and saw the light first. It was no brighter than it had been on the other side, just a pale silver strip that began on their left and gradually widened until they were standing on a ledge beside the cable. They slapped each other on the back, then started climbing again.

They crossed over the top of the cable, always rising, always trending to the south, over the broad hump and down again on the far side. The cable was completely bare now; no trees, no earth clinging anywhere. It was the first time Gaea had really looked like the machine Cirocco knew it to be: the incredible, massive construct made by beings who might still be alive in the hub. The bare cable was smooth and straight, rising at an angle of sixty degrees now, getting closer to the flaring bottom edge of the spoke. The wedge of space between the cable and the spoke had narrowed to less than two kilometers.

On the south side the stairs entered another tunnel. They thought they were ready for it, but it almost fooled them. They hurried through the first zone of heat and congratulated themselves when they felt the temperature begin to drop again. It reached about fifty degrees, and began to rise once more.

"Damn! It's a different set-up. Let's go!"

"Which way?"

"Back would be just as bad as forward. Move!"

They would have been in danger only if one of them had fallen and hurt herself, but it frightened Cirocco, and reminded her never to take Gaea for granted. She had forgotten the cable was made up of wound strands, and that the path of whatever hot and cold fluids ran through it could be quite complex.

They made it past the zone of vibration which was still

in the center, and through the cold zone, which was not as choked with ice as the first had been, and emerged once again on the north side of the cable.

Across the top, and down into the third tunnel. Through it, and across the top again.

They did that seven more times in two days. It would have been faster but for a delay in the fourth tunnel, which was so choked with ice even Gaby had to chip before she could squeeze through. It took them a frigid eight hours to break a path.

But the next time they reached the south side of the cable, there was no tunnel. The angle of rise was now between eighty and ninety degrees, and the staircase began to wind along the outside of it like the red stripe on a peppermint stick.

Neither wanted to camp on a ledge a meter and a half wide that hung over a drop of 250 kilometers. Cirocco knew she tossed in her sleep and one toss could carry entirely too far. So, though both of them were weary, they kept trudging around and around the outside of the cable, always pressing their left shoulders to the reassuring solidity.

Cirocco did not like what was happening overhead. The nearer they got, the more impossible it looked.

They knew from their observations outside that each spoke was oval in cross-section, fifty kilometers thick one way and slightly less than a hundred the other, before it flared out to join the rim roof. They had just passed through that flaring section, and the spoke walls they could dimly see were nearly vertical. What they had not counted on was the lip that ran all the way around the monstrous bore of the spoke tube. It was easily five kilometers wide.

The cable seemed to enter the lip seamlessly, probably continuing above and traveling on to whatever tied it to the hub. During one of their rest stops they studied the lip, seemingly just above their heads, yet still two kilometers away. It was a massive ceiling to their labors, stretching endlessly until the opening became visible, narrowed by perspective. The opening was forty by eighty kilometers, but to reach it they would have to traverse five kilometers hanging from the underside of the lip.

Gaby looked at Cirocco and raised one eyebrow.

"Don't borrow trouble, Gaea's been good to us so far. Climb, my friend."

And Gaea was good to them again. When they got to the top of the cable there was another tunnel, this one piercing the vast gray roof.

They lit the lamp, noting that there was not much fuel left, and began to climb. The tunnel curved to the left as if the cable was still there, though they could no longer be sure of it. They counted 2000 steps, then 2000 more.

"It occurs to me," Gaby said, "that this could go all the way to the hub. And if you think that's good news, you'd better think again."

"I know, I know. Keep climbing." Cirocco was thinking of lamp fuel, the state of their provisions, and the half-filled waterskins. It was still 300 kilometers to the hub. At three steps to the meter, that made it almost an even million steps yet to go. She looked at her watch and timed their pacing.

They had a rhythm of about two steps per second; just light touches of the toes to push them high enough to touch the next step. The gravity at that level had fallen to almost one eighth—half the already low gravity when they set out.

Two steps per second was half a million seconds of travel time. Eight three three three point three, etc., minutes, 138 hours, or nearly six days. Double that to include rest periods and sleep, at a conservative estimate . . .

"I know what you're thinking," Gaby said, from behind her. "But can we do it in the dark?"

She had hit on the important point. The food could last two weeks. The water might be enough with rationing, but not for coming down.

But the crucial consumable at this stage was lamp fuel. They had no more than a five-hour supply, and no way to get more.

She was still working on it, trying to construct a mathematics that would get them to the top, when they emerged on the floor of the spoke.

Nothing had ever made Cirocco feel smaller. Not O'Neil One, not the stars in space, not the floor of Gaea herself. She could see everything, and her sense of perspective failed utterly.

It was impossible to detect the curvature of the walls. Like an upended horizon, they stretched away from her until suddenly they began to wrap around, making the space look more semi-circular than round.

Everything was bathed in a pale green luminescence. The source of the light was four vertical rows of windows which sent beams slanting down to cross each other in the empty center.

Not quite empty. Running straight as a ruler through the central space were three vertical cables wound together like a braid, and drifting in and out of the light beams were odd, cylindrical clouds that twisted slowly as they watched.

Cirocco recalled thinking of the dark, narrow spaces beneath the cable they had explored as a cathedral. Gaea had exhausted her store of superlatives, but she knew that had only been an abandoned chapel. *This* was the cathedral.

"I thought I'd seen it all by now," Gaby said, quietly, pointing up at the wall behind them. "But a vertical jungle?"

There was no other way to describe it. Clinging to the walls, reaching outward or branching up, the inside of the spoke was crusted with more of the ubiquitous trees. They dwindled, becoming at some indeterminate distance just a smooth carpet of green.

Beyond that was a gray roof.

"Would you say that's 300 kilometers up?"

Gaby squinted, then made a grid with her fingers and calculated with some system of her own.

"It covers the right number of degrees."

"Sit. Let's think on this."

She needed to sit more than she needed to think. Until this moment she had actually thought she could make it. She now saw that delusion had been fostered by an inability to visualize the problem. She could look at it now and she quailed inside. Three hundred kilometers, straight up.

Straight. Up.

She must have been insane.

"First. Does it look like there's any way through that roof?"

Gaby looked, and shrugged.

"Means nothing. There was a way through this, wasn't there? We'd never see it from here."

"Right. But we hoped there would be a ladder to the top. Do you see one?"

"No"

"Right again. I thought those stairs meant a way had been provided to walk to the top, if necessary. Now I think it's likely that a walk to right here, this spot, was all the builders had in mind."

"Maybe." Gaby's eyes had narrowed. "But they must have left a way to get to the hub. Probably these trees weren't meant to be here. They've overgrown everything, like they did on the cable."

"In which case . . ." What?

"We have a hell of a climb ahead," Gaby finished for her. "With all this growth we might never find the entrance. It would probably be easier to locate from the top."

"Right for the third time. I'm just trying to reason it out, you see. It had entered my mind that if—say four or five years from now—if we get to the top and find there isn't a stairway . . . we've got another long climb. Down."

Gaby laughed this time.

"If you're saying let's turn back, I wish you'd come out with it. I won't freeze you with contempt."

"Let's turn back?" She hadn't meant the question mark, but there it was.

"No."

"Ah. I see." She did not mind. They had long forgotten

the relationship of Captain and crew. She laughed, and shook her head. "All right. What's your plan?"

"First look around. Later—four or five years from now—we'd look pretty foolish if one of the builders asked why we didn't use the elevator."

Chapter Twenty-One

It was roughly 250 kilometers around the base of the spoke. They began to circumnavigate it, looking for anything from a rope ladder to an anti-gravity helicopter. What they found was horizontal trees, growing in the vertical forest.

When they penetrated the outer branches and followed the trunks to their roots in the wall, they had to climb a gradual slope made of fallen branches and rotting leaves. The real substance of the spoke was a spongy gray material. It yielded like soft rubber when they pressed it. When Cirocco pulled a bush from the wall, a long taproot came out with it. The wall bled a thick, milky fluid, then closed around the small hole.

There was no soil, and very little sun; bright as it had seemed when they came out of the dark staircase, the real light level was quite low. Cirocco assumed that, like many of the plants on the rim, these depended on sub-surface sources for life.

The wall itself was moist and supported growths of moss and lichen, but few intermediate-sized plants. There were no grasses, and what vines existed were parasitic,

rooting in the tree trunks. Many of the trees were the same species they had seen on the rim, adapted for a horizontal existence. There were familiar fruits and nuts growing on them.

"That takes care of the food problem," Gaby said.

There could be no rivers in the spoke, but the wall glistened with tiny trickles. High above, spouts could be seen, arching out and turning to mist long before they reached the floor.

Gaby looked up at them, noting that they seemed evenly distributed, like lawn sprinklers.

"So much for dying of thirst."

It began to seem that the climb would not actually be impossible. Cirocco found it hard to be elated about it.

Excluding the possibility of a staircase—which she quickly concluded they would not find, since the trees prevented a close exploration of the wall—there were two ways to the top.

One involved climbing the trees themselves. It should be possible, Cirocco reckoned, to go from branch to branch out where spreading had meshed the branches of one tree with those of its neighbors.

The other possibility was a straightforward job of mountaineering. They found that their metal spikes could be driven into the wall surface simply by holding them and jabbing.

Cirocco favored the wall, not wanting to trust the trees. Gaby liked the branches, which would be quicker. They debated it until the second day, when two things happened.

Gaby noticed the first thing while looking out over the gray floor of the spoke. Her eyes narrowed, and she pointed.

"I think that hole's not there anymore," she said.

Cirocco squinted, but could not be sure.

"Let's climb up and take a look."

They roped themselves together and began ascending through the branches.

It was not as bad as Cirocco had feared. Like anything else, there was an optimum way to go about it, and they

quickly discovered what it was. There was a line to pick
between the thicker branches closer to the wall—which
were rock solid, but tended to be too far apart—and the
thinner, more willowy ones farther out, which provided a
thousand places for hands and feet but sagged under their
weight.

"A little farther in," Cirocco called ahead to Gaby, who
had taken the job of scouting the path at the end of a
five-meter tether. "I'd say about two-thirds of the way to
the top of the tree is about right."

"In, top," Gaby said. "You're mixing your directions."

"The bottoms of the trees are in close to the wall. The
tops are out in the air. What could be simpler?"

"Suits me."

After climbing through ten trees they began to work
their way out to the top of the last one.

When the branches they walked on began to bend, they
tied a line to a strong one. Now the sag worked to their
advantage, as it opened a window in an otherwise
impenetrable wall of foliage. They had chosen a tree that,
in a horizontal forest, would have towered above its
neighbors. In the spoke it had to be content with jutting
further from the wall.

"You were right. It's gone."

"No, I wasn't. But it will be in a minute."

Cirocco saw what was left of the hole. It was a tiny
black oval in the gray floor, and she could see it
contracting like the iris of an eye. From below, the only
time they had a good look at it, that hole had been nearly
as large as the spoke itself. Now it was less than ten
kilometers across, and still closing. Soon it would seal
around the vertical cables that emerged from its center.

"Any ideas?" Gaby asked. "What good does it do to
close the spoke off from the rim?"

"I haven't the faintest idea. I presume it will open
again, though. The angels got through it, they come
through regularly, so it . . ." She paused, and then smiled.

"It's the breath of Gaea."

"Say again?"

"It's what the Titanides call the wind from the east.

Oceanus brings cold weather and the Lament, and Rhea brings hot air and the angels. So you've got a tube 300 kilometers high, with a valve on each end. You could use it as a pump. You could create high and low pressure areas, and use them to move air."

"How would you go about that?" Gaby asked.

"I can think of two ways. Some kind of moveable piston to compress or rarefy the air. I don't see one, and I sure as hell hope there isn't or it'd smear us."

"If there was, it wouldn't have done these trees any good."

"Right. So it's the other method. The walls can expand or contract. Close the bottom valve and open the top one, expand the spoke, and you draw air in from the top. Close the top and open the bottom, put on the big squeeze, and you force it out over the rim."

"Where does the air that comes in the top come from?"

"It's either sucked up through the cables—some of it must be, we saw that—or it comes from the other spokes. They all connect at the top. With a few more valves, you can use the spokes against each other. Open and close a few, and you end up sucking air out of Oceanus, through the hub, and into this spoke. Then open and close some more, and force it down over Rhea. Now if I only knew why the builders thought it was necessary."

Gaby looked thoughtful.

"I think I can give you that. It's something that's bothered me. Why doesn't all the air pool at the bottom, down at the rim? The air's thinner up here, but it's still okay because the air pressure at the rim is higher than Earth-normal. And in low gravity, pressure drops off less quickly. Mars' atmosphere isn't much for instance, but it goes out a long way. Then if you keep the air circulating, it doesn't have time to settle. You can keep adequate air pressure all the way through Gaea."

Cirocco nodded, then sighed.

"All right. You've just disposed of the last objection to the climb. We've got food and water, or at least it looks like we will. Now it looks like we'll have air, too. What do you say we get going?"

"How about exploring the rest of the wall?"

"What's the use? We might already have passed what we're looking for. There's just no way to see it."

"I guess you're right. Okay, lead on."

The climbing was hard work: tedious, and yet requiring full attention. They got better at it as they went along, but Cirocco knew it would never get as easy as the climb up the cable.

The one consolation at the end of the first ten-hour climb was that they were in shape. Cirocco was weary and there was a blister on her left palm, but aside from a slight backache she felt all right. It would be good to sleep. They climbed out to the top of a tree for a look down before making camp.

"Will your system measure a height like that?"

Gaby frowned, and shook her head.

"Not well." She held her hands out, made a square with them, and squinted. "I'd say—*yeow!*"

Cirocco grabbed her under one arm, steadying herself by holding a branch over her head.

"Thanks. What a fall that would have been."

"You had your rope," Cirocco pointed out.

"Yeah, but I don't really want to swing on the end of it." She caught her breath, then looked at the ground again.

"What can I say? It's a hell of a lot farther away than it was, and the ceiling ain't a meter closer. It's going to be that way for a long time."

"Would you say three kilometers is about right?"

"I will if you will."

That meant one hundred climbing days, assuming no trouble. Cirocco moaned softly and looked again, trying to believe it was five kilometers but suspecting it was closer to two.

They went back in and found two branches nearly parallel and two and a half meters apart. They slung their hammocks between them, sat on one branch and ate a cold meal of raw vegetables and fruit, then got into the hammocks and strapped themselves in.

Two hours later, it began to rain.

Cirocco woke to a steady dripping on her face, moved her head, and glanced at her watch. It was darker than it had been when she went to sleep. Gaby was snoring quietly, on her side, her face pressed into the webbing. She would have a sore neck in the morning. Cirocco debated waking her but decided that if she could sleep through the rain she was probably better off.

Before moving her hammock, Cirocco edged out to the top of the tree. She could see nothing but a dim wall of mist and a steady downpour. It was raining much harder toward the center. All they were getting at the campsite was the water which gathered on the outer leaves and ran down the limbs.

When she returned Gaby was awake and the dripping was much worse. They decided moving the hammocks would do no good. They got out a tent and, after ripping a few seams with their knives, converted it to a canopy which they tied above the campsite. They dried as best they could and got back into the wet hammocks. The heat and humidity were terrible, but Cirocco was so tired she quickly fell asleep to the sound of water beating on the tarp.

They woke again, shivering, two hours later.

"One of those nights," Gaby groaned.

Cirocco's teeth chattered as they unpacked coats and blankets, wrapped themselves tightly, and returned to the hammocks. It was half an hour before she felt warm enough to sleep again.

The gentle swaying motion of the trees helped.

Cirocco sneezed, and snow fluttered away. It was very light, very dry snow, and it had drifted into every crevice of her blanket. She sat up, and it avalanched into her lap.

Icicles hung from the edges of the tarp and the ropes that suspended her hammock. There was a constant cracking sound as wind whipped branches up and down, and a constant clatter of ice hitting the frozen tarp. One of her hands was exposed, and it was stiff and chapped as she reached across the gap and prodded Gaby.

"Huh? Huh?" Gaby looked around with one bleary eye, the other held shut by frozen lashes. "Oh, *damn!*" She was racked by coughs.

"Are you okay?"

"Except for a frozen ear, I guess so. What now?"

"Put on everything we have, I guess. Then wait it out."

It was hard to do, sitting in a hammock, but they managed it. There was one disaster as Cirocco fumbled with numb fingers, then saw a glove quickly vanish in the swirling snow beneath them. She cursed for five minutes before recalling they still had Gene's gloves.

Then they waited.

Sleep was impossible. They were warm enough in the layers of clothing and blankets, but they wished for face masks and goggles. Every ten minutes they shook the accumulation of snow from their bodies.

They tried to talk, but the spoke was alive with sound. Cirocco found the minutes stretching into hours as she reclined with the blanket over her face and listened to the wind howling. Over that sound, and much more frightening, was a sound like popping corn. Branches, overloaded with ice, were snapping off as the wind whipped them.

They waited five hours. If anything, the wind grew colder and stronger. A branch snapped near them, and Cirocco listened to it crash through the ice-crusted forest below.

"Gaby, can you hear me?"

"I hear you, Captain. What do we do now?"

"I hate to say it, but we're going to have to move. I want to be on thicker branches. I don't think these will break, but if one breaks above us, we've had it."

"I was just waiting for you to suggest it."

Getting out of the hammocks was a nightmare. Once out of them and standing on the tree limb, it was worse. Their safety ropes were frozen and had to be painstakingly bent and twisted before they could be used. When they began to work their way in, it was strictly one step at a time. They had to attach a second safety line before going back to remove the first, then repeat the process, tying knots with gloved hands or removing the gloves and doing it quickly before their fingers grew numb. They used hammers and picks to chip ice from branches they had to walk on. With all their caution, Cirocco fell twice and Gaby once. Cirocco's second fall resulted in a strained muscle in her back when the safety line stopped her.

After an hour of struggle they reached the main trunk. It was steady and wide enough to sit on. But the wind blew harder than ever with no branches to break its force.

They drove spikes into the tree, lashed themselves to it, and prepared once more to wait it out.

"I hate to bring this up, but I can't feel my toes."

Cirocco coughed for a long time before she could talk. "What do you suggest?"

"I don't know," Gaby said. "I do know we'll freeze to death if we don't do something. We've got to either keep moving, or look for shelter."

She was right, and Cirocco knew it.

"Up, or down?"

"There's the staircase at the bottom."

"It took us a day to get this high, with no ice to complicate things. And it's another two days back to the stairs. If the entrance isn't buried in snow."

"I was about to get to that."

"If we move, we might as well go up. Either way, we'll freeze unless this weather breaks soon. Moving would postpone that a while, I guess."

"That was my thought, too," Gaby said. "But I'd like to try something else, first. Let's go all the way to the wall. Remember earlier you talked about where the angels might live, and you mentioned caves. Maybe there's caves back there."

Cirocco knew the main thing was to become active again, to get the blood flowing. So they crawled along the tree trunk, chipping ice as they went. In fifteen minutes they reached the wall.

Gaby studied it, then braced herself and began attacking the ice with her pick. It fell away to expose the gray substance, but she did not stop chopping. When Cirocco saw what she was doing she joined her with her own pick.

It went well for a while. They hacked a hole half a meter in diameter. The white milk froze as it oozed from the wall, and they chipped that away, too. Gaby was a demon of snow; it caked her clothes and the woolen scarf drawn over her mouth and nose, turned her eyebrows into thick white ledges.

Soon they reached a new layer that was too tough to cut. Gaby attacked it viciously, but eventually conceded she was getting nowhere. She let her hand drop to her side and glared at the wall.

"Well, it was an idea." She kicked disgustedly at the snow that had fallen around them as they worked, shaken down by the vibrations. She looked at it, then craned her neck and stared up into the darkness. She took a step back, grabbing Cirocco's arm to steady herself when she slipped on ice chips.

"There's a darker patch up there," she said, pointing. "Ten . . . no, fifteen meters up. Slightly to the right. See it?"

Cirocco was not sure. She could see several dark places, but none of them looked like a cave.

"I'm going up to take a look."

"Let me do it. You've been working harder."

Gaby shook her head. "I'm lighter."

Cirocco did not argue, and Gaby hammered a spike into the wall as high as she could reach. She tied a rope to it and climbed high enough to hammer in a second spike. When it was secure, she knocked the first one loose and drove it in a meter above the second.

It took her an hour to reach the place. Cirocco shivered below, stamping her feet and shrugging off the showers of ice Gaby sent down around her. Then a dislodged shelf of snow broke over her shoulders and brought her to her knees.

"Sorry about that!" Gaby called down. "But I've got something here. Let me get it cleared and you can come up."

The entrance was barely large enough for Cirocco to squeeze through, even after Gaby had chipped away most of the ice. Inside, it was a hollow bubble with a diameter of about a meter and a half, and a floor to ceiling height slightly less than that. Cirocco had to remove her pack, then pull it in after her. With both of them and two packs inside it seemed possible they might have found room to stow a shoebox and still be able to breathe, but not much more than that.

"Cozy, eh?" Gaby asked, removing Cirocco's elbow from her neck.

"Sorry. Oh, sorry about that, too. Gaby, my foot!"

"Excuse me. If you'd just scrunch . . . that's better, but I wish you wouldn't stand there."

"Where? Oh, my." She suddenly burst out laughing. She was crouched with her back against the ceiling and her knees bent while Gaby edged to the rear and tried to stay out of the way.

"What's so funny?"

"I was thinking of an old movie. Laurel and Hardy in their nightgowns, trying to bed down in an upper berth."

Gaby was smiling, but obviously didn't know what she was talking about.

"An upper berth, you know, on a cross-country train . . . skip it. I just thought they should have tried it in arctic gear, and with a couple suitcases thrown in. How do you want to work this?"

They shoveled the remainder of the snow out of the tiny cave and stacked the gear in front of the opening to block it. When they did so, what little light there had been vanished, but the wind stopped blowing in, so they counted it a gain. After struggling for twenty minutes they managed to settle down side by side. Cirocco could barely move, but was not inclined to worry about such things in the blessed warmth.

"You think we can get some sleep now?" Gaby
wondered.

"I sure feel like I could. How are your toes?"

"Okay. Tingling, but they're getting warm."

"Me, too. Good night, Gaby." She hesitated only a
moment, then leaned over and kissed her.

"I love you, Rocky."

"Go to sleep." She said it with a smile.

The next time Cirocco woke, sweat beaded her
forehead. Her clothes were soaked. She lifted her head
groggily and realized she could see. Wondering if the
weather had changed, she moved her pack slightly, then
more urgently, and discovered the entrance to the cave
had closed.

She almost woke Gaby, but thought better of it just in
time.

"Try to get out *first*," she muttered. There was no sense
telling Gaby she had been eaten alive again unless it was
really true. Gaby would not take the news well; the
thought of being confined in such a small space—bad
enough in itself—was terrifying when she thought of
Gaby and her contagious panic.

It turned out there was no cause for alarm. While she
explored the wall where the hole had been, it began to
move, irising until it was as large as it had been before.
There was a clear window of ice with faint light behind it.
She hit it with her gloved fist and it shattered. Frigid air
rushed in, and she hastily blocked the hole again with her
pack.

In a few minutes she moved the pack. The hole had
closed to a few centimeters.

She looked thoughtfully at the tiny hole, putting it all
together in her mind. Only when she thought she
understood it did she shake Gaby's shoulder.

"Wake up, kid, it's time to make adjustments again."

"Hmmm?" Gaby came awake quickly. "Hell, it's an
oven in here."

"That's what I meant. We'll have to take off some

clothes. You want to go first?"

"Go ahead. I'll try to stay out of your way."

"Right. Why do you suppose it's so hot in here? Have you thought about that?"

"I just woke up, Rocky. Have a heart."

"Okay. I'll tell you. Feel the walls." She performed the complex task of removing her parka while Gaby made the same discovery she had made earlier.

"It's warm."

"Yeah. I couldn't figure out this wall from the first. I thought the trees were un-planned-for, like the growths on the cable, but they couldn't grow here, as I see it, without the wall to nourish them. I tried to think what kind of machine would do that best, and I came back to a natural biochemical machine. An animal, or plant, possibly a genetically tailored one. I find it hard to believe something like this could have evolved in any reasonable time. It's 300 kilometers high, hollow in the middle, and hugs the *real* wall."

"And the trees are parasites?" Gaby was taking it better than Cirocco had expected.

"Only in the sense that they draw nourishment from another animal. But they're not true parasites, because it was *planned* that way. The builders designed this large animal as a habitat for the trees, and in turn the trees provide habitats for smaller animals, and probably for the angels."

Gaby considered it, and looked narrowly at Cirocco.

"Pretty much like the very large animals that we presume live below the rim," she said, quietly.

"Yes, something like that." She watched Gaby for signs of panic, but did not even see her breathing heavily. "Does that...ah...worry you?"

"You mean my well-known phobia?"

Cirocco reached behind her pack and stimulated the entrance into opening again, then moved the pack and let Gaby see it. It began to close slowly.

"I found this before I woke you up. See, it's closing, but it'll open again if you tickle it. We're *not* trapped, and this isn't a stomach or anything like—"

Gaby touched her hand, smiling faintly. "I appreciate your concern."

"Well, I didn't mean to embarrass you, I only..."

"You did the right thing. If I'd seen that first I'd probably still be screaming. But I'm not basically claustrophobic. I've got a new phobia that may be my very own; fear of being eaten alive. But tell me—and make it very convincing, please—if this isn't a stomach, what is it?"

"There's no parallel on any creature I know." She was down to her last layer of clothing now, and decided to stop there. "It's a refuge," she went on, trying to make herself small as Gaby began to remove her clothes. "It's for precisely what we're using it for: a place to get in out of the cold. I'm willing to bet the angels winter in caves like this. Maybe other animals, too. Possibly the creature gets something out of it. Maybe the droppings fertilize it."

"Speaking of droppings..."

"Yeah, I've got the same problem. We'll have to use an empty food jar or something."

"My God. I smell like a camel already. This place is going to be lovely if the weather doesn't break soon."

"It's not so bad. I smell worse."

"How diplomatic of you." Gaby was down to her garishly patterned underclothes. "My dear, we're going to be living damn close for a while, and there's no use in modesty. If you're keeping that on because—"

"I wasn't, not really," Cirocco said, too hastily.

"—because you're afraid of arousing me, think again. It's practically not there, anyway. I hope you don't mind if I take this off and give it a chance to dry." She did so without waiting for permission, then stretched out beside Cirocco.

"Maybe that was part of it," Cirocco admitted. "The other reason, the big reason, sort of makes me blush. I've started my period."

"I thought you had. I politely didn't say anything."

"How diplomatic of *you*." They laughed, but Cirocco felt her face flushing. It was awkward as hell. She was used to a shipboard routine of fastidiousness. Being messy and unable to do anything about it appalled her. Gaby suggested Cirocco use a bandage from the medical kit, if only for her own comfort. Cirocco let herself be talked into it, happy that the idea had come from Gaby. She could not have used needed medical supplies for such a purpose without Gaby's approval.

They were quiet for a time, Cirocco uncomfortably aware of Gaby's nearness, telling herself she had to get used to it. They might be in the shelter for days.

Gaby did not seem bothered in the least, and soon enough Cirocco lost her sharp awareness of her body. After an hour of trying to sleep, she began to feel bored by it all.

"You awake?"

"I always snore when I'm awake." Gaby sighed, and sat up. "Hell, I'll have to be a lot sleepier before I can sack out with you so close. You're so warm, and soft..."

Cirocco ignored that.

"Do you know any games to pass the time?"

Gaby rolled onto her side, facing Cirocco. "I could think up some dandies."

"Do you play chess?"

"I was afraid you'd say that. You want black or white?"

The ice formed around the entrance as fast as they could knock it away.

They worried about air at first, but a few experiments proved there would be adequate oxygen even with the opening completely closed. The only explanation was that the survival capsule functioned like a plant, soaking up carbon dioxide through its inner walls.

They discovered a nipple set into the back of the cave. When squeezed, it exuded the same milky substance they had seen earlier. They tasted it, but decided to stick to their supplies until there was nothing left. This was the milk of Gaea Meistersinger had told Cirocco about. Undoubtedly it fed the angels.

The hours slowly turned into days, the chess games into tournaments. Gaby won most of them. They invented new games with words and numbers, and Gaby won most of those, too. What with all they had been through together, the things that drew them close and the things that pulled them apart, Cirocco's reservations and Gaby's pride, it was not until the third day that they made love.

It happened during one of the times they were both just staring at the faintly luminescent ceiling, listening to the wind howling outside. They were bored, too energetic, and slightly stir-crazy. Cirocco was spinning an endless stream of rationalizations through her head: Reasons Why I Should Not Get Physically Intimate With Gaby. (A)...

She couldn't remember (A).

It had made sense not to until a few days ago. Why didn't it now?

There was the situation; surely that had colored her judgement. She had never been so intimate with another human being. For three days they had been in constant physical contact. She would wake up in Gaby's arms, wet and excited. What was worse, Gaby could not help knowing it. They could smell changes in each other's mood.

But Gaby had said she didn't want her unless Cirocco could return her love.

Hadn't she?

No. She thought back over it and realized all Gaby had said she required was a sincere enthusiasm on Cirocco's part; she would not accept lovemaking as therapy to ease her own pain.

All right. Cirocco had the enthusiasm. She had never felt it so strongly. She was holding back essentially because she was not homosexual, she was bisexual with a strong preference for the male sex, and felt she should not get involved with a woman who loved her unless she felt she could carry through beyond the first act of love.

Which had to qualify as the silliest thing she had ever heard. Words, words, just stupid words. Listen to your body, and listen to your heart.

Her body had no reservations left, and her heart had

only one. She turned over and straddled Gaby. They kissed, and Cirocco began to stroke her.

"I can't say I love you and be honest about it, because I'm not sure I'd know what it felt like with a woman. I'd die defending you, and your welfare is more important to me than any other human being. I've never had a friend as good as you. If that isn't enough, I'll stop."

"Don't stop."

"When I loved a man, once, I wanted to have his children. What I feel for you is very close to what I felt then, but it doesn't have that. I desire you . . . oh, so bad I can't even express it. But I can't say for sure that I love you."

Gaby smiled.

"Life is full of disappointments." She put her arms around Cirocco and pulled her down.

For five days the wind howled outside. On the sixth, the thaw began, and lasted until the seventh day.

It was dangerous to go out during the thaw. Chunks of ice came crashing down from above, making a terrible racket. When it stopped, they emerged, blinking, into a world that was cool, and shining with water, and whispering to them.

They worked their way out to the top of the nearest tree, heard the whispering grow louder. As the smaller branches began to bend beneath their weight, they entered a gentle rain: big drops falling in slow motion from leaf to leaf.

The air in the center of the column was clear, but all around them, as far as they could see, the walls were wreathed in rainbows as the melted ice worked its way down through the foliage to the new lake on the spoke floor.

"What now?" Gaby asked.

"In. In, and up. We've lost a lot of time."

Gaby nodded. "I don't mind, you know that, as long as it's where you're going. But would you tell me once more—why?"

Cirocco was about to say it was a stupid question, but

realized it was not. She had admitted to Gaby during their long incarceration that she no longer believed she would find anyone in control at the hub. She did not know herself when she had stopped believing it.

"I made a promise to Meistersinger," she said. "And now I have no further secrets from you. Not one."

Gaby frowned. "A promise to do what?"

"To see if there is anything I can do to stop the war between the Titanides and the angels. I didn't tell anyone about it. I'm not sure why."

"I see. Do you think there's anything you *can* do?"

"No." Gaby said nothing, but continued to search her eyes. "I have to give it a try. Why are you looking at me like that?"

Gaby shrugged. "No reason. I'll just be curious to know your reasons for going on after we find the angels. We *will* be going on, won't we?"

"I suppose so. Somehow it seems like the right thing to do."

Chapter Twenty-Two

The world was an endless series of trees to climb. Each was a variation on the same problem; as different as snowflakes, yet with a numbing sameness. What communication was needed to get through them could be accomplished by hand motions and grunts. They became a perfect tree-climbing machine, one body moving forever upward. They climbed for twelve hours at a stretch. When they camped, they slept like the dead.

Below them, the floor opened and a sea of water fell over Rhea. It remained open for a few weeks, then closed when the roof opened and the frigid winds blew once more, forcing them to take shelter. Five days of darkness and they were out again, and climbing.

They were six days past their third winter when they saw their first angel. They stopped climbing, and watched him watching them.

He was near the top of the tree, indistinct through the branches. They had heard angels wailing before, sometimes followed by the sound of giant wings flapping. Still, so far, Cirocco's knowledge of angels was limited to one frozen moment when she had seen one impaled on a Titanide spear.

He was smaller than Gaby, with a huge chest and spindly arms and legs. He had claws instead of feet. His wings emerged just above his hips so that in flight he would be prone with the same amount of weight on each side of the wings. Folded, they reached over his head with the tips trailing below the branch he perched on. The flight surfaces on his legs, arms, and tail were neatly folded.

Having noted all those differences, Cirocco had to admit that the most startling thing about him was his humanness. He looked like a child dying of malnutrition, but it was a human child.

Gaby glanced at Cirocco, who shrugged, then motioned for her to be ready for anything. She took a step forward.

The angel shrieked and danced backward. His wings unfolded to their full nine-meter span and he poised, beating them lazily to remain on branches too thin to hold his weight.

"We'd just like to talk to you." She held out her hands. The angel shrieked again, and was gone. They could hear the roaring of his wings as he gained altitude.

Gaby looked at Cirocco. She raised one eyebrow and made a motion with one hand, questioningly.

"Right. Up."

"Captain."

Cirocco froze instantly. Ahead, Gaby was jerked to a stop as the rope between them grew taut.

"What?" Gaby asked.

"Quiet. Listen."

They waited, and in a few minutes the call came again. This time, Gaby heard it, too.

"It couldn't be Gene," Gaby whispered.

"Calvin?" As soon as she said it, she recognized the voice. It was oddly changed, but she knew it.

"April."

"Right," came the reply, though Cirocco had not said it very loud. "Talk?"

"Of course I want to talk. Where the hell are you?"

"Below. I see you. Don't come back."

"Why not? Dammit, April, we've been hoping you'd turn up for months. August has been going crazy." Cirocco was frowning. Something was wrong, and she wanted to know what it was.

"I come to you, or not at all. You come to me, I fly away."

She perched in the small branches, twenty meters from the two women. Even at that distance Cirocco could make out her face, exactly like August's. She was an angel, and Cirocco was sick.

She seemed to have trouble speaking. There were long pauses between sentences.

"Please do not come closer. Do not move in my direction. We can talk this way for only a short time."

"Surely you don't think we'll hurt you?"

"And why not? I . . ." She stopped, edging away. "No, I suppose not. But I could no more let you approach than I could hold my hand in a fire. You smell wrong."

"Does it have to do with the Titanides?"

"With what?"

"The centaurs. The people you make war with."

She hissed and backed away. "Do not speak of them."

"I don't think I can avoid it."

"Then I must leave. I will try to return." With a loud cry, she plunged through the leaves. They heard her wings for a short time, then it was as if she had never been with them.

Cirocco looked at Gaby, who sat with her feet dangling. Her face was somber.

"It's awful," Cirocco whispered. "What happened to us?"

"I was hoping she could give us some answers. Whatever it was, it hit her the worst. Worse than Gene."

She returned a few hours later but could not answer the questions that mattered most. It appeared she had not even been thinking about them.

"How should I know?" she said. "I was in the darkness,

I woke up, and I was as you see me. It didn't matter, and it doesn't matter now."

"Can you explain that?"

"I'm happy. No one wanted me or my sisters. No one loved us. Well, now I don't need it. I am of the Eagle clan, proud and alone."

Cautious questioning brought out what it meant to be of the Eagle clan. It was not a tribe or association, as April had seemed to imply; rather, it was a species within the genus angel.

Eagles were loners, solitary from birth to death. They did not come together even to mate, could suffer each other's company for only minutes at a time, and then only while cruising at a comfortable distance. April had heard of the humans' presence in the spoke through such a passing conversation.

"There are two things I don't understand," Cirocco said, carefully. "May I ask?"

"I don't promise to answer."

"All right. How is it there are more angels, if you don't come together?"

"There is a non-sentient creature born at the bottom of the world. It spends its life climbing to the top. Once a year I find one and implant an egg on its back. Male angels deposit sperm on it or not, as chance has it. A fertilized egg goes to the top with the creature. The infant is born as the host dies. We are born into the air and must learn to fly on the way down. Some don't. It is at the will of Gaea. This is our—"

"Just a minute. You said Gaea. Why did you choose that name?"

There was a pause.

"I don't understand the question."

"I can't make it plainer. Calvin named this place Gaea. He thought it fit well. Are you into Greek mythology, too?"

"I never heard the name before. Gaea is what the people call this creature. She's sort of a God, though not exactly. You're making my head hurt. I'm happy as I am, and I must go now."

"Wait, wait just a minute."

April was edging toward the top of the tree.

"You said 'creature.' Are you talking about this thing in the spoke?"

April looked surprised. "Why, no. This is only a part of her. The whole world is Gaea. I thought you knew that."

"No, I—wait, please don't go." It was too late. They heard the beating of her wings. "Will you come back later?" Cirocco shouted.

"Once more," came the distant reply.

"One being, you say. All one creature. How do you know this?"

April had returned in only an hour this time. Cirocco hoped she was getting used to company again, but she still would approach no closer than twenty meters.

"Believe it. Some of my people have talked with her."

"She's intelligent, then?"

"Why not? Listen . . . Captain." She held her temples for a moment. Cirocco could imagine the conflicts. April had been one of the finest physicists in the system. Now she lived as a fierce wild animal, according to a code barely comprehensible to Cirocco. She thought the old April might be struggling to get through the creature she had become.

"Cirocco, you say you speak to . . . to those on the rim." It was as close as she could come to the concept of Titanides without fleeing. "They understand you. Calvin can speak to the floaters. The changes Gaea worked on me are more complete. I *am* one of my people. I awoke knowing how to behave among them. I have the same feelings and drives as any other angel. This is one thing I know. Gaea is one. Gaea is alive. We live inside her."

Gaby was looking a bit green.

"Just look around you," April went on. "What have you seen that looks like a machine? Anything at all? We were seized by a living beast; you postulate a creature under the rim. The spoke is filled with a huge living thing; you decide it is a coating over the framework beneath."

"What you say is intriguing."

"More than that. It's true."

"If I accept that, I won't find a control room in the hub."

"But you'll be where she lives. She sits like a spider and pulls strings like a puppet master. She watches over all her creatures, and she owns the two of you as surely as she owns me. She has tampered with us for her own purposes."

"And what are they?"

April shrugged, a human gesture that hurt Cirocco to watch.

"She would not tell me. I went to the hub, but she refused to see me. My people say that one must be on a great mission to gain Gaea's ear. Apparently mine was not great enough."

"And what would you have asked her?"

April was quiet for a very long time. Cirocco realized she was crying. She looked up at them again.

"You hurt me. I think I won't talk to you any more."

"Please, April. Please, for the friendship we had."

"Did we? Did we really? I can't remember it. I remember only me and August, and long ago, my other sisters. We have always been alone with each other. Now I am alone, alone."

"Do you miss them?"

"I did," she said, emptily. "That was long ago. I fly, fly to be alone. Solitude is the world of the Eagle clan. I know that is right, but before . . . before, when I still yearned for my sisters . . ."

Cirocco held very still, afraid of frightening her away.

"We band together only at one time," she said, with a quiet sigh. "When Gaea takes her breath, after the winter, then blows us over the lands . . .

"I flew with the wind that day. It was a fine day. We killed many because my people listened to me and rode the great floater. The four-legs were surprised because the breath was over; we few had remained on the floater, tired and hungry, but with the lust still in our blood, still able to work together.

"It was a day for the singing of great songs. My people followed me—me—did what I told them, and I knew in my heart that the four-legs would soon be wiped out in

Gaea. This was but the first skirmish in the new war.

"Then I saw August and my mind left me. I wanted to kill her, I wanted to fly from her, I wanted to embrace her and weep with her.

"I flew.

"Now I dread the breath of Gaea, for someday it will take me down to slaughter my sister, and then I will die. I am Ariel the Swift, but enough of April Polo remains in me that I could not live with such a thing."

Cirocco was moved, but could not help being excited. April sounded as if she was important in the angel community. Surely they would listen to her.

"It happens that I am up here to make peace," she said.
"Don't go! Please don't go."

April trembled, but stood her ground. "Peace is impossible."

"I can't believe that. Many of the Titanides are sick in their hearts, as you are."

April shook her head. "Does a lamb negotiate with a lion? A bat with an insect, a bird with a worm?"

"You're talking about predators and prey."

"Natural enemies. It's printed in our genes, killing the fourlegs. I can... as April, I can see what you're thinking. Peace should be possible. We have to fly impossible distances just to do battle. Many of us do not make it back. The climb is too hard, and we fall into the sea."

Cirocco shook her head. "I just think if I could get some representatives together..."

"I tell you, it's impossible. We are Eagles. You cannot even get us to act as a group, much less meet with the four-legs. There are other clans, some of them sociable, but they don't live in this spoke. Perhaps you would have luck there, but I doubt it."

The three of them were silent for a time. Cirocco felt heavy with defeat, and Gaby put her hand on her shoulder.

"What do you think? Is she telling the truth?"

"I suspect she is. It sounds just like what Meistersinger told me. They have no control over it." She looked up, and spoke to April.

"You were saying that you tried to see Gaea. Why?"

"For peace. I wanted to ask her why the war had to be. I'm quite happy, but for that. She did not hear my call."

Or she doesn't exist, Cirocco thought.

"Will you still go seek her?" April asked.

"I don't know. What's the point? Why would this superhuman being stop a war just because I ask her to?"

"There are worse things to do in life than to have a quest to fulfill. If you turned back now, what would you do?"

"I don't know that, either."

"You've come a long way. You must have overcome great difficulties. My people say Gaea likes a good story, and she likes great heroes. Are you a hero?"

She thought of Gene spinning down into the blackness, of Panpipe running to his doom, of the mudfish bearing down on her. Surely a hero would have done better than that.

"She is," Gaby said, suddenly. "Of all of us, only Rocky has held to her purpose. We'd still be sitting in mud shacks if she hadn't pushed us. She kept us moving toward a goal. We may not reach it, but when that rescue ship comes, I'll bet they find us still trying."

Cirocco was embarrassed, but strangely moved. She had been fighting a sense of failure since the capture; it didn't hurt to know someone thought she was doing well. But a hero? No, not hardly. She had only done what had to be done.

"I think Gaea will be impressed," April said. "Go to her. Stand in her hub and shout. Do not grovel or beg. Tell her you have a right to some answers, for all of us. She will listen."

"Come with us, April."

The angel-woman edged away.

"My name is Ariel the Swift. I go with no one, and no one goes with me. I will never see you again." She dived once more, and Cirocco knew she would keep her word.

She looked at Gaby, who rolled her eyes upward with a slight twist of her mouth.

"Up?"

"Why the hell not? There *are* a few things I'd like to ask."

Chapter Twenty-Three

"I'm not a hero, you know."

"All right, heroine."

Cirocco chuckled. They were bedded down on the last day of their fourteenth winter together, their eighth month in the spoke. There were now only ten kilometers separating them from the hub. They could do it in their sleep, as soon as the thaw started.

"Not even that. If there's a heroine here, it has to be you."

Gaby shook her head.

"I've helped out. This probably would have been a lot harder for you if I hadn't been here."

Cirocco squeezed her hand.

"But I've just tagged along. I've helped you out of some messes, but I don't qualify as a hero. A hero wouldn't have tried to throw Gene over the side with no parachute. *You* would have made it here by yourself, I wouldn't have."

They were silent, each with her own thoughts.

Cirocco was not sure what Gaby said was true. Part of it was accurate, though she would never agree with it out loud. Gaby could not have brought them this far. She was not a leader.

But am *I?* she wondered. She had certainly tried enough to be one. Could she have made it alone? She doubted it.

"It's been fun, hasn't it?" Gaby asked, quietly.

Cirocco was genuinely surprised. Was it possible to call eight months' struggle fun?

"I don't think that's the word I would have used."

"No, you're right. But you know what I mean."

Oddly enough, she did. She was at last able to understand the depression that had plagued her during the last weeks. The trip would soon be over. They would discover the means to return to Earth, or they would not.

"I don't want to go back to Earth," Cirocco said.

"Me either."

"But we can't just turn back."

"You know best."

"No, I'm just stubborn. But we do have to go on. I owe it to April and Gene—and the rest of us, too—to find out what's been done to us, and why."

"Get out those swords, will you?"

"You expecting trouble?"

"Nothing that a sword would cure. I'd just feel better with it in my hand. I'm supposed to be a hero, right?"

Gaby didn't argue. She went down on one knee and rummaged through the extra pack, came up with the short swords and tossed one to Cirocco.

They were standing near the top of what had to be the last staircase. Like the one they had climbed at the bottom of the spoke, it made a spiral around the cable, which they had re-discovered at the top of a long, bare incline that marked the margin between the forest and the upper spoke valve. Climbing the slope had been pick, rope, and piton work, occupying them for two arduous days.

With no lamp oil remaining, the climb up the stairs had been done in total darkness, one step at a time. It had passed without incident until Cirocco had discerned a faint, red glow in front of them. Suddenly she had felt the need of a sword in her hand.

It was a fine weapon, though the hilt was too large. It

weighed nothing at all this high in Gaea. She struck a match and touched the figure of a Titanide chased into the flat of the blade.

"You look like a Frazetta oil," Gaby said.

She looked down at herself. She was ragged, wrapped in the tatters of her fine clothing. Her skin was pale where it was clean enough to see. She had lost weight; what was left was hard and wiry. Her feet and hands were tough as leather.

"And I always wanted to be one of those Maxfield Parrish girls. So much more lady-like."

She shook the match out and lit another. Gaby was still looking at her. Her eyes glowed in the yellow light. Cirocco suddenly felt very good. She smiled, then laughed quietly, reached out and put her hand on Gaby's shoulder. Gaby returned the gesture, a half-smile on her face.

"Do you...have some kind of feeling about this?" Gaby gestured with her sword toward the top of the stairs.

"Maybe I do." She laughed again, and then shrugged. "Nothing specific. We ought to be on our toes."

Gaby said nothing, but wiped her palm on her thigh before settling her fingers firmly around her sword hilt. Then she laughed.

"I don't know how to use this."

"Just act as if you do. When we get to the top of the stairs, leave all the gear behind."

"You sure?"

"I don't want the extra mass."

"The hub's a big place, Rocky. It might take a while to search it."

"I've got a feeling it won't be long. Not long at all."

She blew out the second match. They waited until their eyes had adjusted, until they could see the faint glow from above. Then they walked, side by side, up the last hundred steps.

They ascended into a pulsing red night.

The only light came from the laser-straight line overhead. The ceiling was lost in gloom. To their left, a cable loomed, a black shadow in the blacker air.

The walls, the floor, and the air itself reverberated with the rhythm of a slow heartbeat. They faced into a cold, thin wind, blowing from the unseen entrance to the Oceanus spoke.

"It's going to be tough to nose around," Gaby whispered. "I can only see about twenty meters of floor."

Cirocco said nothing. She shook her head to clear the odd, heavy feeling that had come over her, then fought off an attack of dizziness. She wanted to sit down, she wanted to turn back. She was afraid, and did not dare give in to it.

She held up her sword and saw it shimmer like a pool of blood. She took one step forward, then another. Gaby kept pace, and they walked into the darkness.

Her teeth hurt. She realized she had been biting down hard, jaw muscles knotted. She stopped, and shouted.

"I'm here!"

After long seconds an echo returned, then a series of them trailing into oblivion.

She held her sword above her head and shouted again.

"I'm here! I am Captain Cirocco Jones, commander of the *DSV Ringmaster,* commissioned by the United States of America, the National Aeronautics and Space Administration, and the United Nations of Earth. I would like to speak with you!"

It seemed like ages before the echoes died away. When they were gone, there was nothing but the slow pulsing of the monstrous heart. They stood back to back, swords ready, looking into the darkness.

Cirocco felt a surge of anger flow through her, erasing the last traces of fear. She brandished her sword and screamed into the night as tears ran down her cheeks.

"I *demand* to see you! My friend and I have come through many hardships to stand here before you. The ground coughed us forth naked into this world. We have fought our way to the top of it. We have been treated cruelly, tossed about at whims we do not understand. Your hand has reached into our souls and tried to take our dignity, and we remain unbowed. I challenge you to come forth and answer to me! Answer for what you have done, or I will devote my life to destroying you utterly. I do not fear you! I am ready to fight!"

She had no idea how long Gaby had been tugging her sleeve. She looked down, having trouble focusing. Gaby looked frightened, but stood staunchly at her side.

"Maybe," she said, timidly, "uh, maybe she doesn't speak English."

So Cirocco sang her challenge again in Titanide. She used the high declamatory mode, the one reserved for the telling of tales. The hard, dark walls threw her song back until the black hub rang with her defiant music.

The floor began to shake.

"IIIIIIIIII..."

It was a single note, an English word, a hurricane of speech.

"Heeeeeeear..."

Cirocco fell to her hands and knees, looking dumbly at Gaby hugging the floor beside her.

"Yoooooooooouu..."

The word echoed for many minutes, gradually trailing into the far-off bass muttering of an air-raid siren winding down. The floor steadied, and Cirocco lifted her head.

White light blinded her.

Shielding her eyes with her forearm, she squinted into the glare. A curtain was being drawn from one of the walls. The curtain reached from the floor to the ceiling, five kilometers high. Behind it was a crystal staircase. It sparkled cruelly as it ascended into light so intense Cirocco could not look at it.

Gaby was tugging at her sleeve again.

"Let's get out of here," she whispered, urgently.

"No. I came to talk to her."

She forced herself to put her palms flat to the floor and push herself up. Getting to her feet was easy; staying there was another matter. She would have liked nothing better than to do as Gaby suggested. Her bravado now seemed like a fit of intoxication.

But she began to walk toward the light.

The opening was 200 meters wide, flanked by crystalline columns that had to be the upper ends of support cables. Looking up, she could see them unwind, each strand twisting through a complex pattern until it joined a basket-weave that covered the distant roof. Here was the unimaginably strong anchor that held Gaea together.

She frowned. One of the strands was broken. Upon closer examination, the whole ceiling looked like a sweater a kitten had played with, full of snarls and ravels.

It made her feel better to look at it. Mighty as Gaea was, she had seen better days.

They reached the bottom riser of the staircase and stepped onto it. It emitted a low organ note that lingered while they climbed. The seventh step raised the pitch one half tone, and the thirteenth step sharped it again. They proceeded slowly through the chromatic scale, and when the first octave was reached, harmonics began to creep in.

With no warning, orange flames roared on each side of them. The women literally jumped two meters into the air before the low gravity brought them to a stop.

Finally, gratefully, Cirocco began to get angry again. Awesome it was—a knee-knocking, teeth-chattering display of raw power that was sure to make the bravest grovel. Yet it had the opposite effect on Cirocco. God or no God, it had been a cheap trick, calculated to play on nerves already scraped raw. As such, she thought it in the same league with the novelty palm buzzer.

"P.T. Barnum had nothing on this girl," Gaby said, and Cirocco loved her for it. Showmanship, that's what it was. What kind of a God would need it?

The flames died, only to leap twice as high, licking the ceiling to make a tunnel of yellow and orange. They kept walking.

Ahead were towering gates of copper and gold. They swung open without a sound and clanged shut behind them.

The music rose to a maddened crescendo as they approached a large throne surrounded in light. By the time they reached the broad, marble platform at the top of the stairs it was impossible to face the throne. The heat was too intense.

"Speak."

As the word was uttered—in the same deep tones they had heard outside, and yet with a more human

sound—the light began to dim. Cirocco stole cautious
glances, made out a tall, wide, human shape in the fog of
light.

"Speak, or return from whence you came."

Cirocco squinted, saw a round head set on a thick neck,
eyes that blazed like coals, thick lips. Gaea was four
meters tall, standing erect before her throne on a
two-meter pedestal. Her body was round with a
monstrous belly, huge breasts, arms and legs that would
have awed a professional wrestler. She was naked, and the
color of green olives.

The pedestal changed shape abruptly, became a grassy
hill covered with flowers. Gaea's legs became tree trunks,
her feet firmly rooted in the dark soil. Small animals
stood around her while flying creatures circled her head.
She looked directly at Cirocco, and her huge brow began
to cloud.

"Uh . . . I mean, I'll speak, I'll speak." She opened her
mouth to do so, wondering where her righteous anger had
gone, when she glanced at Gaby. She was trembling,
looking up at Gaea with eyes that glittered.

"I was here," she whispered. "I was here."

"Hush," Cirocco hissed jabbing her with an elbow.
"We'll talk about it *later*." She wiped sweat from her
brow, and faced Gaea again.

"Oh Great—" No! Don't grovel, April said. She likes
heroes, April said. Please, April, please be right.

"We came . . . uh, me and six others came from . . . we
came from the planet Earth, quite some . . . I don't really
know how long . . ." She stopped, and knew she would
never get anything out in English. She took a deep breath,
straightened her shoulders, and began to sing.

"We came in peace, I know not how long ago. We were
a tiny crew, by your reckoning, and presented no threat to
you. We were unarmed. And yet we were attacked. Our
ship was destroyed before we had a chance to explain our
intentions. We were confined against our will, in
conditions injurious to our minds, unable to communicate with each other or our comrades on Earth. Changes
were made in us. One of my crew was driven insane as a

result of this treatment. Another was near to insanity at the time I left her. A third no longer desires the company of his fellow humans, and a fourth has lost much of his memory. Yet another has been changed beyond all recognition; she no longer knows her sister, whom she once loved.

"All these things are monstrous to us. I feel we have been wronged, and deserve an explanation. We have been treated badly, and deserve justice."

She sagged a little, happy to have gotten it all out. What happened next was out of her hands. She was through kidding herself; she could not fight this thing.

Gaea's frown deepened.

"I am not a signatory of the Geneva Accords."

Cirocco's mouth fell open. She didn't know what she had expected to hear, but it certainly wasn't that.

"What *are* you then?" It came out before she could stop it.

"I am Gaea, the great and wise. I am the world, I am the truth, I am the law, I am—"

"You're the whole planet, then? April was telling the truth?"

Maybe it wasn't wise to interrupt a Goddess, but Cirocco was feeling like Oliver Twist asking for more gruel. She had to fight it somehow.

"I wasn't through," Gaea rumbled. "But yes, I am. I am the Earth Mother, though I am not of your Earth. All life springs from me. I am one of a pantheon that reaches to the stars. Call me a Titan."

"Then it was you that—"

"Enough. I listen only to heroes. You spoke of great deeds when you sang your song. Speak of them now, or leave me forever. Sing to me of your adventures."

"But I—"

"Sing to me!" Gaea thundered.

She sang. The story took several hours because, though Cirocco wanted to condense it, Gaea insisted on detail. Cirocco began warming to the task. The Titanide language was well suited to it; as long as she stayed in declamatory mode it was impossible to sing in awkward

phrase. By the time she was finished she was feeling proud, and a bit more confident.

Gaea seemed to be pondering it. Cirocco shifted nervously. Her feet hurt, which proves, she thought, that you can get bored by anything.

At last Gaea spoke again.

"It was a good tale," she said. "Better than I have heard in many an age. You are truly heroic. I will speak with you both in my chambers."

With that, she vanished. There was only a flame which flickered for a few minutes, then died away.

They looked around them. They were in a large domed room. Behind them the stairs, unlighted now, reached down to the dark hub interior. Corroded nozzles lined the staircase, smoking fitfully, giving off the sharp pings of cooling metal. The smell of burnt rubber hung in the air.

The marble floor was cracked and discolored, covered with a film of dust that clearly showed their footprints. The place looked like a seedy opera house when the house lights come up and banish illusion.

"I've seen some screwy things since we got here," Gaby said, "but this takes it. Where do we go now?"

Cirocco pointed silently to a small door set into the wall on their left. It was ajar, and light was shining through the crack.

Cirocco pushed it open, looked around with a growing sense of recognition, then stepped in.

They entered a large room with a four-meter ceiling. The floor was composed of milky glass rectangles. Light shone through from below. The walls were paneled in beige painted wood and hung with gilt-framed oil paintings. The furnishings were Louis XVI.

"*Déjà vu,* eh?" said a voice from the far end of the room. It was a short, dumpy woman in a shapeless sack dress. She looked like Gaea in the same way a carved bar of soap might resemble Michelangelo's "Pièta."

"Sit down, sit down," she said, jovially. "We don't stand on ceremony in here. You've seen the razzle-dazzle; here's the bitter reality.

"Can I get you something to drink?"

Chapter Twenty-Four

Cirocco had given up on having opinions.

"You know what?" she asked, feeling more than a little giddy. "If somebody said right now that *Ringmaster* had never left Earth orbit, that this whole thing had been staged in a Hollywood backlot, I don't think I'd bat an eye."

"A perfectly natural reaction," Gaea soothed.

She was waddling around the room, getting a glass of wine for Gaby and a double shot of Scotch on the rocks for Cirocco, straightening paintings, brushing dust from tables with the ragged hem of her skirt.

Gaea was short and squat, built like a barrel. Her skin was weathered and brown. She had a nose like a potato. But there were laugh lines at the corners of her eyes and her sensuous mouth.

Cirocco tried to place the face, giving her mind something to do while she studiously avoided making theories. W.C. Fields? No, only the nose qualified for the role. Then she had it. Gaea looked a lot like Charles Laughton in *The Private Life of Henry VIII*.

Gaby and Cirocco sat on opposite ends of a slightly

©Fupp 24/3 1978

frayed couch. Gaea put a glass on the end table beside
each of them, then huffed across the room to hoist her
bulk into a high-backed chair. She wheezed, and laced her
fingers in her lap.

"Ask me anything," she said, and leaned forward
expectantly.

Cirocco and Gaby looked at each other, then back at
Gaea. There was a short silence.

"You speak English," Cirocco said.

"That's not a question."

"*How* do you speak English? Where did you learn it?"

"I watch television."

Cirocco knew what she wanted to ask next, but didn't
know if she should. Suppose this creature was the last
remnant of the builders of Gaea? She had seen no proof
that Gaea was actually one organism, as April had said it
was, but it was possible this person *thought* she was a
Goddess.

"What about all that...that show outside?" Gaby
asked.

Gaea dismissed it with a wave.

"All done with mirrors, dear. Mere sleight-of-hand."
She glanced at her lap, then looked sheepish. "I wanted to
scare you off if you weren't real hero material. I gave it my
best shot. I thought at this stage it would be easier for us to
relate in here. Comfortable surroundings, food and
drink—would you like something to eat? Coffee?
Cocaine?"

"No, I'd...did you say..."

"Did you say coffee?"

"...cocaine?"

Cirocco's nose was tingling, but she felt more alert and
less afraid than she had since they entered the hub. She
settled back on the couch and looked into the eyes of the
creature who called herself Gaea.

"Mirrors, you said. What *are* you, then?"

Gaea's smile broadened.

"To the heart of the matter, eh? Good. I like
directness." She pursed her lips and seemed to consider
the question.

"Do you mean what is *this,* or what am I?" She put her hands just above her enormous breasts, then didn't wait for an answer. "I am three kinds of life. There is my body itself, which is the environment you have been moving through. There are my creatures, such as Titanides, who belong to me but are not *controlled* by me. And there are my tools, separated from me, but part of me. I have certain powers of the mind—which were helpful in the illusions you just saw, incidentally. Call it hypnotism and telepathy, though it is neither.

"I am able to construct creatures that are extensions of my will. This one is eighty years old, the only one of her kind. I also have other sorts. They built this room and the stairway outside, mostly from plans I stole from movies. I'm a big fan of movies, and I understand you—"

"Yes, but getting—"

"I know, I know," Gaea soothed. "I wander. This is a damn nuisance, you see. I *have* to talk to you this way. When I said 'I hear you' earlier... well, I was using the upper Oceanus valve as a larynx, forcing air from the spoke. It plays hell with the weather: those three words sent snow all over Hyperion.

"But letting you see this body makes you want to believe something else. Namely, that I'm a dizzy old woman, all alone up here."

She looked narrowly at Cirocco.

"You still suspect that, don't you?"

"I . . . I don't know what to think. Even if I believe you, I still don't know what you are."

"I am a Titan. You want to know what a Titan is." She leaned back in her chair and her gaze became distant.

"What I really am is lost in the past.

"We are old, that much is clear. We were constructed, not evolved. We live for 3,000,000 years, and have been around for over a thousand of our generations. In that time we have changed, though not through evolutionary processes as you understand them.

"Much of our history is lost now. We do not know what race built us, nor for what purpose. Suffice it to say that our creators built well. They are gone, but we are still here. Perhaps their descendants still live within me, but if so, they have forgotten their former greatness. I listen to messages from my sisters spread through this galaxy, and no one speaks of the builders."

She closed her eyes for a moment, then opened them again, waiting.

"All right," Cirocco said. "You left out a lot of details. How did you get here? Why is there only one of you? You listen to the radio; do you talk over it, too? And if so, why haven't you contacted the Earth before this? If—"

Gaea held up a hand and chuckled.

"One at a time, please. You're making a lot of assumptions.

"What makes you think I'm a visitor? I was born in this system, just like you. My home is Rhea. On Iapetus my daughter is at this moment approaching maturity. There is a family of Titans circling Uranus. They make up the invisible rings. They're all smaller than I; I'm the largest Titan in this neighborhood."

"Iapetus?" Gaby said. "One of the reasons we—"

"Rest easy; I shall explain, and save you a trip.

"We can*not* travel between the stars. We can't move at all except for minor orbital adjustment.

"I release eggs from my rim, where they already have a respectable velocity because of my rotation. I aim them as best I can but over these distances hitting the target is problematic, since the eggs have no guidance once launched.

"When they fall on a suitable world—Iapetus is perfect: no air, rocky, plenty of sunlight, not too large and not too small—they take root. In 50,000 years the infant Titan is ready to be born. At that stage, she has covered an entire hemisphere of the birthing body. That's how Iapetus looked seventy-five years ago; one side was significantly brighter than the other.

"The Titan infant then contracts until she is a thick band that circles the world from pole to pole. That is what Iapetus has become. My daughter has delved deep. She has reached to the core to find the elements she needs for viability. I'm afraid that Iapetus had been quite looted by now; my grandmother, and her mother before her, all used that one moon.

"My daughter is engaged in synthesizing the fuels she will need to break free of Iapetus. That should happen in five or six years. When she is ready—and not a day before, because once born she will contain all the mass she will ever have—she will blast herself into space. It's likely that Iapetus will split in the process, like the one that eventually became the Rings. Then—"

"You're saying Titans are responsible for the Rings?" Gaby asked.

"Didn't I just state it?" Gaea looked a bit annoyed, but was quite absorbed in her story.

"That was long ago, and you can't hold me responsible. At any rate, once free my daughter will kill her present rotation and begin to spin as I do. The part of her that will become her hub is presently touching the surface of Iapetus. In space, this will contract, pulling the spokes out behind it. She will spin faster, stabilizing, fill herself with air, begin moving mountains inside her to prepare for the creatures that will . . . well, you get the picture. I ramble when talking of my daughter, like any parent, I suppose."

"No, no, I'm fascinated," Cirocco said. "Your daughter will have Titanides and angels and blimps inside her?"

Gaea chuckled.

"Not Titanides, I suspect. If she fancies them she'll have to invent them herself, like I did."

Cirocco shook her head. "You've left me behind."

"Simple enough. Most of my species are descendants of creatures Titans sheltered when we were created. Each egg I release contains the seeds of a million species, such as the electronic plants. I don't think my builders cared much for machines. They grew everything they needed, from clothing to houses to circuitry.

"The Titanides and angels are different. You wondered, before you got used to them, how it was possible for them to look so human. The answer is simple. I used humans as a model. Titanides were easy, but angels . . . the headaches! Your storytellers were much more fanciful than practical. The wingspread had to be tremendous to get them off the ground, even with my low gravity and high air pressure. I'll admit they don't look like the Biblical model, but they work! The basic problem, you see, was—"

"You made them yourself," Cirocco said. "Everything about them, from scratch."

"I just said that, didn't I? I designed the DNA. It's no more difficult for me than making a clay model is for you."

"Everything about them is your design. And you got the basic ideas over the radio, which means they couldn't be very old as a culture. We haven't been broadcasting very long, by your standards."

"Less than a century, for the Titanides. The angels are younger than that."

"Then...then you are a God. I don't want to get theological here, but I think you know what I mean."

"For all practical purposes, here in my little corner of the universe...yes, I am." She folded her hands and looked smug.

Cirocco looked longingly at the door. It would be so nice to go through it and try to forget this ever happened.

What did it matter if this person was an insane survivor of the builders? Cirocco asked herself. She had control of the world they called Gaea. It made no difference if she was in fact identical to it; she was the ultimate power, either way.

And oddly enough, Cirocco found herself liking her in her unguarded moments, until she recalled what had brought her to the hub in the first place.

"There are two things I want to ask you," Cirocco said, as firmly as she dared.

Gaea sat up alertly.

"Please, go ahead. There happen to be two things I want to ask you, as well."

"I...you? Ask *me?*" The idea was completely unexpected. Cirocco was nervous enough at the idea of bringing up *Ringmaster*. She knew she and her crew had been wronged, but how do you say that to a Goddess? Cirocco wished she had even a thousandth of the bravado that had enabled her to stand in the hub and shout curses to the empty air. "What could I possibly do for you?"

Gaea smiled.

"You might be surprised."

Cirocco glanced at Gaby, who widened her eyes slightly and surreptitiously crossed her fingers.

"The first . . . ah, the first concerns the Titanides." Damn it, that was supposed to be number two. But it wouldn't hurt to test the water.

"A Titanide called Meistersinger . . ." She sang his name, then went on. "He asked me to . . . if I ever got so far as to see you, to ask why they must be at war."

Gaea frowned, but in confusion more than anger.

"Surely you have deduced that."

"Well, yes, I did. Aggression against angels is built into them. It's an instinct, and the reverse is true for the angels."

"That's precisely correct."

"And since you designed them, you must have had a reason . . ."

Gaea looked surprised.

"Well, of course. I wanted to have a war. I'd never heard of them until I began watching your television programs. You people seemed to like them so much, holding one every few years, that I thought I'd give it a try."

Cirocco could think of nothing to say for a very long time. She realized her mouth was open.

"You're serious, aren't you?"

"Utterly."

"I don't know quite how to put this."

Gaea sighed. "I wish you wouldn't be afraid of me. I assure you, you are in no danger from me."

Gaby leaned forward. "How can we know that? You . . ." She stopped herself, and glanced at Cirocco.

"I destroyed your ship. That's item two on the agenda, I'm sure. There are many things you don't know about that. Would you like some more coffee?"

"Not now, thank you," Cirocco said, hastily. "Gaea, or

your holiness, or whatever I'm supposed to call you—"

"Gaea is fine."

"—we don't like war. *I* don't, and I don't think any sane person does. Surely you've seen anti-war movies, too."

She frowned, and chewed on a knuckle.

"Of course I have. But they were in the minority, and even then, they were *popular*. They contained more bloodshed than most of the *pro*-war movies. You *say* you don't like war, but why are you so fascinated by it?"

"I don't know the answer to that. All I know is I hate war, and the Titanides hate it, too. They would like to see it stopped. That's what I came here to ask you."

"No war?" She peered at Cirocco suspiciously.

"No."

"Not even a skirmish now and then?"

"Not even that."

Gaea's shoulders slumped, then heaved in a great sigh.

"Very well," she said. "Consider it done."

"I hope it wouldn't be too much trouble," Cirocco went on. "I don't know how you go about—"

"It's *done!*" The room was lit by a flash of lightning that made a crown around Gaea's head. The thunderclap brought Gaby and Cirocco to their feet. Gaby had her sword half out of its scabbard, standing between Cirocco and Gaea.

Several uncomfortable seconds passed.

"I didn't mean to do that," Gaea said, her hands fluttering nervously. "It was just . . . well, something of a disappointment." She sighed, and motioned them to their seats.

"I should have said it's *being* done," she elaborated, when things had calmed down. "I'm recalling all the angels and Titanides. The re-programming will take a while."

"'Re-programing?'" Cirocco asked, suspiciously.

"No one will be hurt, my dear. The ground will swallow them up. They'll emerge after a time, free of the compulsion. Satisfied?"

Cirocco wondered what the alternative was, but nodded her head.

"Very good. Now to the other matter. Your ship."

"I didn't do it."

She held up her hand, waited until she was sure Cirocco would not interrupt her, then went on.

"I know I told you I was the whole world, that I *am* Gaea. That was completely true at one time. Now it is less so. Bear in mind that I'm 3,001,266 years old." She paused, and raised one eyebrow.

"Three million . . ." Cirocco's eyes narrowed. "That's what you said your life span was."

"Correct. I am old by my own standards, not just yours. You've seen it on the rim and in the hub. My deserts are drier and my wastelands deeper in ice than they have ever been, and I can do nothing about it. I doubt that I'll live another 100,000 years."

Suddenly Cirocco laughed. Gaby looked startled and Gaea merely sat politely, her head cocked to one side, until Cirocco got it under control.

"Pardon me," Cirocco said, still gasping, "but somehow, I find it hard to be properly sympathetic. Only 100,000 years!" She laughed again, and this time Gaea joined in.

"You're right," she said. "There's still plenty of time to send flowers. I could outlive your whole race." She cleared her throat. "But back to what I was saying. I'm dying. I am malfunctioning in thousands of ways—still holding together, mind you, but not what I once was.

"Think of a dinosaur. A brain in its head, another in its rump. Decentralized control over a bulky body.

"I work the same way. When I was young my auxiliary brains worked with me, as your fingers obey you. In the last half million years that has changed. I've lost much control over my outlying areas. There are twelve separate intelligences on the rim, and I am fragmenting into two personalities even at my central nerve nexus, in the hub.

"In a way, it's like the Greek theogony I've grown so fond of. My children tend to be unruly, willful, antagonistic. I fight them constantly. There are good lands and bad lands down there. Hyperion is one of the good ones. She and I get along well.

"Rhea is temperamental and quite mad, but at least I

can often wheedle her into doing the right thing.

"But Oceanus is the worst. He and I do not speak any more. What I do in Oceanus I do by misdirection, by deceit, by cunning.

"It was Oceanus that snared your ship."

Chapter Twenty-Five

Oceanus brooded for 10,000 years while he felt Gaea's grip grow weaker. There was still a chance she could wipe out the budding independence he concealed so carefully. His grievances festered.

Why must *he* be in the dark? He, the mightiest of oceans, eternally covered with ice. The life that struggled on the bleak ground above him was stunted. Many of his children would die in the full light of day. What was so good about Hyperion that she should be so lush and fair?

Quietly, a few meters a day, he extended a nerve beneath the ground until he could speak directly to Rhea. He recognized the seeds of insanity in her, and began casting his eyes to the west for an ally.

Mnemosyne was no good. She was desolate, physically and emotionally, mourning the passing of her lush forests. Try as he might to kindle resentment against Gaea, Oceanus could not penetrate the depths of Mnemosyne's depression. He tunneled on.

Beyond Mnemosyne was the night region of Cronus. Gaea's grip was strong here; the satellite brain that held sway over the territory was a tool of the overmind, and had not as yet developed a personality of his own.

Oceanus kept moving west. Without realizing it, he was laying a communications net that would unite the six rebellious lands.

He found his strongest ally in Iapetus. If only he had been closer, they might have overthrown Gaea. But the tactics they imagined depended on close physical cooperation, so he and Iapetus could only plot together. He was forced to fall back on his alliance with Rhea.

He made his move around the time the pyramids were being built on Earth. Without warning, he stopped the flow of coolant fluids passing through his immense body and through the support cables he controlled. At the far eastern end of the sea that dominated his frozen landscape, he had control of two river pumps—huge three-chambered muscles that lifted the waters of Ophion into western Hyperion. He stopped their massive beating. To the east, Rhea did the same with the five pumps that raised water over her eastern mountain ranges, while speeding the operation of her pumps near Hyperion. Shut off from the west and sucked dry from the east, Hyperion began to wither.

In a few days, Ophion ceased to flow.

"I got all this second-hand from Rhea," Gaea said. "I had known I was losing control of my peripheral brains, but no one had mentioned any grievances. I had not imagined they could exist."

It had grown gradually darker as Gaea told of the rebellion of Oceanus. Most of the luminescent floor panels had gone out. Those remaining gave off a flickering orange glow. The walls of the room receded in the gloom.

"I knew I had to do something. He was about to destroy whole ecosystems; it might be a thousand years before I could put them together again."

"What did you do?" Gaby whispered. Cirocco jumped; Gaea's quiet voice had nearly mesmerized her.

She held out her hand, slowly made a fist that looked like a lump of stone.

"I *squeezed*."

• • •

The vast, circular muscle had been dormant for 3,000,000 years. It had only one function: to contract the hub and draw out the spokes behind it, just after the Titan was born. Gaea's network of cables depended on it. It was the center of her rigging, the mighty anchor that held her together.

It jerked.

Gigatonnes of ice and rock leaped into the air.

Ten thousand square kilometers of Oceanus' surface rose like an express elevator. The frozen sea turned to slush, embedded with ice cubes the size of city blocks. All over Gaea, cable strands snapped like rotten rope, raveling, snarling, flailing the land beneath them.

The muscle relaxed.

For one giddy moment weightlessness reigned in Oceanus. Kilometer-square ice floes drifted like snow-flakes, turning in the hurricane that had begun to blow from the hub.

When Oceanus bottomed out, fifteen cables twanged the deadly music of Gaea's revenge. The sonic energy alone stripped ten meters of topsoil from the surrounding regions and hurled opposing dust storms a dozen times around the rim before their fury abated.

Like a hand squeezing a ball, the muscle in the hub contracted and relaxed in a two-day rhythm that made Gaea vibrate like a plucked rubber band.

She had one more trick, but she waited until the cataclysm had flayed Oceanus to the bare rock. She had only six other muscles. Now she flexed one of them.

The spoke that towered over Oceanus contracted, squeezed to half its normal diameter. Deprived of water for over a week, the trees were tinder-dry. They fractured, sloughing off their tenuous grip in Gaea's flesh, and began to fall.

On the way down, they began to burn.

Oceanus was an inferno.

"I meant to burn the bastard," Gaea said. "I meant to cauterize him for all time."

Cirocco coughed, and reached for her forgotten drink. The ice cubes clicked alarmingly in the silence and near-darkness.

"He was too deep, but I put the fear of God into him." She chuckled quietly. "I burned myself in the process—the fire damaged my lower valve, and from then on I've blasted him with hurricanes and noise every seventeen days. The sound is not my Lament; it's my warning. But it was worth it. He was a very good boy for thousands of years. Make no mistake, you can't have a dozen Gods running a world. The Greeks knew what they were talking about.

"But the catch, you see, is that his fate is linked with mine. He's another part of my mind, so in your terms, I'm insane. It will destroy us all, eventually, the good with the bad.

"But he was on his best behavior until you came along.

"I had planned to contact you a few days before you arrived here. It was my intention to pick you up with Hyperion's external grapples. I assure you I could have done it delicately, not breaking any glassware.

"Oceanus exploited my weakness. My radio transmission organs are on the rim. There were three of them, but one broke down ages ago. The others are in Oceanus and Crius. Crius is my ally, but Rhea and Tethys managed to destroy his transmitter. Suddenly all my communications were in the hands of Oceanus.

"I decided not to make the pick-up. Not having been in contact with me, you would surely have misinterpreted it.

"But Oceanus wanted you for himself."

The battle raged beneath the surfaces of Oceanus and Hyperion. It was fought in the great conduits that supplied the nutrient fluid known as Gaea's milk.

Each of the human captives was encapsulated in a protective jelly while their fates were decided. Their metabolic rates were slowed. Medically, they were comatose, unaware of their surroundings.

The weapons of the war were the pumps that impelled nutrients and coolants through the underworld. Great pressure imbalances were created by both combatants, so

that at one point a geyser of milk broke through in
Mnemosyne and spurted a hundred meters into the air, to
fall on the sands and fuel a brief spring.

They battled for the better part of a year. Then at last,
Oceanus knew he was losing. The prizes began to flow
toward Hyperion under the staggering pressure Gaea
built from Iapetus, Cronus, and Mnemosyne.

Oceanus changed his tactics. He reached into the
minds of his captives and woke them up.

"I had been afraid all along he'd do that," Gaea said, as
the room lights threatened to gutter into oblivion. "He
had a link into your brains. It became imperative for me
to sever that link. I used tactics that I don't think you'd
understand. In the process, I lost one of you. When I got
her back, she had been changed.

"He was trying to destroy you all before I got you—
your minds, not your bodies. That would have been easy
enough. He flooded you with information. He implanted
the whistle speech in one of you, the songs of the Titanides
in two more. That any of you survived with your sanity is
a source of amazement to me."

"Not all of us did," Cirocco said.

"No, and I'm sorry. I'll try to make it up to you,
somehow."

While Cirocco was wondering what could possibly be
done to put things right, Gaby spoke up.

"I remember climbing a huge stairway," she said. "I
passed through golden gates, and stood at the feet of God.
Then a few hours ago it seemed like I was in the same
place again. Can you explain that?"

"I talked to all of you," Gaea said. "In your condition,
mentally pliable from days of sensory deprivation, you
put your own interpretation on it."

"I don't recall that at all," Cirocco said.

"You blanked it. Your friend Bill went further, and
blanked most of his memories.

"Interviewing you through Hyperion, I decided what
must be done. April was too far indoctrinated with angel
culture and customs. Trying to return her to what she had

been would have destroyed her. I transported her to the spoke and let her emerge to find her own destiny.

"Gene was sick in his mind. I took him to Rhea, hoping that he would remain separated from the rest of you. I should have destroyed him."

Cirocco sighed.

"No. I let him live when I could have killed him, too."

"You make me feel better," Gaea said. "As for the rest of you, it was imperative that you were returned at once to full consciousness. There was not even time to bring you together. I hoped you would make your way up here, and in time, you did. And now you can go home."

Cirocco looked up quickly.

"Yes, the rescue ship is here. It's under the command of Captain Wally Svensen, and—"

"Wally!" Gaby and Cirocco said it simultaneously.

"A friend? You'll see him soon. Your friend Bill has been talking to him for two weeks now." Gaea looked uncomfortable, and when she spoke again there was a hint of petulance in her voice. "It's a bit more than a rescue mission, actually."

"I thought it might be."

"Yes. Captain Svensen is equipped to wage a war with me. He has a large number of nuclear bombs, and his presence out there is making me nervous. That's one of the things I wanted to ask you. Could you put in a good word? I couldn't possibly be a threat to the Earth, you know."

Cirocco hesitated a moment, and it was Gaea's turn to look uncomfortable.

"Yes, I think I can straighten it out."

"Thanks so much. He didn't actually *say* he was going to bomb me, and when he discovered there were survivors from *Ringmaster* that possibility became more remote. I've picked up some of his scout ships, and they are in the process of constructing a base camp near Titantown. You can explain to him what happened, as I'm not sure he believes me."

Cirocco nodded, and said nothing for a long time, waiting for Gaea to continue. She did not, and eventually Cirocco had to speak.

"How do we know if *we* can believe all this?"

"I can give you no assurances. I can only ask you to believe the story as I told it."

Cirocco nodded again, and stood up. She tried to make it casual, but no one had been expecting it. Gaby looked confused, but got to her feet.

"It's been interesting," Cirocco said. "Thanks for the coke."

"Let's don't be hasty," Gaea said, after an astonished pause. "Once I return you to the rim I won't be able to speak to you directly."

"You can send me a postcard."

"Do I detect a hint of anger?"

"I don't know. Do you?" Suddenly she *was* angry, and was not sure why. "You're the one in the position to know. I'm your captive, no matter what you call it."

"That's not quite true."

"I have only your word for that. Only your word for a number of things. You bring me to a room straight out of an old film, show yourself to me as a dumpy old woman, give me my only vice to indulge in. You bring down the lights and tell me a long and unlikely story. What am I supposed to believe?"

"I'm sorry you feel that way."

Cirocco shook her head tiredly. "Skip it," she said. "I'm feeling a little let down, that's all."

Gaby cocked one eyebrow at her, but said nothing. It irritated Cirocco, and it didn't help when Gaea seemed interested in the statement, too.

"'Let down'? I can't imagine why. You've done what you set out to do, against formidable odds. You've stopped a war. And now you're going home."

"The war bothers me," Cirocco said, slowly.

"In what way?"

"I didn't swallow your story. Not all of it anyway. If you really want me to go to bat for you, tell me the real reason the Titanides fought the angels for so long, to so little purpose."

"Practice," Gaea said, promptly.

"Say again?"

"Practice. I have no enemies, and nothing in my

instinctive behavior to help me cope with war. I knew I would meet humans soon, and everything I learned about you underlined your aggressiveness. Your news, your films, your books: war, killing, predation, hostility."

"You were getting ready to fight a war with us."

"I was exploring the techniques, in case I had to."

"What did you learn?"

"That I was terrible at it. I can destroy your ships if they approach closely, but that's all. You could destroy me in the twinkling of an eye. I have no feel for strategy. My victory over Oceanus showed all the subtlety of arm-wrestling. As soon as you people arrived, April revolutionized the angel attack and Gene was about to introduce new weapons to the Titanides. I could have given them those weapons, of course. I've seen enough cowboy movies to know how a bow and arrow functions."

"Why didn't you?"

"I hoped they would invent them."

"And why didn't they?"

"They are a new species. They lack inventiveness. That's my fault; I was never high on originality. I stole the giant sandworm in Mnemosyne from a movie. There's a giant ape in Phoebe that I'm quite proud of, but it's another imitation. The Titanides I took from mythology—their sexual arrangements are original with me, however." She looked smug, and Cirocco almost grinned. "I can do the bodies, you see, but giving a manufactured species a sense of ... well, the sheer orneriness you humans have ... It's beyond me."

"So you borrowed a little of it," Cirocco said.

"Pardon me?"

"Don't play innocent. There's one thing—of some importance to me and Gaby and August—that you forgot to mention. I've believed you so far, more or less, but here's your chance to convince me you've told the truth. Why did we become pregnant?"

Gaea said nothing for what seemed a very long time. Cirocco was ready to run. After all, Gaea was still a Goddess; it would not do to anger her.

"I did it," Gaea said.

"Did you think we'd approve?"

"No, I was sure you wouldn't. I'm sorry now, but it's done."

"And un-done."

"I know." She sighed. "The temptation was just too great. It was a chance to gain a new hybrid—one that might incorporate the best of both species. I hoped to re-vitalize...never mind. I did it, I'm not trying to make excuses. I'm not proud of it."

"I'm glad to hear that, anyway. You just don't *do* that, Gaea. We're thinking beings, just like you, and we deserve to be treated with more dignity than that."

"I understand that now," Gaea said, contrite. "It's a hard concept to get used to."

Cirocco admitted, grudgingly, that it probably was, after 3,000,000 years of being a Goddess.

"I have a question," Gaby said, suddenly. She had been quiet for a long time, seemingly satisfied to let Cirocco do the negotiating. "Was this trip really necessary?"

Cirocco waited, having had doubts about that part of the story herself.

"You're right," Gaea admitted. "I could have brought you here directly. Obviously, since I brought April more than halfway. There would have been some risk with the additional time in isolation, but I could have put you back to sleep."

"Then why didn't you?" Cirocco demanded.

Gaea threw up her hands.

"Let's stop kidding each other, shall we? Number one, I don't know if I owed it to you. Number two, I was—and still am—a bit frightened of you. Not you personally, but humans. You're inclined to be hasty."

"I won't argue with that."

"You made it up here anyway, didn't you? That's what I wanted to see: if you could do it. And you should be thanking me for it, because you had a great time."

"I can't imagine how you could think a thing like—"

"We're being honest now, remember? You're really overjoyed that you're about to go home now, aren't you?"

"Well, of course I—"

"Everything about you says you're not. You've had a goal to achieve—getting up here. Now it's over. The best time of your life. Deny that if you can."

Cirocco was nearly speechless. "How can you say that? I saw my lover nearly killed—I was nearly killed myself. Me and Gaby were raped, I went through an abortion, April has been turned into a monster, August is—"

"You could have been raped on Earth. As for the rest of it . . . you expected it to be easy? I'm sorry about the abortion; I won't do that again. Do you blame me for the rest of it?"

"Well, no, I think I believe what you—"

"You *want* to blame me. It would make it easier to leave. You find it hard to admit that even with all those things that happened to your friends—none of it your fault—you've had a great adventure."

"That's the most—"

"Captain Jones, I submit to you that you were never really cut out to be a Captain. Oh, you've done well, just like you do a good job of most things you tackle. But you're not a Captain. You don't enjoy ordering other people around. You like your independence, you like to go to strange places and do exciting things. In an earlier age you would have been an adventurer, a soldier of fortune."

"If I'd been born a man," Cirocco corrected.

"That's because it's only recently that women have had a crack at adventure on their own. Space was the only frontier available to you, but it's done by the numbers, very civilized. It's not really your cup of tea."

Cirocco had given up on trying to stop her. It was all so far-fetched, she decided to let Gaea ramble on.

"No, what you're cut out for is exactly what you've been doing. Scaling the unscalable mountain. Communing with strange beings. Shaking your fist at the unknown, spitting in God's eye. You did all those things. You got hurt along the way; if you keep on that path you'll be hurt more. You'll freeze and go hungry and bleed and fall down from exhaustion. So what do you want? Spend the rest of your life behind a desk? Go home; it's waiting for you."

Far down the curved abyss that was Gaea's hub, wind howled faintly. Somewhere volumes of air were being sucked into a vertical chamber 300 kilometers high, and that chamber was peopled by angels. Cirocco looked around her, and shivered. To her right, Gaby was smiling. What does she know that I don't know? Cirocco wondered.

"What are you offering me?"

"A chance at a long life span, with the possibility that it might be quite short. I'm offering good friends and evil enemies, eternal day and endless night, rousing song and strong wine, hardships, victories, despair and glory. I'm offering you the chance at a life you won't find on Earth, the kind of life you knew you wouldn't find in space but hoped for anyway.

"I need a representative on the rim. It's been a long time since I've had one, because I demand a lot. I can give you certain powers. You'll define your job, pick your hours and companions, see the world. You'll get some help from me, but little interference.

"How would you like to be a Wizard?"

Chapter Twenty-Six

Seen from the air, the expedition base camp was an ugly brown flower. A ragged wound had opened in the soil just east of Titantown and had begun discharging Earth people.

It looked like it would never stop. As Cirocco watched from Whistlestop's gondola, a blue glob of gelatin shaped like a pill oozed from the ground and fell on its side. The encapsulating material quickly turned to water and sloughed away from a silvery crawler-transporter. The vehicle churned through the sea of mud and made its way to a rank of six similar machines parked beside a complex of inflatable domes before discharging its five passengers.

"These folks came in style," Gaby observed.

"Looks that way. And that's just the landing party. Wally won't bring his ship in close enough to get picked up."

"You sure you want to go down there?" Gaby asked.

"I have to. Surely you know that."

Calvin looked it all over and sniffed.

"If it's all the same to you," he said, "I'll just stay up here. I might get nasty if I went down."

"I can protect you, Calvin."

"That remains to be seen."

Cirocco shrugged. "Maybe you'd like to stay, too, Gaby."

"I go where you go," she said, simply. "Surely you know *that*. Do you think Bill's still down there? He might have been evacuated by now."

"I think he'd wait. And besides, I have to go down to get a look at *that*."

She pointed to a shiny heap of metal a kilometer west of the camp, sitting in its own flower of overturned dirt. There was no pattern to it, no hint that it had ever been more than a scrap heap.

It was the bones of *Ringmaster*.

"Let's hit the silk," Cirocco said.

". . . and says she was actually working in our interests throughout the alleged aggressive incident. I can offer you no concrete proof of most of these statements. There can be no proof, except the pragmatic one of her behavior over a suitable time. But I see no evidence that she is a threat to humanity, now or in the future."

Cirocco sat back in her chair and reached for her glass of water, wishing it was wine. She had talked for two hours, interrupted only by Gaby amplifying or correcting details of her account.

They were in a round dome that served as mission command headquarters for the ground party. The room was adequate for the seven assembled officers, Cirocco, Gaby, and Bill. The two women had been brought there promptly when they landed, introduced to everyone, and asked to begin the de-briefing.

Cirocco felt out of place. The crew of the *Unity* and Bill were dressed in spotless, wrinkle-free red and gold uniforms. They *smelled* clean.

And they looked entirely too military for Cirocco's tastes. The *Ringmaster* expedition had avoided that, even eliminating military titles except Captain. At the time *Ringmaster* was launched, NASA had been at pains to erase its military origins. They had sought U.N. auspices for the trip, though the notion that the expedition was anything but American was a transparent fiction. Still, it had been something.

Unity, by her very name, testified that the nations of Earth were cooperating more closely. Her multi-national crew proved that the *Ringmaster* experiment had drawn the nations together in a common purpose.

But the uniforms told Cirocco what that purpose was.

"Then you counsel a continuation of our peaceful policy," Captain Svensen said. He spoke through a television set on the fold-up desk in the center of the room. Aside from the chairs, it was the only article of furniture.

"The most you can lose is your exploratory party. Face it, Wally. Gaea knows that would be an act of war, and that the next ship would not even be manned. It would be one big H-bomb."

The face on the screen frowned, then nodded.

"Excuse me for a moment," he said. "I want to talk this over with my staff." He started to turn away, then reversed the motion.

"What about you, Rocky? You didn't say if you believe her. Is she telling the truth?"

Cirocco didn't hesitate.

"Yes, she is. You can bank on it."

Lieutenant Strelkov, the ground commander, waited until he was sure the Captain had nothing more to say, then stood. He was a handsome young man with an unfortunate chin and—though Cirocco found it hard to believe—he was a soldier in the Soviet Army. He seemed little more than a child.

"Could I get you anything?" he asked, in excellent English. "Perhaps you're hungry after your trip back here."

"We ate just before we jumped," Cirocco said, in Russian. "But if you had any coffee...?"

"You didn't really finish your story," Bill was saying. "There's the matter of getting back down after your conversation with God."

"We jumped," Cirocco said, sipping her coffee.

"You..."

She and Bill and Gaby were in one "corner" of the round room, their chairs drawn together, while the *Unity*'s officers buzzed at each other around the television set. Bill looked good. He walked with a crutch and his leg apparently hurt when he stood on it, but he was in high spirits. The *Unity*'s doctor said she could operate on him as soon as he was aboard, and thought he would be nearly as mobile as before.

"Why not?" Cirocco asked, with a faint smile. "We brought those chutes all the way up as a safety measure, but why not use them?" His mouth was still open. She laughed, relenting, putting her hand on his shoulder. "All right, we thought about it a *long* time before we jumped. But it really wasn't dangerous. Gaea held the top and bottom valves open for us and called Whistlestop. We did it free-fall for the first 400 kilometers, then landed on his back." She held out her cup while an officer poured more coffee, then turned back to Bill.

"I've talked enough. What about you? How did things go?"

"Nothing so interesting, I'm afraid. I spent my time in therapy with Calvin, and picked up a little Titanide."

"How old was she?"

"How...the *language,* you idiot," he laughed. "I learned how to sing *goo-goo* and *wa-wa* and *Bill hungry*. I had a great time. Then I decided to get off my ass and *do* something since you wouldn't take me along. I started talking to the Titanides about something I knew a little about, which was electronics. I learned about coppervines and batteryworms and IC nuts, and before long I had a receiver and transmitter."

He grinned at the look on Cirocco's face.

"Then it wasn't..."

He shrugged. "Depends on how you look at it. You kept thinking in terms of a radio that would reach Earth. I can't build that. What I have isn't very strong—I can only talk to *Unity* when it's above and the signal only has to punch through the roof. But even if I'd built it before you left, you probably would have gone, wouldn't you? *Unity* wasn't here yet, so the radio would have been useless."

"I suppose I would have. I had other things to do."

"I heard." He grimaced. "That gave me the worst moments of the trip," he confessed. "I'd started to like the Titanides, and then out of nowhere they all get this dreamy look and hurry out into the grassland. I thought it was another angel attack, but none of them came back. All I ever found was a big hole in the ground."

"I noticed a few when we came in," Gaby said.

"They've been drifting back," Bill said. "They don't remember us."

Cirocco's mind had been wandering. She was not concerned about the Titanides. She knew they would be all right, and now they would not have to suffer in the fighting. But it was sad to know Hornpipe would no longer remember her.

She had been watching the *Unity* people, wondering why no one came over to talk. She knew she did not smell very good, but didn't think that was the reason. With some surprise, she realized they were afraid of her. The thought made her grin.

She realized Bill had been talking to her.

"I'm sorry, what was that?"

"Gaby says you haven't told the whole story yet. She says there something more, and that I should hear it."

"Oh, that," Cirocco said, glaring at Gaby. But it had to come out soon, anyway.

"Gaea, uh ... she offered me a job, Bill."

"A 'job?'" He raised his eyebrows, smiled tentatively.

"A 'Wizard,' she called it. She tends to the romantic. You'd probably like her; she likes science fiction, too."

"Just what did the job entail?"

Cirocco spread her hands. "General troubleshooting, nature unspecified. Whenever she had a problem I'd go there and see what I could do. There are—literally—some unruly lands down here. She could promise me limited immunity, a sort of conditional passport based on the fact that the regional brains would remember what she did to Oceanus and not dare to harm me while I traveled through them."

"That's all? Sounds like a chancy proposition."

"It is. She offered to educate me, to fill my head with a tremendous amount of lore in the same way I was taught to sing Titanide. I'd have her support and backing. Nothing magic, but I'd be able to cause the ground to open up and swallow my enemies."

"That I can believe."

"I took the job, Bill."

"I thought so."

He looked down at his hands, seemed very tired when he looked up again.

"You're really something else, you know?" He said it with a trace of bitterness, but was taking the news better than Cirocco had expected. "It sounds like the kind of job that would appeal to you. The left hand of God." He shook his head. "Damn, this is really a hell of a place. You may not like it, you know. I was just starting to, when all the Titanides disappeared. That shook me, Rocky. It really seemed like someone had just put away his toys because he was tired of the game. How do you know you won't be one of her toys? You've been your own boss, do you think you still will be?"

"I honestly don't know. I just couldn't face going back to Earth, back to a desk job and the lecture tour. You've seen over-the-hill astronauts. I could land a job on the board of directors of some big corporation." She laughed, and Bill smiled slightly.

"That's what *I'm* going to do," he said. "But I'm hoping for the research department. Leaving space doesn't scare me. You know I'll be going back, don't you?"

Cirocco nodded. "I knew it when I saw your nice new uniform."

He chuckled, but there was little mirth in it. They looked at each other for a time, then Cirocco reached out and took his hand. He smiled with one corner of his mouth, leaned over and kissed her lightly on the cheek.

"Good luck," he said.

"You too, Bill."

Across the room, Strelkov cleared his throat.

"Captain Jones, Captain Svensen would like to talk to you now."

"Yes, Wally?"

"Rocky, we've sent your report on to Earth. It will take some analysis, so there won't be a definite decision for a few days. But we up here have added our recommendation to yours, and I don't think there will be any problem. I expect to upgrade the base camp to a cultural mission and United Nations Embassy. I'd offer you the job of ambassador but we brought someone along in case our negotiations were successful. Besides, I expect you're anxious to get back."

Gaby and Cirocco laughed, and Bill joined in soon after.

"Sorry, Wally. I'm not anxious to go back. I'm not *going* back. And I couldn't take the job even if you offered it."

"Why not?"

"Conflict of interest."

She had known it would not be that simple, and it was not.

She formally resigned her commission, explained her reasons to Captain Svensen, then listened patiently as he told her, in increasingly peremptory terms, just why she had to go back, and for good measure, why Calvin had to return as well.

"The doctor says he can be treated. Bill's memory can be restored, Gaby's phobia can probably be cured."

"I'm sure Calvin can be cured, but he's happy where he is. Gaby's already *been* cured. But what do you plan to do for April?"

"I was hoping you could help coax her to come back to us before you came aboard. I'm sure—"

"You don't know what you're talking about. I'm not going back, and that's all there is to be said. It's been nice talking to you." She turned on her heel and strode from the room. No one tried to stop her.

She and Gaby made their preparations in a field a short distance from the base camp, then stood side by side, waiting. It was taking longer than she had expected. She began to get nervous, glancing at Calvin's battered watch.

Strelkov came racing out the door, shouting orders to a group of men busy erecting a shed for the crawlers. He stopped suddenly, caught flat-footed when he realized Cirocco was not far away, waiting for him. He motioned the men to stay put, and came toward the two women.

"I'm sorry, Captain, but Commander Svensen says I have to place you under arrest." He seemed genuinely apologetic, but his hand was close to his side-arm. "Will you come with me, please?"

"Look over there, Sergei." She pointed over his shoulder.

He started to turn, then drew his weapon in sudden suspicion. He backed away and to one side until he could steal a glance to the west.

"Gaea, hear me!" Cirocco shouted. Strelkov eyed her nervously. She carefully made no threatening gestures, but raised her arms in the direction of Rhea, toward the place of winds and the cable she had climbed with Gaby.

There were shouts from behind them.

A wave was traveling down the cable, almost imperceptibly, but producing a definite kink like the wave that moves through a garden hose when it is given a quick flip from the wrist. The effect on the cable was explosive. A cloud of dust expanded all around it. In the dust were trees torn out at the roots.

The wave hit the ground, the place of winds bulged, shattered, sent rocks high into the air.

"Cover your ears!" Cirocco yelled.

The sound hit all at once, throwing Gaby to the ground. Cirocco was staggered, but stood her ground as all the thunder of the Gods rolled around her, the tatters of her clothes streaming out as the shock wave hit and the winds began to blow.

"Look!" she shouted again, holding out her hands and raising them slowly toward the sky. No one could hear her, but they saw as a hundred waterspouts broke through the dry ground, turning Hyperion into a mist-shrouded fountain. Lightning crackled through the thickening fog, the sound of it swallowed in the mightier roar that still re-echoed from the distant walls.

It took a long time for it to die away, and in all that time no one moved. When it was quiet again, long after the last fountain had turned to a trickle, Strelkov was sitting where he had fallen, still looking at the cable and the settling dust.

Cirocco went to him and helped him to his feet.

"Tell Wally to leave me alone," she said, and walked away.

"That was very slick," Gaby said, later. "Very slick indeed."

"All done with mirrors, my dear."

"How did it make you feel?"

"I nearly wet my pants. You know, one could learn to get off on that. It was tremendously exciting."

"I hope you don't have to do it very often."

Cirocco silently agreed with her. It had been a close thing. The demonstration, awesome for having occurred at her command, would have been merely inexplicable if it had arrived before Strelkov came out of the dome to threaten her.

The fact was that she could not repeat the performance for five or six hours, even if she asked for another at that very moment.

She could communicate readily enough with Gaea. There was a master radio seed in her pocket. But Gaea could not react quickly. To do anything as awesome as she had just accomplished, she needed hours of preparation time.

Cirocco had sent the message requesting the stunt while still on Whistlestop, after carefully considering the likely sequence of events. From that time, it had been a nervous dance with the clock, drawing out her story here, skimping on the answer to a question there, always with the knowledge of the forces gathering in the hub and under her feet. Her advantage had been the leeway she had in timing her resignation, but the drawback was estimating the time it would take Wally Svensen to order her arrest.

She could see wizarding was not going to be easy.

On the other hand, not all of her job would be as

finicky as calling in an air strike from heaven.

Her pockets were stuffed with the things she had brought as backup measures in case the blood and thunder failed to intimidate the ground party, things she had obtained foraging through Hyperion before reboarding Whistlestop and traveling to the base camp. There was an eight-legged lizard who could spit a tranquilizing agent when squeezed, and an odd assortment of berries that would do the same job taken internally. She had leaves and bark that could be turned into flash powder and, as a last resort, a nut that made a passable hand grenade.

There were libraries of wildlife lore in her head; if there were Gaean girl scouts, she would own all the merit badges. She could sing to the Titanides, whistle to the blimps, and croak, twitter, chirp, rumble and moan in a dozen languages she had not even had a chance to use. To creatures she had not yet encountered.

She and Gaby had worried that all the information Gaea proposed to give them would not fit into human brains. Oddly, it had been no trouble at all. They were not even aware of any changes; when they needed to know something, they knew it, just as if they had learned it in school.

"Time to head for the hills?" Gaby suggested.

"Not yet. I don't think we'll have any more trouble from Wally, once he adjusts to the idea. They'll see that we're more valuable if they maintain good relations with us.

"But there's one more thing I want to see before we go."

She had been prepared for an emotional moment. It was, but not as bad as she had feared, and not in the way she had expected. Saying goodbye to Bill had been harder.

The wreck of *Ringmaster* was a sad, silent place. They walked through it without speaking, recognizing pieces here and there, more often unable to tell what a twisted hunk of metal had been.

The silver hulk gleamed dully in the beautiful

afternoon of Hyperion, partly embedded in the dusty ground like a robot King Kong after the fall. Already the grasses had established a foothold in the turned soil. Vines crept over shattered components. A single yellow flower bloomed in the center of what had been Cirocco's command console.

She had hoped to find some memento of her former life, but she had never been acquisitive and had brought little of a personal nature with her. The few photos would have been eaten, along with the log book and the envelope of newspaper clippings. It would have been nice to come across her class ring—she could see it sitting on the shelf beside her bunk where she had last removed it—but the chances were against it.

They saw a crewman from *Unity* some distance away from them. He was clambering over the wreckage, pointing his camera and snapping indiscriminately. Cirocco thought he was the ship's photographer, then realized he was doing it on his own time, with his own camera. She saw him pick up an object and put it in his pocket.

"Come back here in fifty years," Gaby observed, "they're likely to have carted it all away." She looked around speculatively. "This looks like a nice spot for a souvenir stand. Sell film and hot dogs; you'd do pretty good."

"You don't think that'll happen, do you?"

"It's up to Gaea, I guess. She did say she'd let people visit. That means tourism."

"But the cost..."

Gaby laughed. "You're still thinking of the *Ringmaster* days, Captain. It was all we could do then to get seven of us out here. Bill says *Unity* has a crew of 200. How would you have liked to get the film concession at O'Neil One thirty years ago?"

"I'd be rich by now," Cirocco conceded.

"If there's a way to get rich here, somebody'll do it. So why don't you make me Minister of Tourism and Conservation? I'm not sure how I like the role of sorcerer's apprentice."

Cirocco grinned. "You've got it. Try to keep the bribes and nepotism down to a minimum, will you?"

Gaby swept her arm in a circle, a far-away look in her eyes.

"I can see it now. We'll put the taco stand over there— a classical Greek motif, naturally—and we can sell Gaeaburgers and milk shakes. I'll keep the billboards down to fifty meters, tops, and limit the use of neon. 'See the angels! Smell the breath of God! Shoot the rapids on the Ophion! This way to the centaur rides, only one thin sawbuck! Don't forget to bring—'"

She yelped and danced to one side as the ground moved.

"I was *kidding,* damn it!" she yelled at the sky, then looked suspiciously at Cirocco, who was laughing.

An arm came from the spot where Gaby had been standing. Loose dirt shifted to reveal a face, and a mop of multi-colored hair.

They knelt and brushed sand away from the Titanide as she coughed and spit, until she had managed to free her torso and front legs. She paused to gather strength, and looked curiously at the two women.

"Hello," Hornpipe sang. "Who are you?"

Gaby got to her feet and held out her hand.

"You really don't remember us, do you?" she sang.

"I recall something. It *does* seem as if I knew you. Didn't you give me some wine, long ago?"

"I did," Gaby sang. "And you returned the favor."

"Come out of there, Hornpipe," Cirocco sang. "You could use a bath."

"I remember you, too. But how do you manage to stay balanced for so long without falling over?"

Cirocco laughed.

"I wish I knew, kid."